THE STRANGE DISAPPEARANCE
OF MARY YOUNG

THE STRANGE DISAPPEARANCE OF MARY YOUNG

Milton M. Propper

COACHWHIP PUBLICATIONS
GREENVILLE, OHIO

To
Mother
Who Is Largely Responsible
For This Book

The Strange Disappearance of Mary Young, by Milton M. Propper
© 2026 Coachwhip Publications edition

First published 1929
Milton M. Propper, 1906-1962
CoachwhipBooks.com

ISBN 1-61646-635-9
ISBN-13 978-1-61646-635-0

I

WOODLAWN PARK

The astounding crime that opened with the murder of an unidentified girl and closed with the pursuit of an unknown criminal across half the continent had its beginnings at Woodlawn Park on a hot and busy Sunday night in the middle of August. Woodlawn Park is that type of institution to which the common people flock, but at which blue-law advocates and reformers raise holy hands of horror. It is situated within the Philadelphia district, a blot upon the landscape of the main-line towns, whose citizens neither welcomed its foundation nor, from their haughty seclusion in mansion and garden, approve its continuance.

For it rears a network of amusements towering into the sky, roller-coaster foundations, mingled with Ferris wheels and other constructions; and at best it presents no lovely sight, even in the evening when lights illuminate every structure with gay and rakish effect. In addition, there is the noisy discord of chattering crowds and sounds which only politeness can term music. For the poorer classes it is undoubtedly a haven of refuge from the cares and responsibilities of the workaday world. Those whose existence is spent in cheerless factories at monotonous labor; the sailor, on leave from the fleet, seeking recreation; the day-laborer and his family—all flock to the park with pleasure.

All find forgetfulness and a fleeting enjoyment in the inviting amusements.

This particular Sunday night found the park at its most raucous. Great crowds stormed every divertissement, in long twisting queues. The grounds were ablaze with brilliant and colored lights. Venders called their wares from stands located in every conceivable nook, their voices mingling with the laughter and murmur of the mob. The tinny sound of the carrousel's music found visitors in a spending mood and attracted its clientele with ease. Above that clamor came the roar of the scenic railways, the "Lightning Glider," the "Daredevil," and that newest addition to the park's concessions, "Thrills in the Dark." It grows to thunder as a car, after poising upon the brink of an incline, hurtles forward at increasing momentum into breakneck speed. And even that cannot drown the shrill, throaty screams of patrons enjoying vicariously thrills not part of their normal, daily lives.

To Peter Rawley, the brakeman at the end of the ride of "Thrills in the Dark," the repeated process of checking the momentum of the trains was quite tiresome. He acted automatically, aiding the riders from their seats and pushing the cars beyond the paling to where the next eager batch of riders waited. Without conscious effort, he called out: "Stay in your seats for the second ride. No waiting. Only ten cents." He was accustomed to seeing couples emerge from the darkness of the exciting ride with disheveled hair or mussed clothes; so much so that he failed to notice them. His elementary thoughts were far from his actual work. Even at the present moment the incident of assisting from the car a man whose girl was, however, taking another ride by herself, made no particular impression. The escort paid for the extra ride by dropping the price into a slot-receiving machine and passed through the gates. Rawley wished the boss would move away, so that he could light his pipe. But Mr. Alexander Simones, proprietor of the concession, knew his business too well to leave at this busy moment. Besides, it gave him a pleasant feeling to see the coins rolling into the little window at the entranceway.

When the car emptied, Rawley pushed it forward; in a trice, it was filled again and shoved off, to enter the blackness of the tunnel which covered the entire route. In three minutes it would be back again and the riders would have little or nothing for their money. But they always came back for more. If he possessed what was taken in on one Sunday night, he'd be able to quit work for several months at least. And then there was that girl behind the ticket booth of the "Jigsaw." She was a good-looker and most likely enjoyed a good time. What was her name? Mamie Saule. He'd speak to her that very evening after—

The return of the cars interrupted his train of thought for the instant. They came shooting out of the darkness, to a screeching stop as he applied the brakes. Realizing that the boss was watching him closely at the moment, he turned his attention to the passengers. Blinking and shouting, some with streaming hair, they were already leaping agilely out; some were shoving down toward the exit. He gave the usual announcement as to second rides, with the same monotonous tone as always and, noting that a woman seated on the first seat of the first car had made no motion to get out, he turned toward her.

She was sitting in an oddly slumped position, as though asleep; her head was lowered so that her chin was resting upon her chest. Her hands were extended and folded in orderly fashion upon her lap, and held a pocketbook loosely in them. She looked neither up nor to either side, but maintained her pose with a strange rigidity.

"Another ride, miss?" asked the brakeman. "Only ten cents."

There was no reply, nor did she move an inch. What was the matter with her, he wondered.

"End of the ride," he announced, with growing impatience.

Still his words brought no results. He realized something was wrong, but could not tell what it was. Probably it was some "drunk," though how she had ever got on in the first place puzzled him. He would have to take drastic measures. The people surging on their way to the opening halted on the first hint of the unusual, to watch the proceedings with curiosity and interest.

"Hey, there! Get a move on!" yelled the proprietor sharply from the cashier's box. "What on earth's the matter with you? Are you—"

Mr. Alexander Simones never finished his sentence. At that instant Rawley leaned over and seized the girl's arm. At the same instant he was aware of a creeping chill that sinuously moved through him and caused him to shiver with a fear he did not understand. Disturbed by the movement, the scarf that was tightly wrapped about the girl, as if to protect her from the night air, became loose. As by the power of an unseen hand, it partially unwound itself, and as it unwound it revealed her blouse beneath. It was a blouse dabbled in red—upon which a hideous red stain was ever spreading and widening, growing until it covered the entire left breast!

The brakeman gave vent to an uncontrollable cry. From where he stood, Simones also saw the red stain. His eyes bulged, first in surprise and then in horror. His face went white with a sudden strained look. The staring crowd, who had expected to view some amusement, also saw. They stood in a rooted, dreadful silence as a shudder seemed to run through them. Then a girl spectator screamed hysterically and, with some indistinguishable remark, fainted.

Her escort barely caught her and gently eased her against the railing. Some man also cried out in terror, and the tension was broken.

In the very instant, a crowd began to gather outside the rail. Drawn by the sudden screams, they collected in an amazingly short time. From all corners of the park, from the walks and the pavilions, they poured forth, to crowd about the "Thrills in the Dark," to push upon one another and view the attraction. And with them came the nearest two park policemen.

The proprietor broke the spell and moved forward toward the dazed brakeman. He could think of nothing appropriate to say.

"What's the matter with her?" he inquired hoarsely. "Is she hurt?"

Before his employee sufficiently recovered from the shock to reply, the policemen pushed their way through the milling assembly to the platform. They had drawn their clubs in case it should turn out to be a mere brawl and their whistles were ready to summon assistance if any were needed.

"What's going on here?" demanded the stouter one, Donahue, as they broke into the open.

Then they too caught sight of that amazing tableau under the arc lights of the platform and they stopped in alarm. The scarf of the girl had slipped off all the way, and she seemed to have slumped forward more in her seat. Though both had had many experiences in their lives on the force, neither had ever come upon so serious or surprising a situation before. And for the instant they were stumped.

Patrolman Donahue was the first to recover, and his natural confidence and ability, born of many years of service, swiftly reasserted themselves. He turned to his companion.

"This looks pretty bad, Mike; too much for us to handle. Better get Headquarters in a hurry. And the park doctor too—you know where to find him. Though I'm afraid it's all over with her."

Mike nodded and hastened away; the crowd, strangely awed and silent, parted respectfully to make a lane for him. Not far distant came the jangling discord of the merry-go-round; for once, its noise did not sound attractive.

Donahue turned to view the body. He realized that nothing must be changed or touched, so that the Central man, when he arrived, would find the situation as it originally was. Privately, he hoped that the man would arrive soon and take the responsibility off his hands. He turned to Rawley.

"Here, you," he commanded authoritatively, "shut that gate over there," pointing to the "Exit" gate. "You people will have to stay here for a while—all of you that just got off."

The brakeman hastened to obey in a scrambling manner and the patrolman, disregarding the murmur of protest that rose behind him, walked over to the car.

"Here, somebody help me detach this car and move it to the siding switch; it'll be out of the way there." He glanced through the spectators within the cage. "You there, and you—you'll do."

The two men designated left their partners and joined him. In an instant the car with the body was uncoupled from the other two that had come along with it and shoved over. The proprietor hovered about them nervously as they accomplished the task, and constantly wiped his face with a handkerchief. When it was finished, he looked desirous of speaking, but the policeman spoke first:

"Now, Simones, let's have it. What happened here? What do you know about this?"

"I?" replied the proprietor, with a slight accent that speedily revealed his Grecian origin. "Nothing at all. Can you imagine this happening on a Sunday night? It'll ruin me. My business will—"

"Never mind that now," interrupted the officer, sharply. For at this moment his colleague returned with the park doctor—an official whose services were often in demand on busy nights, but seldom for such a matter as this. It was evident that Mike had already explained some of the situation to him, for he went straight to his examination, without a question or pause. And Donahue addressed the other:

"Did you get Headquarters?"

"Yes; they're sending some one right down."

It was a hot night and when the phone rang Headquarters was particularly drowsy, for thus far there had been very little doing. The officer in charge came quickly enough to life, however, on learning what had occurred, and switched the speaker to the Central Detective Bureau.

Lieutenant Thomas, who was on duty, had difficulty in getting the bare facts straight, for Mike, at the other end of the wire, was excited and had not the controlling powers of his associate. Thomas, a stout, burly fellow whom years of experience had so inured to all surprises that many people thought him cold-blooded, quieted him down.

"Now," he said, calmly, "just go easy and let's get this straight. You say a girl has been hurt? Is she badly hurt, or not?"

Mike didn't know; he replied that he was just going for the doctor, but that it looked quite serious to him. There was much blood on the wound.

"All right. Just hold on for a few minutes, and we'll have some one there in a jiffy. It looks to me like a job for the Homicide Squad"—and with that Thomas rang off.

The details were none of his business; they were up to the man he sent out there. He considered that Tommy Rankin was a good one for it; it didn't look too important. Probably a killing in some sort of fight, he decided; and besides having some cleverness, Rankin knew his crooks and his underworld. There were always killings that involved gang feuds. And Tommy wasn't busy on anything else just then. While he waited for telephone connections, Thomas recalled how the detective had broken up the Curtis gang which had terrorized the city a few years before; and how, later, he had caught the notorious forger, Penrhyn.

"Good enough chap," he mused, "and young. Barely thirty, I'll bet."

The click of the telephone informed him that connections were complete. He heard a voice which he instantly recognized.

"Thomas speaking," said the lieutenant succinctly. "A call from Woodlawn Park; a girl stabbed down there. Go and make the usual report. And by the way, you can take Bill along if you want to."

This last was added as an afterthought on Thomas's part, and was meant as a joke. For he knew Rankin well enough to be aware that he always worked alone. It was one of his peculiarities that he never combined with anyone in his investigations. He never had had a colleague; even the routine business he did himself. "Solo" Tommy, some wit of the force had once called him, and the appellation was a suitable one. He often said that he was sure of thoroughness only because he trusted no one else to do what was, rightly, his duty.

The case Thomas thus briefly outlined over the phone did not promise much, but it was all in the routine. Rankin recognized the quip of his superior, but rang off without replying. He set out at once, assuring himself, on the way, that his notebook was in his pocket. That was the single bit of equipment without which he could not do. For his other peculiarity—and he had only these two—was his writing down of everything that occurred. He did not trust his memory; if a thought came into his mind that might be of value, he put it down, lest it should slip him and later be unrecallable. He even reasoned on paper; his deductions, his conclusions, his actual logic were all to be found in black and white within the pages of his precious book. And already he was preparing to store his first impressions there.

Rankin's arrival coincided with the close of the doctor's examination. The same curious, gaping crowds outside the concession's inclosure made way for him; no one had left for all were getting a ghoulish satisfaction from being witnesses of the tragedy. Nevertheless, the sudden transition from merriment to fatality effectively dampened their spirits. Several more park patrolmen were handling them and preventing them from pressing too close to the fence.

Within the platform, however, the spectators were becoming restless. Several expressed their desire to leave in audible terms, among them the young man whose partner had fainted. Willing hands and a glass of water had brought her to speedily enough, but she leaned tremblingly against the rail, with her escort doing his best to soothe her.

"That's all right," the guardian Mike told several. "There ain't goin' to be anybody leaving till the Central man gets here and says it's all right."

Rankin broke through and instinctively turned to Donahue as the most sensible man of the crowd. The latter recognized in him the air of authority of the force, and stepped up with a salute.

"My name's Donahue, sir." ·

"Right, Donahue. I'm Rankin." Out came the notebook, and his eyes swept the entire scene briefly. He saw in that glance the car, and the body, under the arc lights, the doctor, just rising from his examination, though his back was still turned, and the trembling brakeman. "Let's have the whole thing in a few words."

"Well, sir, I haven't found out much, to tell the truth. I've been waiting for you. From what I can see, the car came from a ride through the tunnel, and the girl, there, was in it, dead. And that's about all."

"You mean the girl was killed there, in that car?" There was incredulity in the detective's voice.

"Yes, sir," replied the officer. "I haven't done anything yet in the way of questioning. I got in the doctor, and sent Mike, over there, to get Headquarters, as well as get in touch with the morgue people."

"Well, I'll be damned!" Rankin had heard of peculiar places in which tragedies had occurred; he recalled the case in which a body was found cramped up in an un-lighted oven; and he remembered in the Pleasance crime the victim had been discovered in a main-line pipe. But this was more unusual than any of them. It stimulated his interest and made him think it wasn't going to be the commonplace case he first feared. Perhaps there was more in it than met the eye.

"Those people there," the officer continued, "in the enclosure, were the ones that came in on this ride. We've been holding them for you, and you may be sure no one slipped out. And I had the car moved over there, so it would be out of the way. But nothing has been touched, except by the doctor."

"Good work." The other nodded his head in commendation. "Who made the discovery, Donahue?"

"One of them two over there." The policeman pointed toward the proprietor and his employee. "That's Mr. Sim-ones—he's the boss of this shebang; and the other's the brakeman. I haven't been able to find out much, but I guess all these people saw it at the same time."

"I see." Rankin noticed that the doctor was standing in some indecision, waiting to speak to him. He was a gray-haired, wizened man in spectacles and he nervously fingered his medical bag.

"Yes, Doctor—a—?"

"Fisher," the physician supplied in a piping tone.

"Glad to know you." He was succinct in his reply. "What's the result?"

"It's comparatively simple, actually. The woman is dead—has been dead now for more than twenty minutes, I suppose. A young woman she is—I should say not much over twenty-one, if that. She was stabbed with a longish, narrow blade, perhaps five inches long, in the heart—in the very apex of the heart. Viewing it from the medical standpoint, I should say it was a beautiful blow, and who-ever did it knew his business. It penetrated between the fifth and sixth ribs, exactly."

"Does that mean that death was immediate?"

"Practically," came the answer. "Hardly more than a minute could have elapsed, anyway, for it was a clean-cut stab. The body was still quite warm when I arrived."

The detective nodded his understanding. He thought a moment before asking the next question.

"How long ago were you called in?"

"Well, I was in my rooms, down near the pond, when this officer they call Mike came to inform me of the affair. He said he came straight down, except to get you, and that the accident—or whatever it was—had just occurred. That was at exactly ten minutes after ten. And it hardly took ten minutes to get me."

"In other words, supposing that the discovery was made almost at once, that would place the crime at approxi-mately ten o'clock, would it not?"

"I suppose it would."

"I'll have to look into that." Rankin glanced at his watch and returned it to his pocket. "And it's now a good deal after ten-thirty. I've gotten an early start, at that. Have you got the weapon, Doctor Fisher?"

"No, I haven't. It isn't there, in fact. Naturally, the woman has been bleeding much on that account. Ordinarily, after such a blow, the body would slump down, if seated; but the girl seems to have been fairly well placed in an upright position, so that if the wound were invisible, things would appear fairly normal." The medical man paused, and then added in a stern tone, incongruous with his treble voice: "It's rather horrible to think that some one could have carried out a crime like this, and then paused to rearrange things the way it has been done. He deserves little mercy, whoever he is."

The detective wrinkled his forehead in the seriousness of thought. It was undoubtedly a grave case, whatever the facts behind it were. There seemed to be a long, thoughtful premeditation about it. But why should the crime, if such it were, have been committed on a scenic railway? That was the amazing thing—why a scenic railway? The chance the criminal took—the danger of it! He must have been a fool. And yet, was the criminal such a fool, after all?

He looked about him. In the distance, amusements were still continuing in full blast, unconcerned with the tragedy that had occurred in this one. People were still enjoying themselves elsewhere, everyone with his own crowd, taking no notice of other groups. Each appeared to be self-sufficient. It is often said that the safest place to commit a crime is in a large crowd. Everyone is so engrossed with his own affairs that he has no time to see other people. The natural selfishness of mankind makes each individual oblivious, in a large measure, of the difficulties of strangers. Where better can a hunted criminal

hide than among many people? Where better can he commit a crime than in the same crowd? It would be a simple
matter to stab—

Rankin realized he had no business racing ahead of his
information and forming preconceived notions that would
be difficult to obliterate. He would have to take things
in logical order, and work out the possibilities from his
discoveries. And the first thing would be to look at the
victim of the affair; at least make some sort of perfunctory
examination upon which he could improve later.

He looked up, nodding at the doctor's last remark.

"He won't get much mercy if we catch him," he replied,
with a steely quality to his words. "Let's have a look at the
girl before we go any further."

2

THE UNKNOWN VICTIM

Tommy Rankin was no amateur at the detecting game, despite his youthful age and appearance. At twenty-nine he had gained much knowledge of the criminal classes to which he had pledged a lasting enmity. He had started with the force at the minimum age, and in the ensuing period had gained quite a reputation for himself, particularly with regard to his ability to trail fugitives from justice. He knew his underworld perfectly—the various gangs who combated the law, and the chief haunts of the hunted; and among them he had gained a name for square dealing and fair shooting, so that all were sure of straight treatment at his hands.

He was of medium size and weight, tipping the scales at a hundred sixty. He was conceded by many to be rather good-looking, which fact did not make him especially vain. He had dark, piercing eyes, which were the most alive part of him, forever darting keenly and studying people; and his thin lips were generally set together. Of fair skin, he had dark-brown hair, which curled up in irritating knots. His entire pose was one of alertness and comprehension.

The detective was capable of no Sherlockian brilliance. His investigations were carried on by common sense and perseverance, so that he succeeded by sheer doggedness where others failed. He had his own share of mental ability, which enabled him to deduce meanings from his discoveries and reason logically to correct conclusions. But his capacities left him a rather serious-minded young man, with small imagination in other directions, and little sense of humor. He was typically a clever, ambitious worker who put all his attention to his occupation.

As Rankin approached the sideswitch in company with Dr. Fisher, he reflected upon this strange case to which he had been assigned. A girl killed on a scenic railway! How—and by whom? He could see the bulk of the body which the physician had mercifully concealed with some handy covering, to shut out the view from gaping, merely curious eyes. He lifted it without hesitation, for it was no time for squeamishness. The sight that met his eyes astonished him greatly.

He had expected to see a girl of the type who might be driftwood upon humanity—upon whom was written the stamp of a fast, hard life, with much of its ugliness and squalor. It was that type which usually incurred enmities resulting in such tragedies as this. Instead, he looked into the face of a girl whose youth and innocence were apparent even in death. Her features were finely molded and bore all the indications of genuine intelligence; her perfectly straight nose was finely shaped and pointed, so that in profile it would have appeared clean-cut. Her lips, untouched by paint, indicated humor and graciousness; it would have been wonderful to see them curve up in a smile. Her chin was small, and delicately curved away to a white neck. She had fine brown hair; her eyes, partially opened, were gray, and leaning forward, he thought he could detect in them, under the bright lights, a look of surprise.

Clearly she was beautiful—death could not rob her of that; clearly she was refined and genteel. If nothing else indicated that, her fine tapering fingers and soft hands, untouched by sores or abrasions, were sufficient evidence.

She was clad in a light summer frock of inexpensive material—a prettily patterned cotton cloth of some sort. It was the kind of dress a working-girl might wear on an outing—neat and attractive, but not costly. Neither were her shoes or hose costly. That was not in keeping, however, with the type of girl she appeared to be, and it was an incongruity that subconsciously worried the detective. The scarf she wore, now so miserably discolored in red, completed her attire; but he saw that whereas most of her garments were cheap, this last item was of the most expensive and finest silk, and magnificently embroidered. The thought flashed through Rankin's mind that the combination was at least peculiar; for if her clothes were her normal type of dress, how could she afford such a scarf? He quickly dismissed it, however, for girls, in these days, no matter what their circumstances, mysteriously manage to possess some fineries.

He bent over and gently disengaged the girl's hands from her purse, on her lap, pocketing it for later scrutiny.

Bending forward for an examination of the wound, he saw, as the doctor had pointed out, that it was a deep, sharp incision. It had stopped bleeding, however, and the medical man had managed to clear away much of the unpleasant outflow.

"Do you think it could have been suicide?" This was purely a routine question. He had, himself, no such belief.

Dr. Fisher looked astonished at the query; evidently the idea had never entered his mind.

"Yes," he replied, after a moment's thought, "it could have been, certainly, for it is a direct front stab; but it's hardly probable, is it? Why should she pick out this, of all places, to kill herself? Of course, that's hardly in my province; but then, where is the knife?"

"Couldn't it have fallen out?"

"No; that would be impossible. The blow is a straight one, you see, and, as I said before, quite deep. It is, one might say, a horizontal stab inward, so there is little chance of its having fallen out. No, it was withdrawn, without a doubt."

"I wonder why," mused the detective. He pondered the question, then made a brief note in his little black book: "Why did the criminal take the knife? Was it incriminating?" To the doctor he said: "Do you think there was any time for resistance—some sort of a struggle, perhaps?"

"Hardly," came the reply. "I doubt if there was more than enough time to, let us say, scream, before death intervened; perhaps there might have been a single convulsive movement."

Rankin looked disappointed. He had been thinking that if there had been some sort of a struggle it would net him a clue. But the floor of the car was of bare wood and showed no footprints or marks. Nor did the seat beside the body.

He turned back the lapel of the blouse she wore, but there was no maker's label on it. Neither was there any mark of identification upon her. She wore no jewelry of any sort, not even a necklace, though by bending closely for a minute scrutiny of her hands, he saw that on the fourth finger of the left hand was an imprint of a ring that had been recently there. It looked as though it had been barely taken off—certainly the mark was still red, a clear-cut circle. But thus far there was no clue as to who she was; and unless the pocketbook and his quizzing were productive of results, he would remain ignorant on this vital point.

Suddenly something glinted on the floor beneath the girl's feet. Only at a certain angle did his eye catch the reflected light. He picked it up with extreme care, for it was a silver cigarette lighter, such as many people now carry in the place of matches. A silver surface retains fingerprints clearly and he could not afford to obliterate a possible clue. On the under side were the initials J. N., carefully cut in. It was in perfect working order, as he saw by opening it; on the grating of the steel wheel against the rod of cerum alloy, sparks ignited the petrol-soaked wick.

Rankin expressed the thought that was in his mind to the watching physician.

"If this belongs to the criminal, it will hang him."

"Do you think it does?"

"I certainly hope so," returned the detective, "though it's possible that anyone dropped it, any number of rides ago." And then, as an added idea, "But if it had been there long, don't you think it would have been found, or fallen out of the car?"

Before the physician could answer, there came a sound of disturbance behind them. Pushing forward, the gentleman whose companion had fainted addressed the guardian patrolman in querulous tones.

"How long do we have to stay here? I've got to get this young lady home; she's not feeling good, and can't stand here, waiting—"

"You're none of you leaving yet," interrupted the phlegmatic Mike, waving him back. "Not till the boss says so. There's murder here; it's not a Sunday-school picnic."

Rankin turned to look at them. There were many of them, mostly strangers, and he realized he couldn't hold them all for an indefinite time; it was likely that they could tell him nothing. Mentally, he counted them, and the number of car seats. There had been three cars on the fatal trip, each of which contained four seats. That gave room for twelve couples; and he saw eleven couples within the railing, besides one extra man, of rather unprepossessing appearance. At the height of business, every seat had been filled; the dead girl was in the twelfth seat. Where, then, had this extra passenger come from? He must be accounted for. Was it possible that he had been the girl's companion?

He studied the man more closely. He was a burly, sullen-looking fellow with lowering eyes and drooping shoulders; his hands were gnarled and his nails were grimy. "Probably a day-laborer," thought the detective; it was absurd to think that he had been with the girl. Still, one could never tell. But it was foolish to suspect any of the couples.

"Is there any one of you that can tell me anything about this?" he called out, addressing them all. "Anyone who knows anything about it, or knows anything about the girl?"

There was no answer; and, following the dead silence, he turned to Mike.

"Take their names and addresses and let them go. We might need them as witnesses—some of them, anyhow. Find out which couple was sitting in the second seat of the first car; they might be able to tell us something. And"— he nodded toward the burly individual—"keep that one here till I can talk to him."

The man indicated evidently heard the words, or surmised they were talking about him, for he pushed forward truculently to register a protest. But Mike pushed him back with a sufficient display of brawn to overawe the combative stranger, and he relapsed into muttered argument regarding this discrimination. Rankin, however, paid no attention to these details, for he caught sight of Donahue waiting uncertainly beside him, trying to make up his mind to speak.

"Yes, Donahue?" His voice was encouraging.

"I beg your pardon, sir. Perhaps I oughtn't to say it— but there's one couple, I think, that knows something. I guess they can tell you something—"

"What do you mean?" Rankin glanced over the crowd.

"It's that girl there, that fainted. No one else did, and it struck me sort of funny that she should be so badly affected."

The detective gave the couple mentioned a closer look. The man was handsome, in a dark way, with swarthy skin that made it probable he was of Italian parentage. The girl was exactly the opposite—of exceedingly fair skin, and light, golden hair, while her features were well formed and attractive.

"It's not surprising, Donahue, that she should faint, if she's particularly excitable; it's not a pleasant sight."

"Yes, but there is something else, sir," went on the officer. "I was here when she came to, and I could swear that before she fully knew where she was or what she was doing, she spoke something that sounded darned funny to me. She said, 'My God! she looks like—' and that was all I could get, sir. But I'm sure she said that."

The other was startled from his equanimity.

"You are positive, Donahue?"

"Yes, sir. That's why it struck me so funny."

The names of the couple in question were just being taken when Rankin motioned to them. He received the distinct impression that the girl, at least, was nervous, more so even than the circumstances warranted. They came hesitantly.

"What do you want with us?" It was the young man who spoke, and his voice was perturbed. "I've got to get this girl home—she isn't well—and we don't know the slightest thing about it."

"Are you sure of that?" Rankin asked. "Nothing at all?"

"Absolutely. I'll swear to it. We were sitting way back in the last car, so how could we see anything at all? Isn't that right, Blanche?"

The girl looked disturbed at being addressed. She glanced nervously at their inquisitor, and saw his eyes were fastened upon her, as though they sought to bore into her thoughts.

"No—no—that's right—nothing at all."

He glanced at her exclusively as he put the next question, seeing which, her escort frowned his displeasure.

"Did you, for instance, never see the girl before? Or doesn't she look like some one you've seen somewhere before?"

"No, never. I don't know anything about her. I've never seen her before at all—that's the truth."

"Didn't you say, for instance, when you saw the girl, that you believed you knew her?"

Before she could answer, her companion interfered.

"Look here," he cried in harsh tones. "I told you this girl knows nothing about it—and neither do I. You can see how nervous she is from the shock, and if you don't let us go she'll be ill again. You've got to permit us to get away."

Rankin glanced at the doctor, who nodded to indicate that the man indeed spoke the truth when he said that she was in a high-strung, dangerous condition. He was positive that the girl, at least, was lying, but he realized that it was no time now for him to press his point. Accordingly, he submitted with as good grace as was possible under the circumstances.

"If you will give me your names and addresses, so I can get in touch with you if I want, you can go."

"Willingly, sir," the young man began. "I live with—"

"His address is 406 Porter Lane," broke in the girl, swiftly, "and mine is 5470 Stager Street. My name's Blanche Rushby."

"And mine's Alfred Ramon." It was evident that the young man was puzzled, and so was the detective, by this unexpected interruption by the girl. For a moment he thought they were trying to deceive him as to their true identities, but when he asked, the other was able to produce from an inner pocket an auto license and an envelope, both of which verified the name and address just given.

As soon as they had gone, he turned to the proprietor. Mr. Alexander Simones was almost blue in the face from excessive excitement and nervousness; he was evidently holding back something with great effort.

"Look here," he shouted, gesticulating wildly. "How long must I wait here for you to get ready? The busiest Sunday night this year—and this happens to ruin everything. And then I got to stay here till you get a lot of monkey business from your hands. My rival, Mr. Blumberg over there—" he waved in all directions—"coining money. Such a system."

The detective waved his hand authoritatively. "Stow it," he said brusquely. "If you've got any complaints to make, file them at Headquarters to-morrow. I'm ready to hear your story."

"I ain't got no story. I don't know anything about it."

"You're the proprietor, aren't you?"

The man subsided a trifle. "Yes, I'm Mr. Alexander Simones, and I'm the boss of this. But that don't make me know anything, does it? I was by the ticket office when that car came out—and there the girl was."

"By herself?"

"How should I know? I tell you I wasn't up there. Ask that loafer over there," and he pointed to Rawley. "He seen everything."

At hearing his name mentioned, the brakeman looked up. From the time he had aided Donahue and closed the gates, he had seated himself, taken out his pipe, puffed away, the while staring into space. It was evident that he had not yet recovered from the shock of touching the dead body. The appellation of the proprietor seemed to arouse him from the stupor, so that he rose and seemed on the verge of contesting its applicability with the speaker. But he caught the eye of the detective and paused, instead, to await his pleasure.

"What's your name?" Rankin asked.

"Peter Rawley, sir."

"You're the brakeman here, are you not?" And when the other nodded, "Tell me, now, exactly what happened. I understand you found the body. Is that right?"

"Yes, sir, but I don't know anything about it. I never saw the girl before in my life."

"Nobody said you did, Rawley. But exactly what did you see?"

The braketender looked his surprise at the question.

"Me? I didn't see anything at all. Why, the girl was just sittin' there, and when she didn't get off it comes to me she was some drunk, so I started to help her out."

The detective saw that he would have to be patient. Here was a one-track mind that would never lead, but merely follow.

"She was all right when she got on, wasn't she? You didn't notice anything wrong then?"

"No, I didn't. Why should I notice anything at all? They're all alike—the people that gets on here." His tone bore witness to his disgust for the position.

"See, I told you he was a loafer." The proprietor could not resist interjecting this remark

"Was she alone when she got on?" persisted Rankin. "Wasn't there anyone with her?" The crime would have been impossible unless she had had a companion, but thus far, unless he proved to be the burly individual, none had appeared.

The brakeman looked puzzled at the query; and it was almost a minute before he finally replied:

"Well, there wasn't anybody got off that seat there when the car came around. I'm sure of that."

"How can you be so sure if you weren't paying attention?"

"Well, I saw the boss looking then, so I watched the car. Some folks were just stepping out, and the first thing I saw was this here woman. She wasn't moving. But I'd swear to it no one had a chance to slip from that seat before that."

The detective had certainly counted on getting some trail in this direction. Under the canvas was the clearest evidence that a crime had been committed, yet he could discover no clue. Either the man was mistaken or there was something he had missed. He groped for another possibility, and seeing none, pressed the point.

"Think again and take your time about it."

Rawley obeyed literally. He returned to his original seat, sprawled his legs, and started puffing away at his pipe. Simones looked for a moment as though he were going to object to the pipe by pointing to a "No Smoking" sign, but he thought better of it. It was with deep relief that Rankin saw the brakeman suddenly rise and grin sheepishly.

"I guess you're right, boss," he said. "There was a man there with the girl but it wasn't on this ride; it was on the ride just before. This is her second ride; but he got off, and paid me for another ride he said she was taking."

His inquisitor's heart leaped with satisfaction. Here at last was something definite to work upon.

"What did he say?"

"Why, nothing much—not anything, I guess, except, maybe, 'Another for her.' I didn't take any particular notice of the girl then, but I guess she was sitting almost the same way the next time she came around. I s'pose it may 'a' been the same girl."

"It was," Rankin returned. "And then where did he go?"

"I dunno. I guess the only way there is—out. You see, yuh buy your rides for fifteen cents at the booth down there, and come in over there. And then, if you get a second ride, you drop a dime into this slot, here,"—he indicated a glass coin-receiving machine—"and stay on. Then when the ride is done you just go down this passage, out to the park again."

"I see. Can you describe the fellow?"

"Huh?" Rawley looked dismayed and scratched his head uncertainly.

"What did he look like? Was he tall or short?"

"Well, I guess he was middle-sized. I dunno. I didn't take any particular notice of him." He thought an instant. "Gosh! I'll be darned if I can remember anything about him."

"Did he look anything like that fellow over there?" Rankin pointed to the detained workingman. He realized if the brakeman had something concrete with which to compare his thoughts, they might be a little more productive.

Rawley stared at the prisoner. When he spoke, his voice was scornful as well as emphatic:

"Nuthin' like 'im. This chap was nice-looking—and nicely dressed, too. I guess he wasn't so tall, neither; and he had a big bulgy cap on—and I guess it was a brown suit."

"Was his face clean-shaven? Was he bearded? Is there anything you can tell us about his looks?"

"Well, he had no beard—nor mustache, nuther, but he just walked out so fast I couldn't notice anything more about him."

"Do you think you would know him if you saw him again?"

"Maybe I would. I guess so; but he'd have to be dressed the same, anyway. Otherwise, maybe—and maybe not."

Rawley finished in a weak, undetermined manner, and made a concluding gesture.

It was indeed concluding, for more than that Rankin could not elicit. Though he urged and cross-questioned for ten minutes, the brakeman could add nothing to his description of the missing person. He didn't know the color of his hair or cap; nor was he sure of any other item. Rankin made a mental determination to put the matter of identification to the test if occasion should ever arise.

His next step was to discover precisely where and how the crime was committed. He would have to go over the route of the murderer and murdered. He turned to the proprietor.

"Mr. Simones, do brakemen travel on the rides with your cars?"

"Oh, no, sir! There ain't any need. There's an automatic brake at the end of the first rise, before the cars go down the second hill." He added, proudly, "It's one of the best braking arrangements in the industry, too."

"Then I suppose I can just go ahead by myself, eh?" And when Rankin saw the look of surprise on Simones' face, he proceeded to explain.

"I just want to take a ride over the course. But understand, it's to be a free ride. I don't propose to pay for it."

The other winced, and he smiled. As Rawley, at his orders, arranged a train of cars for him, the physician, who had been waiting for some time in the background, announced his intention to depart. The detective obtained his assurance that he would be willing to cooperate with the morgue and inquest officials and then stepped into the car that was drawn up, preparatory to shoving off for the ride.

3

INVESTIGATION

At that moment Mike, freed by the departure of the last rider, approached Rankin hesitantly.

"There's reporters outside the gate, sir, that wants to come in. What shall I do about it, sir?"

Beyond the patrolman Rankin could see Billy Fairchild of the *Ledger,* Ormond of the *Sun,* Wolley of the *Inquirer,* all of whom he knew. Fairchild waved a greeting to him and called in a cheery voice. For a moment he was uncertain, but he realized how public the affair was already and if they didn't get the news here they'd get it elsewhere. And they might as well have it correctly. Intuition told him, furthermore, that this was a case where publicity would be desirable; he might need the press to aid him in learning who the girl was.

"Open up the gate," he instructed, "and tell them what they want to know and see that they get it straight." As the officer obeyed, he addressed Fairchild, who was the first to enter. "Where did you get the news so quickly?"

"Headquarters, of course. One of our men was hanging around. It's over half the town already, I'll wager. Not everybody can be killed on one of these contraptions."

"Hardly." The detective smiled, realizing that it was just that fact that was going to give him so much difficulty. "All right there, Rawley. Shove off."

Almost at once the pitch blackness of the tunnel enveloped the car. It was beginning to climb and there was no way of telling when he would reach the top of the incline. In the Stygian darkness there was nothing he could see; he could only hear the rattle of machinery as the car grappled with the lifting chain. How safe it would be, he thought to himself, to kill in this tunnel. The criminal was not such a fool. No one could watch him in the act, and all that was needed afterwards was a rearrangement of the body, and then that colossal bluff at the end of the ride. Even that was safe—to step nonchalantly out of the car, hand in a dime or drop it into the slot, and move on. Who was to notice anything wrong? But granting that something were discovered almost at once, it would do no good. A single step into the crowd outside the concession would take the culprit beyond all tracing. It was brilliant in its diabolical completeness.

The car was suddenly taking the first plunge. The sensation of rushing into unknown space was breathtaking, gasping. It was as though the entire world had suddenly collapsed under his feet. He felt himself careening madly about a curve, forward into a lesser dip, and then brought to a halt at a snail's pace that almost threw him forward in the seat of the car. Had the cars behind him been filled, the tunnel would have resounded with screams. What, then, if the poor girl had screamed in pain or horror? Was not everyone crying out at that very moment? Did not other cries mingle with hers, so as to make them inaudible?

Rankin had thought for a moment that the girl might have been stabbed from behind—that the person back of her might have risen, bent over her, and struck. But he discarded the possibility at once. The roof of the tunnel was too low to permit standing, and had such a thing occurred, the blow would have to be, perforce, a downward one. The doctor had said, however, that it was a straight blow. But the act was easy enough to one who sat in the same seat. The girl was in the man's arms; most likely she trustingly lay with head against his shoulder. A single stab and it would be done.

What, if all this were true, had become of the weapon with which the crime had been committed? For the moment that puzzled Rankin more than any other question. Either the criminal had taken it with him when he had withdrawn it—or else he had dropped it somewhere in the tunnel. This latter was a distinct possibility and it meant that the course of the ride would have to be searched. The detective could not see why, if this had been done, the knife had not been left in the wound.

The car swerved madly down the second hill—a plunge on a double turn like the letter S. Rankin clung on tightly and caught his breath; there was a queer sinking sensation in the pit of his stomach. It seemed an endless drop, and the darkness was so oppressive as to be unbearable. The next instant he was shot out into the level home stretch and the unexpected light at the end of the journey, blinking as though he had emerged from the bowels of the earth.

The reporters, who had in the interim made good use of their time quizzing the two officers, greeted him with shouts and catcalls. Rankin paid no attention, for at the moment the morgue wagon drew up before the concession and two officials approached him with regard to the disposition of the body. He had learned all there was to be learned from the remains at the present time, and, accordingly, it was removed, with solemnity and care, the tragic remains of one in whom had been, but a few hours before, the joy of life.

Rankin then approached the waiting proprietor.

"Mr. Simones," he said, "is there any way of making an investigation of that tunnel? There may be something there that could help us."

"Oh, yes! You could walk through if you are short. We got it lighted when we want to, because it's all wired through. Every six weeks we got to go over it and see if everything looks all right. And we try it out, with lights on, every day before we open."

"Good! Then put them on now, I'm going to walk through and see what is what. Donahue,"—to the officer—"stay at that entrance, and let no one follow me in. I don't want anyone putting anything over on me."

The patrolman obeyed, but the proprietor looked at Rankin as though he believed him mad. It took him a moment to make up his mind, but he finally moved toward an electric switch and turned it. At once a brilliant blaze illuminated the opening and as far inward as could be seen. Rankin hesitated and then plunged in.

It was no easy walk. He had to pick his way carefully among ties, in places where the bottom in which tracks rested was no more than a network. This did not occur often, however, for which he was thankful. Generally there was a substantial flooring beneath his feet. Dazzling bulbs completely chased the darkness and lit up every corner; it was merely a matter of keeping his eyes open as he walked. Going up or down, the strolling was just as difficult; the angles of the hill made it hard for him to always maintain a balance, and the climbing winded him in a very short time. He glued his eyes to the flooring, darting into corners and unexpected turns. Now and then he had to duck where the roofing lowered inward too far. Most of the time it brushed his head, anyway.

It took the detective twenty minutes to cover the distance. But he had discovered nothing for his pains. A few papers, dropped by joy-riders, earlier in the day, somebody's cap, and a scarf pin were the extent of the trophies collected in the tunnel. None of these applied to the case; they supplied no clue to the girl or her murderer. There remained, then, only the girl's purse, which still rested in his pocket.

Accompanied by Fairchild, who watched over his shoulder, he opened it, laying the articles upon the railing as he extracted them. It was a plain mesh bag, as inexpensive as the victim's clothes had been. In it there were only the ordinary belongings of a girl—powder and powder puff, but no lipstick; some small change, with a bill or two and some keys. There were also a movie program, folded into a bundle, and scissors. He examined each with care; but on none did he find the slightest clue that would tell him of the girl's identity.

"I've got most of the dope from Donahue, there," Fairchild broke in on the search. "But who in the world is she, Rankin?"

The detective smiled a bit wearily. It had been a long evening, and he was rather tired.

"You know as much about that as I do. I haven't learned a thing about that yet. And unless this bag tells me something, I'll be stumped, I suppose."

Once more he dug deep into the bag, and this time brought up a flimsy handkerchief and another folded bit of paper. Opening it, he discovered it was a note, written on fine paper that reminded him almost of office stationery of the highest grade, so smooth was its texture. The hand was sprawling, though strong and masculine, yet did not appear carelessly scribbled. Instead, it seemed to be the writer's normal fist. It read:

At the corner of Reed Street at nine o'clock.

J.

The initial of the note was the same as the first initial on the silver lighter. That was the first point, but it might just as well be a coincidence as not; probably it was, for half the people of the world are named John or James. He handed it to the reporter.

"What do you make of that, Bill?"

The other studied it for a moment, before replying:

"It looks to me as though the writer had made an appointment with the girl for to-night at that corner, eh, what?"

"Yes, that's what I make of it, too. But where in the world is Reed Street?"

"Somewhere in Germantown, isn't it? Wait a minute and I'll tell you."

Fairchild hunted briefly through the pages of a city directory. Then he nodded a corroboration. "That's right—forty-seven-hundred block, in Germantown, between Applegate and Downley."

"Um! I guess that must be right. This movie program is one of the Germantown neighborhood, too. Well, that's something to go on."

Rankin took out his watch, and was astonished at the passage of time.

"Phew! Almost one o'clock already! And I've got to write up my report before I go to bed. I guess I'll mosey along."

"Yes, but what about that guy over there?" The reporter pointed to where Mike was still guarding his unfortunate prisoner.

The detective looked. He had forgotten all about him. In the light of Rawley's evidence as to the missing man and his appearance, this fellow couldn't possibly have anything to do with the case. Nevertheless, he had behaved suspiciously and had to be explained.

At his motion the man shambled suddenly toward him. Rankin spoke in a sharp, threatening tone.

"What's your name?"

The man growled. "None of your business. Why must I hang around here like this when I ain't done nothing wrong?"

"Oh, it isn't any of my business, eh?" The detective was brusque as he jerked his finger about to where the body had been. "That girl that was over there was murdered, and unless you answer my questions you're going to be held under suspicion for doing it. And it won't be easy to get out, either."

At that the prisoner was thoroughly cowed. A frightened look came into his face.

"I swear I don't know nothing about it," he whined in a suppliant manner. "I swear it, that I'm innocent."

"Very well, then, answer my questions. What's your name?"

"Elmer Spearman, sir."

"That's better. Now, where do you work?"

The stranger seemed eager to make up, by his talkativeness, the stolid silence of a minute before.

"On the Broad Street subway construction, at the Columbia Avenue section. Al Costigan's my head boss. I don't have my union card with me, since it's Sunday, or I'd prove it. They gave me the day off."

"Very well, then, how did you get in here?"

"What do you think I did? Of course, I—"

"Don't tell me you paid," interrupted the detective, sternly, "because you weren't on this trip unless you sat up front with the girl. There wasn't enough room for you. Or maybe you were with her. Come on, let's have the truth."

The laborer became alarmed again. "No, I wasn't. You're right, I wasn't, but I didn't mean any harm. I was just trying to sneak over the rail for a little ride. I thought maybe I could do it and get away with it." He repeated, earnestly: "But not for any harm, just a joke."

Rankin studied the man's face. If his tale was true, he would be accounted for, even though it actually proved that Rawley was a loafer to let him get away with it. Simones would get a great deal of satisfaction from that. And he did not recognize the fellow as ever having come within the arm of the law.

"But you got on the wrong side," he said, hoping to catch the laborer. "This is the 'off' side. The 'Entrance' side is over there."

Spearman shook his head sheepishly and tried to grin.

"Yes, I know it now, but I didn't then. I thought I could sneak on, over here, and when I got over, that car came around, just like the brakeman said, and there was the girl dead there. So it was too late to get away."

The detective decided to believe him and let him go, even though he wasn't altogether satisfied. Certainly they could verify his identity easily enough, in case it proved necessary. Getting his address, he motioned Mike to release him. The laborer had been punished enough for his petty attempt at crime; he didn't appear in the least capable of plotting any greater one. And once freed, he darted off like a startled rabbit, and for the instant a half-smile played about Rankin's lips.

He turned to Fairchild, who looked as though he entirely disapproved the proceedings.

"Make the most of this, Bill. Let's have plenty of publicity and headlines. Tell the rest of them that."

The reporter stared quizzically at him. "What's the big idea, Tommy?"

"I rather think I'm going to need it. Since I can't find out who she is, other people will have to tell me. A girl can't drop out completely, you know. She's bound to be missed by some one. There'll be somebody who'll recognize her description or know her, of course, those who merely think they know her, as well as publicity cranks who don't know her at all, but claim they do. It'll be up to me to sort the genuine from the others, but too much news is better than none. There will be all sorts of it pouring into Headquarters about noon to-morrow."

"All right, Tommy. Depend upon me to play it big. It's a sensation, anyhow."

"And another thing. I wish you'd insert for me the following ad in the lost-and-found column of your paper: 'Found, a silver cigarette lighter initialed J. N. If the owner desires to have it returned, he should call at 530 Hector Street between eight and nine any morning or evening.'" The reporter scribbled it down in his book. "Got it?"

The other nodded, wisely refraining from asking questions. The detective verified the various addresses he had collected during the course of the evening—that of Rawley, of the laborer, and of the young couple. Despite his inability to learn one all-vital fact, he was well content with the progress of the evening. For as he took his departure and passed down the platform to his little car, his right hand clenched a tiny, flimsy silk handkerchief. Its existence he had, on the spur of inconceivable impulse— perhaps merely his native caution—kept from the knowledge of Fairchild and the other reporters. It was the handkerchief he had so carefully drawn from the bottom of the bag; and there were initials upon it, finely embroidered in silk. They were M. Y.

4

IDENTIFIED

Despite his late retirement the previous night, the detective arose before eight o'clock in the morning. He foresaw a busy day ahead of him, and was relieved to find that the weather promised clearness. He had spent more than an hour with his notes and his preliminary report before he went to sleep; and he had marked down each of his clues and trails, with brief remarks following. The report was a bare outline; the notes were more complete; and these he reviewed again to learn whether the conclusions he had come to in the night would satisfy him in the light of day.

> Handkerchief—Has initials, M. Y.—Who is she?
> Silver lighter—Has initials, J. N. Are there possible fingerprints? Does it belong to a party in the case?
> The appointment note—signed J. Is this the same as J. N.? See the policeman on Reed Street beat.

To each of them he had a possible trail. As to the girl's identity, he was sure that Blanche Rushby could tell him something. She had lied when she said she did not know her—of that he was certain. It was only the insistence of

43

her escort that had caused her to escape interrogation of a stern sort last night. The next time she would have no such supporter.

As to the lighter, he might receive some result from the advertisement. Of course, if the actual criminal had dropped it, there would be none; but if it belonged to a previous rider, he would at least have the matter cleared up and would know whether it had anything to do with the case.

Nor could he overlook the third possibility. The meeting to which the note referred was between the girl and her unknown companion, for nine o'clock, just when it was becoming dark; but if either party arrived before that time, it was possible that the bluecoat on the Reed Street corner had noticed them and could give him some assistance.

A single knock on the door informed him of the arrival of the morning paper. Rankin kept comfortable bachelor quarters just off Rittenhouse Square, and he had sufficient private means to insure numerous little conveniences. His three rooms were cozy and sufficed him for his present needs, and at times he did his own cooking, though an old woman came in to clean up daily and look after his wants. He was able to cook quite a variety of little dishes, for which ability he suffered some joshing from other members of the squad.

He barely needed to open the paper to realize that Fairchild had lived up to his promise. There, in crying headlines that outshone every other item on the page was:

UNKNOWN GIRL MYSTERIOUSLY SLAIN
ON SCENIC RAILWAY AT WOODLAWN
DETECTIVES SEEKING SLAYER
WHO FLED AFTER BLOODY DEED
An amazing tragedy occurred at ten o'clock last night at Woodlawn Park when a girl whose identity has not yet been ascertained

was found murdered at the end of a ride on a scenic railway. "Thrills in the Dark," the newest of the park concessions, the entire ride of which is in an enclosed tunnel, was the scene of the occurrence. The discovery was made by the brakeman, Peter Rawley, who was first attracted to the body by the failure of the girl to get out at the end of the trip. She had no companion with her at the time, which point baffled the police until they later discovered that this was the girl's second ride, and that on the first the companion, unknown also, but presumably the murderer, got off, leaving the dead girl behind him.

There followed then a description of the entire affair, the victim's appearance in complete detail, and ingenious conclusions that the writer had chosen to draw. The article closed with the inevitable line about "Police are now working on several clues which promise surprising disclosures."

Rankin was more than pleased. "That ought to be productive of some results," he thought.

When he had completed his toilet and helped himself to breakfast, he left for Headquarters. Having a little car of his own—a roadster—the trip to the Central Detective Bureau occupied but a short time. Lieutenant Thomas was just going off duty, and greeted him cheerily.

"Wait for me, Thomas," he said to his superior, "I'll be with you in a minute—as soon as I get my report in." He carried out his duties in short order. After depositing his report, he left the silver lighter with the fingerprint department, with brief instructions. Then he entered the main office. The official at the desk handed him a paper.

"For you," he explained, succinctly. "Came in early this morning. Two calls from Germantown and one from

Frankford. The first is from some one who thinks he saw a girl answering your description on the L platform at Fortieth Street station with a fellow; reports that they were squabbling, too. The one from Frankford reports the girl in Bryn Mawr. And some Germantown frau is worried because one of her boarders didn't come in last night, and she thinks this girl might be her."

"Thanks," replied the detective. "Send out one of the boys who isn't busy to this address. And find out for me if Elmer Spearman works on the Broad Street subway gang at Columbia Avenue." He handed in the address the laborer had given. He wasn't altogether sure of him, and it was best not to take anything for granted in this game. It was a risky business.

Studying the calls, Rankin rejoined Thomas. The Germantown possibilities looked to him like the better bets; furthermore, he could take Thomas home, on the way, for the lieutenant lived in that direction. Both entered his car and within a few minutes were driving through the parkway, and along the Schuylkill River, toward their destinations.

"It sounds fishy to me," remarked Thomas of the case, after a bit. "The man must have been a fool to take such a chance as that."

"Not such a fool as you'd suppose," returned the detective, warmly. "If you consider it, you'll realize it's one of the safest places imaginable." He described the darkness, the cries that made the girl's inaudible, and the crowds in which the man could escape. "But what worries me is that missing weapon. If the affair were so cleverly plotted as it appears to be, why use a knife which he had to take away with him?"

"I don't see quite what you mean." Thomas appeared puzzled.

"Here: If the crime were planned ahead of time, then so would the weapon be. The criminal would be sure to use a weapon that would not be telltale in any way. And then he wouldn't need to take it away with him. Yet he did just that—took it away. Now I ask you why?"

The lieutenant wrinkled his brow in thought. "Because he was afraid that it would give him away."

"Exactly!" Rankin swerved out of the way of a machine which was hogging the middle of the road. "That's the only explanation I can think of; so you see we're reasoning in a circle. And there's another thing. That note making the rendezvous with the girl. What's the idea of leaving it with her afterward?"

"He might have forgotten it."

The detective's features bore witness to his bewilderment. "Not likely, is it, considering the brilliant way the rest of it was planned."

"Well, it was his one mistake. They all make mistakes, no matter how cleverly they plan." Thomas spoke dogmatically. "It's the mistakes that hang them. Otherwise, how do you think we poor fish would make a living? We've plenty for which to be thankful to criminals."

They drove along in silence for some minutes, passing along the Wissahickon Creek, with its beautiful stream and high, green-verdured walls. The road curved constantly, necessitating a steady attention upon the part of the driver. At length Thomas broke in.

"Did the girl have any jewelry upon her?"

"No, not a bit of it. Not even anything in her bag. Though there was a mark on her fourth finger as though a ring had been there. Perhaps an engagement ring."

"Well," cried the other triumphantly, "did it ever occur to you what really happened? She let herself be picked up by some bum that was hanging around, who intended to

steal her things and when she resisted he had to kill her
with his own weapon. You know some of the people that
hang around that park. It's no Sunday school. I wouldn't
take them home and introduce them to my family."

It was a good explanation, but Rankin shook his head.
It was the one thing he felt sure had not occurred. "No,
I'm afraid that won't do."

"Why not?" Thomas was astonished. "It's perfectly
likely."

"Well,"—the other hesitated as he realized how weak
the excuse was—"she didn't look to be that type of girl.
You can generally tell that."

"How can you tell? By looking at her? Don't believe
it. What with the war and too much freedom, girls are
all alike nowadays." He waxed boisterous, for it was a
favorite theme. "There isn't one of them about whose
character you can say anything positive. As if they aren't
bad enough already, we have gun-girls as well as gun-men;
it'll be gun-grandmothers next. My daughters will know
what's what when they grow up."

He proceeded to discuss his family, but eventually reverted to the original point. The detective clung to his stand,
however, and refused to admit the possibility. However, he
could make sure, he reflected, if it were necessary, by going around to see old Ralph Carter. He was an ex-second-
story man who now watched the cars out at the park; and
there wasn't anything about the underworld or its bad men
he didn't know. He'd be able to tell Rankin whether any
suspicious characters had been around. They were still
arguing the point when the lieutenant was deposited at his
home.

Before driving off, the detective studied the addresses.
He decided to try the L station report first. That came
from Corcoran Street. It promised more than the other,
except for the fact the call from the worried landlady had

come from Morton Street; and Morton Street, he discovered by studying a directory he had brought along, crossed Reed Street along its route. However, he would soon know whether either meant anything.

The Corcoran Street house was a commonplace two-story dwelling. He rang the bell. The lady to whom he explained his errand was attired in a dirty housedress, unkempt and frowsy. She invited him inside and told him to wait a moment till she called Willie. Willie was a shy, stupid-looking boy of about fourteen, and obviously the woman's son. At first he was afraid to speak, but, prompted by his fond mamma, he was made to realize he had to tell the "man" everything he knew.

That alone should have been sufficient to warn Rankin of what was coming. It seemed that the boy had seen a woman standing upon the platform of the Fortieth Street L station. She was wearing pretty earrings, and a brilliant red dress which equaled the hue of her lips. It was impossible that she could have been the poor tragic victim of the scenic railway crime, even though she had gone home and changed her dress. The boy had seen this woman at four o'clock in the afternoon and the person with whom she was arguing wore a uniform which, when described, clearly indicated he was either an L conductor or porter. The entire tale was obviously worthless, and though experience should have accustomed him to false alarms, the detective was depressed.

If the other clues should develop in the same way, he would be at the end of his trail. If Blanche Rushby, whom he intended to see at the first opportunity, knew nothing at all about the murdered girl, if Donahue's suspicions were unjustified, it would be difficult to accomplish anything at all. The thought that he might not even be able to uncover the victim's identity was far from pleasant.

No. 2538 Morton Street, his second objective, proved to be a three-storied, red brick house with lace curtains that peeped from the windows, with a flower pot or two, and an approach of three steps. In one window a card bore the legend:

Boarding, Comfortable and Homelike

Rankin rang the bell with trepidation. Presently the door was opened by a short, squat lady of ample bosom and cheery eyes. Despite her age, which must have been fifty, her cheeks were red and her appearance cherubic. Her hands and apron were white with flour dough. It struck him that she was a clever, motherly sort of woman; most likely, though he couldn't tell why he thought so, a widow.

He explained that he came in response to her call of the morning.

"Oh, yes." She opened the door wider. "Won't you come in?"

He removed his hat and entered what appeared to be, in the semidarkness of drawn shades, a sitting-room. She began to talk before he had an opportunity to ask any questions.

"I'm Mrs. Schmidt," she informed him conversationally, "and I wouldn't have called at all, even because of that awful thing I read in to-day's paper, only it's such an un-usual thing to happen to Mary."

"I understand one of your boarders is missing—or, at least, hasn't been in overnight. Is that it?"

"That's it exactly, sir—that's just it." She nodded to assure him further. "You see, she's such a fine girl—not one of them that chases around all the time. That's the way Miss Young is."

She was, of course, unaware of the sudden satisfaction she had given Rankin by her words. He seemed to know,

intuitively, that he was on the trail at last—that the murdered girl was identified. M. on the handkerchief stood for
Mary; and Y. for Young. That was the girl's name. And he
felt a thrill at his first success; he was still young enough
to experience enjoyment out of his progress. Somehow,
his search was a personal matter to him. Meanwhile, Mrs.
Schmidt continued:

"She stays in much of the time, you know; and she
never stayed out all night like this before. So, of course, I
was worried."

"Naturally," the detective agreed, sympathetically, and he
spoke calmly, though within there was a raging excitement.
"So her name is Miss Young. How do you know she is missing?"

"It was when I went to make up her bed this morning.
I hadn't seen her go out, but I didn't think that very surprising. But when I went to fix up the rooms—as I do for
all my boarders but Mr. Rogers, he does it for himself—
why, I saw that it wasn't slept in yet and she hadn't been
in all night. So, of course, I didn't know what to make of
it. This—this"—she hesitated—"this crime couldn't have
anything to do with it, or her—could it? That's silly." She
laughed tremulously as though she was not certain. "But I
would like to know what's happened to her."

He tried to reassure her, though he had little doubt
that the missing boarder and the dead girl were the same.

"Most likely not. Still, it's best always to make sure. I'd
appreciate it, then, if you'd come with me now, and we'll
settle the matter."

"Now? Go with you now?" The idea flustered her and
she looked dubiously at her apron. "But I'm not dressed."

"That's all right. Just put on a coat and come along.
You'll be all right."

She succumbed to the urgency of his tone. "Well, if
you'll wait a few minutes till I fix myself up—" And she
bustled from the room.

The detective studied his surroundings while she was gone. It was a typical middle-class sitting-room. He remembered seeing a play, *The Show-Off*, in which just such a room was portrayed. There was the outdated, ancient green couch; a mantelpiece with a chime clock, one deep chair and several spindly, very ugly ones. Against the window that fronted the street was a piano with blackened keys and a covering scarf that resembled a colored table-cloth. Family portraits of assorted great-aunts and uncles decorated glaring wall-paper, but withal the room had a homey, comfortable appearance.

He resolved to proceed with caution. Despite his naturally phlegmatic temperament, he found himself on edge at the success of this long shot. But he warned himself to act circumspectly, for there was no foretelling what unusual situations he might unearth.

At length Mrs. Schmidt appeared, garbed in a heavy green dress, carrying a bonnet. This she tied in a bow about her chin as she entered the machine. She spread her skirts and settled herself comfortably.

"Of course, it couldn't be her," she began the moment they moved off. "Such a sweet girl, she was; no one in the world would want to harm her."

"How long has she been your boarder, Mrs. Schmidt?"

"Well, now, let me see." The landlady began figuring. "Two months ago, Annie Jones had her baby and she was here then. But she wasn't here when my uncle Sam died. Such trouble that poor man was having! Gout, rheumatism, and indigestion. It was the indigestion that killed him; but my aunt Sally insists it was rheumatism. Well, she's wrong, that's all there is to it. That was four months ago. She's been here just under three months—came to me some time in May."

Rankin let her speak until he received a reply to his original question.

"Where did she come from, before that?"

The lady stared at him with sudden wonder. "Lands!" she replied. "I don't know. I don't bother my people for their past history if they look acceptable to me in the first place. And anybody could see she was all right. So I gave her the left room on the second floor—that's right above the door. It's the lightest room in the house and comfortable as any. Of course, Mr. Rogers's room gets southern exposure, but then we all can't have everything, can we? I keep a respectable house and I'm particular as to the people I take in, but in Mary's case there was no question." She drew a long breath. "Do you think she could have stayed with a friend overnight? She never did that before."

"Perhaps she did." He decided to postpone further queries till the matter of the girl's identity was settled.

They passed through the park again, along the east drive, with the blue of the river glistening in the sun, and a few canoes and punts dotting its surface. And then along the parkway that leads toward the center of town, until Rankin switched off the main route and crossed Broad Street at Arch.

Presently they drew up before the morgue; it was a grim, foreboding structure of red brick. Mrs. Schmidt evidently sensed its gruesome character before she entered, for she seized the detective's arm apprehensively. Thus they entered, passing from the brightness of a sunshiny day into the chill gloom of an atmosphere pregnant with menace. A huge wheel revolved to keep cool this House of Death to which are brought the bodies of all those mortals who have died by violence. It fulfilled its function admirably; the air had a preservative coolness that was not the cool of nature.

An official hailed Rankin from the door as they passed into the cellar. Here the corpses, covered over, were laid out upon hard, bare tables, grim reminders of the tragedies

which brought their earthly careers to a close. The landlady clung closer to him as they passed into the semidarkness; he could hear her labored breathing. It reminded
him of the inquest that would soon have to be held. Clam-
miness became added to the other eerie qualities of the
surcharged atmosphere.

"Now just one look, Mrs. Schmidt, and it will be over."
Even he was gripped by the gruesome presence of death,
threatening them both as with impending evil.

The landlady regarded the pale, beautiful face, the
calmness of which had a strange, majestic quality. And he
could feel, standing close to her, a tremor move through
her.

"Oh, my God!" she cried, shudderingly, "It's her—the
poor dear, the poor dear! Mary Young—" Her voice suddenly dropped into an abyss of silence, and the next moment, she began to sob softly upon his shoulder.

5

THE BOARDING-HOUSE

After a period, Mrs. Schmidt recovered her poise sufficiently to be led gently from the building by the detective. Once beyond the grim influence of the building, the
warm, bright light still further restored her equanimity,
so that by the time they had entered the car she was almost composed again. She sighed deeply and blew her nose
vigorously into her handkerchief.

"That's the way it is," she turned reddened eyes to him,
"we're here to-day and gone to-morrow. We can never tell
when we're to be called above. But just think of the poor
girl in there! Who could have been so cruel?"

Rankin spoke in a soothing fashion.

"That's just what we are trying to find out, Mrs.
Schmidt, and you must help us. So if there is anything
that you know that can possibly be of assistance, you must
remember it and tell me."

"But what, Mr. Rankin? I wish I knew something about
her." Clearly, she was impressed with this new responsibility.

"You say, for instance, that she came to you three
months ago, but you don't know from where? Didn't she
ever talk to you about her family or her home?"

"Never a word, sir. I remember I did speak to her once
about her people, but it wasn't any good. She just sort

of avoided the subject. I didn't think anything of it, and of course I'm too polite to insist on anything like that. I never believe in butting into other people's business."

The detective nodded, but he wished she had displayed more curiosity. "Quite right. Still, there must be some way to learn something about her. For instance, in her mail, was there anything there you might have seen?"

The woman shook her head in dissent. "Do you know, that really is a peculiar thing, now that you mention it. I don't believe she ever got a letter while she was with me—not one. Just the morning paper."

Rankin pondered the significance of this. No letters—that was, indeed, unusual. He was sure there was something worth fathoming behind the fact.

"What about her work—what did she do for a living?"

"She did tell me—if I can remember it." Mrs. Schmidt paused in thought for an instant. "Yes—she was private secretary for Mr. Charles Bond—in town somewhere, I believe it was. And I think she did very nicely."

He knew the name vaguely. An extremely wealthy man, the head of a powerful electric concern and well known as a philanthropist. He thought he could recall some scandal about the name—also—something about a divorce case in which the man had figured as a correspondent; but the details were too nebulous in his mind for further consideration. He had married a fabulously rich widow, one Mrs. Arthur Hampdale. It was her money that gave him the necessary start. He would have to stop in at the Bond office to make inquiries. The chances were that they would be doing the same when Miss Young did not appear for her daily work.

He mentioned the fact to Mrs. Schmidt. The girl's identity was not in the papers as yet, and he did not wish it to be made public till the following morning; in the interval he should have made some progress.

"If they call up, tell them that Miss Young is indisposed and that she will be in to work to-morrow."

"All right, Mr. Rankin. But I don't think she was staying there much longer. Something she said to me Friday gave me the idea that she was moving to another place, though I don't know where."

The detective pricked up his ears: "Do you remember what it was?"

"I don't recall exactly, for I wasn't paying much attention to it, but it was something about not liking her work or something like that. But I was peeling potatoes for supper—"

"When was this?"

"On Friday evening, sir, and she never said a word about it before or afterward, either."

"I see." The point did not seem of consequence to him, so he failed to press it further. During their talk he had been giving much of his attention to the wheel; but as he asked the next question he bent his eyes upon her in fixed regard. "Tell me, Mrs. Schmidt, did Miss Young ever have a gentleman friend whose initials are J. N.?"

Though astonished at the query, she nodded her head vigorously. "Why, yes! That was Mr. Norris—Mr. James Norris; and he was sweet on her, too. He used to come calling a good deal and they'd spend the evening in the parlor or perhaps go out for a stroll. A fine upstanding young man he was, I thought."

"Who was he, exactly?"

"Now, I'm afraid I can't tell you that. I don't know where he lives or what he does. Maybe some one else at the house can tell you that. But we all liked him; he had a cheery word for everybody and he was quite good-looking, too. A splendid pair they would have made. Of course, some of us were hoping she might consider Mr. Rogers— he's a boarder, I mentioned—more favorably; he thought

the world of Mary, too, only I suppose he was too shy to
say so. This will be a terrible shock to him, poor man." She
sighed deeply again, and it was evident that the thought of
the tragedy still weighed heavily upon her.

Rankin found she did not know how the two had met,
nor where, and neither was she certain as to the progress
of acquaintanceship. She surmised, however, that it had
gone rather far.

"I can't say why I should think so, only for the last two
weeks Mary—I still think of her as though she were alive—
was wearing a ring on the fourth finger of her left hand.
That's the engagement finger, you know"—Mrs. Schmidt
leaned toward him meaningly—"and it was a diamond ring.
So of course we just drew our own conclusions about it."

"But didn't she say anything about it?"

"No, she didn't, and that's just why it was so funny."
Mrs. Schmidt clearly felt the injustice of this lack of confidence. "But I was just sure of it. How could I say anything, though, when she didn't? It wasn't anything to be
ashamed about, was it?"

"No, hardly." The detective weighed what he had just
learned. There was a young man in the case whose initials
corresponded to those of the cigarette lighter. James Norris. Despite the reticence of the two, which was in itself
peculiar, he was sure that Mary Young and he had become
engaged. For there was that ring on the engagement finger.
And it had come off recently—the mark it left was still
very clear. Now why? Had they quarreled? Had she given
it back to him? If that had occurred during or just before
the ride on the scenic railway, would not that be sufficient
provocation to kill? Especially if the man were hot-tempered or extremely self-centered.

He had no actual grounds for supposing such a case.
And yet, it was a real possibility and worth investigation.
He gradually approached the point.

"Tell me, Mrs. Schmidt, was Miss Young wearing that ring yesterday when she went out?"

"Last night, you mean? I'm afraid I didn't see her then at all; most of the evening I was inside in the sitting-room, knitting, but just for a part of the evening I was in the back yard talking with Annie Jones. We talked about the baby's teething, and she was quite worried, although it is not due for another two months at least. And if she went out, it must have been then, for I never saw her go."

"What time was that?"

"Somewhere—just before nine o'clock, I think it was." Remembering the time set for the appointment, he realized that this must be correct. To meet her companion on the corner of Reed and Morton streets on the hour, Mary Young must have left the boardinghouse a few minutes before. During the period Mrs. Schmidt was in the rear. But she could tell him nothing in regard to the one she was to meet—whether it was James Norris, as he suspected it was, or not. He tried one more query.

"During the day, then, did you notice whether she wore the ring?"

This time the explanation was even longer than before, but it was to the effect that in the morning Mrs. Schmidt had not seen the girl at all, and in the afternoon, while she sat in the sitting-room, she had barely caught a glimpse of her as she went out at about five o'clock. They had spoken no words, and the landlady had had no opportunity to discover whether she still wore her ring. But she knew that later in the evening, perhaps at seven o'clock, the girl had returned because she had heard her go upstairs.

"And then, as I told you," she concluded, "I didn't see her go out again, though she must have done so. And I couldn't tell you with whom she went—or if she went by herself."

"And nothing she ever told you indicated that she might be in difficulties or have any enemies?"

"No, nothing at all. If I hadn't seen the poor soul myself, I wouldn't have believed it. She was always cheerful and in the best of spirits."

They threaded their way through the traffic of Germantown Avenue approaching Morton Street, and Rankin had to remain alert for a few minutes, dodging the mixed heavy lines of trolleys and machines. There were still several questions he desired to ask, though they could wait until he had made an investigation of the murdered girl's room. Meanwhile, however, her fellow lodgers loomed importantly as possible sources of information. At least, they would be able to help him fill out the facts. Gossip travels fast and insidiously among lodgers. Accordingly, as soon as he was able to relax his vigilance, he put a question regarding them.

"Well, sir, I've got seven lodgers now—only one room vacant and that's a back room on the third floor. You see, there are four rooms on each floor—a left front room and a left rear one; a right front room and a right rear. It's the left rear on the third floor that's vacant. Miss Mary, poor thing, had the left front room on the second floor, as I told you, and that Mr. Rogers who liked Mary has the right front room just opposite her. He's a clerk and very young—barely twenty-three, I do declare, and real quiet. A peculiar sort of man, if you get what I mean—nervous and bashful-like. But we all think a lot— Look out, Mr. Rankin, for that machine!"

Mrs. Schmidt gave vent to a subdued scream as the detective swerved out of the way of an oncoming car barely in time to avoid a collision. It was almost a moment before she recovered her breath sufficiently to continue her tale.

"Next to him—that's the right rear on the second floor—is old Mrs. Edgecomb. She's seventy if she's a day,

but she insists she's only sixty. Imagine telling me a story
like that! And such a gossip! You've no idea how that
woman talks. I could swear she makes up some of the things
she says, and I say she ought to be ashamed of herself."

The detective was not particularly interested in Mrs.
Edgecomb's story-telling capacities, so he urged her on.

"And who rooms next to Miss Young?"

"A young lady named Miss Graham. I think she's a
saleslady downtown. She's been with me only about six
weeks—came sometime in June, I do believe; and she came
at a lucky time, too. She would have had to occupy a
top-floor room, but Mr. Callender, who worked in the
Stock Exchange, had just moved out the day before. So, of
course, I gave her the vacant room.

"Now, on the third floor, left front, there's Mr. Samuels.
He's a night watchman, so we hardly ever see him because
he goes out at six in the evening and comes back at six in
the morning. And then, of course, he sleeps all day. The
right front room has Mr. Humphreys, who is a plumber,
and next to him is Miss Minsey, who teaches school in the
Twenty-first Ward."

They drew up before the boarding-house. The detective
assisted Mrs. Schmidt into the house and requested the
key to the dead girl's room. He needed an uninterrupted
freedom of investigation till he had completely finished
his search; much depended upon its success. The landlady
complied, procuring it from a rack in the kitchen, and he
passed up the stairs.

"It's on the right side as you go up," she instructed him
from below. "You can't miss it."

Nor did he. The lock clicked as he turned the key on the
inside and he faced about to view the chamber. A pleasant
room, plainly but neatly furnished; he thought he could
detect in the arrangement of the furnishings an artistic
touch which could hardly be Mrs. Schmidt's. The bed,

occupying the room's center, against the wall, had been, as she informed him, unoccupied the preceding night; the upper cover was thrown back invitingly. On the left was a closet the door of which swung partially open; opposite it, against the right wall, was a highboy, on which were the usual articles of a woman's toilet and some inexpensive but colorful ornaments. Several small rugs of simple, trim pattern covered the floor. A connecting door, leading to the next room—the left rear, he recalled—was locked. A small table with two chairs, placed so as to catch a maximum of sunlight from the two front windows, completed the equipment and the entire effect was one of tidiness.

He began by opening wide the closet door. Within were five dresses, on hangers, together with some pairs of shoes. The latter were of no particular make but merely for serviceable and for practical wear. The dresses were spread across the complete length of the closet and were characterized by the same qualities—all were neat and plain, such as a secretary would don.

He was about to close the door, believing there was nothing to be learned from them, when he caught a sudden quick glint of sunlight behind the clothing. He looked again, pushing the garments aside. Behind them were two more dresses he had missed at first; and they were of an entirely different character. Both were richly and beautifully made; one was of pink silk of the finest quality and material, and the other was white, more in the style of an evening gown. Even his male eyes could appreciate their expensiveness. They were incongruous in this closet and in these surroundings; and the incongruity of it had a familiar touch. There had been the scarf which was out of keeping with the rest of her clothes, and now she possessed dresses which were similarly inconsistent. The incident was beginning to take on some importance; it was worthy of a memorandum in his little black book.

The dresses gave him no assistance in his quest, however; the labels with the names of the makers, if any had ever existed, had been removed. This circumstance was, in itself, most unusual.

Rankin's examination of her other apparel netted him nothing in the way of information. From under the highboy he drew forth a fine leather suitcase with the initials M. Y., but that was hardly news. The bedclothes and the towels belonged to the boarding-house. He went thoroughly and completely through the highboy, examining every article with extreme care, and learned little for his pains. All of it—underclothing, ornaments, toilet articles, and some cheap jewelry—was new, recently purchased, and lacking any identifying marks. It was as though their owner had deliberately attempted—and with success—to blot out her former life, whatever it was. Nowhere was there any writing.

It annoyed him at first and then irritated him. What could be the cause of this willful effort to separate her former existence from her present one? Why should she obliterate the events which had occurred more than three months ago? She had received no letters. What could be the answer to that? Either she had no relatives or she was an outcast; and the first was unlikely. And the second? He began to believe that Lieutenant Thomas may have been right when he said the girl could just as well have been a bad one. Of course, Mrs. Schmidt did not think so; but it is easy to deceive people, and hers was the impression of a single person. What was the past she evidently desired to hide? Who were her people? If his examination of the inmates of the house brought him no results, the only place to which he could turn was the office of Mr. Charles Bond. Surely they must have demanded some credentials from her when they employed her.

There remained only the little table. The detective opened the single shallow drawer, and on the surface, discovered a box of letter paper. He removed the cover. It was untouched; not a single sheet or envelope had been used. There was something ironical in that fact. But he removed it, nevertheless, and beneath it were papers—four of them—the newspapers, evidently, which Mrs. Schmidt said that she received daily.

Casually he picked one up, and opened it to get the date. And then his heart leaped with gratification. For they were not local papers at all! They were four papers of the past week, of the *Daily Tribune* of Gary, Indiana. Something tangible here, at last; something to connect Mary Young with her previous existence! Perhaps her last stopping-place, perhaps her home town; it made little difference at this moment. It was sufficient that he had a clue to her past. He studied the sheets to discover whether he could select any special item that might have interested her, but a hurried survey revealed nothing unique or unusual. He'd have to give more time to it, later; and meanwhile a telegram would have to be directed at his earliest opportunity to the Gary chief of police, inquiring for Mary Young.

Having completed his inspection, he replaced all things as he had found them, satisfied that there was nothing more to be discovered. He unlocked the door and stepped into the hallway. There, standing in the doorway of the room to the rear of the dead girl's, stood a young woman with flaming red hair, who watched him through lowered eyelids, and with a half-smile playing about her rouged lips.

6
MISS RUTH GRAHAM

For a brief moment Tommy Rankin found himself staring speechless, almost rudely, at the vision that stood before him, as though he believed her to be an apparition. She had such keen, searching eyes that they disconcerted him and caused him to come to a complete halt. She was the first to speak, nodding in a friendly fashion as she did so.

"Good afternoon, stranger."

She had a pleasant deep voice that was strangely musical. It was rich in its intonations. The detective returned the greeting.

"You are Miss—a— ?"

"Ruth Graham," she informed him lightly. "Correct the first time. Never mind the 'Miss.'"

He thought he certainly ought to learn something from one who had been Miss Young's nearest neighbor, no matter for how short a time. Girls are fond of confiding in each other their various tribulations.

"Has Mrs. Schmidt spoken to you about the tragedy?"

"Yes. I just came in, and she told me about it. Poor kid!" There was a world of sympathy in her voice: "That sure is a tough break, I'll say."

"Did you know her?"

"Well, slightly; you see, I—" She broke off and motioned him into the room with a slight provocative smile. "Won't you come in?"

Rankin hesitated before accepting the invitation. In her last few words he recognized the girl's type. Tall, large, almost masculine in physique, she was that specimen of femininity who could play fast and loose with a fellow. She could be slangy, tantalizing, and daring, but always would avoid stepping over the danger line. All her attractions lay in the little insinuations of her behavior, the subtle invitations, yet she appeared fully capable of caring for herself. He wouldn't give much for the chances of one who attempted familiarity with her against her wishes.

Accordingly, he entered slowly. When it came to women, Rankin was not far from being naive in his artlessness. His life had been too busy, and too serious in his efforts to make good, to have allowed him much time for companions of the opposite sex and this one was not too comfortable. He took the seat she offered, but refused a cigarette.

"Now," she said, with a smile, as she took one, lighting it, "we're ready for a good old-fashioned quiz, aren't we?"

"I suppose we are," he agreed. "Perhaps the best thing would be for you to tell me just what you know; anything at all that might help me."

It was Miss Graham's turn to hesitate. "Well," she said slowly, at last, "I don't know if what I can tell you will do you any good. You can take it or leave it. Of course, I didn't know the poor kid well; I'm out all day, and she kept a good deal to herself. Not snobbish, you understand, just quiet and reserved. Still, we did get acquainted a bit. I suppose Mrs. Schmidt told you about Jimmy Norris already?"

"She did mention him," he replied, cautiously feeling his way.

"Well, he was her fiancé; they were engaged to be married."

Rankin nodded. "So it had gone as far as that. Mrs. Schmidt thought so, too, but she wasn't sure."

"Oh, yes. She had the ring already. She didn't want everyone to know it, though, so she said nothing about it. She told that old snooper, Mrs. Edgecomb, that she had bought it herself. I guess that gave her an earful for her newsy ways!" A smile of amusement played for an instant about her lips.

"Do you know anything about him—this Norris? Who he is and where she met him?"

"No, I couldn't tell you that, I'm afraid, because, to tell the truth, she never discussed him with me at all; at least, not until yesterday. But I know he lives at the Enderley Apartments; that's somewhere in West Philadelphia."

"Not until yesterday?" Rankin was alert, though disturbed by the fact that Miss Graham's eyes were upon him. "Why, what happened then?"

"Well, it was yesterday afternoon. She came into my room—for the first time, I suppose it was—and she was weeping bitterly, crying as though her heart would break. I asked her what was the matter, of course, and she told me she had broken her engagement and given Norris his ring back, on account of a quarrel she had had with him."

"A quarrel?" This was a corroboration of his own deductions. "What was it about?"

"The poor kid wouldn't tell me that; it was the one thing I couldn't get out of her. But it must have been pretty serious, for she was crazily in love with him before that. I suppose it was something he had done—or maybe it was another woman. But I got the general idea that he wasn't interested in her any more, though I couldn't be sure of that."

Miss Graham took several puffs, and watched the smoke rings, which she had so skillfully formed, dissolve into the air. She shifted to place a pillow beside her.

"That's men for you," she went on. "Get a poor girl where they want her and then drop her. It's happened many

a time. Of course, I tried my best to comfort her—I told
her that he wasn't worth worrying her head about if he was
that kind of a fellow, and that she'd best forget him. But it
didn't do much good, because she seemed to feel it was as
much her fault as his and she was already sorry and willing
to patch up things if she could. Mary even said she'd go so
far as to forgive him for what happened, and start again.
I suppose she became hot-tempered during the argument
and threw him his ring. But now she seemed ready to find
him and ask to be taken back. Catch me running after a
man like that!" she added, scornfully.

"When did this occur? Do you know that?"

"It was on Saturday night; they went out to a dance or
something of the sort. He came for her just before nine, so
she said; but the spat must have begun almost at once, for
she came right home—she was back in an hour. And she'd
been miserable ever since."

Rankin nodded his comprehension. "And what happened afterward?"

"After a bit I managed to calm her down, and I tried to
persuade her to rest a bit; but she was too jumpy for that.
She insisted she was going to find him—call him up, perhaps, and if she couldn't get him that way, she'd go and see
him. Either that or get him to call her. I don't think she
knew exactly what she wanted to do, and she was taking it
so hard that I was awfully sorry for her."

He wished that she would cease staring at him the way
she was doing—had been doing, in fact, ever since their
conversation began. From the first words, Miss Graham's
eyes had been fixed upon his face. She was looking at him,
and, it seemed to him, almost through him; and all the
while there had been playing in those eyes and about these
lips the same half-smile with which she had greeted him in
the doorway. It was challenging, it was tantalizing; at first
it merely disturbed him, but later it made him feel most

uncomfortable. He felt in that smile a vague, inexplicable defiance. It was a recognized fact that he had some claims to handsomeness, and he wondered, squirmingly, whether she was attempting a flirtation.

She extinguished her cigarette before going on.

"Finally Mary went out—I suppose to do as she had said she would; and since she had been with me for more than an hour, it must have been after four-thirty."

"And after that, did you see her again or find out whether she had succeeded in finding Norris?"

"No, I'm afraid I didn't," the girl replied at once. "I don't know what happened after that. She came in at seven o'clock in the evening, because I heard her in her room. But she didn't do more than greet me through the door, and she didn't say anything at all about her difficulties. And I went out, myself, just a little bit later."

The time details, at least, were correct. Mrs. Schmidt had also seen the girl leave the house at five o'clock, and had heard her return, while she sat in the living-room, at seven o'clock.

"So you can't tell me where she went then?"

The reply was in the negative. He leaned forward toward her. Whatever her traits, she appeared to be a shrewd girl; consequently, her opinion would be valuable.

"Do you think it possible that Norris might have killed the girl?"

Miss Graham shrugged her shoulders. "God knows what happened to her; but he might have, for all we know. If a man's low enough to throw her over, why, he might be low enough to do anything."

It was evident that she did not have an exalted opinion of the opposite sex.

That terminated their conversation regarding the crime. He mentioned the other boarders casually, and when he came to speak of Mr. Rogers she was at once full of contempt.

"What about that poor fish?"

He wondered why Miss Graham should think so little of the boarder.

"I understand he thought a good deal of Miss Young."

"I suppose he did, but he hadn't a chance with her; and it was a wonder he wouldn't realize it. A mooning fool—he used to watch the poor girl wherever she went, and pester her for a chance to talk to her. Joe Rogers isn't half a man. I'd have soon put him in his place, if I had been her, but she was too gentle to hurt him."

"What do you mean, pester her?"

"Well, for instance, he used to watch for her to come out of her room. You know, his room is diagonally across from mine and just opposite hers, so I could see him, in the evening. He'd keep his door open all the time to wait until Mary came out. She must have been sorry for him. I know I wouldn't have stood it very long."

The detective grew aware that Joseph Rogers would be an interesting man to meet. He appeared to have an unusual personality, and it was possible that he could tell him something of importance. Rankin decided to save further interrogation in regard to Rogers for the man himself. And meanwhile Miss Graham still watched him, in that subtle but veiled challenge. Why didn't she stop it? He could feel himself getting hot under the collar.

The interview was at an end; he thanked her and rose. "Oh, must you go already?" Languidly she rose with him, and her tone expressed regret. "I thought perhaps we might have a pleasant chat together on more sociable subjects— ourselves, for instance."

He was confident that she was "pulling his leg"; nevertheless, he felt the warmth of blood rushing to his cheeks and he was a trifle confused. She dared him, in both her voice and her attitude, to continue their acquaintance- ship, and he thanked Heaven for the moral strength and resolution it required to disregard the invitation he read in those expressive eyes.

"Too busy now," he replied as brusquely as he could. "Perhaps some other time."

"All right, then. Some other time."

There was a finality to her words, as though she intended that he live up to that promise. She watched him out of the door and down the stairs; it was not until he had turned the last step, into the hallway below, that he experienced relief from her boring eyes. As the door closed above him, he thought he heard a faint musical ripple of amused laughter behind it.

Mrs. Schmidt appeared from the kitchen, again engaged in cooking. She directed him to the phone, in a cubbyhole under the steps, and he asked for Headquarters.

He reviewed to himself, while awaiting his party, the information he had collected regarding Mary Young's fiancé. On Saturday night there had been a serious quarrel between them and the engagement was broken. On Sunday, regretting her decision, it was evident that she had sought him, to come to an agreement. In some unexplained manner an appointment was arranged between them to meet at Reed Street at nine o'clock. Assuming that Norris had no intention of permitting a settlement between them, that, for instance, he was involved with another girl—her importunities would make him furious and desperate. There he had a sufficient motive for the crime. True, it was weak and many links were yet missing, but it hung together fairly well.

He gave Headquarters instructions to wire to Gary a complete description of the murdered girl, and inquire for her.

"Anything new?" he asked.

"Nothing special," came the reply over the wire. "Johnson [the fingerprint expert] has a beautiful enlargement of a thumb from the silver lighter in case you need it. It has a noticeable scar across the center of the ridges, like a crescent."

"I'll drop in for it later."

Rankin rang off. Mrs. Schmidt had already informed him that she had spent Sunday afternoon in the house, and this fact took on a curious importance in the light of what Miss Graham had told him. If Mary Young went out to seek her lover, or to call him, she may have used the house phone to do so. And Mrs. Schmidt may well have overheard something which would connect the events of the afternoon and the evening.

He put the question to her directly.

She was positive no call had been made. "As I told you before, I was in the living-room during the afternoon, and I can hear very plainly every time the telephone rings or is used. Ordinarily, I'd go out in the park on a Sunday afternoon, to sit with Mrs. Edgecomb and take in the air; but yesterday the heat kept me in. It didn't keep her, though, I declare, Mrs. Edgecomb goes out every afternoon and evening and sits in Vernon Park. She ought to be in now."

"When she went out, at five o'clock, did she say anything to you?"

"Nary a word. She walked right past me. And though I heard her come in later, I never saw her again. Not until I saw her, poor soul, this morning."

The detective changed the subject abruptly.

"Have any of your boarders come in yet?"

"All but Mrs. Edgecomb and Mr. Rogers and I'm expecting them very soon now. Mr. Rogers clerks down at the National Securities Bank, and he's generally done there about four o'clock and Mrs. Edgecomb never stays out later than five."

He received from her fresh information as to the location of the various rooms and names of the boarders on

the third floor. It was just after four o'clock and if it took
the interesting Mr. Rogers an hour to travel from town
and the National Securities Bank was on Chestnut Street,
he had an hour to wait till he would be able to quiz him.
Meanwhile he would learn what the night watchman, the
plumber, and the school-teacher on the upper story had
to tell him. From them he did not hope for a great deal;
the storm center appeared to be focused on the second
floor. It amazed him to contemplate the mingled drama of
life that had been progressing almost imperceptibly in this
commonplace little boarding-house. It resembled boiling
water, he thought, only a few bubbles and ripples on the
surface to indicate that there was any kind of disturbance
at all; and then suddenly an explosion which caused the
superheated liquid to fly in all directions and scald whoever was within reach.

He was not disappointed, therefore, with the results
of his investigation in the upper regions. Mr. Samuels,
the night watchman, had just risen, in preparation for his
coming labors, and he hadn't the slightest idea what the
young man desired in his room. Rankin did not take the
time to enlighten him. Humphreys proved more interesting, but hardly more informative. He knew nothing that
would add to the detective's store of knowledge, having
barely ever spoken to Miss Young; but he was nevertheless
willing to discuss the matter at great length. When he was
refused the opportunity, he looked obviously distressed.

There remained Miss Minsey. The school-teacher
proved a tiny, faded, mouse-like creature whose squeak-
ing voice still further accentuated her resemblance to the
rodent. She knew all about the crime from the landlady,
who had evidently spent less time in the kitchen than she
appeared to have done, and she was full of sympathy for
the unfortunate victim. But she could tell him nothing
that would assist him. On Sunday, she had been out till

after supper, returning at seven-thirty. Later in the evening she had seen a man come from Miss Young's room and
descend the stairs.

Rankin halted her at that point. A man coming from
Mary Young's room on Sunday evening! That was something entirely unexpected.

"At what time did this occur?"

"It was just ten minutes to nine."

"How can you be so sure of the time?"

"I remember exactly how it happened. I had just stepped
out into the hall here to borrow a book from Mr. Humphreys. It was a primer I'm considering having my pupils
use in school. I had been winding my wrist-watch while I
did so, and I carelessly dropped it." She showed him the
watch, still upon her wrist, but with a shattered crystal.
"Of course I was alarmed that I had broken it, but it was
still going when I picked it up."

"And then—?"

"It was at that very instant that I saw this person—just
for a second, you understand. Because he was standing at
the door. He had just closed it. And he moved away down
the steps to the first floor. So, you see, I just had the barest glimpse of him. You can't see further than the top of
the stairs below here, from up here."

She led him into the hallway. Leaning over the banister,
he could see Miss Graham's door plainly, but the entrance
of the farther room on the left was barely within his range
of vision. And the steps leading to the ground floor were
completely cut off by the projection of the second-story
ceiling.

Rankin was perplexed and baffled. Mary Young's appointment at Reed Street had been set for nine o'clock. To arrive
there in a comfortable time she must have departed from
the house at a quarter to the hour. Yet five minutes later a
man was seen leaving her room. What could it mean?

A possible solution to the problem came to him. He re-called that on Saturday night Norris had called for the girl to take her out; Miss Graham had said that had occurred at approximately 8:45. Assuming, however, that he had actually arrived a few minutes later, was it not possible that he had come up to the girl's room to escort her down? Probably she was just ahead of him on the steps going down, as he closed her door behind them both.

He put the question to Miss Minsey.

"Are you positive of the date? Didn't this happen two nights ago?"

She shook her head in a negative that would brook no alternative.

"Oh, no, Mr. Rankin, I'm positive it was last night. Why, I went to the theater on Saturday night! It was the Garrick."

His mystification increased, but he was not yet willing to give up.

"Wasn't the young man Mr. Norris, with whom Miss Young had been going out?"

"I couldn't say. I've never met the gentleman."

Neither did Miss Minsey know whether she would rec-ognize the man if she ever saw him again. And she ap-peared so distressed that he should doubt her word that he forbore any further questioning. Whether the incident was of importance or not, it left him bewildered, for it failed to coincide with what he had already discovered. He decided that the woman was in error; there was no other hypothesis.

During the latter portion of the inquiry Rankin had been aware of recent arrivals below. The front door had slam-med, followed by voices and the chattering of women's tongues at a furious rate. He thought he detected a sob or two.

"I'll wager Mrs. Edgecomb is in," he reflected with a smile.

Nor was he in error. As he proceeded down the staircase to the second floor, Mrs. Schmidt hailed him from below.

"Mr. Rankin, I was just telling Mrs. Edgecomb what's happened to the poor girl, and she says she's got something very important to tell you at once."

7

MRS. EDGECOMB'S STORY

Mrs. Edgecomb proved to be a colossal woman of enormous girth and uncertain but very substantial age. Her walk resembled the waddle of an ancient gray gander, and she wheezed noisily with every stride. A few lone hairs straggled upon her chin, in place of hairs that should have been on her head. The chair in which she firmly ensconced herself protested squeakingly under her weight.

Mrs. Schmidt introduced them to each other, her companion cupping her ear and craning to get the name.

"Now, Mrs. Edgecomb, what is it that you desire to tell me?" Rankin seated himself opposite her.

"Just imagine, Mr. Tankman, such an awful thing happening to us in our quiet lives here. I declare, we aren't safe anywhere, nowadays, are we? What is the law coming to when a citizen can't be sure he won't be murdered in bed? What's the matter with the police force, that's what I want to know! Of course, you understand, I'm not casting any reflections on you. You aren't on the police force, are you? You're a detective, aren't you? That is different, isn't it, Mr. Tankman?"

He smiled at her vehemence. "Well, there is some difference, of course."

She went on as though he hadn't spoken.

"And such a refined girl, too—not at all like that hussy Miss Graham. I declare, I can't see how anybody can abide that woman. Such a fresh person. She has no respect for her elders at all. Not that I'm old, you understand. But it just goes to show that you can't tell, from the outside, what anybody is like."

Rankin smiled the smile of the weary and the patient. "Quite right, Mrs. Edgecomb. But you had something in your mind that might help me with the case."

"Yes, yes. I'm coming to that. It's about Mr. Rogers. A nice man he is, and I think a great deal of him, and I wouldn't say anything in all the world that might bring him trouble. But still, as I say, you never can tell."

Mrs. Schmidt, an interested listener, nodded her agreement.

"Now you know, Mr. Tankman, that I go out every day, twice a day, to the park; it's so pleasant and cool out there, and I do so enjoy watching people pass all the time."

"Yes, Mrs. Schmidt was telling me so."

Mrs. Edgecomb cast a frigid look at the landlady, as though she wondered what else the latter had divulged.

"Oh, was she? Well, I spend the afternoon there; and then again I go out in the evening till dark. I did yesterday and I did on Friday night. You remember, I'm sure, how nice it was Friday night—so calm and delightful that I remained out later than I usually did. I had just made up my mind to leave when who should come along and sit on the bench in front of me but poor Miss Young and Mr. Rogers. You can imagine how surprised I was, because none of us ever thought there might be anything between them."

Her listener became interested.

"Now don't misunderstand me, Mr. Tankman. I wasn't trying to listen to them; I wouldn't do such a thing. And, anyway, they didn't talk loud enough, at first, for me to hear."

She spoke with an injured tone. He could picture her straining forward in the darkness, trying to catch their words, but he was too diplomatic to say so.

"Mr. Rogers was talking away at a great rate, and Miss Young was listening; and then she says something to which he answers. After that it sounded as if they were arguing, and Miss Young jumps up and says, as proud as any queen, 'How dare you, Mr. Rogers?' From then on I could hear most of what went on. Of course, perhaps I shouldn't have listened, but if people will talk out loud in public, then it's their funeral if they are heard.

"Mr. Rogers said to her: 'I swear it's the truth, Mary, so help me God! I'm crazy about you; you know I'd do anything for you to win you and he's not the man for you; he doesn't love you as I do. And what I say I can prove,' or words something like that."

Mrs. Edgecomb spoke with relish, deriving much satisfaction from repeating the words. She settled herself again in the protesting chair and continued.

"He tried to hold her hand—I could even see that in the dark—but she draws it away, cold-like, and says with lots of scorn at him: 'I've been very patient with you, Mr. Rogers, because I was sorry for you, and I never put you in your place. But when you come here with that des-despic—well, anyhow, disgraceful lie, to try to injure the man I love in such an underhanded manner, that's as much as I'll stand. I'll have nothing to do with you from now on.' Goodness, Mr. Tankman, it was just like an old play—romantic and all that—only more interesting because it was real."

"What occurred then?"

"Miss Young started to move away. The poor man was all wrought up over that, and he went after her, saying that he was sorry he had hurt her, and whether she'd forgive him and at least treat him the same as before. But she said to him: 'The sooner we come to an understanding between us, the better. Under no circumstances could I possibly consider you, so you may as well make the best of it.' And with that she walks off, leaving him standing there, under the trees."

"You say this was on Friday evening?"

"Yes, sir, the very night I didn't get back till almost ten o'clock. Don't you remember, Mrs. Schmidt, you remarked on my staying out so late?"

Thus appealed to, the landlady verified the date. "But you didn't tell me anything about this, Mrs. Edgecomb," she added, aggrieved.

"Well, we were angry at each other then over what you said to me on Thursday, and so I wasn't going to tell you."

For the moment, it appeared that the argument, whatever it was, that had begun on Thursday, was about to burst anew, but the detective delayed hostilities by inquiring as to the remainder of the adventure.

"Well, there isn't much to tell besides that," Mrs. Edgecomb continued. "Mr. Rogers just stood watching her go; and then he stood muttering to himself, angry-like. I watched him till he was out of sight."

"Precisely what were the relations of Mr. Rogers and Miss Young before that?"

"Nothing much," broke in Mrs. Schmidt, disregarding the other's frigid look. "We all knew Mr. Rogers liked her, and he was always trying to take her out. But as I told you before, she liked young Mr. Norris instead, so there didn't seem to be much hope for him. I'm sure she never gave him any encouragement."

"And you don't know what it was that offended her so?"

The reply was in the negative. Rankin regarded his watch and meditated for an instant. He turned to Mrs. Schmidt.

"It's now five-thirty. What time did you say Mr. Rogers comes in?"

"Why, before five o'clock, usually. I'm surprised he is so late."

"I guess he isn't coming in at all," put in Mrs. Edgecomb, complacently smoothing her dress.

"Why not?" Rankin's voice was sharp; he sensed impending disaster.

"Because he isn't here, that's why."

"What do you mean?"

"I saw him leave with a packed grip last night at eleven-thirty."

"What!"

For the briefest iota of time a pall of silence fell over the two listeners. In Mrs. Schmidt's eyes were written bewilderment and amazement; in Rankin's face, confusion and bafflement. Only Mrs. Edgecomb remained unmoved, as though what she had just divulged were but the least important item of information.

"There, I thought that would get you," she said in a proud and triumphant tone at her sensation. "Yes, sir, he went away last night."

The detective turned fiercely upon the landlady.

"Why didn't you tell of this before?"

"Good gracious! Mr. Rankin, I didn't know anything about it. I haven't seen him to-day, that's true; and as I told you before, I never clean up his room. He does that himself, even though I have a key to it. He doesn't want anybody to touch his belongings. And as for believing he was gone—" She completed the sentence with a disclaiming shrug.

"Was his rent paid?"

"Up to this Saturday."

"Get me that key to his room at once."

As the landlady departed, flustered, upon her errand, he faced Mrs. Edgecomb again.

"How did you happen to see him?"

"Don't hustle me, young man," she replied severely, waving a finger at him. "At my time of life I have to be quiet. I had just stepped into the hall to call good night to Miss Minsey, and there he was standing on the steps, with his coat and hat on, and carrying his bag."

"What did he say to you?"

"Well, you can guess how surprised I was at that. I asked him where he was going, so dressed up and at such an hour; and he was surprised to hear me speak, for he hadn't seen me before that, nor did he know I was watching him. He said, 'I just received a telegram that my mother is ill; and I've got to go home at once.' Well, of course, I believed him, so I said, 'I'm sorry to hear it, Mr. Rogers. I do hope she'll be better soon.' And he thanked me and went on."

The detective waited anxiously for the return of the landlady. When Mrs. Schmidt entered with the key, he snatched it from her hand. Up the stairs he raced, three at a time. In his mind there was shaping an increasing dread which he could not define. Intuitively, as he nervously fumbled with the lock, he realized that something was desperately wrong. He hardly knew what to expect, but he apprehended the worst.

As the door swung open, a single glance sufficed to prove accurate his most disastrous premonitions. The room that lay before him was literally devastated; a melee of articles lay about in an inextricable tangle. The covers and sheets were ripped from the bed, and strewn pellmell upon the floor. Every drawer was opened and emptied; some of them had been removed altogether and were scattered here and there. The skeleton of the highboy, with all its containers removed, stared at him bleakly. It was as though a cyclone had passed through. Clearly Mr. Rogers's departure had been sudden and panic-stricken.

In all this welter of confusion, however, there was not a single sheet of paper. In the rear of the room was a fireplace; and in it lay the blackened remains and ashes of many papers. It was evident that the lodger had burned them all; he had been careful that no telltale bits of writing remained for the prying eyes of investigators.

But why? Rankin was thoroughly baffled by this unexpected development. Why should this unknown person have been seized with such a headlong alarm? Was he the murderer of Mary Young? It would certainly appear so; but if he had planned flight in advance, to follow the murder, there would have been no necessity for one carried out so obviously upon the spur of the moment. But assuming there was some other unrevealed reason for his flight, why had he found it necessary to burn all his papers? And what of James Norris—had he nothing to do with it?

Obviously, of course, the excuse given regarding the sick mother was a lie, concocted on the spur of the moment to satisfy the insatiable curiosity of Mrs. Edgecomb. One doesn't tear one's living quarters apart to pack, no matter how great is one's anxiety. Mrs. Schmidt would be able to tell him whether any such telegram had arrived; or at least whether there had been a messenger boy. For she had been in the house the entire evening except for a short period spent with Annie Jones at the back fence. And she would also know whether the message had come by telephone. Inquiry at the Western Union, he was sure, would verify his belief in the falsity of Rogers's statement; but he hardly believed it would be necessary to carry his investigations to that length.

Exclamations of horror behind him informed the detective that Mrs. Schmidt had reached the second story and was glancing into the room over his shoulder. Puffing painfully up the stairs, Mrs. Edgecomb followed.

"My goodness! Look what that man did to my furniture!" the landlady cried, wringing her hands. "Isn't this perfectly terrible?"

Agreeing that it was, he informed both of them that it was neither the time nor the place for women's hysterics.

"You've got to answer my questions now, and do it swiftly. I want from you, Mrs. Edgecomb, an exact description of Mr. Rogers's appearance, and the clothes he was wearing when you saw him in the hall."

She complied with a minimum of delay. Both women realized that events had taken a serious turn; for, though the fugitive had gained a sufficiently advantageous start so that instant pursuit would be no better than later pursuit, and perhaps not so good, nevertheless a beginning on the trail must be made at once.

"He's a thinnish man, about medium height, I should say—anyhow, not very tall; and he's quite young."

"But such little hair for a man of his age," put in Mrs. Schmidt.

"That's right." Mrs. Edgecomb nodded. "He was always complaining about its coming out."

"What color was it?" queried the detective.

"A darkish blond, if you get what I mean. Wouldn't you say so, Mrs. Schmidt?"

Between the two, a fairly complete, if unprepossessing, picture of the missing boarder was produced. Further details indicated his age at twenty-three or a bit more; he had dark eyes that were rather shifty (so they thought now); a long bony nose and thin lips. His chin receded; his color was generally a pasty white. He wore, at the time he left, a dark-brown suit of plain pattern, ordinary black pumps, and a straw hat with a stiff brim and a green-and-yellow band. Mrs. Edgecomb couldn't be sure of this last detail, due to the poorness of the light which was filtering from her room through her open doorway into the hall. The bag he carried was an oblong black one and unusually large—more than a yard in length. But otherwise there was nothing distinctive about the lodger's outfit.

"You didn't happen to notice how Mr. Rogers went away—whether he went by taxi from the house, did you?" he inquired.

"No, I didn't, Mr. Tankman," replied Mrs. Edgecomb. "I guess I should have, but it seemed all right to me then, so I didn't bother. Who would have believed he was such a villain?"

"Has he been your boarder long, Mrs. Schmidt?"

"It's almost six months, now; he came in February. And he's always been regular in his rent. He never gave me a bit of trouble before this."

"Do you know where he came from, before that?"

The landlady could not enlighten him as to her lodger's past, nor his previous residence. They had never had occasion to inspect his mail, nor had he ever mentioned it to her. She thought, perhaps, that the mailman might be able to aid him.

In regard to the telegram of the night before, there was another blank. Mrs. Schmidt was positive she would have heard the bell ring, had there been any message, for her quarters were on the ground floor. Equally sure was she that a call from the telegraph company would have come to her attention. But there had been no calls after nine-thirty yesterday evening; the last one, at the time, was for Mr. Humphreys. This Rankin expected; it merely substantiated his belief that the boarder had lied.

There remained but to search the room. Perhaps there, in his haste, Rogers had overlooked some article which would enable the detective to trace him. Whereupon he closed the door in the faces of the protesting women and

viewed the wreckage. He chose the closet as his starting
point and from there passed to the loose items upon the
floor. He scrutinized extra shoes, a forgotten handkerchief,
coat-hangers, and used socks; scrupulously he searched
through the drawers and studied deserted cuff links and
neckwear. They revealed to him nothing of consequence.

While he investigated he meditated upon the sudden
flight. The time element was an important one. Mary
Young's murder had occurred at approximately ten o'clock.
The journey from Woodlawn to Morton Street would
occupy, with all traffic in Rogers's favor, perhaps three-
quarters of an hour. At the most, an hour. This would
bring him to the boarding-house at eleven o'clock; by
eleven-thirty he could have packed his things and fled.
And it was at eleven-thirty that Mrs. Edgecomb saw him
go. Yes, it all fitted together very precisely.

But gone where? Not a paper, not a word, to indicate
a destination. He knelt beside the fireplace and gingerly
stirred the charred and blackened remnants. Ashes disin-
tegrated under his touch. Cautiously he searched among
them, in the hope that some sheet had escaped the dev-
astating flames. But all lay before him burned to a crisp.
No, not quite all; at the very bottom of the ash-heap lay
a minute bit of white paper which, by some strange freak
of the fire, remained untouched. Eagerly he lifted it and
examined it. It was barely a quarter of an inch wide and
not over three-quarters of an inch in length; and on it, in
tiny printed figures, were a series of four numbers, one
below the other. And that was all.

A line to the left indicated a margin; and though the
detective studied them anxiously, he found them meaningless. Nevertheless, he pocketed the scrap for future refer-
ence and analysis, with extreme caution:

226.5

343.0

456.4

500.2

Why had Rogers thought it so necessary to burn up all his papers? Why must every scrap of writing be destroyed? There was nothing left in his own handwriting. There was only one possible inference—that Rogers was the actual criminal and had enticed the girl, in some unknown manner—as by the note of appointment, to the park. His name was Joseph Rogers; the J of the note could as well be his initial as it could have been that of James Norris. And then, he had completely forgotten that message—the telltale handwriting which would reveal the criminal! He had left it with his victim! What was it that Thomas had called it—the error that hangs the criminal? What more natural than that he should become panic-stricken when he recalled it; that in his panic he took to flight, burning first every incriminating bit of evidence?

It was very plausible; more than that, it was probable. But that did not free James Norris altogether. He was already too deeply involved to escape suspicion so easily. Rankin's next steps were obvious—to send out an alarm for the fugitive, so that a search for him could be begun, until he had more time to take charge himself; and meanwhile he would make a quiet investigation of Mary Young's fiancé. He didn't wish the bird in the hand to take alarm, even though the bird in the bush were already gone. Rogers's start was sufficient to preclude any advantage to be gained by an immediate pursuit. He would turn in to Headquarters a description of the man and his habits, as far as were known. If necessary, he would set some one else working on that trail. However, with Norris it was different.

As far as the detective knew, Norris was unaware that he was implicated; theoretically, he did not even know the name of the girl who had been stabbed at Woodlawn. This fact had not yet been released to the papers. When he did know, Norris would have to make the first open move. But not the first actual move; that would be Rankin's. He would be prepared.

Having so concluded, Rankin acted at once upon his decision. He reminded Mrs. Schmidt and Mrs. Edgecomb that they must be ready to attend the inquest, to be held in the morning; and warning them to say nothing, he left the boarding-house.

8

THE ENDERLEY APARTMENTS

Between 6:30, at which hour he left Mrs. Schmidt, and 8:30, when he arrived at the Enderley Apartments, Tommy Rankin completed several errands of lesser importance with regard to the crime, and took his first meal since breakfast. More specifically, he visited Headquarters for the photographs of the fingerprints found on the cigarette lighter, and gave notice of Rogers's flight. Johnson, the expert, presented him with clear enlargements of several prints, only partial, however; but the thumbprint already mentioned was complete. He explained that the scar, so resembling a narrowed quarter-moon, had most likely been caused by a cut from glass. It was distinctive to its owner, and, once he was located, would make his identification a simple matter.

The officer in charge took down the details of Rogers's flight and such description of the fugitive and his habits as was available. Before Rankin left, the telegraph was working to broadcast the news all over the country, and to set the intricate, efficient network of the law stretched for him.

"You had better get some one to handle the Philadelphia end of it, too," Rankin instructed, "until I can get around to it."

"How about Gordon?" put the officer.

Lester Gordon was a persevering, if not an overly brilliant, worker, fully capable of handling all the drudge work concerned with this phase of the case. Once in a while he had flashes of inspiration which resulted inexceptional success; but they were not to be depended upon. When he was summoned, Rankin explained the situation fully, and gave directions.

"Your primary job is to trace his movements from the boarding-house. I've already covered that, but it wouldn't hurt you to question them more in detail. You may learn something I missed. Anyhow, that will be your starting point. Call at the place where he worked, the National Securities Bank, on Chestnut Street, and see what they have to say about him."

"The bank's closed now," Gordon replied. "I'll do it the first thing in the morning."

"And report to me as soon as you've hit something; if necessary, we'll work together on it."

As soon as Gordon left, Rankin turned to the officer in charge.

"You know my policy," he explained, "I'm shy on getting assistance, or using it, and I never do if I can possibly avoid it. But this affair isn't going to be as simple as it first appeared; it's branching out into several angles."

He took his departure, studying the enlargements. His next step was to seek out the officer who patrolled the Reed Street-Morton Street beat. The bluecoat verified his suspicions of the meeting the preceding evening. He recalled that at five minutes to nine he had observed a young lady standing at the crossing of the two streets in a state of nervous anxiety.

"I recognized her," he said; "I've often seen her come out of Mrs. Schmidt's. When I walked past, I merely nodded to her and she nodded back. Then I went around the corner; and when I came back she wasn't there any more."

"No," he went on in answer to the next query put him, "I didn't see anyone with her at all, though I guess she must have been waiting for somebody who came while I was around the corner. It takes me ten minutes to walk around the block, so I'd be back here at five after nine. And if, as you say, sir, the meeting was for nine o'clock, I'd have just missed them."

It was only a matter of detail, so that Rankin was not especially distressed at the blank he had drawn; though he would have appreciated a description of the one Mary Young had met. Who had it been—James Norris or Joseph Rogers?

Abruptly he shifted to his other trail.

"Since you appear to know some of Mrs. Schmidt's boarders, have you ever noticed a pasty-faced, thin young man, about twenty-three years of age, with blondish hair?"

"Yes, sir, I've seen him, but I can't say that I've ever taken particular notice of him or ever spoken to him. He never appeared like a very sociable person."

"Well, here's the point. Last evening this chap left Mrs. Schmidt's at eleven-thirty at night, with a large black suitcase. He wore a brown suit and a straw hat with a striped band about it. Did you, by any chance, see him come out or observe where he went?"

The detective read in the patrolman's face another failure, and this time he was keenly disappointed. The latter again went over the explanation in regard to his beat, and ended by saying that he couldn't see the length of it; and even if he were able, it would probably have been too dark to notice anything, anyway. And thus a possible trail to the fugitive's flight came to an end before it had ever commenced.

The Enderley Apartments, which proved to be in a newly developed section of West Philadelphia, he had no difficulty in locating. They were a ten-story structure of

brown brick, fashionable in appearance, and attractively
constructed. Little flower balconies dotted the walls at
intervals between the windows in a regular row, all filled
with blooming plants. At the rear, a sunken garden added
charm and a semblance of wealth to the building. The wide
entrance was of marble, which, with a slight awninged
approach, presented an inviting aspect. Certainly, it was
no residence for the poor, and it reminded the detective
that he had yet to learn how Norris earned his sustenance.

He noted with satisfaction the arrangement of the interior. First came a short, polished hallway decorated with
flowers. On the right, a stairway led to the upper regions;
opposite it, on the left, was the elevator shaft with two
elevators. Beyond that was the telephone switchboard,
at which sat the operator, engaged in conversation over
the wire. At the entrance stood a porter. It indicated that
among the employees—elevator boy, operator, and porter—it would be difficult, if not impossible, to leave or
enter the apartments without being noticed.

After observing in the vestibule that Norris had D
apartment on the fourth floor, Rankin approached the
porter. But beyond informing him that Mr. Norris was not
in at the present moment, there was nothing he could tell
the inquirer. The latter, making it appear that he sought
Norris as a friend, claimed that he had attempted to com-
municate with him ever since the preceding evening, and
desired to know whether Norris had then been in. But the
porter could not recall positively; he suggested, however,
that his inquirer sound the telephone girl, for she, he
inferred, with contemptuous feeling, was apt to regard the
movements of any man upon whom she laid her eyes.

Obeying the hint with something of amusement, the
detective approached the telephone operator and contemplated her till he drew her attention. She returned the
inspection with a quizzical gaze, and returned his nodded

greeting cordially enough, the while chewing gum vigorously with evident enjoyment. He put his first question.

"Do you know Mr. Norris?"

"I'll tell the world," was the slangy reply. "He's that handsome that any girl would know him if she could. What can I do for you?"

"I've been looking for him ever since yesterday. I have some business with him and I haven't been able to connect up with him. It's something I want to see him about, personally. You don't happen to know where he went, do you?"

"No. I'm sorry, but I couldn't tell you."

He tried a long shot. If the murdered girl had really sought Norris the preceding day, she might have done so by telephone, even though she had not used the boarding-house instrument. And he was banking that Norris had then been out.

"Well, he wasn't in last night, either, was he? Because I tried to reach him at around five o'clock, and there wasn't any reply."

The operator looked her astonishment, and he was aware that her alertness had revealed to her the slip he had made.

"Oh, was that you that was trying to get him?" she inquired. "It sounded like a girl, and she was in a frightful hurry."

"It was a girl," he explained, apologetically, "my secretary. She was doing her best for me. I hope she wasn't rude."

"Oh, no! That was all right. He had been out all afternoon and hadn't come in yet."

So he was right. And failing to make connections with her lover by phone, what had she done next?

"What time did he come in?"

"Well, I suppose it was near seven o'clock in the evening; he came in for a few minutes only, and then went out at once."

"And when did he return after that?"

"Now, I'm afraid I couldn't tell you. But I know it was very late, because I'm on duty here till two o'clock in the morning, and when I stopped last night, he wasn't back yet."

"Are you positive of that?"

"Yes," was the reply, "because I was waiting to speak to him myself when he came in. There was something I wanted to tell him."

The switchboard buzzed and the girl plugged a switch. "All right," she shouted into the mouthpiece. "I'm trying to get your party."

"You know," she went on, talkatively, "you're not the only person who has been asking after Mr. Norris. A gentleman came to see him at eleven o'clock last night, but I told him he wasn't in. Such an hour to come calling!"

Rankin wasn't interested in this detail, but it gave him the opening he sought and he was quick to seize it.

"Don't women ever visit him here?"

She gave him a quick, suspicious glance, but evidently decided, from the urbanity and innocence of the tone, there was no ulterior motive behind the question.

"It's funny that you should mention it, because a strange thing happened yesterday early in the evening. A girl came to see him about six o'clock, and I have never seen any one so anxious. She appeared terribly worried. When I told her that Mr. Norris wasn't in, she looked despairing and said she just had to get in touch with him and that she'd leave a note for him in case he arrived before she got home."

"Hm! That's interesting. Fancy such a thing happening to Norris." The comment was casual; how interesting it was, the operator would never realize. "It must have been something quite important. Did you give it to him?"

She replied with vehemence. "Certainly I did—when Mr. Norris came in at seven o'clock. When I promise a thing, I keep my promise."

"I have no doubt." Rankin hesitated upon the next query, for he expected an explosion. "You didn't happen to notice what the note said, did you?"

"What?" She abruptly thrust back her chair and regarded him distrustfully. "What do you take me for that you think I would do such a thing?" And then, as he hesitated, she added, harshly, "Look here, what's your game, coming around here and asking these questions?"

Her protestations were too violent to be true, and her agitation told him that she had read the message.

"Why, I didn't mean anything by that. I was just asking a simple question, and it wouldn't do any harm if I knew about it, would it?" Unassumingly, he drew a bill from his pocketbook. "And it would give me something to kid him about. Imagine Jimmy mixed up in an affair like that! It will be worth just ten dollars for me to have a laugh on him."

He smiled jovially as he waved the money before her. Of course, she didn't believe him—she was too shrewd a girl for that. But she eyed the money longingly, nevertheless, while she appeared to weigh the consequences of repeating what she knew. Her previous anger passed away.

"And he'll never learn how I found out," he added, persuasively.

"Promise?"

The detective nodded and placed the money beside her. For another instant she hesitated, and then made her decision.

"Well, I did read it, though I suppose I had no business to. It said: 'Dear Jim, I must see you. Get in touch with me at once, or arrange to meet me somewhere.' And it was signed, 'Mary.'"

It was what he had inferred; but it was worth the money actually to know of the existence of another link rather than merely to guess at it. He thanked the operator and cautioned her not to repeat the incident to Norris—which she fervently promised; and a moment later, when she was engrossed with the call of a particularly irascible party, took the stairs to the apartment of his suspect. This he did rather than chance attracting the attention and suspicion of the elevator boy. For what he was about to do was technical breaking and entering, from which charge not even his official position would protect him, if he were caught. The Department didn't actually frown upon this method of procuring information—it merely professed to, to salve the official conscience. What it did find unpardonable was a blunder in following this mode; if a man erred, he deserved no consideration.

Rankin reached the fourth flour of the building without an encounter. A long hallway stretched before him, along which was D apartment, almost opposite the stairs. The corridor was lighted, permitting him to view its entire length. And although he realized he could not afford to be discovered in this undertaking, he approached the door unflurried and began to work calmly at the lock with his collection of keys. If any one should happen to come from other apartments, nothing would appear amiss; it would seem a perfectly natural effort to open the door. One of his master keys was sure to do the trick. The first and second wouldn't do, but on the third attempt there was a faint click and he was able to swing the door inward and enter, shutting it quietly behind.

The apartment he saw in the semidarkness of late dusk had three rooms and a bath. They were ample, luxuriously furnished. The chamber in which he stood was the living-room; a central davenport stood outlined in the fading light, fronting a fireplace, and behind it a mahogany table and library case. Across its length, two doors opened, one into the bedroom on the left, which he could barely see through the half-closed portal; and the other into what appeared to be a lounging- or writing-room. That entrance was swung wide, revealing to his view a black walnut desk, some deep-seated chairs, and the telephone.

So far, so good. The silence about him was absolute, and there was an eerie quality in the faint twilight which still filtered through the windows. The closed windows made the air oppressive and he thought he could detect the faint odor of cigarette smoke, indicating a recent caller. He couldn't, of course, risk the electric light; but he had provided himself with a powerful searchlight in contemplation of this very possibility.

He decided to try the bedroom first. He moved across to it quietly, opening the door completely, with caution and peering about before he entered. The soft carpet beneath his feet deadened whatever sound he may have produced. Closing night compelled him to flash the light ahead of him. It produced a brilliant, glowing circle, leaping here and there among the furnishings, but completely cut off by the surrounding darkness. There were two containers—a chiffonier and a dresser, the latter a low and long-bodied bureau of rosewood. The drawers were deep and roomy, containing such articles as are customary in men's apparel—shirts, drawers, socks, pajamas, ties. But though he turned them all over with infinite thoroughness, they revealed nothing to him.

Replacing every article just as he had found it, Rankin turned to the tall chiffonier. Its drawers moved with difficulty and protest, and for the moment he feared the sounds they raised were audible in the hallway. He proceeded with greater caution, scrutinizing bedding, sheets, and toilet articles. The bottom drawer contained nothing but towels, as unpromising as the rest. At the very bottom, however, placed deeply in the corner of the drawer, he found another towel, wrapped into a bundle. It covered a hard, thin article, but he opened it without hope or expectation.

And there, in the shining area of the light, he gazed upon the plain handle and wicked blade of a sharp, small knife! It gleamed upward at him like something evil, chaste and bright. Inwardly exultant at the discovery, which for him could have but one meaning, Rankin lifted it carefully in the towel, for examination. It had undoubtedly been wiped clean, yet with haste. For though the blade itself was undefiled, close under the handle was a single minute spot of ugly red. Its user had missed this tiny corner.

Rankin rewrapped it with care and placed it within his coat. He needed only the fingerprints and handwriting of Norris to complete his case against him. The bathroom was a likely spot to locate the former. Rankin replaced the other towels, closed the drawer, and moved vigilantly toward it. It connected with the bedroom. His light played ahead, a shining beacon, revealing the tub, the washbowl, the medicine chest, and the toilet shelf. On the latter was a rinsing glass for the use of the mouth. One always uses such a glass for washing the teeth, and in using it the finger tips are always wet, so that they leave their mark when the glass has dried. And this one was smeared a trifle, as such glasses generally are—an admirable surface for telltale impressions.

Holding out the tumbler to reflect the searching rays, he saw the prints he sought, silhouetted against the transparent surface. They were not clear-cut prints in which every line stood out distinctly, as in the photograph with which he compared them; but an application of a fine yellow powder made them sufficiently plain to allow a general comparison. Detailed examination could be made when the culprit was in his hands; but even by this rough survey he could detect the print of the thumb several times on the glass. And every one was complete enough to reveal the miniature semicircular scar across the center. Undoubtedly the same hand had produced the impressions both upon the tumbler and upon the silver lighter, and that hand was the hand of James Norris.

Rankin turned to the lounging-room, in which he had observed the desk; there, undoubtedly, would be the most logical place to locate his final clue. A discarded check-book, with its stubs filled in, an unfinished letter—either would be sufficient for his needs. He crossed to it and tried the top; it was unlocked and came open at his first effort. Again the light revealed immediately his objective. It was an ancient black checkbook, cast aside and secluded in one of the pigeonholes, from which every check had been removed. But the stubs remained and beside them he placed the message found in the murdered girl's pocket-book.

There was no resemblance between the two fists; it was impossible that the same hand could have penned the scripts. That of the note was slanting, widespread, and careless; the "ee" of the word "Reed" almost merged into "ii"; the "t's" were uncrossed. But the check stub credit to the Exchange National Bank was in a neat, precise hand, meticulous in every detail. No man, even in a purposeful attempt to disguise his writing, could have penned both without leaving some similarity. But none existed here.

At that very instant, so close to his ears that it caused him to spring back in startled alarm, a harsh, jangling peal cut the grave-like stillness of the room. It was the telephone bell, shrilling in the darkness. And between the first and second rings the detective heard the click of a key fumbling against the lock of the outer door, seeking the proper groove to turn it and the knob rattled under somebody's hand. The owner of the apartment—the man he sought to incriminate—had returned!

9

TOMMY RANKIN'S NOTEBOOK

In the instant the detective left himself in utter darkness. He knew he could not afford to be discovered in this predicament. A thousand thoughts and possibilities of escape occurred to him on the spur of that fatal second; he would rush past the man and dash through the door; he would hide till Norris had retired; he would impersonate a burglar and bluff his way out. But he discarded them all—none was feasible. But he realized he must act swiftly, for this very room in which the telephone was repeating its harsh clatter would be the newcomer's first objective. It wasn't safe there, even for the instant; nor was the living-room, through which Norris would have to pass. The bedroom alone remained.

Darting low, like a moving shadow, he slipped from the lounging-room. The key turned in the lock and the door swung open; and in his swift passage the detective caught a glimpse of the intruder as he was silhouetted against the rays of the hallway lights; a brief glimpse, which revealed him to be a well-built, broad-shouldered man with a keen, handsome face. Then the door shut and the living-room lights went on, in an illuminating blaze.

The telephone continued to peal out—a fortunate circumstance, in Rankin's opinion, for it would swallow whatever sound he would make in the next moment.

After that Norris would make his own noise, engrossed in his telephone conversation, thus giving him still greater leeway to move about without fear of discovery. But not for long. Perhaps a moment, perhaps two or three, but certainly no more; if he had not found a way of flight, he was lost.

For an instant he crouched behind the bedroom door as Norris—for he was sure it was his suspect—crossed toward the telephone. Then he turned to the bedroom windows. There were two of them; the nearer was on the inside, toward the lounging room; the farther was close to the partition wall of the next apartment. He approached the former; it was clasped on the inside, but the clasp turned without a sound. He recalled the flower balconies which he had observed on the walls of the building as he had entered, and now he tried to visualize their arrangement. There had been a perfect row of them on every floor, every fourth or fifth window; there was, apparently, one for every apartment—balconies barely large enough to bear one's weight and not meant as verandas; nor were they directly under any window. They stretched from the end of one window, including less than half of it, to the beginning of a neighboring window, including in its scope the same amount. And it was the only possible avenue of escape.

Rankin peered from the window. There was nothing there, except four stories of dark space stretching far below.

The telephone had ceased ringing. Clearly through the partition came the sound of Norris lifting the receiver; and in the silence his greeting easily penetrated the wall. The detective was not particularly interested in telephone conversations at that moment, but he fervently prayed that it would continue for some time.

He turned to the other window and peered out. There it was, the tiny landing stretching from the corner of the window, beyond for four or five feet to the first window of the adjoining apartment. A profusion of geraniums mingled with the green of ivy and fern lay before him on the slight railing, in an orange-painted wooden box. Mentally he blessed the architect of the structure. He turned the latch; he raised the glass. It squeaked slightly and he held his breath; but the conversation in the next room continued uninterrupted.

Gently, the detective climbed over the sill, taking exquisite caution to make the feat a noiseless one. He had to take a long and precarious step over the rail, which was more than a foot below and almost beyond him, as he climbed out. It was difficult to gain a foothold, and he groped in the darkness, balancing dangerously upon the sill. Below, there was nothing to prevent a fatal fall, were he to lose his balance. The fear of scraping the wall or upsetting the plants made the effort doubly dangerous, and Norris must have almost finished with his conversation.

Nevertheless, he took the step. With a single heave he found himself clinging to the box of plants, breathless, but with both feet planted firmly within the balustrade that fringed the shallow platform. With the same caution he leaned back to close the window, and as he did so there was wafted through the opening the concluding words of the telephone conversation. They caused him to pause in his effort; he held his breath. Norris was saying:

"No, don't be a damn fool. No one knows anything about it, or suspects. So why worry about it? It's hardly safe to talk over the matter here. Wait till I see you to-morrow. Don't be alarmed, meanwhile."

Rankin had no time to ponder upon the meaning of the words. Norris was ringing off, and he standing upon a flimsy balcony, four floors above the street. Below was blackness, and in the distance, the lights of the central part of the city. Westinghouse was nearest, then the Elverson Building, and City Hall with its rearing tower of William Penn. There was the shadow line of tall structures, and two brilliant searchlights darted in a sweeping radius. How was he to get down and to the city? If only the next apartment should prove unoccupied; that would be an unprecedented bit of luck.

The apartment was not empty, however. Through drawn blinds came the gleam of lights, and from the further window—the one he could not reach—he heard a victrola. People were at home. The nearer one, the window to which the balcony extended, was closed, and the shades were down too far for him to see what was going on. But he knew it was a party of some sort— noises of laughter and merriment issued forth, mingled with the music.

There was apparently no way for him but to bluff his path through the situation. And that swiftly, before Norris came into the bedroom and switched on the lights. That would reveal him, undoubtedly, for the man had already lit the lounging-room bulbs, and the flare they cast illumined the wall as far as the balcony in a semi-shadow. It caused him to cringe closely to the wall and bend low for he did not want to be discovered from below, either.

His first gentle tap brought no result, so he had, perforce, to repeat it louder, though he feared it would attract the attention of Norris. And then the shade flew up abruptly; a startled and slightly tipsy young lady with her bobbed hair in disorder and her painted lips formed into a vacuous smirk stared at him from the other side of the glass. Beyond was another young lady in close embrace with a young fellow whose face he could not see; and to complete the party of four, a second chap sat hangdoggedly upon a sofa. The first girl gesticulated wildly to her companions; whereupon they turned their attention to him and crowded forward to inspect him as though he were an exhibit. After a moment of argument and hesitation, in which the two men appeared to be insisting that he remain where he was, they opened the window and permitted him to enter.

Rankin was deeply apologetic. He explained that he was a resident of the adjoining apartment and that he had climbed on the balcony for fresh air, and that the window had somehow snapped behind him. To people in a normal condition the story would have been a weak one, but to those four, in their befuddled state, it sounded a perfectly natural thing to risk one's life for fresh air. They never paused to consider how impossible it was for a window to close and lock.

"Thash all right, mister—no hard feelings," muttered the girl who had first seen him. "My name's Cora Blakely. Won't you have a drink?"

Having once brought him in, they appeared attracted to the newcomer. When he declined with thanks, the two girls pressed him to remain, much to the evident dislike of the two men. But he remained firm in his insistence. Still apologetic for the interruption, he broke away and took his departure. Two minutes later he was out of the Enderley Apartments, bound for his own lodgings.

There was still plenty for him to accomplish before he retired.

In retrospect, the achievements of the single day were amazing. So many steps had been taken in his search, so many clues and trails unearthed. Most of them were in his little notebook; a few he retained in his memory. But they were mere scribblings; he had yet to compile them in logical order—to collate them in a methodical arrangement. The inexplicable contradictions of some of his facts were baffling and they left his mind in a chaotic condition.

It would be a long and difficult process to separate the dross from the gold. Not all of it had been pure information; much merely reflected the personalities of those with whom he had come in contact. The good-hearted Mrs. Schmidt, the enigmatic Miss Graham, the talkative Mrs. Edgecomb, the tiny Miss Minsey, must also be considered, as well as the telephone operator and words of James Norris himself as he spoke over the phone. This last confounded the detective. Its implications were clear enough, but who was Norris's confidant? Who else had such knowledge of the crime that he worried over the suspect's welfare?

For more than two hours after reaching his quarters Rankin pondered over the case. And as he did so, he methodically rearranged and rewrote many of his conclusions to clarify his conception of them. And when he had finished his little black book presented the following appearance.

The Case Against James Norris

1. Was engaged to the girl who loved him tenderly.
2. On Saturday night he quarreled with her for an unknown cause.
3. On Sunday afternoon the girl left the boarding-house at 4:45 approximately, to seek him.
4. At 5 she tried to reach him by phone and failed.
5. At 6 she called at the Enderley Apartments with a note asking him for a meeting.
6. He received it from the telephone operator at 7. Presumably he complied—hence the note of appointment.
7. He went out at 7 o'clock and was not back at 2.

8. He committed the murder because—
   (a) The silver lighter and the fingerprints
       in the death car are his
   (b) The weapon with which the crime was
       committed was found in his drawer
   (c) He had a motive, though what it was,
       beyond the quarrel, is uncertain as yet.

It was a good case—a very complete one, indeed; one, thought the detective, upon which a jury might find Norris guilty, even without further detail. Certainly the facts were well-nigh impossible to explain away. But there were a few loose ends, nevertheless, which had to be elucidated before it was perfect.

If These Facts Are So, Then—
1. Why is not the note of appointment in Norris's handwriting?
2. How explain the flight of Joseph Rogers?

The first was not so difficult—it was easily possible that Norris had got some one else to write it for him, merely as a precaution. For instance, the messenger boy, or whomever he had sent with it to Miss Young, he had instructed what to write, not being willing to entrust it to his memory. But the second question baffled him; consider as he would, he could discover no solution. He turned to the second half of his notes.

The Case Against Joseph Rogers
1. He loved the girl silently, worshiping her hopelessly.
2. On Friday night he tried to win her by defaming Norris; was laughed at for his pains and told he hadn't a chance.

3. The murder occurred at ten o'clock, Sunday
   night; he came in panic-stricken at eleven,
   packed his belongings and fled.
   (a) It is an hour's trip from the park.
   (b) The note was his; the realization that
       he had left it there caused his fright, the
       burning of his papers, and the flight.

But there was a yawning, tremendous gap between Friday and Sunday night that had to be filled in. What had occurred in those intervening hours which might explain the poor girl's death? It seemed incredible that Miss Young, who Friday had spurned Rogers, should have consented to accompany him to the park on Sunday. But was it impossible? Rankin thought not—women were changeable and fickle. Suppose, for instance, that Norris had not answered the note he had received through the telephone operator, not being willing to meet the girl again after their quarrel. Then was it not probable that she, desperately injured by his unconcern, or in a pique, should consent to a date with the man she scorned? That certainly was plausible.

Then what followed? Rogers wouldn't be satisfied with that if he were the kind of man the various portraits indicated. A cad he must be; certainly something of a moron, and an egotist. The kind of chap, perhaps, who felt that the world owed him an existence. If so, his knowledge of the real cause for Miss Young's condescension toward him would rankle in him and make him bitter. He would understand that it came from no real feeling she had for him; and in the light of her words on the past Friday, it would serve to turn his affection to hatred. Would not his jealousy overpower him?

The detective congratulated himself upon his facile imagination. But even such a possible case left much unsolved and unanswered.

1. What was the need of a note of appointment? Rogers could have arranged to meet her, by word of mouth.
2. How did Norris's cigarette-lighter get into the death car?
3. How did the knife with which the crime was committed get into Norris's bureau?
4. What did Norris's words over the phone mean?

The first point wasn't of too much consequence. The note had been necessary for some reason; and there was no way of proving it was Rogers's, as he had left no writing with which it could be compared. And the second question was not unanswerable, either. It was certainly possible that it had, in some manner, come into Miss Young's possession, through Norris, so that she had it with her on the fatal evening. And that, in some inexplicable manner, she dropped it.

But the knife? That was a different proposition. He examined it carefully at his leisure, and any doubts that it might not be the lethal weapon were dissolved. It was a plain knife, with a handle, resembling a paper-cutter; but it was shorter and far more keen. The blade was just under five inches in length—approximating the depth of the stab, according to Dr. Fisher. A detailed scrutiny of the top failed to reveal any fingerprints; which was a curious precaution in one who had been so careless in disposing of it.

Assuming, however, that Rogers was the criminal, how did the weapon come into the bureau of James Norris, wrapped in one of his towels? The detective realized that Rogers despised Norris with the hate that jealousy arouses; his animosity toward him must have been even greater than his dislike of the victim. This was proved by his attempt to slander. Could he, therefore, have planted the weapon, to shift suspicion upon Norris? If so, when? Certainly not after the crime, for it was an hour's trip from Woodlawn to the boarding-house, and that full hour had been consumed. Rogers could not also have visited the Enderley Apartments in that time. Of course, he might have done so after he left Mrs. Schmidt's at 11:30; but of this Rankin knew nothing.

And nothing would explain the words he had overheard Norris speak.

The detective contemplated his deductions to see if he had missed any valuable item. To-morrow, with the publishing of the girl's identity, he would expect results from various quarters. His own moves depended upon these results. Inspecting his notes once more, on the spur of the moment, in a mood half-sardonic and half-grim, he inscribed at the bottom of his two "Cases" the words:

"Take Your Choice."

10

THE ARREST

Headquarters was in a turmoil of activity the following morning when Tommy Rankin arrived to make his reports. Several new robberies, a recent development in bootlegging, and a murder were the latest problems of an unprecedented crime wave. Thomas, on duty overtime, as a result, commended him for his progress on the case.

"A clever thing to identify the girl in so short a time. It's in all the papers this morning. What's the next move to be?"

"Well, I expect some results to-day, and very soon at that."

"For instance?"

Rankin lighted a cigarette before replying. They sat in the lieutenant's office, Thomas lounging in his swivel chair, feet upon the desk. His companion perched himself on the end of the desk to receive the benefit of the slight breeze that came through the opened window of the room. It promised to be a scorching day.

"To-day being the first day that the papers have come out with the entire story," he explained, "it's the first chance this Norris I told you of has of knowing the murdered girl was his fiancée. That is—he certainly knew it long ago, if he's the man I'm looking for, but now it's safe for him to come out of cover and inquire about it. The

beauty of it is that he daren't lay low. He's got to do the
natural thing that a former fiancé would do—he's got to
appear on the scene. He knows we'll learn about him; it
would be too suspicious for him to stand pat and take no
interest."

He puffed at his cigarette, and went on.

"He'll have to come to us for information. I've given
instructions at the boarding-house to refer everything
to me. What happens then depends on what he has to
say. You'll agree with me that the case against him is very
strong. It'll take some tall explaining to destroy it."

Thomas nodded sagely, and for a moment silence fell
upon them both. The inquest was being held that morning, but Rankin had already arranged for it to be a formal,
perfunctory affair. Hence, he was not attending. It was too
unusual a case to permit the following of the regular routine. The landlady and probably Mrs. Edgecomb would be
called from the boarding-house to identify the girl. Rawley and Dr. Fisher would be summoned from the park to
describe the discovery and the condition of the body. And
then the jury would return with the customary verdict of
"death at the hand of a person or persons unknown."

When the detective renewed the conversation, it was to
ask Thomas about Mr. Charles Bond. The inquest would
certainly not conclusively settle the problem of Mary
Young's identity. The jury's finding that one Mary Young
had met her death by stabbing would clarify nothing at
all. Neither her former home nor her acquaintances would
be revealed. And it was this information he desired most.
There was nothing in the Gary newspapers, no marked
or noted item for which news alone she might have taken
them. Rankin decided that Gary had once been her residence and for a goodly period. And thus far there had
been no reply to his inquiries, nor did he expect any till
evening or the following morning.

Meanwhile the only source of information remaining was the financier. It appeared Thomas did know something of Mr. Bond, for he had eagerly followed the scandal in which the latter had been recently involved. He had an unsavory reputation with regard to women, and a jealous and elderly wife who possessed and controlled the wealth of the family. Such a combination was bound to breed difficulties.

Trouble had begun when Bond paid attention to Martha Mannering. She was an actress, a leading Broadway beauty who had made a tremendous success in *The Black Coat* which ran into five hundred and fifty performances. Her husband was Ronald Oakley, a wealthy sport, man-about-town sort of chap, generally well liked, though with something of a temper. He had never come in contact with the law in any of his dealings, though was slightly entangled in the notorious Corbellie Club, the end of which had come only after a raid resulting in the death of two bluecoats.

In some manner, Bond and the actress came together and did, as Thomas expressed with relish, "a little cutting up on the sly." Their relations, far from innocent, continued unknown for some time, until one day Oakley unexpectedly appeared and found them in each other's arms in a North Philadelphia apartment. Where he received the tip-off was never revealed. The rest of the unpleasant scandal, however, all came out in the subsequent divorce proceedings. Out of revenge, Oakley made such publicity of his divorce that it became impossible to hush matters up, and, naturally, it came to the ears of Mrs. Bond.

The financier's plight was almost as bad as that of his companion. Mrs. Bond, holding the purse strings—for it was she who had given her husband a successful business—threatened to withdraw all her investments.

The result would spell ruin for him. Somehow they came to an agreement and things quieted down.

"It's a wonder she didn't divorce him."

Thomas laughed and slapped his knee.

"Not she—she knew better than that. Her face was far from being her fortune. She was a widow when she married Bond, and over forty then. Husbands are too scarce at her age to discard them like that even with her money behind her. After their arrangement, I'll wager he toed the mark for a long time. I suppose it didn't last long, though; it seldom does with his kind."

Rankin sat back and stared at the ceiling.

"So he's that sort—and Mary Young was pretty." It was a grotesque thought and he immediately dismissed it. He had too many complications already. Aloud, to his companion, he said, "How old is Bond?"

Before Thomas could reply, an officer entered and announced the arrival of a young man who insisted on seeing Rankin. The detective gave Thomas a meaning glance.

"All right, Simpson. Let him in. Let me handle this, Thomas."

An instant later there entered a young man whom the detective had no difficulty in recognizing as the man barely glimpsed in the door of the apartment the preceding night. Observed closely, he proved to be an exceptionally fine-appearing young man. His eyes were of clear gray, his nose firm but sensitive, in a narrow mold. He was of more than medium height, and his square jaw and broad shoulders betokened strength and power, and one could see that as an ordinary rule he carried himself squarely and with stability.

But at this moment it was evident that he was laboring under the stress of strong emotions. His face was drawn and white, with the look of one who has just received a shock; his lips were tightly compressed, to prevent the quivers which threatened to break out. The eyes, staring uncertainly from one man to the other, were strained.

"Which of you is Rankin?"

"I am." The detective waved his visitor to a seat, but Norris disregarded the invitation.

"Listen," he said in a tremulous voice. "It's all true about what the papers said of Mary Young's murder—there's no mistake? They wouldn't tell me anything at the boarding-house, but you are sure there is no mistake?"

"I regret to say there is none. Mary Young was murdered."

The words appeared to deprive Norris of the last vestige of hope. He dropped into the chair, and for the moment buried his face in his hands. There was silence, except for his labored breathing. Rankin watched him shrewdly, reflected that if this was acting, it was excellent.

Presently Norris looked up, and it was clear that he had succeeded in getting a grip upon his feelings.

"It is terrible! Why, it's unbelievable. Who could have done such a terrible deed?"

"That's what we are endeavoring to discover." Rankin put sympathy into his tone. "It must have been rather sudden for you—to see any item like that so unexpectedly. You are Miss Young's fiancé—James Norris—are you not?"

The other evidenced no surprise at Rankin's knowledge as he acquiesced.

"Well," went on Rankin, "the only way we can find out what occurred is to investigate. And there are a few questions I'd like to ask you that might assist us."

"I? I'd do anything to help you, but I'm afraid—"

"Let me be the judge of that." Still the detective maintained his bland, even tone, so that Thomas observed him disgustedly. Why waste this politeness on a suspect? They weren't his methods. He believed in strongarm tactics. "You say you were engaged to the girl? How did you meet Miss Young?"

For a moment Norris appeared as though he would refuse to reply, but, apparently thinking the better of it, he explained:

"I'm really afraid I can't tell you much about her. I met her purely by accident—we merely ran into each other; and at once we fell in love with each other."

"Well, who is she? Where did she come from?"

"That's just what I can't say. We never inquired into each other's past. It was such love as takes everything on trust." He saw the look of incredulity in the detective's eyes. "Oh, I know that sounds peculiar, but it's the truth. She was just Mary Young to me. I tell you I never inquired any further than that. Why should I? I could tell at once what a fine girl she was. There was no doubt about her from the very beginning."

"So that you know neither her people nor her past?" Such a situation was indeed incredible, and obviously the man was concealing something. "When did you become engaged?"

"It was three weeks ago when I gave her the ring and I shall never forget her delight at receiving it. She was so romantic about it—like a little child—and it pleased me, too. We would have been happy if this—this—" He left the sentence unfinished.

Rankin leaned forward, and for the first time there was a hint of suggestiveness in his tone.

"A ring? That's mighty strange. She had no engagement ring upon her finger when we found the body."

Norris appeared chagrined. "No. That's right. We— that is, I—" he hesitated in doubt. "Well, we had a little disagreement Saturday, and she gave it back to me. But it wasn't serious; it would have been patched up very shortly."

"It must have been rather serious if Miss Young was willing to break the engagement because of it."

The other winced at the sharp tone and gave a nervous, deprecating laugh. "She didn't actually break the engagement. It was just a little lovers' tiff, and there was no real trouble at all."

"I see. What was the argument about?"

"I tell you it was no argument—just a trifle. You know how women are at times—the least little thing hurts them. It isn't important enough to talk about."

Was Norris aware that he was treading dangerous ground? He was doing his best to impress the detective that it was but a minor incident, yet it had made the girl cry as though her heart would break according to Miss Graham, and seek her lover frantically on Sunday. Rankin, gradually feeling his way, decided not to press the question.

"When did you see Miss Young last?"

"On Saturday night. We went out to a dance, but it was on the way that we had our little falling out; so I brought her home early."

"What time was that?"

"I suppose it was around ten o'clock."

"And you haven't seen her since?"

"No."

"Not, for instance, on Sunday night? You didn't meet her then?"

"No, certainly not." Norris was indignant. The trend of the detective's questions occurred to him and he glanced at him dubiously. "Why, you don't believe I know anything about it, do you?"

"Well, perhaps not," Rankin replied, with a deprecating gesture. "Nevertheless, we would like to know how every one connected with the case spent Sunday night."

It was still too early to alarm his quarry. The affability of his questioner had its effect of lulling Norris into a belief of his safety and he fell into the trap set for him.

"I don't suppose that's unnatural. On Sunday evening I—" Norris broke off, and Rankin, observing him closely, was positive that a sudden look of dismay mingled with dread had passed swiftly across the face, to be gone in an instant. He nodded encouragingly.

"I—spent the evening in my rooms at the Enderley Apartments."

"Alone, by yourself?" The detective was exultant; he had caught his man in the first slip, from which still greater things would develop. But Norris had recovered his self-control. Having adopted this stand, it was apparent that he intended to maintain it.

"Yes, all alone. I was writing and doing some work I had in hand till almost twelve. Then I went to bed."

"Didn't any one see you, or didn't you see any one?— some one who could corroborate your statement?"

"No, I'm afraid not. Why, what of it? It makes no difference."

"That's too bad," murmured Rankin, sympathetically, "because I have it on the word of several witnesses that you were not in on that night, but out, and that you had not returned by two o'clock in the morning."

At the words he discarded his affectation of friendliness, and brought his fist down upon the desk with a resounding crash. Norris leaped to his feet so abruptly that he almost overturned the chair.

"So you do suspect me," he ejaculated in a voice of fear. "I might have known it!"

"Stick to the question, Mr. Norris. Where were you on Sunday night?"

"Just where I told you, in my rooms. And whoever says that I was out is lying. I don't know anything about the crime, and I never saw Mary again after Saturday night."

"You may as well know that we shall attempt to disprove that statement to the best of our ability. Tell me, sir, have you ever seen this before?"

Rankin produced the silver lighter; it glittered in the sunlight as he placed it gently upon the desk. Again Norris's eyes, telltale beacons of his mind, reflected a look, this time of recognition.

"Why, of course!" he replied, puzzled. "It's mine. How do you come to have it?"

Automatically he reached for it and picked it up.

"Where did you have it last, Mr. Norris? Come now," Rankin added sternly as Norris hesitated, "let's have the truth this time. It will be much better for you."

"Why, I suppose," again Norris paused doubtfully, "I must have lost it, since you have it now. I believe I remember, for I didn't see it in the last few days. On Saturday, I think it was, but I don't know where; perhaps at the dance or in the cab. I couldn't say—"

"Oh, you couldn't?" It was, indeed, too weak an excuse, clearly created by an alarmed brain on the spur of the moment.

"No, I couldn't, Rankin." Norris braced himself. "Look here, what does this badgering mean? I came here to inquire about my fiancée, and now I find myself threatened and the subject of suspicion. I tell you I don't know a thing about it."

"So you don't know where you lost it? I'll tell you, sir. You left it, unfortunately for yourself, in the death car in which Mary Young was murdered!"

There was no reply. Norris sank back into his chair, mentally stunned. In his eyes was written fear, an unmistakable, livid fear, as though he comprehended the hopelessness of his position. It was not the reaction the detective had expected, but there still remained the final trap to be sprung.

He drew forth the knife. It was yet wrapped in the towel found in Norris's bureau. Its owner appeared to recognize it. Both articles attracted his gaze, fascinated him;

he shuddered, and then stared at the blade for a moment before he spoke.

"What's that? It looks like—it—it isn't—?"

"Precisely. I'm pleased to find that you recognize it. It is the weapon with which the crime was committed. We found it in this towel, your towel, in the bottom of the drawer of the chiffonier in your rooms . . ."

"You didn't! I don't believe it. You are just trying to—"

"Perhaps you can tell us how it came there," Rankin continued inexorably, as though there had been no interruption.

Lieutenant Thomas lost his patience.

"Maybe you lost that, too," he sneered, with heavy sarcasm, "and it somehow fell into your drawer. Look here, young man, you may just as well confess and make things easier for yourself. Tell us where you did spend Sunday and what happened. Why, man, you're sunk! We've got the goods on you cold."

Norris gazed from Rankin, studying him so intently, to the officer leaning toward him threateningly. He made a gesture of despair, accompanied by a rueful smile.

"It seems you have," he agreed. "Am I under arrest?"

"Yes, you are," replied Rankin, "and I warn you that anything you say will be used against you."

"In which case I shall be as mum as an oyster."

From that moment Norris refused to make any statements. For fifteen minutes they cross-questioned him in a vain effort to win from him some sort of confession. He refused to lay bare the cause of the quarrel; he strenuously denied ever having received a note from the dead girl; and he stubbornly refused to vary the tale that he had spent Sunday evening in his apartments.

Thomas became increasingly furious as time progressed, and wanted to use harsher methods. But even these threats left the prisoner unmoved. Rankin maintained an even tenor throughout the inquisition, secretly admiring the other's imperturbability. Finally, he seated himself at the desk and scribbled a brief note, and then rang for Simpson.

"Take this up to the coroner's office and inquire if they have a witness there named Peter Rawley. If they do, give this note to the coroner." And when the order had been obeyed, "That will settle things for us without a word from Norris."

After a few minutes of waiting the patrolman returned, followed by the scenic railway guard, who entered the office awkwardly, shyly fingering the much-worn cap he carried. The sight of the prisoner seemed to embarrass him more. But the detective speedily put him at his ease and explained what it was that he required.

"Take a good look at the prisoner here," he instructed, "and tell me if you've ever seen him before."

Rawley obeyed. He stared long and completely while his mind groped for recognition. Finally, he replied that he could not say for sure.

"Wasn't this the man who got off at Woodlawn, on the trip before you found the girl's body?" persisted Rankin.

For a brief instant an intelligent look of recognition flashed in the guard's face; but it was followed immediately by one of doubt and dull bewilderment. He shook his head slowly.

"I don't know," he drawled finally. "The man looked something like him, I guess; maybe he was his size, or maybe a little smaller and good-looking. But I can't remember."

"But is it possible that it was this man? Does he remind you in any way of that chap?"

The answer was a doubtful nod.

"You couldn't swear to it, however, could you?"

Another nod—this time in the negative.

Rankin was disappointed. Nevertheless, it wasn't proof by far, even though it was evident that the man could not assist him.

"I guess that will be all. Simpson, take the prisoner away"—he indicated Norris—"and see that he's safely locked up. Get another man to help you handle him if it's necessary. I'll tend to the warrant at once."

The officer proceeded to obey. He escorted both the shuffling guard and the silent Norris from the room. As the door shut behind them, Thomas clapped a heavy hand upon his shoulder.

"Congratulations, old man! Good work. You've got him good. That day-laborer, or whatever he is, is too dumb to know anything, and there isn't any doubt that he's the one that did it."

But his colleague merely shook his head disconsolately.

"I'm not so sure," he replied slowly.

11

A STARTLING DISCOVERY

The offices of Charles M. Bond, Inc., were situated on the fourth floor of the Alvin Building, one of the most modern business structures of the city. The detective had no difficulty in locating them, for upon the frosted glass of the doorway, which one saw immediately upon stepping from the elevator, was clearly printed the name of the concern. His knock upon the door was answered by a secretary, one who wore tortoiseshell glasses, was of uncertain age, and was dressed in a straight-laced, high-necked dress of somber hue.

She informed him that Mr. Bond was not in, though he ordinarily arrived at ten o'clock, and that he would not be in until twelve o'clock. Rankin looked at his watch and discovered it was after eleven-thirty.

"I think I'll wait for him. He can't be gone very long, now."

The secretary inspected him severely, and almost grudgingly opened the door, permitting him to enter. He took a seat against the wall and studied the office. It was one of a suite of rooms, completely furnished with the newest and most modern equipment. The central desk was of fine-grained oak. A steel filing cabinet completely filled the opposite corner. At the front, three windows looked out upon Broad Street. Two other doors led into inner offices, one of which, partially opened, revealed to him a corps of employees at work, clearly the office staff; and the other, marked "Private," the sanctum of the head of the concern.

The secretary paid no further attention to him after motioning him to a seat. She returned to her own desk and in a prim fashion began to sort papers. An unpromising source of information, but he nevertheless would attempt to see what he could learn.

"Mr. Bond once had a private secretary here—didn't he?" he began.

She stared at him through her tortoise-shell glasses with as much astonishment as though he had informed her that the moon was made of green cheese. Then she returned to sorting her papers.

Unrebuffed, Rankin repeated the question, and this time she replied constrainedly to indicate it was against her will.

"Yes, he did."

"A Miss Young, wasn't it? Ah, I thought so. I thought I remembered her when I came to see Mr. Bond the last time. What's become of her?"

"I'm sure I don't know," was the staid reply. "Besides, I don't believe you ever called on Mr. Bond before, or I would remember it. At least not during the time that Miss Young was here." She resumed her work with a promptness that clearly indicated she had no inclination to gossip.

The detective affected a merriment he was far from feeling. It was plain she knew nothing of the tragedy.

"You have a good memory, young lady," he laughed, "and I was just wondering if you could assist me. I'm rather interested in her and I'd like to locate her."

Another cold gaze rewarded him.

"I'm sorry, but I could not help you at all; I don't know anything about her. She gave notice on Friday that she was leaving; but even so, one would think she would have the decency to come in yesterday and let us know for sure. But she didn't. Still, I'm not surprised."

She spoke spitefully, and Rankin saw that he had luckily touched a vulnerable spot. This repressed, none-too-good-looking young lady had been jealous of Miss Young—perhaps even because the susceptible Mr. Bond had failed to shower her with the attentions he had given the other.

"Why not?" he asked.

"That's just how she was—no consideration for others; and she was clumsy, too. Why, I could have done her work better than she did! She hadn't the slightest idea how to use a typewriter."

"You mean she wasn't a skilled stenographer? At what sort of work would you say she was adept?"

"I don't know that; but I don't believe she ever did a stroke of work before she came into this office. One of those lily-dainty girls who don't know what it is to labor week in and week out."

"Then why did Mr. Bond keep her?"

"Well, now,"—the secretary put a world of suggestion into the few spiteful words—"you know men. Not that it was Mr. Bond's fault at all. I think it was she that kept encouraging him."

She caught herself suddenly in confusion. What she was discussing with this stranger was indiscreet, to say the least; while he recognized this reaction as she continued with her work, nevertheless he wasn't willing to give up yet. She had said just enough to whet his curiosity for more.

"Why did she leave, then? Wasn't she satisfactory?"

There was no reply. Casually he strolled to her desk, meditating upon the new complication her words suggested. It was the first suggestion that there was anything the

matter with the murdered girl. True, in view of others'
testimony, he could discard it merely as spite on the secretary's part; but it wasn't like him to throw away any
probable trail.

"What are you doing?" he asked politely.

Her reply was brusque and disapproving. "Sorting papers."

"Indeed? Is it interesting work?"

He regarded her work. Bills, notes, and accounts littered the desk top, and these she was arranging in some
sort of order.

"It is, if one isn't interrupted all the time."

The quip flew above him. Suddenly he snatched from
her hand a sheet she was just about to lay down. It was
a brief business letter scribbled roughly on finely woven
white paper.

"Who wrote this?"

"Give me back that paper!" The secretary snatched at
it angrily. He kept it beyond her reach. "You can at least
behave like a gentleman."

"Who wrote this?" he repeated. "Tell me that and you
can have it back." There was an ominousness in his tone
that drove her to reply.

"Mr. Bond did, of course. Now let me have that or I
shall call one of the clerks."

The detective returned it, apologizing for a rudeness
he did not at all regret. For the notepaper and the writing
of the letter were both exactly the same as the paper and
the script upon the note of appointment found in the dead
girl's pocketbook!

There was no mistaking the scrawled, slanting hand;
the uncrossed "t's," the "ee's" that closed into the letters
"ii"; he would have recognized them anywhere. Charles
Bond was the author of both, and he had written both
on paper from his office. Not James Norris, but Charles

Bond. What was the import of this astounding discovery? How did it coincide with the problem as he had already formulated it?

He strolled to the window to ponder upon the problem, followed by the secretary's glaring eyes. Below, in the street, crowds of people hustled on their way to lunch, in a never-ending flow. Across Broad Street a construction project was in progress, the foundations being built into a vast cavity that yawned almost beneath him. Further down, the traffic signal light and Chestnut Street engulfed in the lunch-hour rush. A constant stream of machines passed. One drew up before the Alvin Building, a blue-and-white Daimler limousine, conspicuous for its size and beauty, and a man in a gray topcoat and Panama hat descended.

Rankin's mind was in a whirl. Did it mean that Mary Young had gone to Woodlawn with her employer? On first glance, it would appear so. But the straight-laced secretary had just informed him that the girl had ceased work on Friday. Why, then, should she accompany Bond to the park on Sunday? And the note was signed "J," and not "C" for Charles. The financier's name was not Charles J. Bond, but Charles M. Bond, as he had read on the glazed door of the office. And why should one whose initials are C.M.B. sign himself "J"? It was ridiculous. And if Bond had written that note, what of the tale of the telephone operator at the Enderley Apartments? The girl had visited them on Sunday afternoon, and left a message, requesting an appointment with Norris.

The further he investigated into the case, the deeper he found himself engulfed. Instead of the pieces of the puzzle falling into place so that the total diagram was beginning to take form, the enigma grew more complicated. So engrossed was he in contemplating this latest development, that he was unaware of the arrival of the man he sought until Mr. Bond stood before him and spoke to him. He was the person who had just descended from the blue-and-white Daimler below.

The financier was a heavy-set, middle-aged person, rather short in stature, so that he gave the impression of being pudgy, if not stout. His eyes were small and beady, his nose bulbous. His pendulous lower lip overhung an enormous jowl, and a few wisps of hair, carefully combed, decorated the crown of his head. He was faultlessly attired in a dark-gray suit of perfect tailoring, a silk handkerchief protruding from his upper coat pocket, and a diamond stickpin in his tie. Ostentatious rings were displayed on his fingers and his entire being fairly reeked of perfume and powder. A most unprepossessing individual, the detective decided; and he felt an instant dislike for him.

He informed Mr. Bond that he desired to see him in private; whereupon the other, beaming urbanely upon him, opened the door into the office marked "Private," and waved him affably ahead of him.

The room was a replica in miniature of the outer office, lacking only the filing cabinet and the secretary's desk. Upon the central desk was a picture of a deadly-eyed and forceful woman with pouchy cheeks and two chins. Her age was about forty-five.

"My wife," explained the financier, seeing the other's eyes stray toward it. "Now, sir, just have a seat there and tell me what I can do for you."

His manner was jovial and bland, but to the detective it did not seem altogether a natural pose. He had a definite aim now in his inquisition and he determined to make the most of his opportunity.

"I'm from Police Headquarters," he informed the other. "Name's Rankin."

Mr. Bond gave a sudden, apprehensive start which he could not control, and he clutched the arms of his chair with his short fingers. But the next instant his distress had passed and he smiled benignantly.

"Ah, yes, from Headquarters. I'm pleased to know you. You will have to be prompt, for I've a business appointment at twelve-thirty which I can't afford to miss." He glanced at his watch. "And it's almost twelve-fifteen now."

"I'll make it as brief as possible. Have you, by any chance, seen the morning paper?"

"Yes, the financial *Ledger* only, however. May I ask why?"

"It's a matter about your secretary, Miss Young. You had such a secretary at one time, did you not?"

"Miss Young? Certainly I did, and quite recently." The financier's reply was casual, but once more the fingers tightened on the chair.

"What became of her?"

"Why, she left me the other day. It was Friday, I believe."

"Why did she leave you? What was the difficulty?"

"Difficulty?" Mr. Bond extended his hands in a deprecating fashion. "Difficulty? Why, none at all. She just decided to leave. I think she had a prospect for another position somewhere else. Oh, no, there was no trouble."

"Are you positive?" Rankin's tone was searching. "Wasn't there some sort of annoyance?"

"My goodness, no! Nothing of the sort! I don't see how you could ever have gotten that impression." The denial was suave and self-contained. "But what about Miss Young? I do hope she isn't in any trouble."

"Miss Young was murdered on Sunday night, at Woodlawn Park!"

The effect of this simple statement was astounding. Suddenly and completely Mr. Charles Bond was seized with terror. His face became a pasty gray, his eyes bulged in fear, and his lower jaw dropped in nameless apprehension. He cast a hunted glance about the room and raised his hands to his throat as though he were strangling. Rankin rose in alarm.

"What's the matter, Mr. Bond?"

The electrical magnate managed to wave him away as he struggled for control. With visible effort he straightened himself.

"Nothing's the matter," he gasped. "I'm all right. It's just my horror at hearing such terrible news. It really was quite a shock. I thought so much of the poor girl." He shook himself and his voice dropped almost to a whisper under his breath as he added, "and at Woodlawn Park."

There was a curious quality about the words, and the tone in which they were spoken, and they made Rankin pierce the other with a glance as he seated himself.

"Yes, at Woodlawn," he said. "Do you ever go there?"

Mr. Bond mopped his forehead feverishly.

"Of course not," he replied indignantly, with far more vigor than the statement required. "There's nothing very attractive there. I don't think I'd care for it."

"I thought perhaps you might have been. Many people go just for the fun of the amusements."

"Well, I can't see anything to them. I prefer more genteel entertainment—clubs, for instance. Why, last Sunday I spent the evening at the Marlton Club."

This was a most unusual thing to say under the circumstances. Rankin had given Bond no cause to believe that he suspected him, nor had he questioned him as to his movements on the fatal evening. Nevertheless, the man seemed to think it necessary that he volunteer an account of them without being asked. For what possible cause should the financier be so anxious to supply himself with an alibi? It must be a good alibi, at least, else he would not have spoken so surely about it. And it forestalled further inquiries in that direction, unless he wished to reveal his newly developed suspicions.

He had already decided that such a movement would not be wise. He had too little material with which to attack the man and demand an explanation of the note; for it was no simple matter to accuse one so powerful and wealthy as his opponent with so little provocation. If he erred, the Department would demand his resignation, regardless of his previous accomplishments.

So all he said was, "Indeed? The Marlton Club?"

"Yes, sir." The magnate began to elaborate on the subject. "On Sunday my chauffeur drove me there at eight-thirty, and I spent the evening there till quite late."

"May I ask with whom?"

"Oh, I hardly remember. No one in particular." They were sparring for information, each determined to give out as little as possible and to learn as much. Rankin's casual question had found Bond too alert to fall into any trap. "But you wanted to find out something about Miss Young, did you not?"

"Yes. I was hoping you might be able to tell me about her. It's such a curious crime."

"It's sudden, anyhow." The magnate pressed a button upon his desk, immediately the frigid-faced secretary stood in the doorway. "A morning paper please, Miss Cochrane. And get in touch with Alfred and tell him to bring the car around."

"A peculiar woman, Miss Cochrane," he explained while they waited. "Stern and hidebound, if you understand what I mean. But a good worker."

"Yes, she seems efficient."

The secretary returned with the *Public Ledger* and promptly withdrew. Bond had no difficulty in locating the story of the crime, for it was yet a front-page sensation; and while he digested it the detective lighted a cigarette and waited. He observed that the magnate had completely regained his smug suavity. The fatal moment in which he might have revealed something had completely passed.

"Uh! Terrible indeed!" he murmured sympathetically. "The poor girl! You know, we did think such a great deal of her here. But I'm afraid there's nothing in regard to the crime that I can tell you. I know nothing whatsoever about it. And it is now almost twelve-thirty—"

Rankin took the hint. Plenty of time, the next time, to pin Mr. Bond down to the truth, if it became necessary. But despite his smugness, he was clearly anxious to get away.

"Very well, sir. There will be just one thing I want to know. Where did Miss Young come from before she worked for you?"

"I'm afraid I couldn't say, Mr.—what did you say your name was?—Rankin. Really, I never inquired about it."

"But didn't you ask her any questions when she came to you—demand some sort of credentials from her?"

"No, we didn't. Of course, I realize that's a poor way to do business, but then I consider myself a fairly good judge of character and I believed I could read many good traits in this girl. She was intelligent, refined, and—good-looking"—he slurred over this last as though he hadn't intended to say it—"so I employed her."

"And yet she left you?"

"Oh, that's another matter. She merely felt she could better her position elsewhere; it's a mistaken idea that quite a few girls seem to get."

"But didn't she ever mention her last position?"

"No, I'm afraid not. Of course, she must have been of good family, as she was quite refined as well as intelligent."

"Miss Cochrane doesn't seem to think so," Rankin said bluntly.

The financier shifted uncomfortably and flushed but immediately regained his poise and spoke calmly: "Well, as I say, she's a most peculiar woman, and she gets such unfounded ideas."

"I see. So you can tell me nothing about her. There was nothing she ever said that might lead you to assume that she was in difficulties or had any enemies?"

"Oh, no, nothing at all. I'm sorry. I'd like to assist you. I'm a firm believer in law and order. As a matter of fact, we really didn't expect Miss Young to leave us yet. We believed she would return on Monday, anyhow, because she hadn't said definitely that she was going. Not what you would call real notice of quitting."

"Why, did she leave something here that she might have returned for?"

"No, no, nothing like that. It simply wasn't settled whether she was taking the other place or not, and I was doing my best to persuade her not to. But then, when she didn't come in, why, I assumed that she had definitely stopped her work. And now, Mr. Rankin, I must call a halt. I'll be late as it is. Stop in again and we'll talk matters over some more."

"I certainly shall." The emphatic tone caused Mr. Bond to regard him for a moment, as though he suspected the veiled meaning in the words.

When they had passed into the outer office, the financier removed his coat from a rack and donned it.

"I shan't be in again to-day, Miss Cochrane. In the future, tend closely to your work; that will be more appreciated."

There was nothing but suave gentleness in his tone, but the secretary's face paled and she bit her lip as she caught the stinging barb hidden in the words. Rankin smiled to himself gleefully at this precaution that had been taken a little too late for Bond's genuine peace of mind and safety. He opened the door, permitting the other to pass out ahead of him, and as he shut it he paused on the threshold to glance back. Miss Cochrane was staring at him with such a gaze of utter contempt and venom, that he chuckled to himself, though in truth he had little cause to rejoice.

12
ADVENTURES OF AN ALIBI

Descending by the steps, instead of the elevator, Rankin reached the entrance of the building just in time to see the financier whisked off in his magnificent car by a liveried chauffeur. He had a brief glimpse of the latter's features, and he fancied that in them he caught some resemblance to some one whom he had seen recently; but he dismissed the idea as a mere figment of his imagination. The magnate leaned from the side of the car to wave pudgy fingers to him and he grimaced.

The warm, bright sunlight of the open air had a refreshing effect, and for some inexplicable reason he welcomed it with relief. The atmosphere of the office, despite its rich furnishings, had been strangely uncomfortable. He had detected in it an air of furtiveness and stealth and all the suavity in the world could not efface this impression. A pall of the uncleanly extended over it, exuding, perhaps, from the personality of its owner. But in the sunlight, despite the rushing crowds and the interminable medley of sounds, there was a cleansing influence.

He had already decided his course of action. First, lunch, which telltale pangs in his nether regions had warned him not to neglect. Afterward, an investigation of Mr. Bond's movements on the tragic Sunday night. There was sufficient justification in this move merely in the distress he had experienced at the mention of the fatality and in his anxiety to supply himself with an alibi. These things were suspicious enough in themselves but in addition there was the appointment note, which the financier undoubtedly had written.

While taking his meal in a nearby restaurant he meditated upon this last piece of information. It brought him to one inevitable conclusion. For, if the financier had met Mary Young at nine o'clock, then he had gone with her to Woodlawn Park; and to consider further, he must have killed her. But what, then, of James Norris? Besides, had not Bond claimed to have spent the evening in company with others at the Marlton Club?

The detective knew the Marlton Club well. But a scanty two squares distance, it was an ultra-refined place, for prosperous and well-known business men of the city. Stockbrokers, manufacturers, lawyers, frequented its rooms. Many sought to gain admission as though it were a prize, believing that its exclusiveness would add prestige to their already established reputations, and many failed. How Charles Bond was ever accepted as a member he could not fathom.

After paying his check, he tipped the waiter and walked out. A brisk five minutes' stroll brought him to the doors of the club. It was a gray stone building, eight stories in height, with marble foundation blocks. The portals were of pillared marble and onyx, leading to revolving doors. This gave entrance to a long corridor, richly ornamented with fine prints, luxuriant in deep rugs and soft, inviting chairs. The hall gave way on either side to small chambers, card rooms, private supper rooms, and reading rooms and at its ends opened into the main lobby.

He approached the uniformed porter in the doorway; he, if any one, could tell him what he desired to know.

Mr. Bond was a conspicuous figure, both because of the comparatively recent scandal and his vulgarly ostentatious display of wealth.

Preliminary questioning elicited the fact that he was on duty regularly and that he divided his hours with another porter who was then at lunch. Each of them, it seemed, had a day off every Wednesday for the other, and every Thursday for the speaker—and their hours did not change on Sundays.

"What are your hours?" then put Rankin.

"Well, sir, that depends," explained the porter servilely. "I come in at eleven o'clock or so, and then, except for a short time for lunch, I stay on duty till four o'clock. Then I come back at seven o'clock in the evening, and stay on till after twelve or so. My buddy takes part of the time with me."

Here was luck already, the detective reflected. The man was on duty during the hours of Sunday evening in which the financier declared he had both arrived and departed.

"I was wondering if you could recall on Sunday evening whether Mr. Charles Bond—you know him, do you not?—whether he was here on Sunday night with a package for me. He was to leave it and I was to call for it yesterday, but I couldn't find the time. There's no use in my going in after it, unless he was here with it."

Much depended on the answer, and he waited in growing suspense. The porter nodded in comprehension, his bright eyes sweeping the detective's features as though he sought something. A smile broadened his lips into a look which, strangely enough, resembled amusement. At length he replied.

"I couldn't say about the package, sir; you'll have to inquire about that inside. But I know that Mr. Bond came here on Sunday night."

"Are you positive of that? When did he arrive?"

"Yes, sir, I'm positive. I remember helping him out of his car when the chauffeur brought him. I suppose it must have been eight-thirty or so, for it wasn't dark yet, though it did become dark shortly afterward."

"How can you be sure it was Sunday night?"

"Well, sir, I remember it distinctly on account of the tip he gave me. He comes every now and then, but he seldom gives me anything. But recently, sir, he's been promising me something; you know, when he drops in, he says to me, 'Nick, just hold your horses and we'll have something for you in time.' And it was Sunday night that he drops in at eight-thirty and says, jokingly, 'Well, here it is,' and then before going in, he gives me five dollars."

"And when did he leave?"

"It was almost twelve o'clock, sir, just before I went off duty. That's how I know what time it was. And he stopped and spoke to me."

If the words were true, the financier was cleared of all suspicion. For during the hours in which the crime was committed, Charles Bond was resting in the lobby of the Marlton Club, smoking, or probably at cards. Yet, the ostentatiousness of his entrance and exit, as though purposely to attract attention, had a curious touch. Between eight-thirty and eleven-forty-five, had he remained in the club the entire time? It was easily possible that he could have left by a side door, if there was one, met Mary Young, committed the crime, and returned to the club, safely assured of an alibi. Was there another exit?

He put the question to the doorman.

"Only a back kitchen entrance," came the reply, "and that's for the chef and the help. I hardly think that he or any of our members would use that, do you?"

"No, I suppose not." Rankin realized that there was nothing more to be learned here, but he was far from satisfied. Bond had undoubtedly made the nine o'clock appointment. "If, as you say," he remarked, "Mr. Bond was here, I suppose my package must be waiting for me inside. It'll be probably at the desk, don't you think?"

"Yes, I suppose so. Go straight through the corridor into the main room and inquire of the clerk."

Rankin tipped his informer and passed into the lobby. Against its rear wall, stairs and elevators led above, and the clerk the porter had mentioned worked busily at his desk. Lounges, comfortable leather chairs, and many types of smoking paraphernalia littered the room in no particular plan or order. Four men puffed away in one corner, engaged in earnest discussion; a colored bellman sat listlessly by the steps. Except for the clerk, there was an air of drowsiness about the place, and he therefore advanced to the desk.

The desk man could not give him the information he sought. In answer to his question regarding the presence of the financier, the clerk replied:

"I couldn't say for sure whether he was or not. We had quite a crowd Sunday evening, and I had a great deal to attend to besides watching who came in or went out."

"Who was here, for instance?"

"Well, I do recall Mr. Altman and Mr. Cantrell and Mr. Porter, and also there were Mr. Collins and John Craig—he came to the desk for a few minutes—and there were,"—he paused and looked at the book in which he was engrossed, writing, as though he were anxious to return to it—"oh, lots more."

"But don't you think you would have recalled him had he really been here?" persisted Rankin. "Understand, it's quite important in a business way that I should be able to locate Mr. Bond on Sunday night."

The clerk shook his head dubiously.

"Not at all, not at all. He may have been here the entire evening and I wouldn't have noticed it. So, really, I could not say. Personally, I don't recall him at all, but if it is so important I'll see what I can do for you."

"Yes, I wish you would."

He rang a bell which effectively served to summon the listless bellman. The latter reported at the desk with a brief salute and a grin.

"This gentleman desires to ask you a few questions."

"Yas, suh."

Rankin withdrew with him beyond the hearing of the clerk and asked him whether he knew Charles Bond. On receiving a reply in the affirmative, he said in a cautious tone:

"I'm just wondering if you could tell me when Mr. Bond was here last, when he spent some time here."

"Yas, suh, ah suttinly could. It was just two nights ago to-day, sah; it was Sunday night. He comes in his cab about eight-thuty, if ah 'members correctly, and he stays around till maybe 'leven-thuty or so, doin' nothin' in pahticalah, just stayin'."

The reply was instantaneous and complete and it was that that made Rankin suddenly view it with suspicion. He had made a vague inquiry and had received an immediate response without any hesitation; and it was so complete a response as to be too glib to be natural. The hypothesis that he had nursed with such little provocation ripened into certainty as he put his next question with the same caution.

"And he was here all evening? Didn't he go out for an hour or more, about quarter of nine till after ten some time?"

"Oh, no, suh," the bellman was emphatic. "Not once, suh. Ah watched him most of the time and ah could sweah he nevah left the club, suh, all evening."

This was obviously ridiculous. So intent was the bell-man on convincing Rankin of the financier's presence on the fatal evening that he was overdoing it. The detective regarded him with a keenness that caused him to flinch before the stern gaze.

"And why should you watch Mr. Bond so particularly?"

"Because—because—" the man floundered about for a way to escape his own pitfall—"because Mr. Bond told me—"

"Yes, what did he tell you?"

"Why, Mr. Bond, he didn't tell me nuthin', nuthin' at all."

"Didn't he tell you to say, to whoever would ask, that he had been here on Sunday evening, and didn't he pay you to say that?"

The negro attempted to affect a look of surprise to cover his sudden confusion.

"Oh, no, suh, he nevah told me that," he stammered. "Why, ah was just tellin' yuh what you-all axed me, suh. That's all—nuthin' else."

"And I think you're lying to me." The detective's face was as dark as a storm cloud. "I want the truth. Was Mr. Bond here on Sunday night, or not?"

"Ah'm not lyin' to you. Ah sweah it's the truth. Don't you tech me." He backed away with a look of apprehension before Rankin's threatening advance. "I'se respectable, Ah am."

"I'm not going to hurt you," returned Rankin, grimly. "Don't worry about that. But unless you speak up you're going to be arrested and go to prison for a couple of years. Now, how much did Mr. Bond pay you?"

For a brief instant a crafty look appeared on the negro's face, but it was swiftly displaced by one of greater terror.

"No, suh, he didn't pay me, Ah tell yuh," he almost shouted, "and yuh cain't arrest me for nuthin'. Nobody pay me, and that's the God's truth."

That was all he would say. Threats, cajoling, and a promise of a bribe were all the same to him; he clung tenaciously to his story that Charles Bond had been at the club on Sunday night. Rather than make a scene, the detective finally desisted; but he left the club convinced that the financier had been anywhere but there on the fatal evening. The probability was that the door porter had also been bribed to supply him with an alibi.

But how could he know that fact for an actuality? Belief and proof were two different matters, and what he would be willing to accept, others would not. Some one who had been present and who had not been bribed that night might be able to help him; accordingly, he reviewed the list of names that the desk clerk had given him.

The first mentioned, Altman, Cantrell, and Porter, he had never heard of; but Collins he knew well. A banker of wide repute and great wealth, it was for him that Rankin had done the service of tracing and capturing the notorious forger, Penryhn. The banker stood to lose thirty thousand dollars unless the criminal were caught; and knowing this, the detective had put all his energy and time, over a period of three months, into trailing him, till he had finally brought the pursuit to a successful conclusion. Collins was properly grateful; certainly he would now be willing to give him assistance.

A call to Collins's office, however, netted him the information that the banker had gone for an afternoon of golf at the Eastview Country Club. The club was a lengthy trip from town, beyond Bryn Mawr and Ardmore on the main line. It would take a good hour at least, and if he went he wouldn't be able to return to the city until the afternoon was gone. But the trail could not rest thus in space, he reflected; it was a matter of too great importance to postpone even for a single day.

Accordingly, after a wait of a half-hour in Broad Street Station and a ride of three-quarters of an hour, he reached Merion, the nearest station to the club. The latter nested at the top of a hill just beyond him, a path leading to the gray sandstone structure that was the central clubhouse. Beyond that, smaller buildings indicated the men's dressing-rooms, the caddy house, and the supply house. Farther beyond, the undulating green of the course itself came into view, bounded on one side by a sparkling rill, and on the other by a clump of trees passing beyond his sight.

Rankin reached the dressing-rooms, just as the man he sought issued from them, clad in brown knickers and a riding cap, and with his clubs slung over his shoulder. He was a pleasant-faced, clear-eyed man of perhaps fifty, with silver hair. He paused in surprise on observing the detective, and extended his hand.

"Tommy Rankin, of all people! What a coincidence to meet you out here!"

"Not such a coincidence as you'd imagine, Mr. Collins. As a matter of fact, I came purposely to find you."

The banker's features expressed both his pleasure and his curiosity.

"Did you? Well, then, you are quite lucky to come just now for I'm about to leave for my game." He hitched his clubs securely upon his shoulders. "I was waiting for my partner and his caddy. I believe they're coming now." He pointed to a stout, bald gentleman and a youngster dragging clubs after him, just emerging from the caddy house. "So you'll have to talk fast on whatever the subject happens to be."

"It will only take a minute," Rankin explained, "but you mustn't expect me to tell you anything, or explain the reasons for my questions."

"That's agreeable to me." Collins smiled engagingly. "So shoot away with them."

"Do you know Charles Bond?"

"Certainly I do. The electrical magnate, isn't he? To be perfectly candid, I'm not very keen on him. You're not a friend of his, are you?"

"Hardly a friend. Not even an acquaintance, in fact. I'm given to understand that you were at the Marlton Club on Sunday evening."

The banker gazed at Rankin curiously.

"That's quite true," he responded. "But how did you know? That's right, I forgot I musn't ask any questions but merely answer them. Yes, I was there with a whole gang—Johnnie Craig, Bob Nolan, Billy Lavinson; we put in most of the evening at cards. But what has this to do with Bond?"

"Was he at the club that evening?"

Collins considered a moment before replying. "No, I'm positive he wasn't."

"How can you be so sure of that?"

"Because if he were I wouldn't have stayed there as long as I did. Mrs. Collins gave me blazes when I got home so late. Bond, you know, is one of those hail-fellow-well-met, slap-your-back nuisances when he is with men. We'd have all heard him soon enough if he had been there, I can tell you. He wouldn't let his presence remain a secret long. I never did understand how the boys voted him through; it happened while I was on vacation or it would never have happened at all."

"Don't you think it possible he might have been in one of the private rooms?" Rankin was determined to allow no loophole of doubt.

"What! And never a peep out of him the entire evening? No, it's impossible, I tell you. We'd have been sure to know of his presence in some manner or another. You can ask any of the fellows who were with me. Here, I'll give you a list of them, and others that I saw there that night."

"I wish you would, though you must be right. I suppose, however, there'll be no need of going any farther."

While Collins completed the list, a faint hail was wafted across the greensward.

"There, I'll have to be going," remarked the magnate. "I fancy I'm being paged." He waved aside the detective's thanks. "Don't mention it. Drop in at my office some time and tell me what it's all about."

Rankin watched him join his companions on the first tee and construct his little mound for the ball, preparatory to the first stroke. He smiled in satisfaction. There was no doubting that he had shattered Bond's alibi. It left the financier in a worse position than ever, merely because of the fact that he had found it necessary to prepare one. It had been a good alibi while it lasted and only the virtues of persistence and doggedness on his part were responsible for its destruction. Charles Bond must have a good reason for wishing his actual location unknown; and he was positive that the cause had to do with the murder of Mary Young.

He was aware now of where the financier had not been. He had now to discover the more vital question of where he had been. Besides Mr. Bond, there was only one person in the world could supply him with that information—the man who had presumably driven him to the club, but who, in reality, must have taken him elsewhere—the chauffeur of the financier.

13
THE FORMER MRS. ARTHUR HAMPDALE

The sun, a golden blazing ball, was already far advanced upon its nightly pilgrimage when Tommy Rankin reached the inclosed grounds of the Bond estate. The heat was tempered by the cool of early twilight, and a gentle breeze, soughing through the trees, freshened the air. Vague shadows were already chasing across the grass in crazy, meaningless patterns, and a night bird, giving a weird, raucous call, darted from the dense foliage of a willow tree.

The detective entered the grounds through the iron front gates that opened to the street, an automobile drive curving inward until it was lost to sight in the dense plant growth of the estate. Sighing willow mingled with stately pine and spruce until the effect was one of a forest, making dark, dank spots on the wide-spreading lawn. The mansion, located far inward, was invisible along the twisting drive, which approached it by a tall portico and passed on to the garage in the rear. A sign cautioned tradesmen to "Enter by the Rear" and Rankin wondered amusedly whether or not he would be considered a tradesman.

His immediate destination was the garage at the extreme rear of the grounds. There he would find, at this hour, the man he sought. The gravel of the drive crunched noisily under his heels as he walked, and he reached the curve which shielded the house from the sight of the street. It burst into view, a tremendous endless mansion of white stone. The auto route turned at the portico on the side, going toward the garage still further in the rear. A walk led from the paving that paralleled the drive to the front entrance; another could be seen on the right side, approaching a lesser portion of the house that might well be the servants' quarters.

The dusk wind carried to his ears the sound of footsteps on the gravel road behind him. Rankin's innate caution coming to the surface, he paused to listen. He could tell, from the measured, steady tread, that they were the footsteps of a man; but there was a curious quality about them that puzzled him as he listened. They were not the normal and regular heavy tread, but were light and careful, as though the walker was taking every precaution not to be heard. They were so stealthy as to be furtive and sly, and this piqued the hearer's curiosity more than anything else. Something peculiar was going on, Rankin decided; and in an instant he had dived into the heavy undergrowth that fringed the road.

For a moment, as the detective crouched there, he fancied that the rustling of the bushes had frightened away the walker. But no; after a brief wait the steps grew louder, and presently their author appeared around the curve. He was a strange, middle-aged man in a dark suit and a slouch hat, whose bulbous nose was but the least part of a set of exceedingly ugly features. The eyes were deep-sunk and dark, and the mouth was awkwardly large, resembling a cow's gullet. Rankin's instinct had been correct—the unknown was stealing his way into the grounds, making every effort to attract no attention. He bent low whenever he approached an open space in the tree growth which permitted the entire lawn to become visible. He stepped as quietly as he could, walking, whenever the foliage permitted, on the grass fringing the side; and this deadened his footsteps effectively. The watcher wondered who he was and what his stealth signified.

Suddenly voices broke into the stillness—a man's voice, and then a woman's in reply, coming closer down the drive, toward the gate. The words were unintelligible but their very sound caused the stranger to start in alarm and seek frantically for a place of concealment. The next instant he too had dived into the thick undergrowth on the other side of the road, exactly opposite the detective. It was a most peculiar situation, two spies, and one spying on the other; and its outcome was bound to be unique.

Presently the two speakers appeared, and Rankin, staring at them in the darkness, was positive he had heard the voices before. But where he could not conceive, and it only made him peer with greater effort to catch a sight of them as they came closer.

And what was his tremendous astonishment when he recognized, in the girl, Blanche Rushby, the girl of the park, who had fainted and who had denied the utterance of those cryptic words with which Patrolman Donahue charged her! And in the dark-faced man, in chauffeur's uniform, Mr. Bond's chauffeur, whose face he had thought familiar that very afternoon, but could not place—the girl's escort, Alfred Ramon!

It was not surprising that the detective had failed to recognize him before. At the park the chauffeur had been in civilian clothes; here he was in uniform. This single change made a vast difference. At Woodlawn he had seen him under flaring arc lights, and then, in the broad daylight, in front of Mr. Bond's office. But what did it mean? What connection did this have with the crime? How were these two implicated in their relationship to their employer? So unexpected was it, that for the moment he totally forgot the other watcher, across from him.

Ramon was speaking in low, husky tones, vibrant with feeling and passion.

"Another kiss, Blanche," he pleaded; "just one."

The girl laughed merrily and shook her pretty blonde head.

"Not now, Alfred. You've got to get back to work on the master's car, if you want to have it ready for him at ten o'clock. You know he will be furious if he has to wait for it."

"Who cares about him?" cried Ramon impetuously. "I've only one real care in all the world, and that's you."

The man's arms were tight about her, but the girl laughed again; and then she gazed up archly into her suitor's determined, pleading face.

"So you've said before, but we don't want to get into any trouble, do we? Things are too happy the way they are. Will you go back if I grant your request?"

"Yes," he replied, eagerly; and she nodded her assent.

Rankin smiled to himself at the ardor of the young lovers. An ideal spot it was, cool and shadowy, with the boughs bending in murmuring encouragement and invitation. For a moment they remained embraced, and when the man released Blanche, a red, joyous flush suffused her features.

"Will you go now?" she whispered.

"Yes, now, but not for long. And don't forget—on my next night off we'll have a wonderful time. That, I promise you."

The chauffeur was off, retracing his steps until the night swallowed him up. The girl watched him go, and then, humming softly to herself, moved down the drive. Rankin wondered what she would say, did she know that two pair of eyes had witnessed that charming little love idyl. He had an impulse to follow her. But the other watcher prevented that. As the footsteps died away, all was silent except for the slight swaying of the trees and the distant hoot of a night owl.

Rankin waited patiently for the next development. It was not long in coming. Across from him, the bushes rustled, and then, with infinite caution, the stranger emerged, first his head, then his arms, and then his entire body. He looked completely about him, up and down the road. Then, apparently reassured that no one was in sight, he progressed with the same furtiveness as before, up the path. Rankin strained his eyes in the gloom to follow him, but on the drive it was already as dark as night. Only in the open spaces of the lawn, beyond, was there anything to be seen. Still he waited, and presently a moving, shadowy form detached itself from the darker shadows of the trees and advanced into the open. The unknown was not remaining on the road, but crossing the lawn in the direction of the side door of the house.

He reached his objective—the side door. Sharply, distinctly in the still night air there came the sound of two raps, done with such precision that they might well have been signals. The detective was convinced that they were such; for there was a very brief wait and then the door opened. A woman stood in the doorway silhouetted against the lights of the entrance; the man slipped in, and the door was shut silently. But brief as the time had been, it was not too short for Rankin to recognize the features of the woman who had answered the signal. For, as a light suddenly blazed in a window beside the portal that had previously been dark, he realized he had seen the deadly-eyed, pouchy-cheeked woman whose portrait was on the desk of Charles Bond—the woman who had at one time been the widowed Mrs. Arthur Hampdale, but who was now the married Mrs. Charles Bond!

This discovery, piling so suddenly upon the other, left him bewildered. But there was no time to consider whether this startling development was part of his case or altogether extraneous to it. At that moment the returning footsteps of the girl became audible, and as she rounded the curve he stepped into the path and confronted her.

For a moment she was startled and stepped back with a slight scream of fright; but taking courage, she advanced and peered into his face closely. He put out his hand reassuringly, determined, however, to be stern with her if necessary.

"My goodness," the girl exclaimed as recognition came to her. "You're the man, the detective, who is—was—" She stopped, and in those few words he recognized the same note of apprehension and alarm with which she had spoken at Woodlawn upon being questioned.

"Exactly," he replied severely, finishing her thought. "The detective who is investigating the murder of Mary Young, and to whom you lied when you said you didn't know her, and in giving me your address—"

This last accusation distressed her for a moment more than the first.

"No, no. I didn't lie. That was my address, my home address; but I didn't want Alfred to mention that we worked for Mr. Bond; so I gave his home address, too; but—"

"So Alfred—Mr. Bond's chauffeur, isn't he?—is also in on this—"

"No, he isn't. He doesn't know a thing about it; he never saw the girl before in his life. He's Mr. Bond's chauffeur and I'm Mrs. Bond's special maid, but I didn't want you to know that." She was trembling in sudden incomprehensible fear. "But he doesn't know a thing about it. I never told him—and you mustn't, either, or he'll be furious."

"But you do know something. Well, I've come for an explanation and I want the truth; and there won't be any playing off or pretending sick this time."

The girl gasped as she realized the admission her agitation had caused her to make, and there was an unrelenting quality about her inquisitor's words that sounded the knell of all hope of pretense.

"What do you want me to do?" she asked faintly.

"Tell me all you can about Mary Young—and why you refused to tell me before. This is murder we have to deal with—a horrible, cowardly murder—and if you shield the criminal or conceal your knowledge, you are as guilty as he."

"I won't conceal anything. I will tell. It's been preying on my mind ever since that awful night, and I can't even sleep for worrying about it. But I never dared to say anything. I was too afraid to."

"Afraid of what? Of whom?"

"Of Mrs. Bond. She has a furious temper, a temper like a wildcat when she gets aroused, and there's no telling what would happen if I spoke. It would be worth my job, certainly, and even more. She's that mean and jealous."

The awed reply bewildered Rankin. Mrs. Bond! Where did she come into this entanglement? What part did she play and what was her relation to the murdered girl? But all he said was:

"Well, you needn't be afraid any more. How did you come to know Miss Young?"

"I didn't really know her; I only saw her once. That was last week on Thursday night. She came out here for Mr. Bond, to do some extra work at the house. I let her in, just after Mrs. Bond seemed to have gone out for the evening. So when I saw her in the park I recognized her as the master's private secretary. And I was so scared then that I fainted, because I remembered what had happened afterward that night, and I thought—that"—the maid hesitated, tremulously—"that Mrs. Bond had carried out her threat."

"Her threat? Of what?"

"Oh, I tell you it was awful," she cried in anguish. "Mrs. Bond did not go out that night, but watched her husband all the time. I don't think anything happened, even though the girl and the master were in his private rooms for two hours; but that the mistress didn't know, and she has such a suspicious nature that she would be ready to believe anything, no matter how bad. But Mr. Bond really thought she was out, or else he would never have dared bring the girl into the house, like that, even for secretarial work."

"It was afterward that the scene occurred and, oh, it was terrible. I was in the next room, waiting to prepare Mrs. Bond for bed, but she must have forgotten that when she went into Mr. Bond's room; but I could hear every word of what she said. Mrs. Bond began to cry around and make a terrible noise in her fury, and she accused him of some unspeakable things, she was that jealous. Then after a while she became calm and dangerous-like; she's even worse when she's like that—then she's real cruel, and I'm always more afraid of her that way. And then she threatened to kill the girl if anything happened like that again!"

"She threatened that? Exactly what did she say?"

"It was something to do with that other trouble Mr. Bond had been in—that divorce proceeding with the actress."

Blanche Rushby paused as though she were about to explain, but he nodded his comprehension and informed her that he knew about it.

"She said," the girl then went on, "'I won't have the patience that Mr. Oakley did when he found you two together; there won't be any divorce. It will just be a stab, or a shot, and the girl will be dead. I tell you I won't go through such a disgraceful scene the second time; rather than that, I'll take the much shorter way—I tell you, I'll kill her!'"

She shuddered as she repeated the venomous words, and it was a brief moment before she had recovered her poise sufficiently to continue.

"Mr. Bond did his best to persuade her that he was innocent, but after what had happened before, she wouldn't listen to him; and I guess you couldn't blame her for that. And she went on raving for almost an hour before she came back into the room; and then I didn't dare to stay because she was absolutely mad with fury. She was trembling like she couldn't control herself, and whatever Mr. Bond had said only served to make it worse. And after a while, he, too, had got mad, so that they had it out for fair. I got out fast, and I stayed out till the next morning."

"So that when you saw the body you believed that Mrs. Bond had, herself, actually stabbed the girl?"

"No, I didn't think that, but I did believe she had got some one else to do it for her, and because I was so afraid of her I didn't dare to let on I knew anything. Alfred never saw her, so, of course, he didn't know why I was so frightened and nervous."

"But what made you think that?" asked Rankin.

"Because one of the things she had said was that the girl would never escape her if there was anything more between her husband and her. She said there would be some one on her trail to get her in case that happened. Oh, there were lots of things like that she said in her anger, and I was so worried that she meant it."

The narration of the tale had exhausted her, for she was trembling. They approached the portico, where there was a stone chair carved out beside the drive. Rankin assisted her into it.

"What sort of a woman is your mistress? Would you say she is determined and vindictive? Do you think she would revenge herself like that?"

"I think she would be capable of anything if she were crossed!" Blanche responded. "She's so used to having her own way. All of this mansion and all the money is her own, and she's been able to rule, all her life. Besides, there's that awful temper and jealousy she has. She was never good-looking herself, and she must know it is only her money that attracts men; so she has come to dislike people who have beauty and girls who can attract men by that."

Remembering the deep-set burning eyes of the photograph, and the original of it, the detective was inclined to agree with her in her character-drawing. But if Mrs. Bond had been responsible for Mary Young's death, how had she accomplished it? Had she gotten some one to follow the unfortunate girl to the park and commit the murder there? And if so, who? A new theory was forming in his mind, which involved the husband, the wife, and the unknown man who had crept so stealthily into the grounds and with whom Mrs. Bond had so peculiar a rendezvous. If it were a correct hypothesis—and there were many grounds to uphold it—then that interview between the mistress of the house and the unknown was of supreme importance. Unless it was already too late, it would be worth overhearing. All things supported him in his belief—the strange way in which the man had appeared, the prearranged signal between him and Mrs. Bond, the stealthy, secretly stolen meeting, and the threats the maid had just related to him, coupled with the fact of Mr. Bond's own peculiar behavior.

He turned to the girl and pointed to the far side of the house through the door of which the intruder had entered.

"What part of the house is that?"

She looked in the direction of his finger. "It's the servants' quarters," she replied. "But there is no one there. Mrs. Bond gave all the help a night off. Alfred is the only one staying. He's at the garage fixing up the car for Mr. Bond, and I didn't go because I wanted to see him."

"But there's a light there under that shade, in the first window by the door. Don't you see it?"

"So there is! I don't know who could be there, because every one went out. They were all glad to get such an unexpected vacation."

"Unexpected?"

"Yes, because it is not any one's regular night out. But Mrs. Bond came into our quarters last night and told us that we could all go out. It sounded to me that she was saying we all *must* go out and she was anxious to get rid of us. But none of them needed much coaxing, though they were all certainly surprised; she never did it before."

The statement strengthened Rankin's theory considerably. If Mrs. Bond desired privacy in her interview, there was no better method of insuring it. And it was just such an interview, he believed, that must never be overheard. According to the maid, Charles Bond was still inside; therefore she could never have held the rendezvous safely in the main portion of the mansion; and the servants' hall was the only place remaining.

Determinedly he faced the maid; and in a tone that threatened to override every objection and would refuse to take "No" for an answer, he said:

"Whoever is there, I've got to know about it. You must get me into the house, and at once, without my being discovered!"

14

THE BLUE-AND-WHITE DAIMLER

It required all of Rankin's powers of persuasion for him to gain this point. The maid was hesitant and fearful of the risk involved, and it was only on his solemn promise to bear whatever responsibilities might ensue from the incident that she finally succumbed to his urgency.

"But I'm not going in with you," she said. "I'm supposed to be out with the rest of the help, and I'm not going to risk Mrs. Bond's catching me. She's fired help for less than that, even. I have a key, and I'll let you in here, at the portico entrance."

With that, she explained to him the way through the house toward the servants' quarters, and then produced the key. The door beside which they stood under the portico was the automobile entrance, but it was not to the main portal of the mansion. This latter was in the central front portion of the house. The portico door opened into a sun parlor, so darkened by the falling night that none of it was visible beyond the entrance. The detective closed the door behind him cautiously, and proceeded on tiptoe across the room.

Totally unfamiliar as to the arrangement of the furnishings, he had perforce to make use of his electric torch. But only for the briefest instant dared he risk it; merely sufficiently to reveal the entrance to the room, and then he moved on in darkness. A davenport had to be skirted, and the path between several chairs negotiated with care; and then he passed through the doorway into the hall which led to the main entrance.

Perfect silence encompassed him. Through the central doorway moonlight filtered sufficiently to indicate the broad staircase, decorated not in the best of taste, with statuettes and a flower vase on the curved landing. From above the stairs there came not a single evidence of habitation, though Rankin knew that behind one of those upstairs doors the financier was preparing to go out at ten o'clock in his magnificent car. It still lacked thirty-five minutes of the hour. The moon also revealed the door to the parlor through which, according to the maid's instructions, he would not have to pass, and the entrance to the library.

It was through this latter that the detective moved furtively, taking care that no sound was made by his feet. Once more the light flashed ahead, to disclose the opposite doorway, leading toward the servants' quarters; and in its brief glare was seen also the tall shelves that covered the wall on one side, filled with books, the ingrained central table, and the lounging chairs of finest leather. Like a silent, shadowy wraith, he avoided these obstructions and gently moved into what appeared to be another hallway.

Here he paused to regain his sense of direction and to recall the maid's instruction. A back stairway, undoubtedly for the help, led above; and to the hall several rooms converged. One was the kitchen—the door on the extreme left, the girl had said; one was the pantry where the cooking supplies and utensils were stored, and the third, the servants' sitting-room, a chamber where, after hours, the employees of the household could gather in fair comfort, for chatting, sewing, and rest. It was this room in which the meeting he so desired to witness was in progress if only he was not too late! For some time had elapsed since that stealthy unknown person had been admitted into the presence of Mrs. Bond.

From behind that closed door came the faint murmur of voices. A thin streak of light issued from the bottom of the door. Directly to his right was the servants' entrance, through which Mrs. Bond had received her visitor. It required considerable mental effort for the detective, a total stranger, to keep himself correct, in the darkness.

"If you go into the pantry," the maid had informed him, "there's a swinging door that leads into the sitting-room. You can see through that, and I think you can hear, too."

The pantry was the middle one of the three adjoining rooms, the kitchen and the chamber in which he was so interested being the other two. He passed through one swinging door, into it, cautious that it should neither swing back nor squeak. The murmur which he could hear in the hall was even more audible, so that, while he could not distinguish words, he knew who was speaking. It was Mrs. Bond. He would not risk the torch any more though that was, in truth, unnecessary. For if the voice was not a sufficient guide, another gleam of light which issued from under the connecting door led him directly to it.

Slowly he opened it the barest division of an inch. It was noiseless, and though the conversation within the room became louder, it continued without interruption. With eye glued against the widening crack, Rankin opened it further. He now had a glimpse inside, but not sufficient to satisfy him. A corner portion of it came into view, and part of the back of Mrs. Bond and there were revealed her tremendous girth and height. She was an exceptionally large woman, correspondingly powerful and militant; and he could indeed believe her to be as terrifying as Blanche had portrayed her. A still further aperture disclosed a portion of her features in profile, the eyes were gleaming in an exalted kind of fanaticism—or perhaps it was merely satisfaction. And she was just finishing her speech.

"And at Woodlawn Park!" she said. "Good!"

The detective could now also view her companion—a full-face view that disclosed crafty eyes and cruel lips—a comparatively low type of human nature. In the face was written avarice and viciousness and he leaned across the little scarf-covered table about which they both sat, with a gleam of desire in his eyes.

"Yes, at Woodlawn. And you promised me that if I—"

"You shall have all that I promised," interrupted Mrs. Bond coldly, "and more, too. Only, remember, never a word of this."

The listener detected a quality of menace in her tone, as though she knew something of her companion's past which would insure the silence she desired.

"Oh, no!" protested the man hastily. "I'll keep perfectly quiet, depend on that."

"Well, see that you do. I believe I promised you—"

"One thousand dollars!" the other interrupted.

"Well, then, here is twelve hundred." Mrs. Bond drew forth from her bosom a small bundle, which she passed over to the man. "You needn't count it here. It's all there; you may be sure of that." She rose, and in a voice which announced the conclusion of the interview went on: "And now, out the same way you came in. And be just as careful as when you came in. The help are not likely to be around, but I believe the chauffeur is in the rear. So keep away from there."

She stilled the thanks at her generosity, and led him to the door of the sitting-room. Watching the little tableau in fascination, Rankin saw the man pass out the door, out of his view, in a servile fashion. A moment later there came a faint sound of a closing door and then silence.

Mrs. Bond stood at the door for a moment, her eyes gleaming cruelly. A bitter smirk was upon her lips and she clenched and unclenched her fist as though she were crushing something mercilessly within her grasp. Obviously, her thoughts were far from pleasant; like an avenging fury she posed, and it recalled to the detective's mind the adage of the "fury of a woman scorned." And then she extinguished the light and disappeared into the hall, stepping majestically, until presently her footsteps died away in the recesses of the library.

Rankin waited until all was perfectly still before he moved. Though he had missed the greater portion of the meeting, and probably the most important part of it, he had witnessed enough to come to a conclusion. The implications of this little interview were evident; in corroboration of Blanche Rushby's tale and the avenging nature of the financier's wife, it clearly pointed to the murder of Mary Young. Or it would have done so had it not left so many other details unexplained. And yet, what other solution was there? What other inference to be drawn? The secrecy of the interview, the payment of the money, Mrs. Bond's satisfaction—to what else could they lead? And then there was Mr. Bond himself. For a moment he had forgotten his suspicions of the financier, but now they returned with even greater force.

It was with Mr. Bond that Mary Young had gone to the park. How, then, had this emissary managed to reach her? There were many things yet to be clarified before an answer would be arrived at; the entire situation needed much explanation. And there was Rankin's original quest of the evening—to prove the financier's whereabouts on the fatal night.

As carefully as before, he crept from the pantry. Mrs. Bond had gone into the main portion of the mansion, and the visitor was gone. But he was cautious until he reached the door which the unknown had just used for his exit. He was safe in using that instead of passing through the entire house again; and a moment later he closed it behind him and stepped into the open grounds of the estate.

It yet lacked fifteen minutes until ten o'clock, sufficient time to catch Ramon before he took Mr. Bond away. Accordingly, he set off briskly for the garage, remembering that it was at the rear of the portico. If any one interrupted him, he was seeking one of the servants or was a friend of the chauffeur's. Presently he came to the lighted stone building he sought.

The chauffeur was outside in his shirt-sleeves, with a wrench in his hand. He recognized the detective at once and, though he expressed no surprise at the visit, his greeting was one in which curiosity and caution were mingled. But he was no longer the truculent protector he had been at Woodlawn. He answered the questions willingly enough and with open frankness, as though he was the possessor of a clear conscience.

As Blanche had predicted, he knew nothing of the actual crime or of the circumstances that caused her so to fear and suspect her mistress. He had never seen the girl before, nor was he aware that the maid had. Rankin's original plan of campaign had been to reveal himself as an officer of the law and demand an explanation of the financier's activities on Sunday night. Due to the peculiar circumstances since arising, there was no longer any need for this; he had excuse enough for any amount of interrogation. And presently he directed the conversation into the channel in which he most desired it.

"What are you doing now?" Both the tone and the question were so casual that the most suspicious would not have suspected any ulterior motive.

"Cleaning out the car and making it ready for the boss. He's going out soon and always likes things spick and span. And it's in need of a terrible cleaning, too."

"The boss?"

"Mr. Charles Bond," explained the chauffeur, "the electrical king."

"Oh, yes, Mr. Bond, of course! I've heard of him. He's quite well known. Doesn't he have that blue-and-white Daimler car that I believe I've noticed about the streets of the city? It's a rather rare specimen about these parts."

"That's the car," Ramon spoke with the pride of possession. "It's an imported car of English make, you know, and one of the prettiest cars on the market, besides."

"So your boss drives, too. Well, I've never seen him."

"Oh, yes, and he's a fair expert at it, too; the last time he had it was Sunday night—when Blanche and I had a night off."

"You don't say! Why, where did he have the car on Sunday, if, as you say, it's in need of such a cleaning?"

"I wish I knew myself, sir," said Ramon. "But since I didn't have it, I couldn't say. It was fair stickied up, if you get what I mean—Sunday papers and what not. Some of it I cleared out yesterday, but I didn't make a perfect job of it."

"Didn't you take the car out with you to the park?"

The idea struck Alfred as ludicrous, for he laughed aloud and slapped his thigh.

"Why, bless you, no sir! When Blanche and I get a day off, we don't get the car with it. No sir, we went out to Woodlawn by trolley."

Rankin joined in the laughter. Then he spoke in a gingerly, hesitant fashion.

"I was just wondering if you'd let me see that car as a special favor. I'm interested, myself, in motors, and I've often wanted to have a close-up look at such a fine specimen as this."

"Why, certainly, sir! There's no special objection, though we'll have to be through before the boss comes for it; he doesn't like strangers fussing around it." Rankin had no special desire to meet the financier, and he acquiesced; whereupon the chauffeur led him into the garage. It was a structure large enough to house three machines, but it contained only the Daimler that interested him so greatly. Perfect order reigned, testifying to the man's capabilities. The hood of the car was up, and it was evident that Alfred had been engaged with the motor when he was interrupted.

"Do you have a car, sir?" he inquired.

"Yes. Nothing, of course, like this. It's a Dodge."

"Oh! Well, that's a nice car too." But his tone sufficiently indicated his disparagement. He said no more till they climbed into the front of the limousine, and then, without waiting for any queries, proudly began to indicate the advantages of the car.

"You see," he indicated the wheel, "it's a right side instead of the left. That's because it is of English make. Over there, you know, they drive on the left side of the road. And then this top—it's a special arrangement for us; it's collapsible without having to go through all the rigamarole of taking it apart. You just turn this pulley here, so,"—he indicated the mechanism in question, and demonstrated its application—"and down it goes. And then you return the lever so, and up it goes, all set with the top on."

"Wonderful!" murmured Rankin. "Not much chance of any one getting wet, is there?"

"Hardly. Now take this brake now—"

While he talked the detective made a sufficient show of interest and attention. At intervals he nodded or interjected some question to show he was following the discussion with absorption. But in the meantime he used his eyes to good purpose about the car; and so concerned was Alfred with his elucidations that he failed to observe this scrutiny. What he had said about its condition was not fully borne out by the facts. The tonneau was swept clean except for some small, useless bits of Sunday newspaper. If the financier had been out alone with Mary Young—as he was now convinced was the fact—the front of the car would contain whatever, if any, traces they had left, though they were likely to have been destroyed by subsequent use of the car.

He examined the front cushions and back supports while apparently listening to the chauffeur. A sticky candy smear, in itself indicative of nothing, was the only reward. A match-stick lay among the foot apparatus, above which Alfred bent to better illustrate a device of which he was speaking. Otherwise there was nothing to justify the trouble he had taken. He sat back for a moment, to think the matter over, when his hand came in contact with the edge of a white piece of sticky paper, probably the cover of the candy that had made the smear on the cushion. Only the fact that it was stuffed into the crack of the cushions between the seat and the back caused him to casually remove it. It barely protruded; and as the other was still bent down, engrossed, he dug into the folds, seized the crumpled paper, and pocketed it without examining it.

Convinced that there was nothing more to be learned from either the car or the chauffeur, he was about to call a halt to the explanations, when the sound of footsteps reached them both. Ramon evidently recognized them, for he looked up in alarm.

"Good God! it's after ten o'clock! The boss is coming and I'm not quite done yet. I'll have to hurry—if you'll only excuse—"

The detective took the hint willingly and, with thanks to his mentor, hastened from the garage and down the path, just in time to avoid being seen by the financier. He had, as he informed himself previously, no wish to make himself conspicuous to Bond until he had proper grounds for moving against him.

It was not until he was beyond the gates of the estate that Rankin paused to examine his find. The brief glimpse he had when he pocketed it already informed him what it was. But now, in the light of the street lamp under which he stopped, he looked again; and he nodded in satisfaction, for in his hand lay a piece of opaque heavy tissue of yellow hue, and across its surface was printed—"Popcorn Confectioners: Woodlawn Park."

15
AT POP ASHBY'S

An hour later Tommy Rankin was at Woodlawn Park, threading his way through a maze of cars in the parking space. His objective was old Ralph Carter, who watched the machines while the fun-seekers made merry within. The knowledge that Charles Bond had actually been at Woodlawn Park on Sunday night, as evidenced by the popcorn wrapper, was as yet insufficient proof to clinch the case; the proof of witnesses, if he could find any, was preferable.

He was well acquainted with Carter. When Lieutenant Thomas had mentioned the possibility of Mary Young's murderer being some criminal who had become known to the girl in the park and then literally "picked her up" Rankin had recalled Carter as being one who would be able to inform him whether or not any such ruffians had been loafing about the park. For the latter knew them all; in his heyday he had been one of the cleverest second-story men in the East. He had executed some amazing coups with such original methods that the police had never been able to bring them home to him. One, completed when Rankin had just entered the force, had caused his superiors plenty of difficulty. Since then, however, age and illness had caused the old criminal to enter into enforced retirement. He decided to earn an honest penny if it didn't prove too difficult, and it was the detective who had obtained this position for him. He would willingly repay him for the service, with information.

But fortune, which had thus far played into Rankin's hands with amazing consistency, deserted him. When he had succeeded in locating one of the auto guards, it proved to be another than Carter. And on inquiry he was informed that Carter had not appeared for duty since the past Sunday.

"I think it's rheumatism," the guard informed him. "He's been having trouble with his joints these last six weeks, and they tell me that on Sunday night there was an especially heavy dew."

"Do you know where I can get in touch with him?"

"No, I don't know. He never told me where he lived. Such a nice old man he seems to be—I do hope he gets better soon. Ordinarily, we're not on together; I take charge of this parking space one night, and he the next night. Except, of course, over the week-ends; then they need both of us, it's so busy."

It appeared, however, that this Sunday had been an exception to the general rule, for the guard had been off duty. His wife, he said, had visiting relatives, and as a result he was not permitted to come on duty. He knew nothing of who had or had not been to the park on the fatal evening.

The result of this brief inquiry left the detective at loose ends for the moment. He knew that he could locate old Carter, did he wish to do so, through Pop Ashby's, in Chinatown. It was a criminal's gathering place, a sort of underworld exchange and directory, where, if one's motives were good, one could get in touch with all sorts of riffraff for nefarious purposes. But it was already after eleven o'clock, and if the trip to Pop's occupied three-fourths of an hour, he could hardly arrive before twelve, and midnight was a decidedly bad time for a lone member of the force in that neighborhood. The best scheme would be to let the matter rest till morning.

But this he was loath to do. Within was a restless urge to complete his case before he retired. His eagerness was like that of the hound on a scent growing fresher as he progressed. At noon this trail had been nonexistent; now its strength superseded all others. He succumbed to it and, against a better judgment, proceeded through the park toward the cars that would take him to town.

As on Sunday, but a scant two evenings ago, the amusements were in full flare, and the joyous, carefree crowd, not as large as Sunday's, however, swirled about him, laughing and chatting. The "Daredevil's" network of tracks reared its flimsy height above him to his right; "Jigsaw" twisted crazily on his left. Again, the roar of the cars on the scenic railways as they took their plunge mingled with shrill and piercing screams. It was just such screams, grimly reflected the detective, which had drowned the genuinely agonized scream for help, or of terror, from the poor girl whose murder he was investigating. The recollection made him feel justified for his stubborn persistence at this late hour.

On the spur of a momentary impulse, he stopped in at the scene of the crime. A long queue of people waited for tickets at the little box fronting "Thrills in the Dark"; and presently Mr. Alexander Simones appeared on the platform above, rubbing his hands in gleeful satisfaction. He greeted Rankin enthusiastically.

"You're singing another tune," remarked the detective. "Things weren't so rosy on Sunday as they appear now."

"Yes," the proprietor agreed, "business is great. Everybody wants to take a ride on the cars in which the girl was killed, and see how it feels. I couldn't have thought of a better advertisement, myself."

"Well, I wouldn't advise you to duplicate it."

The proprietor had nothing to tell him. No one had appeared to ask questions or unduly attract attention. Reporters, he complained, were something of a nuisance, but they also gave him publicity, so he wasn't saying anything. The only bit of information he had was that he had fired Rawley.

The detective was amused.

"Why, what did he do?"

"Such a nerve that man has," replied Simones indignantly. "Besides being a loafer when he does work, he didn't come to-day till three o'clock. And then he tells me that the police wanted him. That dumbbell! He said it was for the—what do you call it?—inquest on the girl."

"Well, he was there. I can vouch for that myself."

"How do you know that? Was you there, yourself?"

After the detective had explained to the suspicious proprietor the source of his information, he advised him to take the guard back.

"Well, maybe," was the doubtful reply; "maybe I was hard on him. But I don't understand it. Why should they call him, but they don't want me? Is that right, heh?"

"If I had known that you were so anxious to testify, I might have arranged it. But you told me on Sunday that you knew nothing about it, so what good would that have done?"

"Neither I do," Simones replied, hastily.

"Well, then, don't worry about it. You'll be called at the trial, you may be sure of that."

After cautioning him to report all suspicious characters to Headquarters, Rankin took his leave. And after an interval he was wandering through dark and tortuous streets towards his destination. Pop Ashby's was a rooming-house, a saloon, and a dance hall combined; and it was something of a blot upon the record of Philadelphia's law and order.

The most vicious denizens of the underworld frequented its rooms, and the lowest dregs of humanity could be
found there. The evil that was there hatched would horrify
the average citizen and cause a widespread demand for its
destruction, and destruction it undoubtedly deserved.

But the police had found Pop Ashby's useful at times.
With all its squalor and wickedness, it was a center of
underworld news and gossip; a headquarters that could
supply a commodity most needed by the law—information. Therefore it was permitted to flourish; and flourish
it did, in a multitude of nefarious crimes.

Viewed from the outside, on the ugly black street along
which the detective approached, it was merely a deserted,
hideous hovel of brick. Not a light appeared anywhere; the
empty window-panes bleakly looked out into the darkness,
announcing to the casual passer-by that the house was ten-
antless. But Rankin knew better. The walls were thick,
so that sounds could not issue forth; and below, in an
almost buried cellar, were the rooms in which gayety and
mirth mingled with crime and squalor. As far as the police
were aware, there were two front entrances and one rear
one, but they suspected many more exits through which
Pop Ashby's clientele could flee if the police became too
inquisitive. There were many secrets, in fact, which the
place held, which would never see the light of day.

Rankin paused at the first door of the building. His
sharp knock was answered by the cautious opening of the
door by a decrepit and vacuous-eyed old man. The latter
looked frightened when he saw him and made a weak
effort to close it upon him. But the detective brushed him
aside brusquely.

"That's all right," he said reassuringly. "I just want to
see Pop Ashby."

He passed down a rickety, black staircase that shrieked
in agony under his tread, feeling in his hip pocket at the

same time to make sure that his revolver was in its proper
place. Not that he expected to use it, but the assurance
was comforting. Then through another door, into a large
room of shaded lights and subdued music, with a bar at
one end. The air was thick with smoke and heavy with
the mingled odor of filth and drink. Men sat at small
tables with women of the lowest type. The illiteracy and
debauchery written in their faces testified mutely to their
lives of vice and depravity. He heard several gasps of
dismay as he crossed to the bar and, in the haze, was positive that at least two of the men slipped from their seats
and stole behind him, toward the entrance.

Pop Ashby greeted him from behind the bar, with neither surprise nor curiosity in his voice. He was a genial,
open-faced, white-haired man of perhaps fifty; and it
was incredible that he could be the proprietor of such an
establishment.

"Tommy Rankin, I'm sure glad to see you. What'll it be?"

The detective waved the offer aside.

"Nothing at all, thanks. I just dropped in to see you."

The old man's eyes contracted ever so slightly as he
replied:

"Not a mere pleasure jaunt, I'm sure, though it's a pleasure to see you. It's a long time since you've honored us. I
suppose some of the boys hardly feel it's an honor."

"I suppose not. The last time I was here it was hardly
as a guest." Rankin paused and looked about.

"Business is rushing, I see. Wasn't that Lew who just
slipped out?"

Pop Ashby nodded.

"Poor old Lew," he laughed. "He was always afraid of
you. But then he has good reason to be. Didn't you send
him up for two years, the last time?"

They continued their social amenities for some time,
but presently Rankin came to the point. "I've come for

information. I'm looking for the old man Carter, and was hoping you could tell me where I could locate him." He saw the cautious look that came into Ashby's face followed by a blankness of expression. "No, don't worry. I don't suspect him of anything and I don't want him for anything. It's just for a little talk, I promise you."

Pop Ashby studied the detective's face, searching it with almost searing eyes. Then he made a decision.

"I'll take your word for it, Tommy. You always were a great one for playing straight, so I think I can trust you. Carter's been laid up in bed for two days and I'm keeping an eye on him. You'll find him upstairs in one of the rooms."

"How do I get up there?"

The proprietor pointed to a door at the opposite corner of the room. "Straight through that door, there, and into the next room, and then down the passageway. Turn up the first steps you come to; it's the second room at the top on the left-hand side." When the detective signified his comprehension, he added, "And mind now, everything straight and aboveboard; no monkey tricks."

A moment later, as Rankin reached the first door in question, the old man hastened across the smoke-filled room and joined him.

"Come to think of it," he said, "this door is locked and there's a couple of boys in there that might not relish the interruption. They're holding a meeting. I'd better go with you."

He knocked upon the door of the adjoining chamber. A gruff voice on the other side asked, "Who's there?" but, upon hearing Ashby's reassuring tones, indicated that he could enter. There was an instant of waiting while the detective heard a key turn in the lock, then the door swung open from the inside.

The room they entered was barely furnished with rough deal tables and some chairs; in one corner, close to the door, stood a bureau, incongruously out of place. Opposite was another door—the one through which they would have to pass to reach the passageway beyond. Four men sat about the table, and one stood at the entrance with them; three of the quintet Rankin recognized.

One, the bull-faced, low-browed chap at the tables, was "Gurt" Kenney, whose cruelty was a byword among the lower classes. He was a killer; of which fact the police were firmly convinced, though they had never succeeded in bringing any murder home to him. Another was "Spark" Porter, a Jack-of-all-trades in crime circles, and one of the most cold-blooded, level-headed scoundrels with whom the detective had come in contact. The third, who had opened the door, was a small, furtive-eyed, shifty-faced man known as "Slim" Starrett, generally; though undoubtedly he had many other appellations. Unquestionably, some deviltry was in the offing, but he said nothing.

At the sight of him the bull-faced man rose in quick fury and crashed his fist upon the table with such force that the empty glasses upon it leaped and rattled.

"My God! What's the idea of bringing a 'busy' into this room? It's not enough that our meeting's interrupted, but then you bring that bird in here to make a quorum."

"Calmly there," replied Pop in a soothing voice. "There's no harm done and no offense meant. Rankin's just passing through. I'll vouch for that."

"Well, let him pass through, but tell him to do it quickly." This came from Spark Porter in soft, unemotional tones. "We don't care much for prying eyes, and you know it, Ashby." He turned to Kenney. "Sit down, old man, and cool off."

Slowly and uncertainly the killer obeyed. The proprietor, flushing at the tones, led the detective to the other door. Rankin held his temper, for the situation was not one in which he could afford to become angered. Followed by the five pairs of eyes, they passed into a dimly lighted, weather-worn passage in which the musty odor of decay and rot mingled with the underground chill smell of the cellar.

They proceeded in silence for a moment before the proprietor spoke:

"You can't very well blame the boys for being put out, can you? Who in the world wants an audience at such a meeting?" He expected no reply and received none; and an instant later he cautioned, "Watch your step here; there's a slight rise."

At the bottom of a pair of steps he stopped and repeated his instructions. Then he turned away.

Rankin ascended the groaning, rickety staircase by himself. He had no difficulty in locating the door in question at once and, without knocking, he passed into the room. It was dilapidated and threadbare and its only pieces of furniture were a tumble-down, dirty bed and a stool. The walls were warped and discolored, and the entire effect of desolateness and bleakness had a depressing influence.

Carter lay white and pinched in the rickety bed. He was about sixty-five, but at this moment appeared at least ten years older. His features had lost all trace of the sharpness they had once possessed; only shrewdness remained in the twinkling eyes, so that he seemed to be nothing worse than a benignant, long-suffering gentleman who had seen better days. That he was in pain, however, was evident from the manner in which he winced suddenly at intervals.

Rankin expressed his regrets at seeing the old man in such a plight, and hoped that he would soon recover.

"That's all right," Carter replied with indomitable cheerfulness, "Pop's taking care of me, and in a few days I'll be out and working again. But how did you find me here?"

The detective related his visit to the park, and the chance he took in locating him through Pop Ashby.

"What do you want with me?" asked the old man. "I don't suppose it's any new trouble I've been getting into, because I'm too old to make trouble." He sighed dolefully, as though his inability were a regrettable matter. "But at one time I could fool the best of you."

"You certainly could," Rankin admitted.

"Ah,"—the statement filled Carter with pride—"I knew it. In those days they used to worry about what stunt I would pull off next; yes, sir." His eyes took on a distant gaze. "I remember Captain Mooney said to me once, 'Carter, I lose more sleep over you than over any other three crooks.' And he offered me a job on the force. But of course I refused it. I wouldn't turn against my own kind. You were just a kid. You wouldn't remember Mooney. But when you joined the force I spotted you then and told Gorber, who is dead now, 'There's an up-and-comer; he'll give us plenty to think about.' And I was right."

He paused in his reminiscences as though awaiting a reply; but when merely a quiet nod from Rankin was forthcoming, as the latter proceeded to light a cigarette, he shifted his subject abruptly.

"What did you come to see me about?"

The detective moved close to the bed.

"Listen," he said, "I'm working on a case—the murder case at Woodlawn last Sunday. You were there then, so you're sure to have heard about it. I can't give you the details, but I'm trying to prove that a certain party was out there that night."

Carter was all alert. "Some one you suspect?"

"Exactly. And one way of knowing whether this party was there is to find out whether his car was there. Since you were on duty that night, I'm banking whether you might have noticed the car or remembered it."

The old man's cackle became a cough, and Rankin had to wait till he quieted down for his reply.

"You expect me to remember that, with all those cars out there? Why, there's hundreds of them."

"Yes, I know, but this car is a rare one—one in hundreds. It's very conspicuous; you must have noticed it. It's a Daimler, that English make of a straight-eight type. It is painted blue and white—a sort of light sky blue. The white stripe is in the middle of the body—"

"Wait a minute." The sick man sat up excitedly in his bed. "Did it have balloon tires, and was its steering wheel on the right side instead of the left?"

"That's the car! So you do remember it? It was there, then?"

"Sure it was. I noticed it first on account of the wheel being over on the wrong side. And then there was its color and immense size. Besides, the top was down."

"Can you remember the people who came in it?"

Carter shook his head dubiously. "Not very well. I only took notice of the car. Still, I do remember that two people came in it—a man and a girl. And I noticed the man because he was fat."

Charles Bond unquestionably, reflected Rankin.

"And the girl?" he asked. "Do you recall her?"

"I can't tell you anything about her, I'm afraid. At my age, all girls look alike. I don't take no interest in 'em. But I suppose she was young and pretty." The old man cackled faintly.

"Did you notice what time they arrived?"

"Well," replied Carter, "I couldn't say exactly, but I suppose it must have been between nine-thirty and ten o'clock. This is the way I figure it out. On a busy night like Sunday it takes a certain time to fill up the parking space. It depends on the crowds, of course, but the last comers fill in the last rows, usually between those two times. Now this here car was in the very last row; we had barely any more room left. So I'd say that was the time."

The time elements fitted well, the detective considered. At nine o'clock, according to both the note and the
patrolman on the Reed Street beat, the financier had met
Mary Young on the Reed Street-Morton Street corner.
True, the officer had not seen the man, but that offered no
difficulties. Charles Bond and his companion had reached
Woodlawn between 9:30 and 10:00, preferably midway between. The same pique or disappointment which he had
once considered had been the motive for the girl's accom-
panying Joseph Rogers to the park when she had failed
to find her lover was, similarly, an applicable motive for
joining Charles Bond on a little excursion. And at ten
o'clock the murder occurred. The facts flowed with beautiful consistency.

The ex-burglar had not noticed when the car left. Neither had he observed any further data regarding the Daimler's occupants. He had been too occupied, he said, with
assisting cars out, when the exodus began, to take further
interest in any specific car, especially since his colleague
had not appeared to help him.

"It's that and the night, sir, that's laid me up like this,"
he explained.

When the detective took his departure it was ten minutes to one.

16
MELODRAMA—AND A SURPRISE

As he reentered the "conference" room the detective instinctively sensed a subtle change of atmosphere. Though it was intangible and indefinable, it was clearly discernible. Where, before, he had experienced a feeling of enmity and dislike, merely, now the sensation was that of threat and menace and this an ominous silence accentuated. Without glancing in the direction of the five conspirators as he walked unhesitantly across the chamber he was aware that they watched him with bated breath and narrowed eyes. He would indeed be fortunate if he escaped without difficulty. The instant he grasped the knob of the door he realized his first intuition had been correct. It was locked and the key was missing.

He faced the five men, feeling, strangely enough, no fear, whatever the outcome of the adventure might be.

"The key is gone." He might have been making a casual statement of the weather. "Let's have it."

Gurt rose and leaned far across the table. His lips were drawn and his eyes were mere pin points of light.

"Not so fast there, Rankin. We want to know what was the idea of coming here. What were you after? We know your kind—"

Rankin's voice developed a steel edge.

"Pop told you what I wanted. I went to see old Carter and that was all. Come across with the key unless you're looking for trouble."

"Strange that you should appear to-night, isn't it?" This came from Spark Porter in tones which matched the detective's for calmness. "It's an unexpected honor."

"If my presence isn't welcome, it must be because you all have guilty consciences."

The taunt brought a flush to Porter's face and caused Kenney to give vent to a roar.

"Is that so, Rankin?" he shouted. "I think you came here to spy and see what you could find out, and you're not going to snitch on us and report what you found. Believe me, I've got more than one score to settle with you!"

He was working himself into a fury. A peculiarly vicious and bestial look appeared in his blazing features, and the fingers of his left hand dug into the table.

"Think what you please; but if you don't open that door you'll land in more trouble than you've ever been in before."

"You'll stay here until we're good and ready to—"

Slim Starrett plucked nervously at the speaker's sleeve and started to rise.

"Don't you think—?" he began.

"Shut up, you rat! This 'busy' isn't going to get away with this—not if I can help it!"

"My God! You damn fool, you'll have the whole force down on us!"

The warning came from Spark Porter too late. He leaped up, clutching outward, in a swift but vain effort to prevent the revolver which suddenly flashed in Gurt Kenney's hand from exploding. With the fall of his chair it crashed with a spurt of flame and a thunderous roar, and the detective felt its hot breath as the bullet splintered into the wall behind him, so close that another inch would have sent it into his brain. Simultaneously his own weapon appeared, so quickly that his shot was a complementary echo. The light bulb swinging about the table shattered into myriad pieces and the tableau was blotted out by the darkness.

The pandemonium that ensued beyond the door a single second afterward failed to interest the detective. Shouts, screams, the rushing of feet, the crashing of tables occurred unnoticed, while his mind raced for a means of escape. Safety depended upon him alone; assistance would eventually arrive, but not from those people in the next room. They weren't apt to risk their skins, interfering in gunplay that didn't concern them. They knew better than that. By the time the police arrived it would be too late unless he acted at once.

The only avenue of flight was the one through which he had just passed—the door leading into the passageway and back to Carter's room. If he could slip out, he could hold the stairs for an indefinite period. But it was obviously an impossibility. The instant he essayed to open the door, even granting that he could reach it in safety, the hallway light would reveal him and he would go down for certain with a bullet in his back. They would expect him to do that very thing. The thought gave him an unpleasant thrill.

But to remain where he was and be a target for bullets was also an impossibility. Kenney fired again, and only the fact that he had leaped away from the door the instant he had put out the light saved him. In another moment he would have more than the killer to reckon with. Once having begun the affair, they would have to finish it. Their only possibility of safety would be to put him out of the way immediately. When the police arrived there would be no sign of him; they could bluff the law that it had merely been a gang fight, and be arrested at the most for disorderly conduct. He would have disappeared and no one would be the wiser.

A third spurt of flame came out of the darkness, and for the instant he thought he experienced a sudden stab of agony in his left shoulder. But he realized it couldn't be an actual wound, merely perhaps the searing of his shoulder as the bullet grazed his skin; after the first sensation he was barely aware of it. The worst of it was that he hardly dared to return the shot, for he would reveal his own open position. If he fired into the crowd he'd get perhaps one or two, but he'd disclose himself; and there were five against him, or, not counting the peaceful weakling Slim, four with whom to cope!

His only hope was the bureau; behind its strong supports he would be secure for the moment. He darted behind it, crouching and bending low; and then, cautiously protruding his head and the muzzle of the gun, fired. A howl of agony which followed gave him a grin of satisfaction; that made one less enemy. But the reply was instantaneous. The bullet buried itself into the wood with a sickening thud. A splinter struck him. He winced and stealthily edged his way beyond the corner of the bureau to fire again. Another flame followed, but this time there was nothing but a dull thud at the opposite end of the room.

The pistol duel came suddenly to an abrupt conclusion as a strange silence fell upon the enemy. What new deviltry were they planning? Outside, the screams continued at intervals, with the mingling of rushing feet. There was a knocking at the door, which became a determined pounding, authoritative and stern. Voices demanded that it be opened but who it was Rankin did not know. It was impossible that aid had already arrived. Barely thirty seconds had elapsed since the first shot, although it seemed to be an eternity; and at least four or five minutes must pass before any one from the outer world could conceivably appear on the scene. Neither could it be Pop Ashby nor the riffraff of the outer room, who knew better than to intervene. And yet the majestic crashing continued without pause.

The next moment he was occupied in a far different way. The four men rushed upon him, as he believed they would—their one hope being to efface him. Hands grasping at him sought to bear him down. Resolutely, he struck out. Fighting was his own special ground and despite the odds he met them grimly. It was even possible that their number handicapped them, while he was free to battle as long as he could and finally go under only after their overwhelming strength had overpowered him. Like ravenous wolves they tore at him, seeking to undermine and beat him down.

Rankin's fist collided sickeningly with a face—and there was a gasping void. That left but three, if he counted correctly; and one of them had him by the legs, exerting a steady, vicious pressure that caused him to stagger. A knife thrust ripped through his clothes. That was different; fists he could combat, but not weapons. He met the arm in midair, and it wilted strangely as the blade went flying against the wall. With its clang was mingled a howl of pain. There was no opportunity to feel satisfaction at each success; his thoughts were furiously, ominously clinging to the details of the battle. Claws in his face barely missed his eyes; a hand reached for his throat, creeping upward with a terrible grip.

Under the constant pounding the door of the outer room shivered, and then stood solid and resisting. But as the crashing increased in fury a panel broke, splitting across the middle and giving way. An axe was buried into the wood and another panel split, and the bodies of men bore irresistibly against the portal, under the hoarse command of a voice. Slowly it collapsed, and light filtered into the chamber in which the struggle was in progress.

The detective's single thought was to prevent the hands from reaching his unprotected throat. His own arms were fully occupied otherwise. It was with his mind alone that he concentrated upon that one problem. But mind is a poor weapon of defense, and his writhing body twisted too late to escape those tensile, clutching fingers. With a vast effort he hurled off the assailant attacking his legs, seized his last enemy. The man was depriving him of breath; and the growing light revealed Gurt Kenney intent upon completing what he had begun. His face was red, and his eyes were bloodshot with the fierce joy in them.

He attempted to force the killer backward to release the grasp. It was like a vise that sank deeper and deeper the greater was his effort to open it. Kenney had got his hold first, unshakably; Rankin's resistance was pitiful in comparison. Already there was a great roaring in his ears and an unbearable pain in his chest. It increased until it filled his entire frame so that it was impossible to locate the exact spot where the hands wrought such exquisite agony. Spots danced before his eyes, the choking sensation merged into a thundering clamor, and he rushed precipitously toward a black void.

Suddenly the pressure was released. In an eternity of waiting, light filtered slowly back to him, and vague impressions. Men rushed about him, helter-skelter, in increasing disorder, and there were sounds which, in a normal state, he would have identified as shots. Across from him was an opened door—or perhaps it was a panel—but he was positive he had never seen it before. And then he fell, and with the falling came merciful oblivion.

When Tommy Rankin opened his eyes he lay on a couch, procured magically from somewhere, with two men bending over him. His head was swimming for a moment, but the specks which danced before him gradually disappeared. He felt incredibly weak and tired, but otherwise seemed perfectly sound. One of the men, obviously a doctor, ministered to him with a cold cloth about his neck as he spoke to the other.

"He'll be all right in a few minutes—just as soon as he gets his breath—and I can ease the pain here."

The latter nodded, and murmured: "I hope so," and Rankin smiled faintly into the anxious face of Sidney Alvin—Captain Sidney Alvin of the Narcotic Squad— whom he had had as a close friend for many years.

"What happened, Sid?" he asked, searching his memory to recall events. But thinking pained him.

"Plenty to you," the captain replied. "Just lie still a moment and don't talk. Take it easy."

Rankin shook his head stubbornly. "But I feel all right. Just let me get on my feet for a moment."

"Not yet . . . What, doctor?"

The physician spoke, and the captain turned to the detective. "He says it's all right; your throat may be a bit sore, but otherwise, you're O.K."

Once assisted to his feet, Rankin took in the scene thoroughly. The room was crowded with policemen and plain-clothes men, watching him anxiously. In their center, handcuffed and closely guarded, were the five men from whom he had so narrow an escape. None had got away. One of the two men whom he did not know had been wounded, the victim of his successful shot; but the injury was in the calf of the leg and did not appear to be serious. Beyond them was an open panel, swinging aimlessly. Gurt eyed him with malevolence and hatred; Spark's appraisal was unconcerned and immobile.

He turned to the captain. "I have still to learn how you got here at such an opportune moment, but it looks like a raid to me."

"That's exactly what it was, and you came very near spoiling the entire party. We weren't set to attack till one o'clock, but at five minutes before the hour two shots went off, and down we came, rushing, fearful that our plans had fallen through or were discovered."

"So I interfered by setting the fireworks off too early?"

"Exactly, though it doesn't seem to have harmed any one but yourself." The captain laughed grimly. "And I still can't imagine where you fit in or how you got here. Around midnight, some of our men slipped in, disguised, of course, to spend an hour around the bar and spy out the lay of the land. At twelve-thirty a whole gang of us had surrounded the place, waiting for the one o'clock signal. It had been arranged that one of the men from the inside would come out when the time was ripe. A couple of our chaps recognized you when you came in, though of course you wouldn't know them. It puzzled them, because they didn't know whether you were part of the plan or not. They couldn't tell what to make of your appearance. Neither do I, for that matter. So what's the answer?"

Briefly Rankin told his story, which the other heard in silence. When he had finished, he asked the captain:

"What's the sudden interest in Pop's place? I thought it was safe for a while. I didn't hear a word of this plan at Headquarters."

Alvin shook his head. "You're quite right. We kept it especially mum because we didn't dare to have a thing leak out. We were after this gang, and had received a tip, from a quarter I daren't divulge, that there had been a meeting called for to-night. We've been after them, for bootlegging, for some time. Their field of activity is between here and the shore, and let me tell you, they've effected some of the slickest stunts to get the stuff through."

"So Gurt has gone in for genteel bootlegging, has he? It's a new game for him. Anyhow, you've managed to get them all."

"No, you're wrong; that's just the trouble. We didn't get one of the chaps behind the gang. We had put so much time and effort on this that we hoped it would be a catch of everybody concerned." Captain Alvin surveyed the prisoners and shook his head disconsolately. "You don't mean to tell me that you think Gurt and Slim over there are capable of anything more than obeying orders and doing the dirty work? We've got the brawn of the organization, at least the land end of it, but not the brain. Of course, there's others concerned with shipping the liquor."

"But what about Spark?"

"Of course he's a good catch, one of the leaders; but there was another one we were hoping to nab." The speaker pointed to the swinging panel in the wall, walked over to briefly to examine it, and returned. "I suppose he got away this way. It's one of the entrances we've suspected and looked for but never succeeded in finding. They were just making their escape through that when we broke through the door. You managed to delay them long enough for us to make our capture."

"You're mistaken, Sid," Rankin replied, emphatically. "There were only five of them, and you've got them all."

The officer of the Narcotic Squad appeared bewildered. "I don't see, then, what could have become of him," he said. "We had it on good authority that he would be here. Unless we catch him outright, I'm afraid he'll give us the slip. It'll be hard to prove anything unless one of the prisoners opens up. Here, you!" He turned abruptly to his men. "Take those fellows out and put them safely away. But keep an eye on them; they've given us enough trouble already."

He waited till the five captives were filed out, accompanied and surrounded by the group of plain-clothes men and officers. Reverting to his original thought, he continued.

"We know well enough who the chap is. But I don't see how it's going to do us any good if we can't prove it. Suspicion never convicts and we'll never get Jimmy Norris without more proof than we now have!"

17
"SPARK" PORTER INTERVENES

The following morning Rankin made his report at Head-quarters and held an interview with the Superintendent of Police. The subject of the interview was Charles Bond. Rankin did not feel justified in taking further steps until he had received official approval.

His discovery that Norris was implicated in the illicit traffic of liquor had not served to assist him. Whether the fact meant anything to his problem he did not know. It certainly increased the criminal potentialities of his suspect. Alvin, on learning that the one he considered the gang leader was already a prisoner, had been filled with satisfaction; but it was fast becoming tempered with a growing fear that they lacked evidence to convict him. The victims of the preceding night's raid were safely incarcerated, but refused to speak. No manner of threat could compel them to "squeal" on their leader. Actuated by the hope, perhaps, that he might be able to assist them from the outside, they professed ignorance of Norris being in any way implicated with them.

The Superintendent heard Rankin's tale with interest.

"It's all very confusing," he agreed at its conclusion, "and I concur with you that some steps must be taken. It is difficult to say precisely what shall be done, however. I think I shall reserve judgment until I am able to see Mr. Bond, myself." He paused. "But what about your prisoner?"

"He is being quizzed this morning by Hartman and Allen. They'll try to get the truth from him. As for myself, I'm not sure, after all, at least not since yesterday's developments."

"I see." The Superintendent nodded. "And what is your next move to be?"

"The girl's funeral is being held this morning and I think it would be a wise thing to attend."

"Perhaps it would; and as to the other matter, I think it would be best to wait. You are sure, at any rate, that Bond has no idea of your suspicions, so it is not likely he will run away. If necessary, I shall put some one on his trail."

Rankin agreed, and left. He drove to the morgue, from which drab building the funeral was to take place. He had no particular motive in attending the obsequies; nevertheless, it would be interesting to view the spectators and discuss the matter with those in attendance. Rankin had little faith in the adage that a criminal always returns to the scene of his crime; like most generalities, it was untrue. Nevertheless, it was good policy to neglect no possibility.

The services were a tragic affair. No one appeared on the scene to claim any relationship or acquaintance with the dead girl. Beyond a few casual and curious spectators, the only attendants at this tragic close of Mary Young's life were her friends from Mrs. Schmidt's boarding-house.

He spoke with them all. The landlady and Mrs. Edgecomb, locked arm in arm in mutual sympathy during the burial service, bemoaned to him the shortness and uncertainty of life. Rankin took the opportunity to requestion them on various points, but their talk contributed nothing to his present store of information.

From Miss Ruth Graham, however, he gained something. The girl, her red hair flaming in the sun, greeted him with a most dazzling smile. Instinctively, recalling her behavior of two days before, her friendliness made him wary. He had not succeeded in analyzing her character thoroughly, though he believed he had approached it with fair accuracy. Whether she merely wished some sport at his expense, or whether she wished to win him as another of her undoubtedly many victims, he had not yet decided.

"Mr. Rankin," she murmured, sweetly, offering him a shapely and manicured hand, "I almost thought you had forgotten me."

He made an attempt to be gallant and felt awkward instead.

"That would be impossible, Miss Graham."

"Flatterer," she laughed, "I don't know about that. You remember you said I could expect a call from you. I have been waiting for that call for some time. Instead, you send around this Mr. Gordon, a nice enough man, you understand, but—" Her deprecating gesture was expressive.

"Well, of course, I've been busy on other lines of the case—"

"That's right," she smiled coyly. "I hope you're making headway. I've been busy myself. You know I work in a department store and—would you believe it?—I could hardly get away for the funeral. A working-girl has no freedom nowadays, has she?"

"No, I dare say she hasn't."

"Take Mary, for instance, what she had to put up with that boss of hers. She was a very fine-toned girl, if you get what I mean, and he seemed to think he could take liberties with her, just as if she were an ordinary person. It's really disgusting the way you can't trust some men!"

Rankin pricked up his ears. Here was something in definite proof of his suspicions of Charles Bond. The girl might be a valuable witness.

"How do you know that?" he asked.

"Oh, Mary told me about that, too."

"Exactly what did she tell you?"

"Not really very much. Just that she wasn't sure she liked her place at all because her employer wasn't a very nice sort of man. He had her come to his house one day for private work, and she couldn't refuse to go; but she didn't want to. Nothing happened, however; he didn't annoy her yet, but there were hints in his voice that she didn't like. She was sure he was approaching the danger point."

"Was that why she was leaving her position?"

Miss Graham hesitated before replying. "Now that," she responded slowly, "I couldn't say. But it might very well have been that, don't you think, especially when such attentions weren't welcome?"

Rankin replied cautiously: "I'll have to investigate into it further. I must admit I have some suspicions of Mr. Bond. But why didn't you tell me this before?"

"Why, it never entered my mind that it might have anything to do with the case. Do you think it does, really?"

Miss Graham received a suitable reply. When the services were over, Rankin bade her good-bye. It was long after noon when he reached Headquarters again. Officer Simpson greeted him with a telegram and some news.

"One of the prisoners that was brought in last night," he informed him, "insists on seeing you. Claims he can tell you something about the case that's very important. What do you want done about it?"

"Something about the case?" Rankin asked curiously. "The one I'm working on? Who is it?"

"Porter, sir. He says you'd better see him, too, or you'll be very sorry you didn't"

Wonderingly, Rankin gave orders to bring the prisoner to him. What could Porter know of the murder of Mary Young? Was there a connection between Norris's bootlegging activities and the crime? If so, what? The detective wasn't interested in the former, unless it had to do with his case; but it sounded as though Spark was very serious. He turned to the telegram.

It was, as he expected, the reply from Gary. It read:

> Nothing known here of a girl named Mary Young, answering your description. No such girl missing as far as we can learn.
>
> Frank Lowry,
Gary Chief of Police

Quite obviously he had drawn a blank. Exactly what he had expected, Rankin himself could not have told; but he hoped to encounter some clue whereby the lesser mystery of Mary Young's past and the identity she so sedulously concealed would be uncovered. It might incidentally answer his major problem.

Simpson ushered Spark Porter into the office. Thomas being out, they would have the room to themselves. The prisoner entered with debonair poise, examining the room keenly, his eyes sweeping every corner. Then he seated himself.

"All alone, are we, Rankin?" he queried. "No dictaphones, no stenographers taking notes, no witnesses listening in? That's right. This is to be a private talk. You'd better tell this cop that we don't want any interruptions."

Rankin gave the requisite instructions to insure privacy. When the officer had withdrawn, he waited for Porter to speak. The prisoner hesitated for a moment as though uncertain how to begin; then, abruptly he plunged in.

"I said I could tell you something about that crime at Woodlawn. It has to do with your arresting Jimmy Norris for doing it!"

Rankin did not show the surprise he experienced. "How do you know anything about that?"

"It was in the late papers yesterday evening; yes, we all saw it; the entire gang, in fact, knows about it. We were aware, of course, that he wouldn't be with us last night, after seeing that. You see, Norris is . . . sort of . . . a friend of ours."

"A friend—?"

Spark Porter's eyes glinted dangerously for a moment.

"I said a friend, Rankin. Oh, I know what Alvin suspects, for all the good it will do him; he'll never be able to prove it, because none of the gang will ever squeal. And that's not your business, anyway. You're interested in clearing up this crime, and I'm interested in getting Norris out of here. Because friends are useful, and he is much more useful to us out of prison than in. So if we cooperate, we may each get our way."

"Are you trying to bargain with me, Porter?"

"You may call it that," the prisoner replied, "but I think it is a compromise. You've always kept your word, once you've promised a thing. I know you'll do it this time."

"And suppose I refuse to compromise, as you call it."

For an instant Porter's face was convulsed with a spasm of fury. But when he replied, his tone was calm and icy.

"Then I promise you it will be your loss. This is no bluff, but an absolute truth. If you don't hear it, you'll make the biggest error of your life. You'll be the laughing-stock of the Central Bureau within two weeks, I promise you."

Rankin realized that Porter must know something of vital import. It would be useless to attempt any deception, since both were aware that an investigation would follow, to verify whatever story the prisoner had to tell. The latter spoke with such confidence of being able to liberate Norris.

"I'll make no specific agreement, Porter," the detective replied. "But if you prove your claims to my satisfaction, I'll do the right thing."

"You'll have no choice, I'm afraid. You can't very well hold an innocent man, and Alvin had nothing on him. I'm not making any admission to incriminate him, either, remember that. I'll deny anything of that sort that you claim."

"An innocent man? What do you mean?"

"I mean that Norris could never have committed the crime of which you accuse him, because he wasn't anywhere near Woodlawn Park at the time!"

If Porter expected the detective to register astonishment, he was disappointed. For Rankin, himself with grave doubts of his prisoner's guilt, it was rather a welcome relief to have one phase of the astonishing tangle on the verge of being cleared. However, it would never do to capitulate too quickly.

"What do you mean by that?" he asked.

"Just what I say. Jimmy Norris was with me on Sunday night, more than a hundred miles from Woodlawn. So, you see, it wouldn't be very possible that he had a hand in the murder."

"Have you real proof of this, Porter?"

"As near as one could come to proof. I can swear to it, and if I do, you won't stand a chance in the world of convicting him."

"All right, then, let's have it."

"Norris and I have what we may call, for want of a better name, dealings together, business dealings, which necessitate our making trips to the shore at intervals. Strictly business, understand; about once every three weeks or so."

"And the object?" Rankin interrupted.

"As I've already told you, I'm making no admission. My object and chief aim is to get Norris out; to make it, frankly, quite impossible for you to hold him. As far as you're concerned, they were either pleasure jaunts or trips to take care of some pending real estate deals. You had better let me tell the story in my own way. . . . It became necessary to make a trip on Sunday night, this time to Asbury Park. I have a red roadster, and we had arranged to meet just below his apartments a little after seven o'clock. He was a bit late, and, as we were in a hurry, I became quite impatient. We hoped to make the journey in three and a half or four hours at the most."

"You were to meet him outside the Enderley Apartments? At what time did you start?"

"He came out finally at quarter after seven—"

This coincided with the testimony of the telephone girl at the Apartments. She had said that he arrived a little after seven and left almost at once.

"We started on the way," Porter proceeded. "My car makes wonderful time on the road and there were only two of us. With luck, we would have made it in minimum time. But after a while we developed engine trouble and had to limp along. Outside of Tom's River, which we came to after dark, there's an atrocious stretch of road; and then we had to stop at a garage for repairs. The sparks needed cleaning."

"Exactly where was this?"

"Simons, just about three miles after you pass through the town. A small wooden shack on your left. The fellow that did the job was an elderly man with glasses. I suppose you can locate him without difficulty."

"Did he see Norris?"

Porter hesitated. "Well, he might have, but, as I say, it was getting dark, and since I was driving, there was no need of his getting out of the car. I did that. The difficulty was in the engine, only."

"And this was about nine or so?"

"Yes, just about nine. The repairs delayed us, however, about three quarters of an hour, and the machine had been dragging along for some time. Though I didn't look at my

watch, I don't suppose it was till ten-forty-five that we
got started again. I was afraid that we wouldn't reach our
destination on time. After the repair, we did fairly well;
nevertheless, it was verging on twelve-thirty when we
reached Asbury Park."

"So that from seven-fifteen till twelve-thirty Norris
was with you all the time?"

"Yes, and I'm willing to go into the witness box to
swear to it. I don't suppose I'd have said anything about it
if it hadn't been for last night's raid; but now that we're in
bad, we can use a man on the outside." He smiled without
emotion. "After all, self-preservation is the first law of
life. If Norris owes his freedom to us, he'll repay us for it.
I expect you to tell him that."

In the face of that implacable smile, Rankin saw his
case against James Norris melt away. Not all of it; there
remained still a substantial number of things which the
prisoner would have to explain. Norris's bootlegging pro-
clivities were not within the scope of his investigation;
he had enough difficulties without that. Certainly they
would explain the words Mary Young's quondam fiancé
had used in his apartment.

Of course, he would send some one to investigate Porter's tale. Tom's River, and other places where the inhabitants would have been likely to see a red roadster, would
be canvassed. Meanwhile, he raised a legitimate objection.

"But Asbury is only a two hours' ride by train," he said.
"So if there happened to be a train leaving for the Jersey
coast at ten-thirty, Norris could still reach your destination, where others might have seen him, at twelve-thirty."

Porter was undisturbed. "That's very true, but is it
likely? Do you think such a series of coincidences could
occur?"

"Certainly it is possible. The crime occurred at ten."

"But I could do far better than this if I wanted to invent something to free Norris—an air-tight alibi. But this isn't air-tight; it's much more likely to be true. Why should I tell you this if it has no basis in fact? I expect you to investigate the whole story."

"Who can tell what your motive is? Since you were the only person with him from two hours before the murder to two hours afterward—"

"What difference does it make," argued Porter, interrupting, "if I'm the only one or if there were a dozen? It's all the same; he can't possibly be guilty."

Further discussion followed. Rankin had Porter cover every detail of the trip to Asbury Park, bit by bit. He made notes of the time involved, the route taken, the mileage, these to be handed to the assistant who would take up the trail. At the end he was fairly convinced of the truth of the narrative. He summoned Simpson.

"Return Porter to his cell," he instructed, "and bring Norris up with you. Don't let them see each other."

He didn't want Norris to know of the raid and the capture of the gang the preceding night. It might make a difference in what his prisoner would be willing to admit, when confronted with Porter's tale.

"Yes, sir," Simpson replied. "Gordon's been in, these last twenty minutes, and waiting to see you. I told him you couldn't be disturbed now, and that he'd have to wait."

"Gordon? Send him in, and hold Norris off till we're finished. Then bring him along."

The officer obeyed. At the threshold of the room, as he was being led out, Porter paused and turned with a meaning smile.

"Remember our bargain, Rankin," he cautioned. "You can't hold an innocent man."

The door shut behind them both, and a moment later Gordon entered and shut it again.

18
THE MISSING LODGER

Gordon seated himself, helped himself to a cigarette from a pack that he produced, offered one to his colleague, and then sat back for a moment, puffing in silence. Rankin waited patiently, knowing from previous experience the leisurely ways of the other. Presently Gordon began.

"You certainly sent me on a chase, Tommy. For the last two days I've been running around, quizzing innumerable people, trying to pick up Rogers's trail."

"With what success, Lester? Nothing's come in from other cities, so I've been hoping for something from you. So far, I haven't been able to tackle Rogers myself."

"I had one or two streaks of luck," Gordon replied, "but the rest of it has been pretty disheartening drudge work. For the longest time I couldn't pick up any sort of a trail. That cop on the corner nearest the boardinghouse didn't know a thing about him and hadn't seen him."

"Yes, I know that. I tried him myself."

"First I went to the bank. They were pretty cold about it, for some reason, and didn't have anything to tell me. Do you remember that robbery that occurred there four years ago? When some unknown gang tackled the paymaster of Baldwin's as he was leaving the bank with a hundred-thousand payroll. He was just getting into the armored car when they opened fire from a car across the street. And they got away with it. We didn't show up very well in that affair afterward, and I don't think they ever forgave us our failure to locate the thieves."

"What did they have to say?" Rankin asked.

"They knew nothing about him, because he gave them notice he was leaving, and did so, last Saturday. I saw there was nothing to be got there, so I tried the boarding-house next. Nice lady, Mrs. Schmidt; she gave me a meal, and both she and Mrs. Edgecomb were quite willing to answer my questions. Mrs. Schmidt hadn't got over how he had ruined her furniture."

Rankin smiled. "I know how she feels about it."

"Well, they couldn't tell me anything. There hadn't been any mail since Rogers had left; as a matter of fact, he never got much mail anyway. I got the whole story out of Mrs. Edgecomb—of how she saw him in the hallway, with that big black suitcase of his, just about to go, and how he told her about that sick mother. Mrs. Edgecomb enjoyed being able to tell it all over again, believe me. But it didn't do me any good, because she hadn't seen whether he had gone by taxi or by trolley. She didn't look out the window after him. I made particularly sure about that suitcase. It was big enough to put in things for a two weeks' stay, so it must have been very heavy. He wouldn't have wanted to carry that very far."

"Describe it for me."

"It was a patent-leather Belber bag, more than a yard in length, black, of course, and held together by thick, heavy straps. Rather conspicuous, so it gave me hopes of some one having noticed him. But later, when I tried the trolleys, the nearest of which was three long blocks away from the boarding-house, I had no luck. That was last night. I wasted more carfare riding up and down the lines and quizzing conductors and late travelers, than I've ever done before. The Department will have quite a bill to pay me. But it didn't do any good. No one had seen him. That didn't prove he hadn't taken a car. It made it less likely though.

"Incidentally, Tommy, I met Miss Graham. Let me tell you she's a corking good-looker. And you seem to have made some impression upon her, too, because she asked about you and hoped I would remember her to you. I think she'd like to have a date. And we never took you for a ladies' man!"

Rankin was annoyed. Miss Graham kept turning up on all sides and she still puzzled him. He preferred not to think about her.

"All right, Gordon," he said brusquely. "Get along with your story."

"Sure, old man, only perhaps I'm a bit put out because she wouldn't notice me. If I were you I'd make use of the opportunity. . . . Well, since I couldn't find him on the street-cars, I decided to try the taxis. I knew that if he called up for a taxi he'd get a central station and they'd instruct the local taxi stand by phone to take the fare. So I went around to all the Germantown stands, inquiring whether any of them got a call on Sunday night, to call for a fare at eleven-thirty. I thought that was going to draw a blank, too, but luck turned and on the fourth attempt I hit pay dirt."

"Good work," Rankin commanded, interrupting in his enthusiasm. "Which company was it?"

"The Quaker Cab. It seems Rogers called up the main office from somewhere—I don't think it was Mrs. Schmidt's, or she would have heard him—at eleven o'clock Sunday night, asking them to send a cab to 2538 Morton Street at eleven-thirty. That was, I suppose, to give him enough time to pack. At any rate, the central office forwarded the call to Germantown and cab 238, the driver by the name of Gerald Smithers, took the call. His companion at the stand remembered the call because it was a slow Sunday, and he almost had an argument with Smithers as to which of them should go.

"Smithers was off duty then, being only on the night shift, which came on at six o'clock; so I had to hurry down to the Quaker office and get his address. Of course it had to be way out in Frankford—967 Parton Street, I think it was; and I hustled out there. Had to drag the poor chap out of bed, but it was worth it. As soon as I described the passenger, using both your description and Mrs. Schmidt's, and especially mentioning the black bag, he remembered him. The call, he said, sounded like a hurry call, so he thought it rather peculiar when he was almost in the neighborhood. Rather intelligent chap, Smithers, and exceptionally observant. However, he did as he was ordered."

"Where did he take him?" asked Rankin. Here was the crux of the matter.

"Rogers ordered him to go straight to Broad Street station, and that's where they went. You were quite right, Rankin, in saying that he was in a deuce of a hurry to get out of town."

"Did he take Rogers directly there?"

"Yes, straight as a die—through the Parkway and downtown. It was just a half-hour's ride, making good time, and they reached the station just as the clock in City Hall tower pointed to midnight."

"Are you sure he didn't have to go out to West Philadelphia first?"

Gordon extinguished his cigarette and stared quizzically at Rankin. "No, of course, he didn't," he replied, "or Smithers would have told me. Was there any reason that he should have?"

Rankin shook his head. Gordon knew nothing of his later discovery of the knife in Norris's rooms, which might have been planted there—must, in fact, have been planted there, if Norris was innocent. If placed there by the fugitive, however, when had the deed been done? Certainly not before eleven o'clock and, now it would appear, not after eleven-thirty, unless it were possible that Joseph Rogers had checked his bag after his arrival at Broad Street station, gone by trolley to the Enderley Apartments, and returned in time to make his train. That, of course, was what had occurred. Rankin upbraided himself for not having thought of it sooner. No doubt, there was sufficient time between midnight and the train's departure to permit the accomplishment of this errand. After all, by the swift "L" it would not take more than half an hour.

"Go on with your story," he instructed.

"I'm afraid there isn't much more to tell," Gordon resumed, "because the trail ends right there. Smithers left him off at the station, was paid a very small tip, about which he complained to me, and then Rogers dropped out of sight."

"Did a porter take his bag?"

"Smithers says not. You may be sure I asked both him and every porter in the station. I figured that Rogers must have taken an early train, one that left within the next hour, because there is no point in his rushing away like he did and then loafing about the terminal for hours for a train. He'd be anxious to get out fast. So I got a list of the trains going out between twelve and one in the morning. There were six trains, two of them only being travelers. They were a train for Boston at twelve-fifteen and one for Montreal at twelve-thirty. The rest were all locals, and I didn't think he'd be likely to go no further than merely some adjoining town. So I concentrated on the two trains.

"But I didn't turn up anything this time. I inquired of the ticket agents whether they remembered selling a ticket to a chap answering Rogers's description. I made the rounds of porters, conductors, guards, to discover if they could recall him. They didn't. No one seemed to have noticed him, as far as I could learn. Yet I'm positive that he bought his ticket after he got to the station."

"I agree with you there." Rankin nodded. "There was no premeditation in regard to the flight. It was sudden and unexpected."

"Yet none of the agents remembered selling him a ticket," Gordon complained. "The earth might have swallowed him up. Anyhow, I'm at the end of the track. I thought I'd better come back and report it to you."

"I think you did as well as could be expected under the circumstances. Let me see your train list."

Gordon complied, and Rankin studied the slip. Where the former had failed in his search was in limiting his trains to the hours between midnight and one o'clock. He had made a correct assumption in that the fugitive would be most anxious to escape the city, but he was ignorant of Rankin's belief that Rogers had first visited the Enderley Apartments. He could not have returned until half past twelve. It was impossible, then, that he could have taken either the Boston or the Montreal train. Here was the error in Gordon's calculations, for which, however, he could not be held responsible. It was not surprising that he had been unable to elicit information of the sale of a ticket to their mutual quarry. Had he made inquiry with regard to the hour between twelve-thirty and one-thirty, or perhaps even stretching it to two o'clock, the results might have been different.

Rankin imparted none of this to his colleague. He intended to resume the trail himself as soon as the Norris affair was off his hands. Accordingly, he commended Gordon for his work, and retained the train list. As soon as he was alone he sent Simpson for his prisoner.

19
A PRISON INTERLUDE

With nothing to do but ponder upon the irony of his predicament, time passed slowly enough for James Norris. His past he could consider; his future was doubtful, though the drab gray cell and the prison bars reminded him of what it would probably be. The bars were before him and all around him; even the little window, which barely admitted light and air, was barred. The sun, shining through it, cast a reflection upon his suit, so that the shadows appeared as stripes. Though they might be a little premature, he reflected grimly that he might become accustomed to them.

He had just come from a hectic battle of wits that consumed more than three hours, and he was exhausted from the long strain. In an upper office, detectives had interrogated and cross-questioned him to draw from him the truth of the murder of Mary Young. They had hurled queries at him with the rapidity of a bombardment; they had bullied and threatened. But he had maintained his own with success. Without variation, he clung to his original tale—that he had spent Sunday evening in his room, that he knew nothing of the silver lighter or the knife, that he had not seen Mary Young that night. All lies, yet they could not beat down his stubborn insistence and constant denials. He remained the only collected and calm man among them. Their excitement, as they tried vainly to wrest an explanation from him, would have been humorous were it not actually tragic.

All his life he had been heading toward prison; in retrospect, that was apparent. Everything that had ever occurred to him pointed in that direction. His father had been a capable but unsuccessful doctor of good blood and genteel family. Failing of prosperity, he was compelled to move to the poorer section of the city, where his clientele were the needy. No lucrative business could there be established, and the physician struggled along, doing his best for the growing boy—which best was not, under the circumstances, very satisfactory. His mother he did not recall; she had succumbed to the privations too early for that.

In the midst of poverty and squalor he had grown to manhood. There was no choice of playmates—only the neighborhood boys, who in gangs infested the district. Gurt Kenney had been a school chum of his, though Gurt had never gone beyond sixth grade; and he had played with Slim in the streets, and many another child who was now a gangster. In their company he had fled policemen and carried on deviltries. His father, too engrossed in his fight for existence, failed to keep a strict eye upon him.

It was only his superior blood and breeding, and his better education that prevented him from falling to the level of those about him. His high school education gave him a mental advantage that marked him as a leader. And he always possessed a consciousness of right and wrong which kept him above the average of his companions, and prevented him from acquiring those traits of viciousness that make the real criminal. But what he did acquire was a peculiar contempt for the forces of law and a desire to resist them if the opportunity offered. He felt the urge to demonstrate their puniness, how easily they could be outguessed and defeated. Thia unique development was not particularly unusual, in the face of the sentiments he had often heard in his younger days. They had been ingrained in him, even though he was aware how wrong it was. An early entrance into the war added to these qualities a lust for adventure.

The conflict of battle supplied, only temporarily, a satisfactory outlet for his energies. When he returned he found himself restless and discontented. He sought something that would fill his needs, and was still searching about when the Eighteenth Amendment was passed. It was a challenge to him. When it became the fashion to defy the law, he was among the first to organize for that purpose. He met Spark Porter then. In him different motives actuated the same desires. They joined forces in building a powerful system which included ships for smuggling, trucks for land shipping, and warehouses which presumably stored lawful goods. Norris did not trust his partner, but they worked together successfully enough.

One thing he shortly discovered. It was not so simple a matter to defy the law as he had at first supposed. In the seven intervening years the perspicacity of the police had ruined many of his cherished plans. Eventually he wearied of the struggle. It kept him in constant jeopardy of his freedom. Most of his associates in the game were far from his own calibre. The more he worked with criminals the greater was his realization of this fact. So he came to the point where he considered discarding this mode of living. He did not permit Porter to become aware of his new attitude or his change of heart. Keeping the idea carefully concealed, he decided to break away after one last great coup. It was in this frame of mind that he met Mary Young.

As he had informed Rankin upon his arrest, it had been an accidental meeting. They squeezed into the same compartment of a turnstile during an evening rush hour, in the subway. He apologized to her, looked into her eyes—

and continued looking. The girl returned the gaze; and
so they watched each other during an entire ride on the
subway. He got out at the same station she did, and after
some hesitation spoke to her. Her reply was neither cold
nor inviting, but the voice sent through him a thrill such
as he had never before experienced. Previously he had been
too busy for women, but he wasn't too busy for just one
woman after that. What followed amounted to a genuine
case of love at first sight with both of them.

Theirs was a peculiar courtship. Strangers at the beginning, they remained strangers in many matters till the very
end. He never questioned her as to her past or her people,
and she never volunteered either. Instinctively, he knew
her for a lady and of good family, despite her residence at
Mrs. Schmidt's boarding-house and her work as a private
secretary. And he, on his side, told her little about himself
and what he was doing. They took each other literally on
trust.

Norris knew that he had betrayed that trust. His secrecy
as to his occupation was actuated by the fear that she
would never approve of it. This factor had finally influ-
enced him to cease his operations entirely. He foresaw that
after marriage such a mode of existence could not continue.
But meanwhile he kept his activities under cover, even
with her—there was just to be that final coup. So matters
stood when the quarrel occurred on Saturday and the fatal
Sunday rolled around.

The trend of Norris's reflections was interrupted by
the clanging of keys against the lock of his prison door.
Without haste or curiosity, he looked up to see Simpson
standing before him.

"Come along upstairs," the officer commanded, "Rankin
wants to see you."

Norris obeyed in silence. More quizzing, probably. He
had refused to speak primarily because he did not wish to

call the attention of the authorities to his activities. He knew from previous experience that they suspected him; but they had no proof, and whatever alibi he might produce would, perforce, connect him with the escapade which had occurred Sunday. Later, it would be safer to talk. With the booty of that final coup completely hidden away, he could tell his story without inconvenience either to himself or to his associates. There was a vast gulf between suspicion and proof. Ignorant of subsequent events, he believed Porter would, in some way, inform him as to when he would be freed from this bond of silence. Until then he would hold out, no matter how tragic the circumstances.

Rankin greeted him in his office and bade him be seated.

"I sent for you, Norris," he began, "to find out what you have to say about the crime. Thus far you've refused to speak. But Porter has been here to see about you."

Norris's features lighted up. It was as he expected; it meant that he could talk.

"What did he have to say?" he questioned.

"He told me a peculiar story about something that occurred on Sunday—something, in fact, that had to do with where you were on that night. It was quite interesting, but I haven't made up my mind whether or not I can believe it."

"And you want me to . . . ?"

"To repeat the same story for purposes of comparison. If they coincide, it will show me that there is some truth in it."

Norris complied. He knew that Porter would never have told the truth unless the situation permitted it. Nor would he have made any damaging admissions as to the object of their trip, even though Rankin might well suspect what it was for. Accordingly, he took care not to implicate himself in relating the journey to Asbury Park. Rankin, with note-book open, followed him closely. In all essential details, even in the minor points, the two narratives resembled each other. The facts dovetailed without error. Cross-examination failed to shake any part of it. There was revealed no indication that the alibi was a hoax, and at the end of an hour Rankin was convinced.

"Why didn't you tell me this before?" he asked, when the story was completed.

"I think the reason is rather obvious, don't you? What I would like to know is, how long are you going to keep me here? You can't hold an innocent man, you know; and there's no harm in an auto journey to Asbury Park."

"Very true," Rankin replied, "but I've still some investigations to make. I'm not altogether satisfied. You must realize your story far from answers everything. And I know there is a great deal you could tell me if you cared to."

"What, for instance?" Norris studied the detective.

"I want the truth about who Miss Young is and how you met her." Norris understood well enough what information the detective desired, but he was wary of any trap.

"I told you that already. It was purely accidental, and our courtship was just such as I have related to you. That's one thing I wouldn't lie to you about; if you were any reader of character, you'd know that. I loved her too much."

There was a quality of deep sincerity in his words. Rankin was surprised to find that his ideas of his prisoner were imperceptibly altering so that he was gradually coming into sympathy with him. This was true, despite the fact that Norris might yet be regarded as a suspect, and, in one sense, a lawbreaker. It was difficult to analyze this subtle change, but there was no doubt that it had occurred.

"Ours was a delightful engagement while it lasted," Norris went on, "romantic and beautiful. But it was all too short. And then there was that awful—" he paused as a feeling of pain welled up within.

"The quarrel? Exactly. What was the cause of that?"

"Yes, the quarrel. It hurts to speak about it, for it was the last time I saw her, and I left her unhappy. It was last Saturday night. Just think of it—four short and yet interminable days ago. We arranged to go to a dance at that big café in West Philadelphia—Shapiro's. I called for her at eight-forty-five, and then—"

Rankin recalled Miss Minsey's tale of the man who left Mary Young's chamber at approximately that time, though she had insisted it was on Sunday night.

"Did you go to her room for her?" he interrupted.

"No, of course not; I waited in the parlor, but I didn't see any one at that time. Mary didn't keep me waiting long, and we took a Yellow Cab to the café. But as soon as we climbed in, Mary asked me what I did for a living. We never talked about my—let's call it occupation—and the question took me unawares. I had no idea how much she might know about it when she put the question. I didn't know how to answer, so I did the most foolish thing I could have done under the circumstances, I lied about it."

"Why should she ask such a question?"

"I haven't any idea," Norris shook his head slowly. "Nor can I tell you where she learned the truth. But she knew, there was no doubt of that, and it was a weak thing to try to evade the issue. She pulled me up short at once and made accusations. I made matters worse by trying to explain away the unexplainable; and the end of it was that Mary—and justifiably, I suppose—broke into tears and, in a fit of anger, returned the ring. She was high-strung and headstrong; I believe she hardly knew what she was doing. It makes me think that at one time she had her own way in everything. That was all there was to it. I had to turn about and bring her directly back."

"But what about the silver lighter?"

"I think I must have dropped it in the cab during our discussion. It became rather heated, I will admit that; and

I was so distressed I was hardly aware of what happened about me. I knew that if Mary were calm and quiet, she'd think things over, so I believed the best thing to do was to bring her home and see her the following day. Unfortunately, Sunday I was too occupied with this other affair and I put my reconciliation off till the following day. I was a fool to put my business ahead of Mary; but believe me, Rankin, it was to be the last time and I couldn't postpone it. I was going to quit afterward. And it was the last time for both of us. I never saw her again."

His voice trailed into sorrowful silence.

"Then you believe that Miss Young picked the lighter up when you dropped it, and kept it with her?"

"I suppose that is what must have occurred. It's the only way I can account for her having it with her in the park. She must have held it, intending to return it, and it dropped out during the course of that awful ride."

Rankin hesitated a moment in thought, and replied slowly:

"That seems likely; but then, how do you explain the knife? I'd like to believe all this, but how in the world did that weapon, with which she was undoubtedly killed, come into the drawer of your bureau?"

"I realize that's the most incriminating thing against me; but I cannot explain it. I can only repeat that I'll take my oath that I never saw that weapon before in all my life."

"Have you any enemies?" Rankin asked. "Any one who would desire to kill Miss Young and incriminate you to revenge himself? Some one who would go to any lengths to be rid of you? That is, suppose the knife were planted by some one—?"

Norris weighed the suggestion, but shook his head wearily.

"I have enemies, I suppose, but none that would do a thing like that. They all move in places where none of them are aware of my interests in other spheres. They wouldn't even know of my engagement to Mary."

"They could find that out. It is, nevertheless, possible, don't you think?"

"I'm afraid it won't do." The reply was stubborn, and Rankin shifted the subject.

"There is only one thing I cannot understand, in regard to what occurred on Sunday evening. The telephone girl at your apartment says that Miss Young tried to locate you at six o'clock, and, failing that, left a message for you, asking you to meet her."

"As I've told you before, I didn't know anything about it. I spent the afternoon in town on some private business, and started back about six-thirty or so to keep my appointment with Porter. I arrived a bit after seven, went upstairs for a few minutes and came down. Miss Victhers never said a word to me or mentioned that Mary had been there."

"But she insists that she gave you the note when you arrived."

"Then she's simply lying," Norris replied in a tone that would admit of no doubt. "I don't know why she should, but I heard nothing about it at all." Again the sorrowful memory overwhelmed him so that he fell silent for a time; and Rankin sympathized with his undoubtedly deep and sincere suffering. "I wish to God that I had got that message, perhaps this terrible tragedy might have been avoided."

"Have you any idea what she wanted with you?"

"No, none at all, unless she wanted to forgive me for the folly of the night before. And if that was it, I'll never forgive myself for failing her as I did."

He had guessed correctly, Rankin knew from Miss Graham's narrative; for, more than that, she really sought his pardon for her hastiness. But he respected the grief of the man before him and mercifully refrained from retailing his information.

"I believe you, Norris," he said, rising, "in everything you've told me. As soon as I can get proof that will satisfy my superiors, you'll be released. Whatever else you've been doing doesn't come within my province."

James Norris regarded Rankin with an earnest gaze of deep understanding. The latter was trying to effect an *amende honorable* as best he could.

"Thanks, Rankin; that's white of you. I appreciate it more than I can tell you."

"But I warn you that you'll be kept under surveillance for some time. Duty compels me to report my suspicions to the Narcotic Squad. Captain Alvin, of whom you must have heard, will be hot after you for proof of what we both believe."

Norris smiled faintly. "I suppose that is the best I can expect. But you needn't worry. I've had a terrible punishment and learned my lesson."

Tommy Rankin shook hands with the man whom, twenty-four hours before, he would never have dreamed of thus greeting or leaving. The clasp was a sincere one. Norris would learn soon enough of the capture of his organization and what Porter had done to assist him. Then he could act as he pleased in the matter.

Norris returned to his cell with a sensation of deep relief.

20
JERRY—A COMEDY OF ERRORS

A half hour afterward the detective was reentering the doors of the Enderley Apartments. The porter was off duty, but the telephone girl, whose name, Norris had intimated, was Miss Victhers, had just arrived for her evening of labor. This time there was neither subtlety nor subterfuge in Rankin's approach. He came straight to the point, giving her to understand he was a detective.

His queries regarding a stranger who might have entered Norris's apartment and planted the incriminating weapon between twelve and twelve-thirty produced no results. The only gentleman the girl recalled was one who stopped in at eleven o'clock, inquired after Norris, and took his departure at once. Though disappointed, Rankin was not convinced; it was possible that Rogers had entered unseen, or, being mistaken for a dweller, had walked in without attracting attention.

He turned to the subject which interested him more at the moment.

"You told me a story two days ago," he informed her sternly, "about a girl who had left a message for you to give Mr. Norris. I want you to repeat it now, so I can get all the facts correctly."

Miss Victhers, far from easy before, now appeared greatly distressed. The command caused her to flush and

look apprehensive. For a moment she affected to have difficulty comprehending his meaning.

"Why, there isn't anything to tell! At six o'clock on
Sunday evening this young lady came in and asked for Mr.
Norris, and when I informed her that he wasn't in just
then, she gave me a note for him. Then when Mr. Norris
arrived at seven o'clock, I gave it to him—"

"Just a moment," the detective interrupted. "There's
the entire point. Did you or did you not give Mr. Norris
that message?"

Miss Victhers caught her breath in agitation; her per-
turbation increased.

"Certainly I did," she replied, with an effort at dignity.
"When I make a promise, I—"

"So you said before. But I want the truth now; nothing
less will do. And if you lie, it will be much worse for you."
Rankin put all the power he possessed into the words.
"You are trifling with a crime as serious as murder. If you
gave that message to Mr. Norris, you automatically convict him of it!"

The shaft lodged home with terrible alacrity. Miss
Victhers became white with sudden fear and horror.

"No! No! I didn't give it to him—I swear it! I forgot all
about it—and lied to you." She turned appealingly to him,
"You must believe me, sir—I did forget."

"There, that's better," he told her in softer tones. "Now,
what did happen?"

"I didn't give it to him," she repeated in her excitement.
"I forgot it. When Mr. Norris came in at seven o'clock he
went upstairs so quickly that I had no chance to tell him.
And when he came down I was busy with a call, and it
slipped my mind till just after he was outside the door. I
ran out to give it to him; but it was too late. He was just
getting into a little red roadster with another man, and

the sound of the motor drowned out my calls to him and he was off before I could reach him."

This was clearly the truth, besides being a verification, if any were needed, of Norris's tale.

"Then why did you lie to me about it?"

The girl shook her head despondently. "It's hard to say," she replied in helpless tones. "I was so worried about having forgotten it that I didn't know what to do. The girl who brought it said it was so important that I was afraid serious trouble might occur, due to my forgetfulness. That might bring me into difficulties, and I didn't want that. So I decided to tell whoever might ask that I had given it to Mr. Norris; and I was going to stick to that." She searched his features dejectedly.

"My dear girl," Rankin commented, "you've got yourself into more trouble this way than you ever would have done had you told the truth in the beginning."

Wondering at the perversity of human nature, he left her staring shamefacedly after him. She had a fright she would not soon forget. The little visit appeared effectually to clear James Norris of all suspicion, but it left Rankin uncertain, nevertheless. Positive, in his own mind, that Rogers had planted the weapon, he was unable to calculate precisely how the deed had been accomplished.

For a moment discouragement overwhelmed him. The seemingly interminable tangle of the entire problem presented no thread at which he could grasp to unravel the mesh. For such a state of mind he knew of but one satisfactory cure. Though it was already dark and he had more pressing affairs, he hastened to his rooms and took a bath. The luxurious touch of warm water somewhat revived his downcast spirits. As he expected, a short period of immersion in steam brought dreamy thoughts. The case seemed far away.

It was precipitately borne back to his attention again in a startling manner. He had just completed his dressing and was considering going out for supper, when there came a sharp, urgent knock at his door.

"Come in," he called.

At the command the door flew open, hurling head-long into the room, almost into his arms, a girl. She was flushed and breathless from a too evident haste in running up the stairs, her little red hat sat askew upon the top of her head and her summer furs trailed after her upon the floor. Her features were pleasing, in a quiet manner, but both the color of a dazzling red silk dress and the jewels she sported upon her bare arms and slender neck belied her quiet features.

Rankin could not resist a gasp of amazement. He recognized her though he had seen her but once before. It was evident, however, that she did not recall him. She had been too far under the weather, the last time he had met her, to recall anything in particular. For this was the tipsy girl of the Enderley Apartments, who but two nights before had opened for him the window of her own rooms to let him enter from the precarious flower balcony! She was Miss Cora Blakely!

She gave him no opportunity to speak but, despite her panting, burst into questions, never pausing for a reply.

"You're Mr. Rankin, aren't you? Thank goodness I found you in! I rushed up here to get a word with you before Jerry comes up. He didn't want me to, and we had quite an argument about it, but I ran while he was getting out of the machine, and now I've got to talk fast and you must listen—"

The detective wondered what in the world she was talking about.

"What can I do for you?"

"Listen," she went on, impatiently, "Jerry is furious and he won't know what he's saying; so you mustn't mind him. You must listen to me instead. And I want to make things all right before he starts." She broke off abruptly and then dashed headlong onward, "Mr. Rankin, you have no grudge against Jerry, have you?"

Her words indicated that this Jerry must be a close acquaintance of his, but Rankin hadn't the slightest conception of whom she spoke. He stared at her bewildered.

"But haven't you made some mistake—?"

"No, no, not if you're Mr. Rankin, the detective." She pressed the question with an urgency that verged upon hysterics. "You have no grudge against Jerry, have you?"

Rather than have a scene, he thought it best to placate her.

"No, of course not," he replied.

Miss Blakely was clearly relieved. "Thank goodness for that. I was so worried. Now I'm sure everything will be all right if you just don't pay any attention to him and remember what I've been telling you." She broke off tremulously as heavy footsteps became audible in the corridor outside. "That's Jerry now—!"

The girl's companion, Jerry, stood in the doorway. It appeared to the detective that he would have an argument on his hands, no matter what the circumstances. For Jerry was a large, stoutish person. Jerry was, in fact, Charles Bond, electrical financier!

That he was irate was evident. He carried a cane which he waved in the air as he tramped furiously into the room. His bloated face was an apoplectic red, and his pendulous lips displayed his teeth in a half snarl. He caught sight of the girl.

"You shouldn't have come up here, Cora. I told you to stay below. I can tend to this young reprobate myself and it won't be pleasant—"

"I'm going to stay, darling," Miss Blakely replied. "So please be quiet and don't carry on. I'm sure everything will be all right."

Mr. Bond went on as though she had not spoken. "I say you had best go downstairs. It's not for you to—"

Rankin thought it high time to interfere.

"May I ask you, Mr. Bond, what is the meaning of this intrusion?"

Immediately the financier shifted his attention, appearing to forget the girl entirely. He waved his cane truculently.

"You'll learn soon enough what's the matter, young man. You'll learn you can't pull off any game as you did yesterday upon Charles M. Bond. That was a fine story you told me then, I must say!"

"I'm afraid I haven't the slightest idea about what you are talking."

The calm tone infuriated the financier further. "Oh, you haven't—haven't you?" he fairly screamed, shaking the cane so near the other's nose that he almost collided with it. "I suppose you don't remember coming into my office with a cock-and-bull story about a case you are working on and then going away and inquiring all over town into my private affairs. I suppose you did nothing of the sort."

Rankin was not the sort to be heckled into any admissions. "I'd advise you to put that cane down, Mr. Bond. If it should explode, the results will be most unpleasant for yourself."

"Jerry!" cried the girl, interrupting, "Please be calm."

"Calm? I am calm—I'm like ice. I only want to know the reason for it. I suppose this fellow didn't ask me a lot of questions in the office, and then try to trace my movements by going to the Marlton Club and inquiring of the porters there. And then he had the nerve to go to my very home and speak to my chauffeur—and loaf about the grounds and—" Mr. Bond broke off in sputterings and it was an instant before he could continue. "Oh, yesterday, I know all about it—they all told me. My chauffeur mentioned it this morning and that you used the same line on him as you did to me. And I demand an explanation at once."

The implications of the financier's charge were bewildering. Did he believe the detective an imposter? Under what sort of delusion was he laboring?

"There isn't anything on my part to explain," replied Rankin wonderingly.

"Oh, there isn't, eh? Well, I'll have you understand that you can't interfere with my private affairs like this. I—I— why, I'll have you arrested, that's what I'll do!"

When the detective merely smiled unconcernedly at the threat, the financier was taken aback. For some reason it was evident that he had expected his opponent to retreat and apologize, or at least explain his behavior. Rankin's undisturbed stand correspondingly threw the financier off his balance.

"So you don't deny it, eh?" His voice held the least trace of uncertainty, and Rankin took the initiative.

"Certainly not. Not only do I admit everything you say, but I'll tell you even more. And when I get finished, Mr. Bond, I expect to hear you reply frankly and completely." A disturbed look flashed across the other's features, indicating that he was on the correct course. "I would have waited for your explanation before, but the subject is far too serious for further delay. I questioned people, it is true; and I learned some interesting facts."

"What did you learn?" The financier lost the final vestige of anger and looked uncomfortable.

"I found out that you were not at the Marlton Club on Sunday night and when you said you were, you lied to me. In a case like this it is no light thing, perjury. You

must have had an important reason for that lie—and for
that alibi you so carefully prepared there. I also discovered
where you were, Mr. Bond—you were at Woodlawn Park in
company with a young lady—!"

The final words, enunciated with clear gravity, were
like an accusation. The financier's face blanched with fear
and agitation; in his apprehension he glanced at his companion with an appealing look.

"Mr. Rankin,"—Miss Blakely stepped forward plead-
ingly—"I thought you said that—"

He waved her aside. "I promised nothing, Miss Blakely, and matters have reached that stage where I'm left no
choice. Now, sir—"

The financier, despite his immense bulk, appeared suddenly to shrink into haggard insignificance. "Mr. Rankin,"
he said, "how much will you take to drop your investigations? I'm a wealthy man and anything within reason I'd
be willing—

"Are you trying to bribe me, Mr. Bond?"

"But I'll give you a great deal, and she'll never be the
wiser. I'll—" He stopped short. "Tell me, Mr. Rankin, how
much does she pay you, and I'll double that amount, I'll
treble it. I don't care what it is."

"How much does who pay me?"

Rankin knew the answer, however. A flash of light
and understanding illumined the entire situation. He had
already grasped the fact that "Jerry" was the financier's pet
name among his lady friends. But in that question lay the
answer to Miss Blakely's presence and the meaning of this
visit. The case which Rankin had laboriously built against
Mr. Bond and his wife toppled to the ground like a house
of cards. It was a catastrophe.

"My goodness, sir!" the financier exclaimed, "at least
do not try to pretend that my wife hasn't hired you to
watch my movements and report my behavior to her! I've

always suspected she had some one on my trail, but she is so sly and does it so carefully when I'm not around, that I never could prove it. But come now—how much does she pay you? I'll make it four times as much if you'll not report to her that I was at Woodlawn."

Recalling what he had witnessed in the home of the Bonds, the detective realized that Mrs. Bond knew that already. His own conclusions of those suspicious circumstances had been incredibly stupid in the light of these revelations.

"So that is why you bribed those servants at the club to lie for you."

"Of course. I have to have some protection against her infernal inquisitiveness. For years she has been hounding me—and always has she been too clever for me. So I arranged this scheme for proving my whereabouts." For a moment the financier was pleased with himself; but he recalled his ticklish situation. "And if you've been working for her—wouldn't you now rather work for me?"

"I assure you, Mr. Bond, that I told the truth when I said that I came from Headquarters. I am investigating the death of your secretary and that alone is my interest in you. I have never met your wife, and I am not hired by her to spy upon you."

"But all those questions—the examination of the doorman at the club—of my chauffeur—?"

"Purely as a matter of routine. I traced the movements of all parties concerned on the night of the crime. You must realize that murder is serious and that nothing must be done which will hinder the course of investigation."

Cora Blakely broke in eagerly with a grateful glance at the detective. "There, I told you everything would be all right, Jerry. I'm sure we can go now, and have nothing to worry about. Can't we, Mr. Rankin? You see, Jerry and I really were at the park on Sunday night, just for a harmless little excursion and fun, you understand. But of course we couldn't let Mrs. Bond find out, for she has such a jealous disposition and thinks such unfair things of my Jerry."

"I understand." Recalling the girl's condition at the Enderley Apartments, her attempted naiveté was both disarming and amusing. "What time did you go to the park?"

"Oh, it was perhaps nine-thirty—or maybe a bit later. Jerry called for me in his car at my place and we came out a bit afterward. We stayed in the park till about eleven-thirty and then took a cozy ride in the country." She smiled at him innocently through two big pools of liquid blue. "And it's all settled now. We can go, can't we?"

"Just one moment. There are one or two questions that Mr. Bond must either answer here or speak in court. He refused the last time I asked him, and did not tell me the truth." Unconsciously he resumed his stern demeanor. "And this time it must be the truth!"

The financier flushed at the tone and changed his position nervously. He was not altogether reassured as to Rankin's status, and he feared a snare.

"Why, I've already told you that I know absolutely nothing about it."

"At least you know," the detective went on, "why Miss Young left you."

"But I did tell you that. She had an offer of a better position."

"I said, Mr. Bond, that I wanted the truth."

The financier regarded his companion uncertainly, and tried to appear unconcerned. "Don't you think, Cora dear, that you had better go downstairs? I'll join you in just a moment."

"No, I'm going to stay here with you. You know you mustn't have any secrets from me, dear." Her swift, shrewd look of worldly complacency only distressed him further. He cleared his throat nervously.

"No, of course not. Do just as you please, my child. I suppose, Mr. Rankin, that she left me because she wasn't satisfied with her position."

"Ah, that's better. And why was she not satisfied?"

"Because—because—"

With an impulse to punish the financier for the trouble for which his secretiveness was responsible, Rankin broke in in a voice of mingled contempt and satisfaction.

"I'll help you, Mr. Bond, with the reasons. Wasn't it because you were forcing your unwelcome attentions upon her; and because she was a decently raised girl who refused to permit such as you to become familiar with her? And you persisted, like most of your kind do, believing yourself superior and every girl your fit prey. And what about this note you wrote her, asking her to meet you on Sunday night? Which I have no doubt she refused—"

"Jerry!" Cora Blakely's voice rang with indignation. "And you said that you never looked at another girl. You said that you thought of me and no one else. Oh, you unfaithful cad!"

The harassed financier started toward her with arms outstretched.

"Listen, Cora. I swear by God—"

"Don't you dare touch me. You can't explain that note Mr. Rankin has there in his hand, can you. It's in your writing. I recognise it, all right." Melodramatically she shrank away from him. "You've been deceiving me—a poor innocent girl—with your riches and money."

"Listen, Cora—"

"I won't listen. I don't want you to ever speak to me again. I'll sue you, Jerry, for ruining my life, that's what I'll do!"

In a fit of petulance and anger, Miss Blakely dashed to the door, flung it open, and was out before either of the two men could prevent her. In desperation, Bond, sweat rolling down his brow, started to follow, but he was brought up short at the door by the sharp command of the detective.

"A moment, Mr. Bond! You haven't explained away this note. And if you don't now, you will before a jury. Such publicity is hardly desirable."

The threat brought him completely to a halt. "Great heavens, Rankin, haven't you made enough trouble for me already? Of course, it is my note. I wrote it on Friday to make a date for that night, while Miss Cochrane was in the office. On Thursday Miss Young had been at my home for some work, and something I said must have offended her, for she refused to speak to me the next day. But I didn't believe it was serious, so I tried that. But it was; and, damn it, that's what caused her to leave!"

The last words were flung over his shoulder. Before they were barely out of his mouth he was out of the door, slamming it noisily behind him. Rankin heard his steps banging swiftly down the stairs till their echo died out far below. And he could only stare at the closed portal in amazement and inexpressible disgust. From the very beginning he had assumed that the note discovered in Mary Young's bag applied to a meeting on Sunday evening and had worked on that premise. And yet, there was no basis for the assumption. The note was undated; it could have applied to Friday or any other day of the week as well. He realized the enormity of his error. The note had dogged his footsteps throughout and complicated the trail; wherever he turned, it confronted him. And it had nothing at all to do with the problem.

Yet, according to the patrolman on the Reed Street-Morton Street intersection, Mary Young had undoubtedly waited for some one at nine o'clock on Sunday evening. For one of the few times in his life, Tommy Rankin cursed aloud in definite and clear-cut terms.

21
GIANT OAKS FROM TINY ACORNS

With all his suspects eliminated but one, Rankin set resolutely to work on the Rogers trail where Gordon had left off. At 10:30 he was in Broad Street station. The terminal, at that hour on a weekday night, is yet fairly crowded with travelers waiting for their trains. Either they are seated in the large waiting-room at the rear of the wide staircase that leads to the train levels, or they stroll in the concourse beyond. Both the ticket offices and the information bureau are on the ground floor.

To the latter Rankin first directed his steps. The list of outgoing trains from midnight to one o'clock that Gordon had given him included only two that departed between twelve-thirty and one. A Trenton theatergoers' special left at 12:41 and the final cars for Paoli went out at 12:45. Both were locals and he agreed with his colleague that it was altogether unlikely that the fugitive had taken either one. Accordingly he eliminated them.

He began to labor upon his own theory. Giving Rogers sufficient time to journey to West Philadelphia and return to the station, it must have taken till 12:30 at the earliest. Still, granting the Gordon premise that he would not have cared to wait more than an hour about the station, that hour would now extend from 12:30 to 1:30. What were the outgoing trains between 1:00 and 1:30?

The employee at the information counter supplied him
with the necessary knowledge. There were three trains—
the Chicago-Western Flyer through Cleveland and Toledo
left at 1:15. The Hot Springs-Louisville Special went at
1:24, to be followed, at 1:30 by the Bar Harbor Express,
through New York and New Haven, into Maine. One of
these must have borne the fugitive away; the next train did
not leave till 2:30. But which one was another question.
How he was to discover this was far from obvious. It was
endless work to inquire of every employee in the station
whether he recalled the man Rankin sought. Gordon had
covered that ground, in his search, fairly exhaustively. Yet
at 12:30 on a Sunday night the terminal is comparatively
deserted, and one of the porters or ticket agents might
well have observed a man with an exceptionally large black
bag.

Rankin made a beginning at the baggage-room. Gordon
would not have tried that; but if Rankin's theories had
any basis whatever, he should find that Rogers had checked
his bag.

As luck would have it, his first effort was successful.
The checker did recall such a gentleman as the detective
inquired after. He had come at a bit after midnight to
check his bag. Since very few came at the hour with their
luggage, and it was a particularly heavy piece, he remembered it when he took it from the traveler. The bag had
attracted his attention more than its owner.

"I don't suppose I'd know him again if I saw him," he
said.

"But can you remember when the bag was called for?"
Rankin questioned. "I suppose it was the same gentleman."

"Oh, yes, it was the same. He came just one hour later.
You see, we close the checking office at one o'clock, and
when he turned in the bag he asked me about it. I told
him and he said he'd be back in time for it. Sure enough,

he came just as I was about to shut the window, and took it with him."

The checker had failed to observe any identification marks upon the bag, or where its owner had gone after he called for it. Rankin was not much wiser than before, for Rogers could yet have taken any one of the three night flyers. They all left after one o'clock. It merely served to indicate that he was on the right track.

He made the rounds of the ticket windows next. Only four sold long-distance fares and Pullman tickets after midnight, the rest closing much earlier. Rankin was thankful for the limit to his field of inquiry. His questions were, of a necessity, vague, though he set the time in which Rogers might have purchased his fare as between midnight and one-thirty. The result was a complete and definite blank. Even with these certain bounds, he could gain no information. The officials would have been only too glad to aid him! Indeed, they did their best to recall what they could. Their recollections were unproductive. Roger's bag was worthless as a means of identification, since every traveler carried a bag. All three trains were popular and crowded, the Chicago Flyer catering to business men, and the Bar Harbor being filled with late vacationists. All the agents felt that if Rankin's quarry had left his purchasing till the last moment, he would have been unable to procure a berth.

He tried the gatemen. Here Rankin was laughed at for his pains. The gateman at track No. 2, from which the Louisville Special had left on Sunday, felt it was ridiculous that the inquirer should expect him to recall some single person with a black bag, when crowds of people all carrying black bags rushed through the gate the instant it was opened. They paused barely long enough to have their tickets punched, and he was too engrossed to study the faces of the holders. Rebuked, Rankin passed on to canvass the guards, who, it appeared, had little to do but watch people. This source, also, was problematical. None of them recalled carrying the bag of any such gentleman as he described, or seeing him lounge about, waiting for a train. Gordon appeared to be right when he said that Rogers had been swallowed up.

It was not until he tried the last guard that he had any success. The guard, a burly, sharp-nosed person, approached him suspiciously to demand an explanation for his peculiar behavior. It was his duty to keep the station clear of bad characters. The sight of Rankin's credentials reduced him to an apologetic servility. He displayed an obsequious willingness to be of assistance.

Rankin explained his quest and carefully described the fugitive, down to the last detail. He knew it by memory.

"I believe I do remember such a man," the guard said, when he was through. "In fact, I'm sure it was the same chap. I spoke to him about the weather, but he was quite bothered by it and didn't appear very sociable, so I gave him up."

He had spoken to him at exactly five minutes after one. The reason he recalled the time so accurately was that he had been talking to the baggage-checker just as he was closing his room. The gentleman Rankin was inquiring about called for his bag then, and stood about for five minutes, when he stepped up to him for a sociable word. To Rankin, this checked the accuracy of the baggage-checker, but it hardly assisted him. For the earliest of the three trains, the Chicago Flyer, did not leave till quarter after the hour. And yet . . .

"Can you tell me," he asked suddenly, "what time the gates open for the Chicago-Western Flyer?"

"At one o'clock, exactly, sir."

"Good! It proves that he never took that train, at any rate."

"How do you figure that out, sir?"

"Don't you see?" Rankin explained. "This chap is in a damnable hurry to get away and his one fear is that he'll be seen. Now there isn't anything more conspicuous than lolling about the platform. He'd want to do as little of that as possible; he'd want to board the train as soon as the gates opened. Instead, at five after, and probably even later, he's still waiting around. What about the Louisville train?"

"The gates open for that a little after one-ten, sir."

"And the Bar Harbor Express?"

"Five minutes later."

At midnight the detective sat down to review what he had accomplished. The search was narrowed down to two possible trains, either of which the boarder could have taken after he was last observed. But which of the two had it been? The Hot Springs-Louisville Special? The Bar Harbor which led to Canada and certain safety? If Rogers had only left some clue to his probable destination; if in his room there had been some trace which would assist him. But there was nothing except that valueless scrap of paper he had found. . . .

On the instant Rankin recalled the unburnt slip of paper, unearthed in the ashes of the fireplace. He had not forgotten it, but had failed to consider it of any importance until this moment, when with the recollection, there came a flooding recollection of its true value. He dug into the corner of his pocket in which the minute scrap lay. Seemingly, the four figures in the row, one beneath the other, were meaningless, possessing no more order than that each figure was higher than the one preceding.

226.5
343.0
456.4
500.2

Yet they were the answer to the very problem which at that moment confronted him. They took on the value of platinum, and his carelessness in handling the scrap amazed him.

Of course, that was what the figures were! They were the clues that solved his difficulties, and he had almost overlooked them! Rankin upbraided himself as a thoughtless, maundering fool. It was the remains of a time-table that Rogers had possessed, and, when faced with flight, hurriedly made use of to find a train that would bear him to safety. He had swiftly studied it, and, after drawing from it the hour of the earliest train, burned it with his other effects when he suddenly determined upon his desperate escape, after his crime.

Every such schedule of train departures has a mileage column paralleling the two columns which name the stations, and lists the time for arrivals. The four figures were part of the mileage column, as was evident from the decimal points which listed so accurately even fractions of a mile. The figures above and below had been burned away by the same flames, which had, by a peculiar freak, left this particle untouched. He had merely to find the time-table in which these four sets of figures appeared in the mileage column in the given sequence, to discover the train Rogers had taken. If Rankin's deductions were accurate, they could only be found on one of two possible tables.

At the information desk he demanded the time-tables of the Louisville Special and the Bar Harbor Express. With them safely in hand, he sat down again. Each was as thick as a pamphlet and filled with data regarding all the trains that traveled over the area covered by its respective special. The Bar Harbor schedules, over which Rankin pored first, contained also the routes and hours of all connecting trains, running between Philadelphia and Maine, with branches to Boston, Providence, and other centers. A thorough examination of every listed route failed to disclose the four figures he sought, in any mileage column. After fifteen minutes of fruitless search, he opened the other.

Nothing in the schedule of the Louisville Special itself resembled his clue. Rankin began to fear he was in error, that his conclusions had no basis. It was too much good luck for him that he should prove correct. If the trail petered out here, he hardly knew what he would do to find it again.

Casually he turned the schedule over . . . and there the four figures were, staring him in the face! They were a vindication of all his theories. There was no doubting that this was the time-table that Rogers had used in considering his destination; and there was equally no doubt that the Hot Springs-Louisville Special was the only train that suited his urgent need. The numbers were part of the column that scheduled the trip of a southbound train from New York to St. Petersburg, Florida, as the pamphlet itself was a routing of all trains between the North and South. Completed, the column read as shown.

85.8	Lv. North Philadelphia......	11.36	2.03
226.5	Lv. Washington (U. Sta.)....	3.05	6.45
343.0	Ar. Richmond, Va..	6.15	10.02
456.4	Henderson, N. C. (SAL).....	f9.13	2.13
500.2	Raleigh, N. C.............	....	4.10

Two minutes after he assured himself he was right, Tommy Rankin set about to collect information regarding the Louisville train. He visited the ticket windows again, passed from there to the agent at the gate, from which the special would leave in but a half hour, and then proceeded to interrogate the man at the information desk. The entire canvass took less than three-quarters of an hour, and when he had finished he had collected the following items.

The Sunday train to Louisville had been particularly filled, for there were many vacationists traveling to Hot Springs for the late season. It would have, therefore, been impossible for a traveler coming to the station an hour before train time to have procured a berth. The Pullmans had been sold out by Saturday night. Unless there had been a last moment cancellation, it would be out of the question. Then the empty berth would have to be purchased on the train from the Pullman conductor.

All Louisville Specials took a different return route, coming by way of Cincinnati. A train with its crew, that left Philadelphia, would take almost three days to return to its starting point. A train that left for Louisville on Sunday night would arrive, according to schedule, about twenty-four hours later . . . very early Tuesday morning. It would lay over in Louisville till late Tuesday morning, make the trip to Cincinnati and lay there for several hours. At ten o'clock Tuesday night it would proceed with its return journey to Philadelphia, arriving at seven or eight Wednesday evening. To-day being Wednesday (or, more accurately, early Thursday morning), it had returned several hours late—almost ten o'clock, in fact. Now it was waiting for one-twenty-four, when it would again proceed on the same round, and return to Philadelphia in three days.

The same crew which accompanied the boarder on his flight Sunday night was thus manning the train now about to leave. It was an unprecedented bit of luck. Rankin's next step was clear. If Rogers had failed to purchase a berth at the station, he must have attempted to do so on the train. Thus he was sure to have attracted the attention

of some conductor on board. A porter would undoubtedly recall him because of his heavy luggage. These events
would stamp themselves upon observant minds. He needed only to discover the correct officials on board and to
probe shrewdly to bring out the facts. His quarry had left
a broad enough trail. It only wanted tracing.

Rankin glanced at the station clock. It was ten minutes
after one. He had just sufficient time to inform Headquarters of his coming journey and purchase a ticket. He did
the former first.

Thomas replied at the other end of the wire. On hearing the speaker, he ordered the detective to hold the line
for a minute. The next instant Gordon spoke, and there
was an urgency in his tone.

"Hello, Rankin! You know Harry Preston, don't you?"

"Certainly I do. What about him?"

Preston was the head of a private detective agency, one
of the foremost concerns in the United States. He was also
the representative of the Bankers' Bonding Association.
Rankin had worked with him on two occasions and their
relationship had been an exceedingly profitable one for
both.

"He came in a few hours ago, from Hot Springs, with
that runaway boarder, Rogers, a prisoner, arrested for the
attempted robbery of his employers, the National Securities Bank, last Sunday night. I've been trying to get you
ever since, at your rooms—"

"What? What's that you say?" Rankin cried.

"That's right, Tommy. I was surprised as you are. The
train was late, or he'd have got in much earlier with Rogers, perhaps before you left here. He didn't have anything
to say, except that we were to hold him till we saw him
to-morrow. Then he went away before I got anything more
out of him. He had the warrant legally made out, so we
cooped up Rogers and things are hanging fire—"

"A robbery on Sunday night!" Rankin interrupted. "Did he say at what time, or how? They didn't tell you anything about that at the bank when you called on them, did they?"

"Not a word. I told you they were cold about it. They haven't got over our last failure yet. If anything of the sort did occur, most likely they decided to make it their own private affair until Rogers was captured. That's more than a direct implication of what they think of us. And Preston is a pretty dependable chap when it comes to that sort of work."

"Did he mention anything about the details, though?"

"Nothing at all, Rankin," the detective replied. "I know no more than you and I'm just as puzzled. You'll have to see Preston the first thing in the morning. And he caught him in Hot Springs, too, of all places. . . . Did you want to speak to Thomas about anything?"

To say that the other was puzzled would be putting it with insufficient force. "It wasn't anything important. I'll get this thing straight the first thing in the morning. Good-bye."

Rankin rang off, his mind tracing the steps to discover where he had fallen into such gross error. It is unnecessary to say that he did not buy a ticket.

22
LAID SCHEMES OF MICE AND MEN

Rankin did not see Harry Preston early the following morning. It was not, in fact, till noon that he succeeded in locating the special inquiry agent and obtained from him the story of Joseph Rogers's crime and capture. In the interim he reviewed the events that had led him off on this false tangent, coordinating and arranging them. There was the quarrel between the boarder and Mary Young, in the neighborhood park, overheard by Mrs. Edgecomb; Rogers's flight that followed closely, the time during which the crime was committed; the hurried packing which took till eleven-thirty, including the burning of all incriminating papers; the bag that was checked, while, presumably, the fugitive visited the Enderley Apartments. But all these events were merely cumulative and circumstantial. They did not make him, *per se,* a murderer; and Rankin was again impressed with the unfortunate results that come from leaping to conclusions from insufficient facts.

The tale that Preston narrated to him was simple in outline if somewhat complicated in detail. Six months before, Joseph Rogers had taken a position at the National Securities Bank, in a dual capacity of clerk and cashier. He was, of course, bonded; his position gave him access to the company's vaults and combinations. He gave admirable service, appearing to be thoroughly honest and capable, with no bad habits, as far as were discoverable. He was always on time and seemed willing to work. His employers considered him an asset.

Exactly a week ago, which was the past Thursday, an event occurred which caused the bank officials suddenly to consider him with distrust. It was the habit of the clerks, when they came to work, in the morning, to discard their civilian coats, in a locker-room set aside for them, for thin gray jackets in which they worked. At noon of the Thursday in question, one of the clerks, Gilbert Henry, in leaving for lunch and while rechanging into his coat, donned Rogers's garment by mistake. He discovered his error at once, but at the same time he made another and more startling discovery. In the coat pocket was a key which would open both of the barred portals at the main entrance of the bank.

As soon as he had recovered from his surprise, Henry reported the find to the head cashier, Mr. Galton. Both agreed that Rogers's possession of the key was suspicious and demanded attention. A conference was had on the matter, with the vice president, and the paying teller also called upon, to decide what should be done. Preston, as representative of the company that had bonded Rogers, was consulted. The decision was to permit matters to take their course, while a careful surveillance was kept upon the clerk. At the first false move the clerk made, drastic action would be taken.

Nothing further to excite interest occurred on Thursday, though Preston trailed his suspect to his boarding-house and kept a close watch upon him the entire evening. Friday passed quietly. After banking hours, however, Rogers visited Broad Street station, and there purchased two tickets to Hot Springs, Virginia. Preston, just behind him, could not discover what he wanted of two tickets, unless he expected to have an accomplice, in view of the fact that later he only made use of one. Since his capture he had stubbornly refused to explain any of his behavior. In the evening he took a young lady from the boarding-house for a walk in the park.

From appearances, and from slices of conversation which the trailer overheard, they quarreled. When it was over his companion cut him altogether and left him sitting alone, disconsolate and dejected.

On Saturday Rogers gave notice that he was leaving. This was a somewhat expected development, in view of his purchase of the preceding day. He was going West, he said, where there were better opportunities. Mr. Galton, to whom he spoke, feigned surprise. There was nothing to do but permit him to go, though the official was certain that "something was up." The vigil was increased, and Dragot, night watchman for the bank, was given instructions to be particularly careful for the next few days. Thus matters stood on the fatal Sunday on which Mary Young was murdered.

During the day Preston continued to trail the boarder, but he indulged in nothing more interesting than some harmless recreation in Fairmount Park. In the evening an assistant took Preston's place, following the suspect to Mrs. Schmidt's. Believing it to be safe, he left for a few minutes for a bite of supper. But during that time Rogers slipped out unseen, though he could have had no inkling that his plans were suspected. It was merely an instance of ill luck, where the tracker permitted his quarry to get out of sight and could pick up no trace of him afterward.

The vaults of the National Securities Bank had a peculiar arrangement of locks, governed by a time-lock mechanism, that made it one of the securest safes in the East. The clock opened the outer doors of the vault, automatically at ten o'clock daily, and shut them at four o'clock. It was practically impossible to derange the machinery unless one had a special key to the clock that set it all in motion. In some way Rogers had procured a key. It was clear that he had been long planning the attempt and had made all preparations for it. With the knowledge he possessed of the combination of the inner vaults, access to the great sums within would be comparatively easy.

On Saturday, just before giving notice, he had tampered with the clock arrangement, so that, while the hands appeared to be in their normal position, the lock was actually set for ten o'clock on Sunday night, instead of for the following Monday morning. Chestnut Street east of Ninth Street is almost deserted on Sunday, so that Rogers must have felt his attempt, even so early in the evening, was safe. It later appeared that he desired to catch the Hot Springs train at one-twenty-four.

Dragot, specially warned, was alert, so that he heard the would-be-thief the moment the key turned in the lock of the barred front entrance. Indeed, he was a little too vigilant and eager to prove himself, or else he would undoubtedly have caught Rogers. As it was, he made a lunge for him the instant he appeared, before he was fairly inside the door. As a result the ex-clerk took instant alarm and fled at the first sound of danger, barely managing to escape. Certain that he had been recognized, he hastened to his lodgings and packed. Dragot had been warned not to call in the police unless it proved vitally necessary. Both the bank officials and Preston felt that it was entirely a private affair of the bonding company, to be handled without the aid of Headquarters, at least until Rogers was captured. For that reason the attempt had not been reported, nor had anything of it appeared in the daily papers. When Gordon made his inquiries, Preston was already successful and en route with his prisoner, back from Hot Springs.

Immediately the watchman communicated with the bank officials, and they with Preston. The latter, aware of

the Hot Springs train that left at one-twenty-four hastened
to the station just in time to make it. He had no difficulty
in finding Rogers, who was trying to purchase a berth for
himself, which, peculiarly enough, he had thus far neglected to do. There were many actions, in fact, Preston agreed,
that needed special explanation. He procured a warrant
during the stop-over at Washington, served it, and made
the arrest on the train, and continued on the round trip by
way of Cincinnati, which had brought him and his prisoner back to Philadelphia late the preceding evening.

As the tale progressed, Rankin found the details increasingly puzzling. Clearly he had erred in assuming that
Rogers's departure had been unexpected, for he had prepared for it beforehand. Nevertheless, working on that
assumption had put him on the right track. Had circumstances permitted him to continue the search, he had no
doubt that he would finally have been able to trace the
fugitive. The evidences of a panicky flight in the disordered
room were of course explained; so too was the time-table
which he had certainly used and burned. But the enigma
itself grew more complicated. The lodger was no longer a
suspect. Why had he taken two berths? Who was to be his
companion? Did he know anything at all about the murder
of Mary Young? Why had he chosen Hot Springs, a resort
and vacation town, as a destination?

The answer was to be found in Rogers only, if he could
be made to talk. As soon as Preston had finished his narrative, Rankin hurried away to see the prisoner. It was the
most important step of his investigation and, despite the
results which automatically liberated Rogers from suspicion, was not to be delayed. Dragot could supply him with
a perfect alibi at the moment the crime occurred. Yet at
some point he was undoubtedly connected with the murder.

Instead of having the boarder sent to him, he visited
him in his cell. There would be a psychological effect in

the fact that he had sufficient interest in the man to come to see him. The dank and gloomy cell he occupied contained only him. He paid no attention to the approach of Rankin and the guard, but remained in the bowed position in which they first viewed him, with his head buried in his hands.

Joseph Rogers did not look up, in fact, until the detective stood alone before him. Mrs. Edgecomb's description of him appeared, on first view, most appropriate. There was the sallow face, the bony nose and the thinned-out hair. The sandy features had written in them a challenge. He had dark, shifty eyes that stared fiercely with a burning intensity at his visitor; he made no attempt to speak. His attitude was inimical, defiant, and Rankin realized that he would, in some manner, have to break down that suspicious reserve before the prisoner would tell him anything. Neither threats nor severity, he saw, would avail him, only, perhaps, kindness. He began in gentle tones.

"Listen, Rogers, I've come to see about Mary Young, whom you must have loved at one time." At the name, Rogers flinched, and Rankin knew that the tragedy was not news to him. He had perhaps seen it in a paper, after his arrest. "You know how she died . . . I have hopes that you might tell me something that would aid me."

The prisoner stared hostilely, without unbending, watching the speaker. The distrust he felt became more apparent, and Rankin experienced a sense of helpless skirmishing with an expressionless image.

"You did love Mary Young, didn't you?" he pursued. "And every one who knew her must have loved her. Had circumstances been different, she might have reciprocated that love."

Was he using the correct approach? He studied the effect of the words. For an instant Rogers shifted restlessly, as though to avoid a painful recollection. He hastened to press the slight advantage.

"It's one of those things that can't be explained. Life is harsh in its way. But whatever Mary Young did, for either good or evil, she didn't deserve that horrible death she met under the knife. And I'm here to avenge her if it's humanly possible."

This time the words penetrated deeply. The listener shuddered and a quiver shook him. He regarded Rankin intensively, to search out his meaning.

"It was . . . terrible, wasn't it?" he said with an effort.

"Mary Young was stabbed to the heart. It was an underhanded blow. One who could stab so treacherously must be found. There should be no mercy for him; he deserves just what he gave—death. That is the law of existence by which we all live."

"That's right," came an awed, fascinated whisper. "He must die."

"And those who knew her must do their share in achieving that end." Rankin spoke swiftly and with increasing force. "Especially those who did more than merely know her. Those who loved her, who worshiped her, they owe her the greatest debt." He shot the question directly at Rogers. "You worshiped her, didn't you?"

The prisoner writhed under the spell of the voice. The words went home. Another quiver shook him and his hands trembled. He half rose toward the detective under the strain.

"My God!" he cried, with a fierce impetuosity. "You ask me if I loved her, whether I worshiped her! Of course I did! More than that—I adored the very ground she walked on. For who else do you think I did all this—plot months and months to rob my employers, worry, plan, and prepare? Who else but for her?"

His tongue was loosened, revealing a torrential passion, mad and uncontrolled. In his words Rankin recognized a highly strung, egoistic, racking bundle of strained nerves. In some way his unstable poise and bitter emotions were indicative of abnormality; of a neurotic type to whom in many phases, life is unbearable. For a moment his heart was softened by pity.

"You did that for her?"

"Yes, for her alone, and she never realized it. For weeks I had carried ideas in my head, to get money with which to marry her, to run away with her. I knew she was a fine lady; I could tell that from her manner. She'd have to have the best, and I was willing to risk anything to give it to her. It was all planned. When I told her what I knew about her lover, then she would come to me. I thought she would give him up for me because I loved her infinitely more.

"Listen." His eyes blazed like beacons in his sallow face. "Do you want to know who killed her? I'll tell you. It was that cur who caused her to discard my worthy love for his unworthy passion. I don't blame Mary for it, I only blame him, and I was determined to break that hold and bring her to me. I had long suspected him of dishonesty, and if I could only prove it, I believed she would leave him. She was too honest and clean for anything low. So I watched him for weeks till I finally found out. I got the goods on him. He was a bootlegger and mixed up with a low gang of crooks and killers."

Rogers broke off suddenly and swung to a new track.

"When I was to tell Mary, she'd give him up for me, and I'd get the needed money for both of us. We'd go off together, in perfect safety to Hot Springs, a pair of honeymooners no one would ever suspect."

Rankin hesitated to break in upon the stream of confession, but he wanted to fit in all the details.

"It was on Friday that you told her of this other man, wasn't it?" he asked.

"Yes, on Friday. Do you know who he is? James Norris. Get him for this terrible crime; make him swing for it! So sure was I of my plan that I bought our tickets beforehand, the tickets only, for I wasn't certain of berth arrangements. Then I told her. It was in the park, in the darkness. Just the place for lovers, so deserted and cool . . . and alone. . . ."

A spasm of pain crossed Rogers's face. He gasped and looked up with haggard features.

"If she had only listened to me then, if she had only come with me! She never knew how close to death she was when she refused me. I loved her so that I almost would have rather killed her than seen her in Norris's arms. But I was mistaken in the hold he had over her. It was strong, much too strong even for me to break. Instead of turning gratefully to me as she should have, Mary refused to believe it. Nothing I could say would persuade her of the truth. And then she left me there with nothing at all remaining but the ashes of my plans. I had to go through with them. But I hardly blame her, after all. It was only him, always him . . . damn him. . . ."

His voice trailed after the last bitter words, smoldering embers of a fire which, the next instant, flared into still brighter flames of venom and hatred.

"You say you want to get the man who killed little Mary Young. You even say you know him. So do I. And if there's a justice on this earth, you've got to capture James Norris."

The effort was too great. The next instant he collapsed upon the prison bench, his head bowed in folded arms. Convulsive sobs racked him for a moment, but presently he looked up again.

"I don't know why I should tell you all this. I can't do myself any harm, because they've got me. But you can't do anything for me. No one can. The best thing I can do is to take my medicine and be quiet."

"It won't be too hard," Rankin murmured encouragingly. "After all, yours wasn't so great a crime. And if it's a first offense, we'll try for leniency. Perhaps you'll get your chance yet."

When he left, many pieces of the puzzle had fallen into place. The quarrel in the park on Friday night, the early purchase of two tickets instead of one, the proven cause of the disagreement between Mary Young and her fiancé, all these problems were answered. Everything, in fact, but the original question. Who killed the girl?

Rankin had to admit he was confronted by a stone wall. The remarkable characteristic about the case was its illustration of how closely people's lives were intertwined. There was Mary Young as the connecting link of three total strangers, Charles Bond, James Norris, and Joseph Rogers. The life of each was far removed from the others and yet, through the girl, they were thrown together, their separate interests becoming bound into a tangled whole. Their not very smooth courses of life were caught up by an unforeseen maelstrom which caused to each of them distressing havoc. The cataclysm here had been the violent death of Mary Young; the resultant revelations were bewildering.

All three were now eliminated. Convinced of Norris's innocence, Rankin felt he could safely disregard Rogers's hysterical accusations, borne of no more potent basis than hatred and jealousy. His own knowledge told him it was a practical impossibility. What, then, was there left? Mary Young's unknown past. Somewhere in that hidden passage of time might lie the solution of his problem. His efforts to probe into it had been unproductive, but then he had not given it the attention he now felt it deserved. He must unearth those concealed years or admit failure.

His knowledge of Mary Young extended no farther than three months back. Previous to that, as far as he was concerned, she was nonexistent. It was obvious she was not an ordinary working-girl and he had long since come to the conclusion that she was refined and of good character. She might even have come from a family of wealth. He recalled the exquisite scarf she was wearing at the time she was killed, and the two expensive dresses he had found in her room. She had studiously avoided mentioning her past to any one; not even her lover was her confidant. And she had received no mail except the papers from Gary.

The recollection of the papers sent Rankin hurrying back to his rooms for another examination. There existed a sheer necessity that he should find something in them that would give him a suggestion from which to work. If necessary, he would go West and make investigations there. But every trail must have a starting point. Previous examinations of the papers, though thorough, had revealed nothing applicable to his case. Then, however, he had an oversupply of clues and there had been no urgency in his search. Now the situation demanded added perception and keenness.

For more than an hour Rankin inspected the papers. Carefully he covered all the personal columns—Births, Deaths, Marriages, Lost and Found, seeking for any possible item that might have even the remotest application to his problem. The real news items could be obtained in any paper; there would have been no need to procure Gary *Tribunes* for them. He searched for initials resembling the dead girl's. He scanned the advertisements and the local news. All in vain; none of it suggested anything to him. Near six o'clock he threw them aside in a fit of disgust and weariness.

Another telegram to the Gary authorities could be of no use. There was nothing for it but to make the trip himself. Even though he had no point of contact, and it might merely develop into a wild-goose chase. He had no choice in the matter.

The telephone bell jangled in his ears. Rankin lifted the receiver. Thomas was speaking.

"Hello! Is that you, Rankin? A telegram just came in that I thought might interest you. Listen to it. It's from Gary, Indiana.

"'Police inquiring into the whereabouts of Mildred Yaeger, heiress, missing from this town for three months. Description: height, five feet, six inches; age, twenty-one; brown hair; eyes gray; carries herself with poise. Further details to follow.'

"And it's signed, 'Frank Lowry, Chief of Police.'"

23
THE HOUSE OF THE DEAD

Tommy Rankin caught the Chicago-Western Flyer that left at one-fifteen Friday morning from Broad Street terminal. With light bag, ticket, and berth, fortunately obtained, he sped westward toward Gary and the Windy City. Despite the strange and unexpected development, he slept soundly. During the following day he mulled over the turn of events to grasp its significance to the fullest extent. Cleveland was reached in the early afternoon; Toledo, toward evening. All the while the clicking of the wheels under him with monotonous regularity fell into a rhythm which seemed to say, without any stretch of his imagination, "The right trail . . . the right trail."

Mary Young, secretary—Mildred Yaeger, heiress! Heiress of what, to whom? The initials were the same for both girls; the description which arrived just before he left was similar. Mildred Yaeger had been missing for three months, Mary Young had appeared three months ago as a boarder of Mrs. Schmidt. Rankin passed the time by studying the *Tribunes* again. This time, however, he searched for the name "Yaeger," and though he discovered nothing applicable to Mildred Yaeger, the name figured on the second page of every paper.

While the meaning of these paragraphs could not be conjectured, Rankin found them interesting. They were daily reports concerning the health and progress of one Lawrence Yaeger. Briefly, they indicated that he was stricken with cancer, that the disease was severely ravishing him; the tone of the dispatches showed that while there was no hope of recovery, at least the sick man was bravely holding his own. Lawrence Yaeger appeared to be a man of consequence, else these items would never have been printed. Their precise meaning in relation to his problem was doubtful. Rankin found all sorts of vague hypotheses running through his mind in regard to them, but he refused to consider them. His greatest fault had been the formulation of conclusions that afterward proved to have no basis in fact.

Other problems were equally intriguing. If Mildred Yaeger had been missing for three months, why should the Gary police delay their inquiry for her until the present date? Unless they did not know that she was missing until now. Why, then, at this particular moment? If they waited three months, why not four? There was some strange connection between the fatal illness the *Tribune* described and the sudden telegram, but what it was was unfathomable. Rankin decided to possess himself in patience till he reached his destination.

The Flyer drew into Gary close upon midnight of Friday. As it was too late to accomplish anything, Rankin sought a convenient hotel and registered for the night. The accommodations were fair; but with the problem ever on his mind, he slept fitfully. In the morning, a cold bath and a tasty breakfast revived him sufficiently, so that he felt prepared for any encounter. Inquiry at the hotel desk gained for him the location of the Police Bureau. A half hour later he was closeted with the Chief of Police.

Frank Lowry, head of the law in the Western steel town, was a stern-faced, lantern-jawed, capable-appearing officer of about forty-five, who looked as though he had won his position by ability, constant application to duty, and hard work. As Rankin introduced himself and explained his mission, he thought he detected an expression of relief. He told only as much as he deemed necessary to make for an understanding of the situation between them, and was relieved to find that Lowry possessed little curiosity and asked few questions. Until he had sounded the state of affairs in this Western town, he didn't want to show his own hand; his innate sense of safety warned him not to permit his true objective to become known in too many places. A cautious policy was always the best; and it always brought the best results. "And so you believe that Mildred Yaeger is the same girl as the one you are investigating in Philadelphia?" remarked Lowry, when he had finished. "Well, it looks mighty like it, I must say."

"Exactly that," Rankin replied. "And if it's true, it looks as though it's a bigger affair than I ever imagined. So what is it all about? Who is this Mildred Yaeger? How does it happen she is missing? And why haven't you been searching for her before this?"

"One question at a time." The Chief of Police smiled, though briefly. The next moment, his features became grim and serious. "They aren't so easily answered and to some of them I don't know the answer myself."

"What do you mean by that?"

"The people who are concerned in the affair are mum about it. They refuse to go into details, but, like a bolt from the clear sky, they come to me and say: 'Mildred Yaeger is missing. Go ahead and find her.'"

"That is peculiar. Who are the people concerned?"

"The most powerful, respectable, and wealthiest people in town. And for that reason I have no choice but to follow their advice and obey orders. Take a look at this." Lowry reached for a copy of the Gary *Tribune*, which lay upon his desk, and pointed to a column on the first page. "It's yesterday's paper. That's the start of the entire business as far as I can see."

Rankin obeyed. In large headlines, staring before him, was the following news:

MILLIONAIRE STEEL MAGNATE DIES IN GARY HOME AFTER FIGHT
Lawrence Yaeger Succumbs to Throat Cancer at 1:30 p. m. Yesterday.
Had been Ill Fifteen Months

A distinguished and respected citizen of Gary, Indiana, passed away at 1:30 yesterday after-noon *[Thursday, Rankin supplemented men-tally]* after a bitter struggle against a cancer infection of the esophagus which lasted over a period of fifteen months. Lawrence Yaeger, well-known steel king, and distinguished phil-anthropist, succumbed to the virulent attack in extreme pain, but remained brave to the very end. He was sixty-eight years old. The disease set in during the spring of 1926, but appeared to be combatable in its first stages. Doctor Sanford, eminent surgeon, who was his constant attendant, held out hopes for recovery throughout last fall and winter and every effort was bent in that direction. Late in May, however, increased infection and a closing of the throat made it clear that Mr. Yaeger's days were numbered. Nevertheless, all hope was not abandoned until a week ago, from which time Mr. Yaeger proceeded to sink very rapidly, until yesterday death came to him. He is survived by a nephew and a niece, the latter of whom is visiting some friends in the East. Both have been summoned and

are expected to arrive shortly. The people of
Gary, who have always possessed the greatest affection and respect for Mr. Yaeger, followed his condition as reported daily by the
Tribune, with great solicitation. The details
of the magnate's will and the disposal of his
estate will not be made public for some time,
according to Driscoll & Ellery, his attorneys.

Under this was a summary of the magnate's life work,
accomplishments, and charities, an imposing list of offices
he had held for both the town and the state. His wealth
was derived from the steel industry, for besides being one
of its directors, he was also a vice-president, and had a
controlling interest in several subsidiary industries.

When Rankin finished these details he folded the paper
and returned it to the desk. The Chief of Police watched
him shrewdly.

"Very interesting," commented the detective, "but I
must confess I'm at a loss to see the exact connection.
There were some papers from Gary in Mary Young's room,
and I did notice some items with regard to the magnate's
sickness. But whether they have anything to do with my
problem, unless his death makes Mildred Yaeger an heiress—"

"That's just it. Although, as the paper says, the details are kept under cover, so I really don't know. But that
item about the niece visiting friends in the East—that's
the crux of the entire matter."

"In what way?"

"As a matter of fact, that niece is Mildred Yaeger, and
she is neither in the East, nor, as far as we know, has she
been notified of her uncle's decease. That's just the story
that has been handed to the papers. She is the missing
girl."

Rankin began to see light. "I understand. But if she's not visiting, where in the world is she and what's the idea of all the secrecy?"

The chief made a hopeless gesture.

"I wish I knew," he replied, "but I don't. On Thursday afternoon Lawrence Yaeger died, with Dr. Sanford, his housekeeper, Mrs. Herman, and, I believe, Driscoll, his lawyer, in attendance. Three hours later, Driscoll came into this office with the information that Mildred Yaeger is missing and must be found. He gave me her description and said that she had left home three months ago. And then he went out."

"And that was all he said? No reasons or explanations?"

"Not a single one. I asked for further details, but he refused them. A good many of us knew Miss Mildred—a sweet girl and popular with the younger set of the town. Naturally, I wanted to know more about it. About three months ago—I should say it was early in May, just before old Yaeger's illness became critical—it was known that she had left town. A news item in the society column announced that she was going East to see friends and perhaps go to a girls' college there in the fall. So, naturally, no one thought anything more about it."

"But it was untrue, of course?"

"I suppose it was, from what Driscoll said."

"Which was—"

"That the girl had left home for an utterly different reason—and no one knew where she had gone. But he said that now, since the old man had died, she must be located and brought home at once."

Rankin pursed his lips and wrinkled his forehead in thought.

"A different reason, eh? What was it? Surely he must have told you that."

"No, he refused to tell me a thing, though you may be sure I asked about it. But Driscoll said that I had enough information for my purpose to work on and that those things were strictly family matters which couldn't possibly come within my scope and aid me."

"What sort of a person is this Driscoll? It looks as though he were a martinet."

"Driscoll, of Driscoll & Ellery?" Lowry's tone expressed the awe he felt. "They are the largest and most powerful law firm in this part of the state. Ordinarily, I'd insist on having the rest of the story or I'd refuse to go on with the work. But one can't very well buck against them."

"Oh, one can't!" Rankin's voice indicated his pugnacious mood. Not only would he buck the firm, but he would get his information. He had come too far and worked too hard to be frightened away by officialdom.

"So I merely went on," continued Lowry, "and proceeded to make the necessary inquiries and notified other cities in regard to the disappearance. Nothing has turned up so far and if results weren't forthcoming to-day they were considering hiring a private firm."

"I'll do my best to make that unnecessary. And you can tell me nothing further than that the girl went away for three months, for some unknown cause, to some unknown place. Do you think this law concern is sincere in its desire to find the girl? Or mightn't it serve their interests better if she were not located?"

The suggestion shocked Frank Lowry. "Certainly they are sincere. The Driscolls and Yaegers have been the closest friends for years; Mr. Driscoll is, in fact, Miss Mildred's godfather, and he certainly was attached to her. I believe this secrecy is in her own interest."

"But this Yaeger family—they appear to be one of the wealthiest in town." Rankin was unconvinced. "At what would you place their wealth?"

"The exact amount is not known, but it is tremendous. I should say it is in the neighborhood of ten million dollars. They are also the town's oldest family and all that sort of thing. But the lawyers know more about those affairs than I—if they'll tell you."

"And yet, that sum is a big stake, you'll agree to that."

The other nodded acquiescence. "But not to Driscoll & Ellery," he added hastily. "It isn't a case of rascally lawyers cheating their clients, you may be sure of that."

Rankin was almost persuaded. Nevertheless, it was not a possibility to be overlooked; he would make up his mind when he interviewed the firm. He glanced at his watch and discovered it was ten o'clock.

"And you believe Mildred Yaeger falls heir to the entire sum?"

"Well, I wouldn't say entire sum; but the greatest proportion of it, most likely. Otherwise, I can hardly see any object in the rush about finding her. Or why else do they keep the details under cover? I believe they are waiting till she is found."

Rankin rose abruptly and extended his hand. "I think the best thing for me is to go around and see Driscoll. There must be something to be learned. Being Saturday, they might close early and I want to get them in. Perhaps the best thing is for you to inform them of my arrival, but don't tell them anything more than that. Merely that I'm an accredited police representative who might know something about Miss Yaeger. Now, where did you say the office was?"

"Eight-forty, the Ellery Building, along this very street, three blocks up. You can't very well miss it if you keep on going. Will I see you again?"

"Perhaps you might. It all depends on what turns up. And where is old Yaeger's place?"

"Two-thirty Armour Avenue, but you'll have to take a trolley to get there. Incidentally, Lawrence Yaeger is to be buried to-day, and you might find it interesting to be present."

When Rankin took his departure he had no intention of visiting the dead man's attorneys. Not, at least, until he had unearthed something more about them and his mission. As Lowry remarked, he might have difficulties in obtaining information from the wary law firm, with his slim basis of knowledge. And what better place could he find more than at the old man's home, the home of Mildred Yaeger, of—? It was yet to be proven that she was Mary Young. Accordingly, he set out for the magnate's residence.

It proved to be an oddly gabled and fashioned mansion of early limestone. The gables protruded, almost without plan, from all corners, as though the house, immense as it was, had merely grown up haphazardly. Yet the effect was merely curious and quaint instead of being ugly, for there was an air of the majestic about the rambling structure. A neatly trimmed garden with a hedge inclosed both the house and grounds with a special exclusiveness that not all of Charles Bond's estate had succeeded in giving to his mansion.

The woman who opened the door fitted well with the sedate character of the place. Quiet and timid, perhaps sixty-five, she was homely in her age. But sweetness and gentleness, without weakness, were written in her kindly features. Her downcast, awed look clearly showed her visitor she expected him to be as silent and sad as was the hushed and sorrowful house. Rankin saw the black crêpe upon the door, and the drawn shades and, as he stepped into the hall, caught the atmosphere of death.

Unconsciously he lowered his voice as he spoke.

"I've come to help you and Mr. Driscoll find Miss Yaeger. You are Mrs. Herman, aren't you?"

The statement caused no surprise in the woman's face. She had not expected him, but she must have known that investigation and search were going on for the missing girl. Not only that, thought the detective, but she must also know why Mildred Yaeger was missing.

"That's right," came the hushed reply, and there was quiet homage in her tone. "I'm Mrs. Herman, and I've been housekeeper for Mr. Yaeger and Miss Mildred these many years. I raised Miss Mildred since her mother died. Oh, I do hope you bring her home, where she belongs on such an hour as this."

Rankin felt strangely hypocritical in the presence of this reverent woman. "I'll do my best," was all he could reply.

"Won't you come in and sit down?"

He followed Mrs. Herman within the door which she closed softly behind them. They passed down a gloomy hall, beyond a room the tall panels of which swung partly closed. She paused there, he in step, and through the door came the cloying odor of flowers, heavy, almost stifling. A flicker of light accompanied it.

"That's where the master is sleeping."

For an instant Mrs. Herman appeared on the verge of continuing her passage, but much to her companion's relief, she changed her mind. Rankin was most anxious to see the old man, and curiosity was not his motive. With tears in her eyes, the woman opened the door, and there was an infinite affection and tenderness in her voice.

"There he is—Lawrence Yaeger. It's rather late to see him now, isn't it, sir? A wonderful man, sir, and a fine master."

He barely noted the darkened room, the magnificent coffin of inlaid mahogany, the mountain of floral offerings, the two candles flickering majestically at the head. Rankin's entire attention was riveted upon the face of the

dead man. All its whiteness could not disguise its kindli-
ness and power—in the open eyes which seemed to glisten
in the moving shadow, in its firm, kindly mouth, in its
snow-white hair. The smoothed features were handsome
in age and death, for the ravages of months of suffering
no longer appeared on the high forehead and proud brow.
Indeed, Lawrence Yaeger seemed to be calmly and peace-
fully sleeping; at any moment he might rise from his couch
of flowers to take charge of affairs.

The housekeeper shut the door, and Rankin believed
he felt a moistness in his own eyes. His mission came to
him with double force in that moment; it was not only to
capture the murderer of Mary Young, but also of Mildred
Yaeger. If they should prove the same, the criminal's havoc
would bring sorrow to two sets of people.

"You can still make him happy," Mrs. Herman broke
into a deadly silence which enveloped them for almost a
moment, "if you bring Mildred back to us. That was his
last thought when he died."

"I'll do my best," he replied, "and you must assist me
in every way. Would you mind if I saw Miss Yaeger's room?
There might be something there that will help."

"Do you think so? It was searched before, but nothing
was found. It hasn't been touched otherwise since Mildred
went away. God knows where she went, and for such little cause, just like the foolish, spoiled child that she was,
three full months ago. Just dusted, but undisturbed. Mr.
Yaeger was always hoping she'd return before he passed
away. They could comfort each other in the last moments.
That's all she was—a headstrong child."

She led the way up a broad staircase with a kingly balustrade, under a glistening crystal chandelier. At a landing
in the steps an ancient grandfather clock stood, ticking
the hour.

"We've taken out the chimes since Thursday," Mrs. Herman whispered. "And such heavenly chimes they were. Every hour, sir, they played for Mr. Yaeger and Mildred. She loved to sit and wait for them to play."

With a heavy sigh she continued on up the steps. Into an upper hallway Rankin was led, richly carpeted and also shaded from light; beyond several doors. The hush was oppressive to him; an eerie feeling stole through him as Mrs. Herman paused before a tightly closed door and, key in hand, opened it.

"This is it, her room, waiting for her just as it was when she rushed away. It was wrong of her to think that her uncle would consider anything but her good. And she went just the same; so quickly none of us knew anything about it till it was too late."

What she was saying was important, the detective was aware. Yet he was not even listening. His eyes were held in a tight bond, his attention unbreakably riveted. For across the room, beyond the deep and luxurious bedstead, the mahogany bureau, the dainty rosewood chairs, the slight davenport, was a chiffonier. On it were toilet articles, perfumes, cream, lying in the disorder in which they had evidently been left three months ago. And there, also, was a picture. It was of a girl, in riding cap, with finely molded features, a straight nose, gracious lips, curved in a captivating smile that revealed pearly teeth. There was a delicate chin and swan-like neck; the eyes beamed with joy and happiness of life. It was a portrait of the mistress of the room—of Mildred Yaeger. It was Mary Young.

24
OUT OF THE PAST

Tommy Rankin felt awkward and apologetic as he proceeded to make a survey of that dainty room under the eye of Mrs. Herman. He could not send her away from the chamber over which she watched with such obvious pride and care; and yet, neither could he forego a necessary investigation. So he compromised by permitting her to remain. It was a spotless, speckless room, in pale gold and pink shades; a young girl's boudoir. In the arrangement of the furnishings was an artistic daintiness; they were placed much after the same plan of the cruder furniture in Mary Young's boarding-house room. There was something pathetic in that.

Rankin passed quickly over the private bureau, which contained nothing but clothing and gave the closet, filled with gowns of the richest quality, but a cursory glance. If necessary, he could return to them later for a minute search. The chiffonier, with the little desk, that occupied one corner of the room, alone interested him. In the former were little fineries which girls possess—gewgaws, toilet articles, pins, and jewelry. They told him nothing. All of it had been left when the mistress, for a cause as yet unknown, fled the house. No evidence of wealth had been discovered in Mary Young's room, except the two dresses which had been taken along.

He turned his attention to the desk. It was of dark walnut, the only article which failed to fit into the chamber's color scheme, evidently added as an extra and needed convenience. The waste basket that lay beside it was uncleaned of paper; even that had not been disturbed. Rankin opened the desk top and removed a pile of papers, pushed into the shelving or lying scattered in no particular order in the drawers. He could glance but briefly through them now; on first view, they all appeared to be letters—social invitations and gossip from friends, for the most part. And one appeared to be a love epistle from one, Bobby. There were also some checks, returned from a Gary bank, some Chicago theater programs, and greeting cards. The most recent was dated as far back as May 10 and now it was late August.

The waste basket received his attention next. And here Rankin unearthed his first clue to the tangle for the solution of which he had traveled West. In it were three pieces of letter paper, crumpled as though thrown away in disgust. One by one he lifted them out and smoothed them carefully for examination. The first one began:

Dear Uncle:

Nothing followed the salutation but a blank and a huge blot; the sheet had been discarded into the basket, for another at once. On the next sheet the writer had made a little progress.

Dear Uncle:
I simply can't go through with it. I must—

Evidently the author considered the start too abrupt for that also ended suddenly. The detective realized the import of these notes. They were farewell notes, letters addressed to Lawrence Yaeger on the eve, perhaps at the very moment, of flight. Clearly, Mildred Yaeger was trying to word a suitable explanation for her deed. Eagerly he turned to the next paper.

Dearest Uncle:

When I consider how good you have been to me these many years, I hesitate to cause you even a moment's pain. I know I seem like a most ungrateful girl in this act but I can see no other way out of it. Your plan with regard to Bob and me has been a most cherished one for so long that I can not expect you to fore-go it. And yet, though I have done my best to obey you, for your sake alone and for what I owe you, I simply can not go through with it. And so, rather than remain here and bring further sorrow—

The letter ceased there, indicating that the girl had tried still another rewriting. And how difficult it was to write at all. Under what stress had Mildred Yaeger left home? What was this plan in regard to Bob and her which she could not go through with? The completed epistle must have been found on the girl's desk after her flight; but this one told Rankin a great deal and left him satisfied with the results of his search. He turned to the silent, watchful housekeeper.

"I think that will be all here, Mrs. Herman. And I want to thank you for making the search so easy for me.

"That's all right, sir," she replied, "if it only serves to bring Miss Mildred back. I'd be willing to do anything for that. Do you think you'll be able to find her?"

"Locate her, certainly." Rankin clung painfully to the barest truth. "But more than that is difficult to promise.

And I expect you to tell me just what happened here. I must have material to work with. You understand that, of course."

The pointed tone caused her to nod vigorously.

"I do indeed, sir, and I'll be only too glad to if you can promise to bring the poor girl to us. Mr. Driscoll warned me not to answer any questions, but he meant, of reporters and such like. This is different, I'm sure, for he wants her found as much as I do." She paused and then added in explanation, "Mr. Driscoll is the family lawyer."

"Yes, I know that. And remember, Mrs. Herman, you must keep nothing from me. I want perfect frankness."

She showed him into a cubbyhole of a room which contained only a sewing-machine and two deep rockers.

"My private sitting-room," she explained with some pride as she invited him to a chair. "We can be comfortable here. And now," she smoothed her apron carefully, "what can I tell you, sir?"

Rankin made an embracing gesture. "Everything, Mrs. Herman. The cause of Miss Yaeger's leaving, and what occurred both before and afterward."

"Well, I hardly know how to begin. The situation has been developing such a long time. Miss Yaeger is Mr. Yaeger's niece, raised here ever since she was a tiny tot just old enough to walk. You see, her mother died in childbirth, and her father just two years later, from grief. Mr. Yaeger never married, himself, but he loved children very much. He felt a deep affection for her and he had her brought here and gave her everything she wanted, just like a father would. And he was just as good to little Bobby Girard. . . ."

"Bobby Girard? Who is he?"

"Besides his brother, who was Miss Mildred's father, Mr. Yaeger also had a sister, Miss Clara Yaeger. Bobby was her son. That was an unfortunate affair in the family, and it caused much scandal. Miss Clara was always a wild one in those days, over twenty years ago; but no one ever dreamed she would run away the way she did. Not even Mr. Yaeger's money could hush up the disgrace of it."

"Who did she run away with?" Rankin was determined to collect all the details; later he would sort the relevant ones from the others.

"A good-for-nothing salesman by the name of Julius Girard, who used to pass through the town and, in some way, got to meet the girl. She always had romantic ideas about her prince that would some day arrive, but no one ever imagined there was anything at all between them until it was too late. But he soon proved what a rascal he was, for he deserted Miss Clara when she had a baby and he's never been heard of since.

"We didn't hear from Miss Clara or anything about her after that for nine years, though they scoured the country for her. Then came the news that she had died, but the boy was left with some very lovely people in New York. Not rich people, but they were very good to him and came to like him immensely; and when Bobby's mother was gone they were beginning to take good care of him. Of course, Mr. Yaeger wouldn't allow them to do that always so he sent them money for him. And after a while he brought the boy out here, to keep Miss Mildred company. He was just eleven then—a little older than she—and they should have gotten along famously.

"I think it was then that all the trouble started. Bobby was such a clever little boy that Mr. Yaeger took a great liking to him; and he got the idea that it would be a wonderful thing if they—the boy and the girl—should grow up together and finally be married, so that they'd have each other and he'd have together the only relatives he had in the entire world. And in the end, I suppose, they'd get everything he possessed, because he had no one else to leave it to. And when older people once get an idea like that, they just hang on to it like glue.

"But Miss Mildred, even that early, didn't like Bobby. All the rest of us thought the world of him, but not she; somehow she couldn't stand him. I remember when she came in one day, crying because she said he had pinched her; she told me she hated him then. And she claimed he was cruel—that he would catch the pretty little butter-flies she loved so well and stick pins in them. Of course, we wouldn't believe that, and I used to say what a foolish little girl she was to imagine such things, especially since Bobby denied ever doing them.

"In 1917, when he was thirteen, Mr. Yaeger sent him East again to a boarding-school, and he stayed there for many years; and when he wasn't at school he remained with these people who raised him. In fact, he never came home since then, and we've never seen him again until just recently."

"What school was that, Mrs. Herman?"

"A private school named Marcus's, a very exclusive place it was; and Bobby was there until he was seventeen. It is in New York City. Then he went to another school—I don't think I remember the name—and after that he went to Columbia for two years. He didn't do so well as we ex-pected there, and when he left we didn't hear of him again for some time—maybe three years. So, you see, he was quite grown up when he turned up again. Mr. Yaeger was properly worried as to what became of him, but he used to say to me: 'Sowing his wild oats, maybe. Well, so much the better for him. When he comes back to Mildred and me, he'll be ready to settle down.'"

"In other words, that plan of marriage continued with him all through the years. There was no change?"

"That's it exactly, sir." Mrs. Herman inclined her head in a slight nod. "The longer Mr. Yaeger had it in mind, the better it seemed to him. So finally it was all settled that the marriage was to take place."

"And Miss Mildred," Rankin put in, "how did she take it? Was she willing or not?"

"That's just the tragic part about the whole affair. As soon as she was old enough to know what Mr. Yaeger was talking about, he spoke to her of it. Naturally, she wanted to please him, for she believed that anything he arranged would be for her good; and she said she'd be willing to do it if it satisfied him. That's just how they got along together. But the older she got the more unpleasant and repugnant—that was the very word she used—the thought was to her. She used to confide in me, that was just like a mother to her, how awful was the thought of such a marriage, prearranged like that, with no love in it at all."

"But I thought you said that she never saw her cousin from the time he was twelve or thirteen years old until recently."

"That's true—in fact, Miss Mildred never saw him since at all, for she was already gone when he arrived. That's why she went—because he was coming. But she remembered him, even though she had been a little girl; and she came to hate the memory of him. Many is the time she told me so, and when she was older—at fifteen or sixteen. But she wouldn't tell her uncle, because he was so happy in the arrangement and it seemed so fine to him, that she couldn't bear to cross his wishes. So she just kept on being unhappy."

She leaned forward confidentially toward the detective and lowered her voice.

"But I know this, sir, that if Mr. Yaeger had ever suspected how sorrowful he was making her, he would have dropped the idea, no matter how precious it was to him. But of course he didn't know; he thought she was satisfied; and she never let him find out any different. And of course

I couldn't interfere, being just a housekeeper, though I told Miss Mildred to let her uncle know how her heart felt about it. Often I told her, but she wouldn't; she owed him so much that she was afraid to be thought ungrateful. So what could I do for her?"

"And then young Girard came home. Is that it?"

"Oh, no, not yet, sir. But when the master was taken ill a year ago he thought it would be wonderful if Miss Mildred and Mr. Bob should marry and settle down in case anything should happen to him."

More and more, light was falling into the dark places. Every sentence uttered by the housekeeper unraveled a part of the tangled skein Rankin had set out to unwind.

"How did you find him then," he asked, "if you hadn't heard from him or didn't know where he was?"

"Well, we wrote to those people who practically raised him, in New York. He used to write from there to Miss Mildred, during his college days—little love letters which I know she hated to get. They made her more angry because, you see, there was no love in the entire situation. She tore them up, and I know she never answered him. Maybe she might have kept one or two, and if so they'd be in that bundle of letters you found in the desk."

At that moment a faint ringing reached them from below. Mrs. Herman started nervously, and, after arranging her apron, rose swiftly.

"That's probably Mr. Driscoll. It will never do to keep him waiting. I forgot, he's coming up to make the final arrangements for the funeral. It is to be at four o'clock."

As soon as she was gone, Rankin removed the letters from his inner pocket, where he had placed them, and searched out the message that had been signed by "Bob." The year of the message, he observed, was 1923.

Dearest Mildred:

Just a line from your future fiancé to let you know that he is in good health; so you needn't worry about him. I'm attending Columbia, and the work is quite difficult so I'm kept sufficiently busy to be unable to write such lengthy love epistles as I know you'd appreciate receiving. On my first recess I might possibly come West, in which case I shall expect a welcome such as befits me. I'll let you know more definitely later.

The sarcasm and the affectation of superiority in the words were apparent. In Rankin's opinion, they indicated the writer as a cad. Evidently he knew of the girl's distaste for him and it was nothing less than a sardonic defiance of her emotions, as though he were sure of his own prospects and position. Yet so cleverly worded that to the uninitiated, ignorant of the situation, there was nothing at all loathsome about it. Small wonder, then, that Mildred Yaeger hated the man she had never seen; she must have kept this letter only because it was more nasty than others he had sent.

Rankin contemplated the other information he had gained. To what it led was clear enough; it only needed more details for the sake of filling in. The girl—he preferred to think of her as Mary Young—left home rather than carry through the arrangement her uncle had made that she wed her cousin. She sought her own freedom and happiness in a way that would suit herself. When it became clear to her that the plan was to be hastened to completion, she determined to escape before it was too late.

He knew why she had left home. How did it aid him in his quest for her murderer? Rankin was certain of one

thing, in an uncertain situation—that Bob Girard, wherever he was, would be a decidedly interesting person to
meet. And so would the lawyer, Driscoll.

The appearance of the housekeeper interrupted his
ruminations. Behind her stood a tall, portly man in high
hat, swallow-tail coat, and spats; in his hand he held a cane.
Although his features did not especially recommend themselves to the detective, they were not the crafty, beady ones
he had expected to find. True, the heavy lips and the ro-
tund cheeks betokened stubbornness and shrewdness; there
was no question that he was an egoist of the first degree,
vain and self-satisfied. But the eyes had a softness in them,
most uncharacteristic in a hard-minded business man.

Mrs. Herman was clearly uncomfortable and nervous.
Her appearance indicated her on the verge of tears, and
the lawyer's foreboding features told Rankin that she had
been upbraided for the indiscretion of talking to him.

"This is Mr. Driscoll, sir," she said. "But you haven't
told me your name—"

"Never mind that, Mrs. Herman," the lawyer broke in
in a cold falsetto tone. "I'll find that out soon enough.
Just leave us to ourselves, will you please?"

He stared at her menacingly and waited till she had
withdrawn and the door closed behind her. Rankin started
to rise, but he motioned him to be seated. He followed the
example, and when he spoke his voice was cold and hard.

"Now, sir, will you kindly tell me the meaning of this?"

Rankin was undisturbed by the assumption of authority. "The meaning of what, may I ask?"

"My dear sir, there's no use your beating around the
bush. I know all about your coming here and asking questions. You've been, to use a vulgar expression, pumping
Mrs. Herman, haven't you?"

"Well, you can call it that if you will." Rankin regarded
the walls with apparent interest.

"Ha!" Driscoll cried emphatically. "So you admit it! By what right and authority do you come here with these questions?"

"So Lowry has told you nothing about me?" The lawyer was less dangerous than he appeared and when he hesitated at the words Rankin resolved to take the bull by the horns. If necessary, he would tell him the truth; though he desired to postpone that evil moment as long as possible. But to an agreement with Driscoll, he must undoubtedly come.

"Yes, Lowry called me up and informed me of your arrival and I have been awaiting your coming at my office ever since. Certainly that gives you no privilege to come here and intrude upon sacred grief."

"If I have done that, Mr. Driscoll, I am sorry; but I believe your chief objection to my appearance here is that I might discover something that you do not choose to tell me!"

"Sir! Do you mean to insinuate that I have something to conceal or keep secret? I'll have you understand—"

"Mr. Driscoll," Rankin broke in upon the indignation of the other, "it is best for you and me to come to an understanding at once. I have come for information and I do not propose to be balked in obtaining it. I can well understand your care in handling the delicate matters of your client, though I admit that all your motives are not very clear—"

"Who are you to question my behavior?"

"I am not questioning it at all. I am merely making a suggestion. I have information, myself, which I will willingly exchange with you; but it must be a fair exchange." Rankin held up his hand to check an eager question from the lawyer. "I shall say nothing until you are ready to be frank with me in the matter of why Mildred Yaeger is missing."

Driscoll faced forward in his seat.

"So you have some information, too! What is it? Do you think you have located her?"

"Whether I have or not is another matter. I have most of your story already. I know, for instance, of Mr. Yaeger's desire to marry his niece to his nephew, and of Miss Yaeger's secret unwillingness to agree. And that, I surmise, is the cause of her leaving home. But I would prefer to hear from you."

Driscoll studied his opponent, and evidently came to the conclusion he was not to be despised. The lawyer's native policy was one of craft and caution; he had always found cunning to be the best means of obtaining his ends. And even with the seriousness of the situation confronting him, he could not bring himself to be thoroughly candid. To an outside observer this battle of wits between two careful men, each determined that the other speak first, would have been most fascinating.

"You seem to be well informed, sir," Driscoll remarked. "What else do you know?"

"I have also learned the entire tale of Bob Girard's boyhood and of the completion of the marriage arrangement. You realize, Mr. Driscoll, I am concealing nothing. It would be best if you'd follow the same policy with me, for then we shall both be satisfied."

Still the other hesitated, and Rankin realized the time for the exact truth had arrived.

"The matter I am concerned with," he went on, "and that you are concerned with, is far more serious than either a runaway or a mere disappearance. Your refusal to speak forces me to be painfully open and frank."

There was alarm in the lawyer's voice.

"What do you mean, Mr. Rankin—more serious?"

"It has to do with murder, sir!"

Driscoll's eyes widened in surprise and wonder, as though he failed to comprehend. With that act the detective's half-formed and vague suspicions of his adversary vanished. The surprise and astonishment were too sincere to have been the product of plan or practice. There was no question of the shock the words produced.

"Murder, sir!" he cried. "Murder? Of what—of whom—?"

"Of a young girl, last Sunday night, in Philadelphia. It will be a week to-morrow. It happened in a park resort, sir, on a scenic railway. You might have seen something about it."

"In a park? Why, I believe I did observe something of the sort in the papers, though ordinarily I never bother with such scandal. But what possibly could this have to do with that—with Miss Mildred Yaeger—?"

Driscoll saw the look akin to pity in Rankin's eyes. A chill ran through him, causing him to quiver in horror and widen his eyes with a sudden, horrible comprehension. Distress makes the whole world kin, and he felt an old man, in need of support, as he grasped the other's arm.

"You don't mean— It can't be that— Good God! it's impossible that the girl is—" He failed to finish the thought.

"Exactly, Mr. Driscoll. Much as I regret to have to tell you, the dead girl is Mildred Yaeger."

25

LAWRENCE YAEGER'S WILL

"I can well understand, Mr. Rankin, how important a matter the will of Mr. Yaeger is, in the light of what you have just told me."

The first shock caused by Rankin's words over, and the story of the crime, and the ensuing investigation, as far as it was applicable to the present situation, narrated, Driscoll capitulated completely. Indeed, his surrender had the characteristics of a collapse; he found himself clinging to the detective for moral support. There was no question that he felt a great affection for the dead girl; and the knowledge of her terrible end was a blow. It was some time before he thoroughly recovered his capacity for leadership.

When they had covered the same ground that Mrs. Herman had gone over, the detective turned to the subject upon which, he believed, the entire tangle hinged. It was his question that elicited the remark from Mr. Driscoll.

"For if Mildred died last Sunday," the lawyer went on, "and Mr. Yaeger passed away but two days ago, it means then"—he paused to follow the trend of his thoughts— "that young Girard inherits the entire fortune."

"Ah!" Rankin's suspicions were confirmed. "I have been expecting that. Precisely, then, what were the terms of the will?"

"That Mildred was heir to practically everything, but that, in case she died—" Driscoll broke off abruptly and produced from an inner pocket a sealed and folded document. "Here, as it happens, I have a copy of the will with me. You can see the terms for yourself. It will save a trip to my office, later."

Rankin broke open the seal expectantly, and scanned the paper thoroughly with a practiced eye. It was a lengthy, legal affair, with the usual preliminaries and "wherefores"; these he passed over, to run swiftly through the column of bequests. There was a long list of them to charities and various institutions, all in substantial amounts, but none seriously diminishing the immense fortune Lawrence Yaeger had amassed during his lifetime.

The date, strangely enough, was quite recent—May 15 of the present year—three months ago, approximately. If Mildred Yaeger had fled on the 10th of May then the will was newly made, following her flight. For—and Rankin had yet to make sure of the exact date—whatever motive, this was certainly a most curious proceeding.

At last he came to the paragraphs he sought.

> To Mrs. Herman, for her long and devoted years of service, I give and bequeath, to be hers, free of all bonds, the sum of 30,000 dollars.
>
> To the son of my sister, my nephew, Robert Girard, I leave in trust until he is thirty years of age the sum of 200,000 dollars, the interest of which he is to receive yearly until such time when the entirety is to be turned over to him. The firm of Driscoll & Ellery is to administer this fund.
>
> The residue of my estate, both real and personal, I devise and grant to my beloved

niece, the daughter of my brother Richard, Mildred Yaeger, and to her heirs. Except in the case that she should predecease me, when the entire estate shall pass immediately upon her death to the aforesaid mentioned Robert Girard, in the addition to the aforesaid trust fund, and to his heirs after him.

As Rankin returned the document, its significance came to him with double force. It gave him the strongest motive for the crime. Mildred Yaeger was the heiress of an immense fortune, and her cousin was left a sum that was paltry, in comparison. In case, however, Mildred died before her uncle, everything—an amount, in lands, money, and bonds, of perhaps eight million dollars—automatically reverted to Robert Girard. When the will was made there had appeared no possibility that the girl would predecease Lawrence Yaeger; and that, nevertheless, was precisely what had occurred.

Driscoll regarded the detective studiously until he repocketed the document. He spoke a single word.

"Well?"

"It is a very strange will," Rankin commented, "and it is very recent. The date is May the fifteenth. Surely that is not the original will."

The lawyer permitted himself a slight smile. "That is correct. It was a will made four days after the foolish girl had taken flight. Naturally, we did not want the true cause of it known, since it was purely a family matter; so it was given out that she had gone East to visit friends. But this act of my client's"—he spoke as though Lawrence Yaeger were still alive and in the briskness of health, instead of a silent, lifeless clay below—"proved that she was an unnecessarily headstrong and foolish girl. Mr. Yaeger was an eminently reasonable and affectionate man, and had he ever dreamt that she was so unhappy about his plan, he would never have pressed her to complete her marriage."

The very words, practically, that Mrs. Herman had used. It was evident to the listener that a terrible mistake, arising from mutual affection and growing into mutual misunderstanding, had been made. That mistake was at least partially responsible for the tragedy. Had it not been made, Mildred Yaeger would probably be safe at home, enjoying her inheritance, instead of in a distant grave, under an assumed name.

"In what way does it indicate that?" Rankin asked.

"You see, my client had no idea how opposed Miss Mildred really was to his scheme—he never thought that she felt so bitter about it—not until it was too late. She had then run away, and in a note she left told him all about it. I believe I have the note in my office. We had private detectives out, searching for her on the quiet, for we didn't care to have anything known. Even young Girard joined in the hunt when he arrived. And meanwhile, to show his good faith, my client changed the terms of his will at once."

"What were the original terms, then?"

"They provided," replied the lawyer, "for the passage of the estate on various dates. On the day of the marriage between young Girard and Miss Mildred there was to be a handsome marriage settlement as a gift; on the birth of the first child, another portion passed. And on the death of my client, it all went equally to the husband and wife. You see, it was written upon the assumption that there would be a marriage. But that was all changed in the second will. It was drawn on the fourteenth of May and completed on the fifteenth."

"So that, by this first will, Girard would inherit an equal share, but by the will in operation to-day he stood to lose almost everything unless Miss Mildred died before her uncle?"

"Exactly!" The detective's statement was such a casual one that Driscoll replied before he realized its implications. He regarded Rankin apprehensively, and the look became a fixed gaze. "You are thinking that Bob Girard killed his cousin because of that. But I won't believe it—I couldn't think that he would be responsible for such a horrible deed."

"Perhaps not; for your sake, even, I sincerely hope not. But you must admit that the facts point to it as a possibility. Did young Girard, by any chance, know of the new will?"

The lawyer shook his head slowly. Clearly Rankin's suspicions distressed him.

"As it happens, he did—that's what makes it seem so bad. And he found it out in a most peculiar manner, too, for ordinarily I would never discuss or make public my client's business. On the tenth of May, Mildred Yaeger fled; and we found her farewell note on the eleventh. She went then, you see, because her future husband was scheduled to arrive in the week. She could not face him. I could never quite understand her aversion to him. To me he seemed quite a personable young man."

Rankin, recalling the letter the "personable young man" had penned his unwilling fiancée, believed that he could; but he said nothing.

"Actually," went on the lawyer, "young Girard did not arrive till a week after Mildred's disappearance, and we were still in an uproar about it. Then, the next day, he came to me in my private office and requested an interview. Somewhat puzzled to know what he could want particularly of me, I granted it. And he amazed me by asking me for one hundred thousand dollars from his estate on the strength of his prospects."

"One hundred thousand?" Rankin broke in, in amazement. "That's quite a sum. Did he say what he wanted it for?"

"No, he didn't. That was the surprising part of it. He merely refused to tell me a thing except that he had to have it at once. He said it was absolutely necessary and that he would return it with interest as soon as he was married."

"If he wanted it so badly, why didn't he go to his uncle?"

"I asked him that, too; I even suggested that he might possibly get it if he did so. But he evidently knew Yaeger as well as I do in the matter of finances. My client, though wealthy, knew the value of money, and would have demanded an accounting of it. And that was the one thing he was not willing to give. He merely kept on reiterating that he had to have it."

Rankin pondered the matter a moment. "It sounds pretty urgent. Do you think it might have been for gambling debts or something of the sort?"

"Yes, I thought of that and mentioned it to him as a possibility. From the look on his face, I think it must have been correct. But he refused to admit anything. And then there was no course left in the face of his insistence but to explain that there was to be no marriage and that he had no real prospects left.

"Of course, it was a terrible shock to him and he raised all sorts of a rumpus while I tried to explain exactly what had happened. He was fearfully excited, though ordinarily he was almost cold-blooded in temperament, I thought. I must confess that the reason I have been so secretive with regard to the estate was that I feared young Girard's arrival; and when he learned that Miss Mildred had not yet been found he might have started some trouble that would make public our difficulties. But of course, since he is the heir, I shall endeavor to get in touch with him at once and bring him home."

"It seems to me the natural thing he would have done, was to have gone to see Mr. Yaeger about his being disinherited. Didn't he try to do something of the sort?"

"He did, indeed—in fact, that was the very first thing he desired to do. But, unfortunately, it was impossible. On that very day Mr. Yaeger's illness took its most serious turn, and after that he was dangerously sick. Till then he had been suffering, of course, but it took a sudden, turn for the worse which was not entirely unexpected. From that time on matters began to look hopeless, even though Dr. Sanford, his attendant, held out faint hopes and encouragement. No one could see him, however."

This statement coincided with the newspaper account that late in May had occurred the most serious relapse. Rankin pursed his lips.

"And where is young Girard now?"

The lawyer wiped his brow before continuing. The strain of his narrative, the heavy silence of the house with the body below, and the stuffiness of Mrs. Herman's private room combined to make the atmosphere oppressive. Not even the open window relieved the heavy, tense heat within.

"I wish I knew that myself, Mr. Rankin; but we haven't heard from him since that day. As soon as he definitely knew all the facts, he went East again, to find Miss Mildred, he said. His intention was to bring her back to my client. And there has been no news of him at all, either as to whether he had succeeded in finding her or had failed."

"You have no idea, then, where he might be located?"

"Not the slightest. We did think we might be able to get in touch with him at Mrs. Murchison's in New York, for he usually goes there and spends much of his time with them. But though we have written, there has been no reply from him, and Mrs. Murchison claims not to have seen him." Driscoll paused before adding in explanation, "Mrs.

Murchison is the lady who raised the boy after his mother died."

If Girard were in the East, Rankin reflected as he nodded, there, obviously, would be his starting point in tracing him.

"Yes, Mrs. Herman mentioned her. Who is she, exactly, and how did she come to take charge of the boy?"

"She lives in Harlem, I believe—at any rate, the address is 213 Camden Street. Miss Clara—the boy's mother, you know, who ran away with the salesman—went to live there after she had been deserted by her husband, while she worked in some downtown store. Mrs. Murchison had a boarding-house then. She hasn't now, since my client permitted her to want for nothing, due to her kindness to the boy. She became greatly attached to him, and when Miss Clara—I shall always think of her as Miss Clara, and never as Mrs. Julius Girard—after Miss Clara died, she rather adopted him. She raised him until Mr. Yaeger took him off her hands and sent him to boarding-school. But he always returns there, as though it were home, whenever he is in New York. I suppose now we shall have to begin a search for him. This business is becoming terribly involved. Do you think he'll show up when he knows he is the heir?"

Secretly, the detective doubted the matter. If his suspicions had any foundation, Robert Girard would be wiser to remain in concealment.

"I think it likely," he replied, however. "And if not, I shall try to trace him. I was wondering whether I could find a picture of him somewhere, so that I could have an idea of his appearance."

It seemed, however, that there was none to be had. The lawyer explained that there had never been any occasion for taking a picture in past years, and recently there had been no opportunity, since Girard had not been home.

Neither was the description that Rankin extracted a very satisfying one. The nephew was of medium height, light complexioned, and with darkish hair. His age was twenty-three. That was all the detail Driscoll could give, and it would have fitted thousands of young men. As a means of tracing the young man, it was valueless.

Further conversation was interrupted by Mrs. Herman's apologetic appearance.

"I beg your pardon, sir," she addressed the lawyer. "But the undertaker is coming up the drive with his men, and the Reverend Mr. Lorch, and I thought perhaps you might want to see them, it being almost time—"

"Certainly, Mrs. Herman. You did quite right."

Hastily Driscoll excused himself, and Rankin followed more leisurely, reaching the funeral chamber after the first solemn greetings were over. As he waited around, friends began to arrive and the exchange of salutations, in hushed whispers, informed him that many were dignitaries of state and prominent citizens. Governors, senators, the mayor of the town, innumerable people of wealth and position, visited the chamber within the following hour to pay their last homage to one they had respected during life.

Though he attended the funeral services—the second such services he had attended within the space of four days—Rankin's attention was far off from the dignified and solemn rites. He occupied himself in wrestling with the newest and most curious details of his many-sided puzzle, cataloguing them into a semblance of order.

There were so many new disclosures. He understood, clearly, the situation which had driven Mary Young from home. For years, the plan Lawrence Yaeger had devised for marrying his two remaining relatives had been in abeyance; there had been no sign of its being fulfilled. Then the old uncle had been taken ill; at first there had been no cause for alarm, but as the symptoms became increasingly

serious it was evident that his days were numbered. He
desired the fulfillment of his scheme before he died.
After various delays, Robert Girard was located in the
East, early in May, and hurried West for the ceremonies.
He arrived about the sixteenth to find an amazing situation. His intended bride had fled on the tenth rather than
marry him; he had been disinherited by a regretful and
repentant uncle who was moving mountains to accomplish
his niece's return; and finally, his uncle was unapproach-
able from that day on till his death, three months later.

What an invitation it was to a bitter man—one raised
by unknown people in an unknown environment and desperately in need of money! His prospects of wealth and
ease were gone. For him there was only one way out. If the
girl who had refused him, and who had robbed him of his
long-awaited inheritance, were to die before his already
dying uncle, then, according to the terms of the newly
made will, the entire inheritance would be his. How he
must have hated his cousin with a venomous, deadly hate!
Therefore he set out, ostensibly to find her, in reality to—

Conjecture though it all was, it hung together logically.
Step by step, each supposition followed the other in a
convincing manner—so much so, that Rankin was ready to
accept it, upon the bare evidence he had, as absolute fact.
Only the recollection of previous blunders prevented him
from falling into the same error again.

During a pause in the service, he requested the lawyer
to point out Dr. Sanford who was present. He was a sur-
prisingly young physician for the reputation he appeared
to have acquired. After the last prayer, Rankin sought him
out and introduced himself as a friend of Driscoll's, which
statement the latter immediately verified. The physician
expressed himself as willing to assist in whatever manner
he could. Rankin inquired as to whether his case against
the missing nephew had any factual basis.

"It's curious that you should ask that question," replied the doctor to one of his first queries, "because it was the very thing that happened. Young Girard came to me on that very day—the seventeenth of May, just after old Mr. Yaeger suffered the change that proved fatal. I knew it was coming, and there was nothing I could do to prevent it—merely, perhaps, postpone the evil day. And the young man wanted to know what were his chances of recovery."

"You told him, then—?"

"Oh, I answered him vaguely, as doctors often have to do when people are too curious. But he pressed me for details, claiming a right, as the nearest relative, to know Mr. Yaeger's exact condition. I admit I thought his insistence rather curious at the time, though from another viewpoint I suppose it was natural. But finally I admitted to him that, though we must hope for the best, there wasn't much hope left. Three months was the very most he could linger.

"You see, the patient was afflicted with cancer of the esophagus, the effect of which, in its growth, is finally to prevent swallowing. Fifteen months is the normal time for such a growth to become fatal. Mr. Yaeger was stricken in the spring of 1926, but until last May he was capable of eating without much difficulty. But the cancerous growth so obstructs the throat passages that finally eating becomes impossible. When it has reached that stage, it may well be considered the beginning of the end. Feeding is possible only through tubes into the stomach, and then only with the greatest agony."

Dr. Sanford's dissertation upon cancer continued for fifteen or more minutes. Rankin listened with politeness, but finally broke away. He was joined by Driscoll with an invitation to supper. This the detective accepted.

"There is a train for New York, that leaves at nine o'clock this evening—it is the twenty-two-hour Limited. If we eat sufficiently early, I can easily make it back."

"Are you leaving already?" Driscoll's tone expressed his astonishment. "Have you found out everything you want to here?"

"Practically," Rankin replied. "I believe I shall drop in at your office to see the copy of the original will and read Miss Yaeger's message when she fled. Otherwise I can't see what else I can possibly unearth here. You see, no one here knew of the whereabouts of Mildred Yaeger, so none could have got at her. I firmly believe that the case will have its ending in the East where it had its beginning."

Toward the close of the fast-waning afternoon he joined the lawyer and they proceeded to the latter's home. Driscoll proved to be a bachelor, living in bachelor apartments. He was, however, very comfortably situated, with a man and his wife as servant and housekeeper. The dinner was charmingly served and very tasty; it included squab, with delicious candied sweet potatoes, a favorite of Rankin's, and ended with sparkling champagne, evidently drawn from private stock, that made him quite satisfied with himself. In the single day he had discovered more that was applicable to his case than in the entire past week.

Throughout the dinner the topic of the case was studiously avoided. It was not, in fact, until the detective was about to leave for the station that Driscoll broached the subject.

"So you are going to New York," he remarked, "in search of young Girard. For my sake, I hope you find him. But I can never believe him guilty of that terrible crime."

"I do not say that he is, necessarily," Rankin replied, "and, as I said before, for your sake, I hope not. But it is best not to lay too much faith in that being the case. There is a lot to be explained." He hesitated. "I wonder if you would do something for me, Mr. Driscoll."

"Certainly, I shall be pleased to do anything to assist you."

"In case you should hear from Girard, will you let me know of it? There's no use my chasing him around New York if he should, in the meantime, turn up here. You can get in touch with me at the Martini."

"Willingly," assented the lawyer, as Rankin opened the door.

It was eight-thirty when the detective left. Twenty minutes later he was aboard the New York Limited. Presently he was started toward what he fondly hoped would be the final steps of his search and the close of the baffling case.

26

FIND THE NEPHEW!

The woman who opened the door to Rankin's knock, at 213 Camden Street, was weary and faded, drooping from a long struggle against poverty. Gray wisps of hair straggled over a deeply lined but kindly face, which expressed surprise at the sight of a man upon the steps. The house itself stood out from its fellows in a drear row of brick houses, in the Harlem quarter, only in that it had an approach of steps, and the others had their entrances upon the street level. Dilapidation and poverty mingled in the streets. The L thundered by, its iron trestles darkening the rooms and preventing any privacy to its inhabitants. If Miss Clara Yaeger found it necessary to take refuge here with her boy, after being deserted by her rascally husband, she must have been in desperate straits, indeed.

With merely dull bewilderment the woman led him into her darkened sitting-room. She stood waiting apathetically for him to state his errand.

"Mrs. Murchison?"

The reply was an abbreviated nod.

"I am looking for Mr. Robert Girard and I have been given to understand that I could find him here or that, at least, you could tell me where I could locate him."

"Are you a friend of Bob's?"

There was a slight suspicion in her tone and she looked up to study him closer. He smiled winningly to gain her confidence; for some reason she appeared wary and hesitant.

"Not exactly that," he replied, "but I am most anxious to find him."

"You aren't—you aren't—a detective?"

He managed to conceal his amazement at this peculiar question. What could this woman have to fear of detectives unless she knew or suspected what he suspected?

"As a matter of fact, I am, Mrs. Murchison." Rankin held out his hand hastily as she shivered suddenly and clutched at her scraggly dress. "But that's nothing to be afraid about. You see, his uncle, Mr. Yaeger, has just died and we are trying to locate him as one of the heirs."

Her extreme relief was evidenced by a deep sigh and a lessening of the tension in her facial lines.

"Oh, I'm so glad of that. I've been so worried about him, in this last year, and there isn't anything I wouldn't do for him. If he would only listen to me. But when young men get that age, they can't hear any advice, but do just as they please." She invited him to a seat and, when he had accepted, went on speaking: "You are sure, sir, that it's not some trouble he's got into?"

Rankin experienced a sensation of guilt at the course he had to follow to worm the truth from the speaker. That she loved her adopted son deeply, whether the feeling was reciprocal or not, was evident. And it was this feeling that he would have to play upon.

"He hasn't, as far as I know of—and I do hope that he hasn't been doing things that he oughtn't."

"Oh, no, sir!" she replied hastily, fearing a wrong impression. "It's not exactly that. I'm sure Bobby wouldn't do anything that's really wrong. It's just that I'm afraid he's in bad company—gamblers and things like that. And nothing I could say would make him pay any attention to me. And since I haven't seen him or heard from him for some time, it's worried me more than ever."

"That's too bad. We'll have to see what can be done, when I find him."

"Will you, sir? I'd be everlasting grateful to you. He used to bring his friends up to his room and they'd spend the whole evening there, together with wine and cards, so that they'd be fair finished in the morning. And then there were lots of other things that I couldn't stop. I've been worried about Bobby ever since he was a youngster. You know, when poor Miss Clara came here—that's Bobby's mother, you know—she had a terrible time of it, what with working so hard in the day. She couldn't very well take care of him then, and in the evening she was too tired. Her husband was a rascal! She was too proud to ask her people at home for help, though I often urged her to. She said she'd rather die than do it. Well, that's just what she did, poor thing—died of working.

"My husband was living then," Mrs. Murchison continued, "but we never had no children of our own, so we got very attached to Bobby. So when that happened, we sort of adopted him as our own and raised him ever since. That is, until his uncle took him away and sent him to school. We couldn't very well afford to do that, so we just had to let Mr. Yaeger know we had him.

"Mr. Yaeger was very good to us, and sent us money to take care of him, as well as extra for ourselves; and he continued that after my husband died and he took the boy off my hands. But Bobby always came back here to stay, even when he was going to college, though he could have afforded much better than this in other places. Sometimes I believed, though, that it wasn't because he cared for me, but that he had a place to bring his men friends, where nobody would say anything, to play. And that's all he's been doing in the last year—drinking and gambling. I'm terribly afraid he's in debt, though I haven't seen him in some time."

She finished her tale with a sad smile. Rankin was silent for a moment.

"But you must know," he finally said, "where I can get in touch with him. As you can understand, it's rather important that I see him soon."

"I wish I knew. I'm so glad, for his sake, that he's come into money, though it is sad about Mr. Yaeger, who was so good to all of us. Maybe he'll settle down now."

"But didn't he leave any word of where he might be? We haven't heard a word from him in Gary, since he left in May, to come East. You must have seen him since then."

"I did, just once; that was early in June." Mrs. Murchison shook her head slowly. "He dropped in just during the afternoon, and said he had to be in Philadelphia by evening, as he was quite busy. But he didn't say what he was doing, nor did he tell me what had happened when he went West."

"He didn't say a word to you? And that was the last time—?"

"That's right—not since—"

Mrs. Murchison started to settle herself back in her chair, when she suddenly quivered and raised her hand to her lips in apprehension. Her eyes dilated, and with a gesture Rankin couldn't quite understand she spoke swiftly: "Just imagine my saying that," she laughed, and it became something of a croak instead—"when as a matter of fact, though I forgot all about it, I did see him again, just once! Can you imagine a thing like that slipping my mind? It was yesterday a week ago, he came here in the evening at ten o'clock, and was here till early morning. He went away then."

Yesterday a week ago. And yesterday was Sunday! A week ago was the day of Mary Young's murder! Rankin's fingers dug deep into the arms of his chair, but his voice gave no indication of the disturbance into which he was thrown.

"On Sunday a week ago? He was here at ten o'clock in the evening? Was that when he arrived?"

"That's right. He came just at ten o'clock. I can't see how it ever slipped my mind, even for an instant. He was here till early in the morning because, I remember, I had to give him breakfast at seven o'clock."

"Are you positive, Mrs. Murchison, that it was Sunday night? It might have been Monday or Saturday, you know, and a single day may make all the difference in the world in tracing him."

The reply came without hesitation. Whatever had disturbed her so was now passed, so that no sign of nervousness was visible.

"Oh, no, it was Sunday, because I spent the evening in. On Saturday night I went out with Mrs. Mulligan, who is my neighbor; but Sunday, I knitted, in the house. I was so surprised to see him, but can recall it very distinctly. He was quite tired when he came in. He said he had come from Grand Central station and he wanted something to eat. So I took some cold things out of the ice box—some tongue and tomatoes and gave them to him. Then he went right up to his room, to bed."

"Did any one else see him? What I mean is, he might have met some one on the street who could recognize him, so we could be sure of the evening."

Rankin's insistence appeared to surprise Mrs. Murchison.

"Why, I tell you, sir, I know it was Sunday; there's no question of that. And it being rather late when he came, I'm sure he didn't see any one. He never knew a soul around this neighborhood."

"Where had he been?"

"Bobby didn't tell me that." She fingered her apron nervously. "But he never tells me anything. He just dropped in, and was gone on Monday morning."

The alibi was complete. Robert Girard couldn't be in both Woodlawn Park, Philadelphia, and Harlem, New York, at the same moment. Nor a half hour later, if Mrs. Murchison should happen to be mistaken about the time by that much. The fastest airplane could not have covered those hundred miles between the two cities in an hour. If what Mrs. Murchison claimed were true, his latest—and remaining—suspect was acquitted before he was ever accused.

Either, then, the woman was lying—and it was clear to see that she was not to be shaken in her tale—or he was again mistaken. It struck him with peculiar force that she should have recalled his visit, which had occurred but a week ago, after distinctly stating several times that she hadn't seen her adopted son in some time. But exactly the reason for her unique behavior he could not fathom. And suppose he were wrong. Where had he erred this time? Was his mistake so overwhelming that the case would finally go down in police annals as an unsolved crime?

After a moment's hesitation he continued upon his original quest.

"If you don't know where he is, can you tell me of any place where I might inquire for him, among his friends, for instance?"

Mrs. Murchison's reply was in the negative. Girard, it seemed, never introduced her to his friends; and this little personal detail served to doubly impress upon Rankin the woman's tragedy.

"But there was one place he spoke of," she went on, "I made a note of it at the time. I was anxious about where he was going once, so I asked him, and he said, to Logan's."

"I'll have to try that. What is the address?"

"I don't remember, but I have it in the kitchen. I'll get it for you if you want it."

He stopped her in the doorway.

"Just a moment, Mrs. Murchison. If you happen to have a picture of Mr. Girard, I'd appreciate it if you'd bring it along."

"A picture, sir?" She hesitated. "I don't believe there is any. I know we never took any, not since he was a baby."

"No, I'm afraid that wouldn't do any good. You know I've never seen him, and it's going to be a difficult job finding him unless I have some idea of his appearance."

"Do you know, I believe you can get a picture of him, at Marcus's. That's the very place. It's that boarding-school out on Morningside Heights that Bobby attended, from the time he was thirteen till he was seventeen. The Reverend Mr. Darrow, who runs the place, was forever taking pictures of the boys either in classrooms of something like that. Of course it will be old, but it might help, if you get an idea."

When she went out, Rankin reflected that he couldn't forever be pursuing a phantom. Presently she returned with the address. It was clear that she could give him no more information.

"May I see Mr. Girard's room?" he requested. "It's quite likely that he left some papers or addresses around that would give me a hint."

A thorough search of the room, however, when Mrs. Murchison consented, failed to reveal any clue to his quarry. For the type of house and the locality, it was furnished with reasonable comfort. In one of the bureaus Rankin unearthed several gambling appliances, a race chart, and a little notebook. The latter contained a record, crudely kept, of losses and winnings at cards and racing. One item was of particular interest. It was a page of various losses Girard had suffered within the period of one month, April 10 to May 10, of the present year.

April 10: to Logan—10,000 on Nellie Bly.
          19: to Sims. Poker. 5000
          22: to Logan—30,000
          30: to Logan—7,500
May 5: to Arlen—12,000—on Hartigan One-Step
          10: to Logan—35,000

The entire sum came to $100,000, the very amount young Girard had tried to borrow from the Yaeger attorney. The record made it clear that the young man had counted heavily upon the loan as a means to pay back his heavy losses. And it proved the fast life he had been leading so far beyond his means. To "Logan," he was the greatest loser.

As soon as he left Mrs. Murchison, Rankin went to the address she had given him. As he had half anticipated, Logan's was a gambling resort of rather middle class, posing as a modern up-to-date rest club. It was patronized by gentlemen's sons who possessed more money than brains. The gilded interior and the lounging-room were invitingly luxurious; on the surface its innocent aspect hid the innumerable devices that parted the fool from his money. The detective was not, however, interested in the illegal proceedings of the resort.

He found the proprietor, after whom the club was named, an affable, bland, stoutish gentleman, who puffed a cigar and smiled constantly from unpleasant eyes. The smile passed quickly when Rankin named the object of his search.

"Bob Girard? No, I haven't seen him since early in May. There's no one I'd like better to see. Are you a friend of his?"

"No," replied the detective, "I'm not, but I'm trying to locate him, and I was hoping that you might be in touch with him or could help me."

"Sorry, I can't tell you a thing. In case you find him, let him know this from me—that the police will be on his trail very soon unless he pays an honorable debt, contracted with me, for the sum of $75,000. And if it isn't the police, it will be some one even more dangerous. I've waited as long as I'm going to for him to turn up with that amount, and he is going to find himself in trouble he won't like if it isn't forthcoming!"

The tone was threateningly unpleasant. Rankin found himself the object of minute scrutiny from the speaker.

"If you can't help me, do you know of any other place I might try?"

"Well, you can go to Arlen's—Girard used to hang around there a great deal—or to the Midnite Club on East Hundred-eighth Street. But I doubt whether they know anything; and I should be careful, if I were a 'busy,' of the questions I asked in some of those places."

With this parting shot Logan joined a servant and walked away. The advice was valuable; it wasn't good to be too curious in establishments such as his quarry appeared to frequent. The proprietor had appeared sincere, but since his shrewd eyes had spotted Rankin, he would probably have refused to tell what he knew, anyway.

His prophecy proved all too true. A visit to each of the places mentioned netted nothing but suspicious looks and careful speech. No one had seen Girard in some time, and they had no inkling of where he was. At the end of an hour Rankin found himself at a loss to proceed.

The trail was infinitely more difficult, he reflected, than that of Joseph Rogers. There he had possessed some clues and the exact knowledge of the fugitive's starting point and the trail had been but three days old. Here, three months had elapsed and he had no definite beginning. It was like searching for a needle in a haystack; the country had swallowed the nephew up and he had the

entire United States to wander in. All that was known was
that he had gone East to find his cousin.

Mrs. Murchison had said, however, that he had come
from Philadelphia and was returning there. But where, in
that large city? Rankin could picture himself wandering
about the streets, peering into faces that passed. The situation was not without its humor. But the realization that
he was in the position of a drowning man, grasping at
straws, caused him to grow serious. Actually, he was floun-
dering in a sea of entanglements.

In a state of indecision, he returned to his hotel,
where, upon arrival, he had arranged to stay. The hotel
clerk greeted him.

"A telegram for you, sir. It's been in for the last hour
or so."

Rankin opened it with eagerness. It was from Gary,
Indiana, and sent three hours ago.

> 9:30 Eastern Time
>
> To Thomas Rankin,
>   Hotel Martini, New York.
> Telegram received from Girard at 8 this
> morning, from Philadelphia, as follows: Am
> returning home. Expect me to-morrow in the
> later afternoon.
>
> Driscoll.

27

THE FACE IN THE PICTURE

"The train to Gary," explained the clerk in the New York Pennsylvania Terminal, "leaves here at four thirty; it reaches North Philadelphia at six forty and Gary to-morrow afternoon at three-thirty."

"If I reserve my ticket now," questioned Rankin, "can I return for it just at train time?"

"Yes, I think that will be possible though ordinarily it's hardly the practice. Or if you want to, you can take the train from North Philly, and go to Philadelphia now, on the same ticket."

When Rankin left the station he hailed a cab and proceeded to Morningside Heights. His greatest need of the moment was a picture of Robert Girard. For if the nephew expected to reach Gary the following afternoon from Philadelphia, the train he would take would undoubtedly be the same as that his trailer proposed to take from New York. It would be of value to know his fellow passenger; he might even be able to get acquainted and elicit some admission that would tighten his case. And certainly he would want to keep an eye on the quarry. He had more than three hours before four-thirty and train time.

The taxi deposited Rankin before the enclosed grounds of Marcus's. A school of some substantial reputation, it nestled upon the rise that overlooked a large portion of the city. Across from it lay Columbia University. It had four brown brick buildings of modern construction, planned in the form of the letter T, two of them being the cross-bar of the letter, and two the vertical support.

An iron fence surrounded them, and a fair-sized estate allowed sufficient space for the inclusion of a baseball diamond and pond. But it was empty, as there was no such thing as a summer session.

A sign, "Headmaster's Office," on the entrance of the building, nearest the iron gates, led Rankin into the presence of the Reverend Mr. Darrow. He was a lanky, pious gentleman, in a dark frock suit, that revealed his profession. His sugary welcome, in a sepulchral voice, was followed by a gentle rubbing of the hands and a desire to know what he could do for his visitor.

The detective began in some uncertainty.

"I have a rather unusual request to make, Doctor Darrow. I've come to see about a boy who was a pupil of yours some years ago. It was in 1920 and 1921 that he was in his last year here."

"May I ask the name of the boy?"

"It was Robert Girard, a nephew of Mr. Lawrence Yaeger, who sent him here. Do you recall him?"

Mr. Darrow was ecstatic.

"Remember him? I certainly do. He was one of the brightest boys we ever had, both in class and in sports. He took part in almost all activities. He was the editor of our school magazine for a while. Quite a fine boy—rather tall for his age—seventeen, I believe, in his final year. But then he shot up very rapidly. Of course. Who could forget him? How is he?"

"Quite well, thank you." Rankin cleared his throat. "The family of Mr. Yaeger, who has just died, sent me here to see if I could procure for them a full-length picture of Robert as a boy. Strangely enough, they neglected ever to have his picture taken as a youth and they have always wanted to have one. And we have heard out there of your capabilities in that—"

The reverend gentleman beamed benignantly.

"It's too bad about Mr. Yaeger, isn't it? Such a splendid gentleman. A picture? Why, we have pictures of all our boys! It's one of my favorite pastimes to snap the dear lads, in groups, you understand, or as organizations, as of our football team, with which we had quite a success last year. But a full-length picture, singly? I'm afraid not."

"Well, perhaps one of those you have will do. Do you mind if I see them?"

"Certainly not, sir. In fact, I'm quite proud of them. Perhaps the best ones are in the dormitories. We always take a group of each respective dorm and hang it there, as an inspiration to future boys who come there."

He escorted Rankin to a building which was on the cross bar of the T and upstairs. On the second and third floors were a series of small rooms, each containing four neat white beds and plain chairs.

"The dressing-rooms are below," he explained.

On the walls of each dorm were many pictures, in groups of all poses and positions, attesting to the lengthy period Mr. Darrow had faithfully fulfilled this service for the school. They made the chambers look like rogues' galleries. With unerring accuracy the guide led his visitor into the third of the dorms, straight to a pictured group of boys. They were seated on the steps of what was obviously the front of the building, posing awkwardly.

"This was taken in 1921, when Robert was in his last year; he was seventeen then. That's he in the middle, next to the boy who is sitting down. Now that's a typical pose."

Rankin peered into the boyish face. Despite the passage of years, even a group photo would be valuable as identification. His start of astonishment would have amazed the

headmaster had he observed the detective instead of the
picture. The picture showed the features of a youth in earliest manhood, keen-eyed, with dark hair carefully combed
back. The nose was sharp but handsomely formed; the lips
were full and sensuous. There was a debonair devilishness
in the pose. He had seen that face before somewhere. They
were the features of—

For the barest fleeting instant the identity was in his
mind. And in a flash the impression fled before he could
grasp it and take definite hold. In vain Rankin tried to
recall it. He was barely aware of telling the disappointed
headmaster that he was afraid the photograph wouldn't do.
Whose was the face that peered out at him, through six
years of time? Where had he seen those familiar features
and met their possessor?

The result of an agony of mental effort failed to bring
back that fleeting memory. Nor would the adding, in his
mind, of those six passing years to the facial lines, return
the brief recollection. He proceeded to recall the features
of every man concerned with the case, passing them in
review, one by one, in the procession.

There was Charles Bond. Rankin ruled him out at once.
The age differences made the idea ludicrous. Was it Joseph
Rogers? Impossible. The pasty face had never possessed
the full-lipped, provocative features. James Norris? The
fiancé's alibi as supplied by Spark Porter was not necessarily water-tight. Was it possible that Norris had picked up
his cousin, and that she, due to the passage of many years,
had failed to recognize him? But Norris was more than
twenty-three. Rankin shook his head and passed on. The
chauffeur, Alfred? Elmer Spearman? Mrs. Bond's hireling?
None of them would fit.

Meanwhile Mr. Darrow insisted on leading him through
the remaining buildings and pointing out to him the
dining-room, the study halls, and the laundry. With pride

he expostulated upon the advantages of the school system. Rankin barely listened, so occupied was his mind; now and then he murmured a platitude to indicate attention. When the principal was not speaking of school, he reverted to his original topic of young Girard's varied abilities and cleverness.

"The highest marks, my dear sir! We were quite proud of him, he was such an all-around chap. There was debating. He had a brilliant mind, and I do believe he could present a problem so involved that not even Sherlock Holmes could unravel it. And there was his dramatic club work; he always took the leading parts. A born actor, especially his impersonations. Why I can remember when . . ."

Presently Rankin managed to break away. The iron gate closed behind him and he stepped into the street.

The astounding thing that then occurred may best be described by an eye-witness who related the incident to her friend.

"I was just crossing the street, Lizzie, when a gentleman comes out of the boarding-school with the iron gates. You know the place I mean—Marcus's. Well, I didn't bother to look at him till he gets into the street. Just when he reaches the car track, would you believe it, he stopped dead! And the car was coming at a good rate! I really believed for a moment that he was crazy, for there he stood without moving, just like one of these wooden Indian cigar statues. And the conductor clanging his bell and yelling at 'im while he did his best to stop the car. I could have sworn he was a gonner; but just as he's gonna be hit he moves like lightning and runs back into Marcus's like the very devil was after him."

"And then what happened?"

"Nothing, except that the conductor swore a blue streak. And I don't blame him. No wonder people get hurt when they act like idiots. I didn't see the chap again."

The account was substantially correct. What had happened was that a memory had flooded back to Rankin at the very moment he stood in the trade. It was the memory of a single sentence, almost a word, that the headmaster had spoken while he barely listened. And it both solved the problem and left it completely explained.

He knew who Bob Girard was; he knew who killed Mary Young; he knew how every act of the crime was committed! That was the incredible part of it. The Reverend Mr. Darrow, who had probably never heard of the murder of Mary Young, or of the existence of Mildred Yaeger, had told him what he had sought in vain to discover for more than a week!

Utterly oblivious of his danger, or of the fright of pedestrians, he dashed madly back into the office. The headmaster was amazed at his behavior. Literally, Rankin collared him and hurled questions at him for almost twenty minutes. They were queries that would have astounded a listener, and they left the subject of that inquisition with wilted collar and flushed face. He answered a variety of perplexing inquiries that seemed to lead nowhere; and when the detective had left he sank into his desk chair in exhaustion.

Once outside, Rankin paused to look at his watch. It was exactly two o'clock. With his recently acquired knowledge, he knew he would have to act faster than he had ever done in his life before. In less than four hours he must prove his case, return to Philadelphia, and make his arrest. He knew now where his quarry was to be found and he knew that unless he had laid hands upon him before six o'clock of that afternoon, he might never do so. The case could never be proven; the criminal would utterly escape his clutches, no matter what he could do to bring the hideous crime home to him. Till six o'clock and not a moment later.

There was a train back to the Quaker City at three o'clock. That left him a little less than an hour to complete his case. Could he do it in that time? Or had his knowledge came too late for him to make use of it?

He hailed a cab.

"Drive me to Columbia University—the main office of admissions and do it fast," he instructed as he entered. "When you get there, wait for me. I'll be right out."

The explanation of Mrs. Murchison's strange behavior was appallingly obvious. The alibi she had provided for Girard was false—fabricated to protect the man he sought. But at first she had not deemed Rankin as among those against whom she must make use of the alibi. His mission was apparently a friendly one that had lulled her into security. But something had rudely jolted her into an awakening.

No wonder the solution had utterly eluded his grasp! As he reviewed the complicated trail step by step, Rankin found himself marveling at its brilliance and originality. It almost defied the imagination; for sheer bravado and generalship it was inconceivable. He had been a fool throughout.

The cab drew up before the university offices. Before it had fairly stopped he was up the steps and in the main office. Several clerks stared in astonishment at the furious entrance.

"Where can I get hold of a class record book of 1923?" he demanded of the glaring young woman. "Don't stand there gaping. Answer me."

He forgot that he was a gentleman in that moment. His badge gained him better attention, however, than his brusqueness; and it was but a five minutes' wait until the volume was in his hands. Furiously he turned the pages, scanning the table of contents at the same time. Then he gave an exclamation of satisfaction; a brief pause and he slammed the book shut. And he was out of the door at the same whirlwind pace at which he had entered.

28
A RACE AGAINST TIME

Andrew Smith, janitor at the university, sweeping the steps, probably experienced no other such excitement in his entire placid life as then befell him. He was still marveling at the haste of the gentleman who had entered the office, and for whom a cab was waiting, when Rankin reappeared, grasped him, and hustled him into the taxi before he could utter a protest.

"Drive to 213 Camden Street," the detective commanded, "and make it in ten minutes if it's humanly possible." He turned to his bewildered and unwilling passenger. "Now don't be afraid. I'll explain to you—"

"But I dropped my broom in the street!" cried the other. "And I'm supposed to be on duty now. I can't go away like this—"

"It'll be all right—everything will be all right—so don't worry. I'll pay for your broom and your time. Just let me have your name and address. I want you as a witness, that's all."

He had succeeded in making the janitor understand by the time the cab had negotiated the intricacies of Harlem streets and drew up before the house on Camden Street. Followed by the other, he entered without pausing to knock. Mrs. Murchison came rushing from the kitchen at the sound of the sudden intrusion.

309

Her look of alarm gave place to one of relief. She spoke eagerly:

"Did you come because you have some news of Bob?"

"No, Mrs. Murchison. I've come because I found out that you lied to me this morning; and I want the truth now!"

Her hands shook in agitation, but her poise was undisturbed.

"Why should I lie to you—?"

"There's no use in denying it for I absolutely know that Bob Girard was not in this house last Sunday night!"

"But he was. I'll swear he was. I told you that before."

Rankin shook his head swiftly. "It won't do, Mrs. Murchison. He was not, and you know it. You may as well come out with the truth. There's a penalty for perjury."

"Oh, my God, sir! You've got to believe me, sir. He came in from the Grand Central station at ten o'clock. That is the truth."

"May I suggest what happened? You see, I know. Bob Girard called you up from Philadelphia last Sunday night and made you promise to tell any one who should ask about it that he was there with you at ten o'clock in the evening. He even threatened you, I'll wager, if you should fail him."

The deadly paleness of her face told Rankin that he was right. But, nevertheless, she shook her head. There was something admirable about the stubborn quality of her fidelity. He saw there was nothing for it but to change his tactics. It was twenty-five minutes to three. Regrettable as it was, the stern necessity of the situation demanded it.

"Mrs. Murchison, do you want to be concerned with murder?"

Her widened eyes stared into his in sheer horror. In that stern accusing gaze she read the destruction of all her hopes for her adopted son.

"Murder! Good God! What do you mean?"

"You are protecting a murderer who is wanted by the law, and that is almost as great a crime as the committing of murder itself! I could arrest you for that this very moment."

It was sheer bluff, of course. He knew that this pathetic little woman was totally devoid of blame. The wonder of it was that she didn't faint at his statement.

"If you don't speak the truth, you are guilty as an accessory after the fact to murder. I absolutely know that Bob Girard was not here Sunday night, and I can prove it in other ways. But if you don't speak, it will be worse for him!"

"How can that be? My Bobby can't be mixed up in murder! Oh, it's not true! It's not true!"

Tears appeared in her eyes, and Rankin spoke more gently.

"It is better to speak now, before it is too late. I assure you you are not helping him by keeping up this pretense; the wiser course is to let me know everything. I might be able to do something for you then."

She gave a glance of deepest despair. Girard, clearly, was not worthy of such loyalty and affection. And when she spoke she felt as though she were betraying him.

"It's too late now. I tried in vain to stop him from going that way. But if you say this is best—and you know— what shall I do but tell you? It's true he wasn't here. I haven't seen him since June—not since he came back from the West.

"But when he asked me to say that he was here, of course I did. Don't you understand how I love him? I'd do anything in the world for him, and he knows it. Even lie for him, though, of course, it's wrong. And then I knew from the way he spoke, it was something serious.

"It was that very Sunday night, at half past ten. He told me I must say, no matter who asked, that he was with me at ten o'clock. That he came in then and stayed till morning. That's why I was so worried when you came around. He got me to swear never to give him away. And now I'm doing that very thing. He'll never forgive me for it, never."

She dropped into a chair and buried her face in her apron.

Rankin turned to the craning and open-mouthed janitor.

"Did you get all that? Good! I'll see that you're paid for your trouble. We'll need you, I think, so be in readiness."

He was out the door the next instant and into the waiting cab, the engine of which was still running. It was twenty minutes to three.

"To the nearest L station, and here's your money. Make it fast."

The driver took his pay and they were off. Three minutes later the detective dashed up the steps on the "downtown" side, through the turnstile. Luckily for him, a train was just drawing in—a local, but beggars could not afford to be choosers. This last business had been most distasteful to him. But his quarry was deserving of no consideration whatever.

At Ninety-sixth Street station he changed to the express. During a wait of but three minutes on the platform he fidgeted about in an agony of anxiety. Inexorably the hands of his watch moved toward the hour. When the train arrived at Seventy-second Street station it was seven minutes to three. He would never make the train, if it were correct. Thirty-second Street and Pennsylvania terminal was yet forty blocks away even though only a single stop intervened.

Rankin held his breath while the train emptied and filled at Times Square. He thought he had never seen a greater or slower crowd. It started on for the next station. There was no time left to telegraph instructions to Headquarters, which would have been the safest way. It was too late, in fact, for anything but to make that train if he could.

He was the first man out of the door, tearing through the turnstiles at a terrific pace. Crowds paused to see this astonishing and furious Marathon. Through the underground corridor into the station passageway, along which many stores displayed their wares, and through the Long Island waiting-rooms. A clock flashing by informed him that the hour was striking; but he barely saw it. Straight on through the vast waiting-room to the track entrances he flew. The guard was closing the gate.

"You're too late, sir. I'm sorry—"

"So am I," returned the detective, assaulting him.

Before the man had recovered his balance on the brass rail against which he was flung his assailant had hurled open the gate and was down the stairs. A conductor stood in the vestibule of a car; the train was beginning to move. Straight past him Rankin dashed. The door slammed behind him and he hurled himself exhaustedly into a seat. He had made it!

The two hours' ride was a strain to tortured nerves. It seemed that the locomotive crept along, barely moving. The stop at Manhattan Transfer was unduly prolonged; people boarded and got off in endless procession; the doors clanged constantly, and although it made many a false start, it never actually started. Through Newark it fairly crawled.

Would he get there in time? The delays infuriated Rankin. His ordinarily phlegmatic temperament was completely lost in his excitement. Even six o'clock would be too late, if anything should occur to cause further delay. He had much to do yet and could afford no blundering this time.

Between Princeton Junction and Trenton the train came to a complete halt for no apparent reason at all. In his uneasiness, he craned from the window to discover the cause. It proved to be a useless exertion. After ten minutes the conductor passed through.

"What's the matter? What in God's name are we waiting for?"

"I'm afraid it's a hot-box," returned the conductor. "But let us hope not."

"A hot box? Will that delay us long?"

"That depends upon how serious it is. We may start in a few minutes—or it may be a half-hour. Or we may even have to get another engine. It's rather hard to tell."

Rankin gave a deep groan as his informant passed on.

Presently the train started again, and this time with greater speed to make up for lost time. But not even that was satisfactory. When they reached Trenton, it was almost quarter to five. The detective summoned the conductor again.

"How late will we be?"

"Perhaps twenty-five minutes. We shall reach North Philadelphia at five-fifteen or five-twenty and Broad Street station at five-thirty."

It was twenty minutes after the hour when North Philadelphia was reached. Rankin got off there; it was nearer his ultimate destination. Within the hour he hoped to be able to write "finis" after the case. For if he did not do so then, he knew he never would. It would be impossible to prove; all the suspicion in the world would never convict. The failure would be detrimental to his established reputation.

He sought a taxi and, giving an address, he entered. The car started off and it seemed all circumstances conspired to cause further delay. Broad Street, along which it progressed, was torn up in the throes of subway construction. Rankin recalled, in this, his original suspicions of Elmer Spearman. Traffic was heavy along various avenues they had to cross and light signals were constantly against them.

"Drive right past them," he leaned forward. "Never mind the rest. I'll fix it all up afterward. This is a police mission."

Grimly the driver obeyed. Officers called after them in vain. Four times Rankin saw the taxi's number taken. They progressed then along Germantown Avenue without incident, until they came to the busy corner where it crossed Chelten.

"Stay here just a moment," Rankin instructed.

He leaned from the cab and motioned to two policemen. When they had piled in, obedient to his command, he motioned again for the driver to continue. The pause occupied but two minutes.

It was five minutes before the hour when the taxi drew up before the house on Morton Street. Another cab, waiting before the door, informed him, even before he entered, that he was on time.

Mrs. Schmidt stood with Mrs. Edgecomb in the hallway. At the latter's feet stood a suitcase. They both looked surprised at the detective's appearance.

"Well, if it isn't Mr. Rankin!" Mrs. Schmidt began an effusive welcome. "It's been quite some days since we saw you. You're just in time to—" She broke off as footsteps sounded at the top of the stairs, descending. "Ah, here she is, now!"

Miss Ruth Graham came into view, looking radiant. She wore a pleated crêpe dress of dark green, with long sleeves. Elegant chiffon hose of peach hue covered shapely legs, and she wore a light green hat. In one hand was a valise; over the other arm a light summer coat hung.

She smiled pleasurably at the sight of her visitor and continued to descend.

"Mr. Rankin! What a delightful surprise! Have you come to see me off? Really, that is most pleasant!"

"Miss Graham is leaving us." The explanation was Mrs. Edgecomb's. "It is for a position in Cleveland. I'm sure we are all sorry to see her go, for we think such a lot of her."

"Really? I didn't know that," Rankin returned. "This is a most opportune arrival, then."

"Yes, isn't it? But it's rather a pity, for I still haven't had the pleasure of your company—and I'm sure it must be worth while." Miss Graham gave an inviting but shy smile. "But then, I do have to go. There is a better position waiting for me out there."

As she extended her hands to him in farewell, the doorway was darkened by the shadows of two men. Miss Graham looked up, startled. At the same instant, Rankin with a swift gesture brought the two wrists together while he held the hands. A sharp, ominous click was heard.

Miss Ruth Graham found herself staring at a pair of handcuffs.

"What is this? A joke? I fail to see the humor in it. Take them off at once!"

A sharp and sudden terror was in the voice, and on the instant the well-modulated tones dropped into tremulous, deeper speech.

"You are under arrest, Robert Girard, for the murder of Mildred Yaeger!"

With a despairing cry the captive leaped forward wildly against her captor. Had he not been on his guard, Rankin would have been thrown from his balance. He met the attack, however, ready, and with greater strength. The girl was repulsed for the instant. The two men in the entrance sped past the astounded landlady and her friend to join in the mêlée.

Snarling, biting, struggling madly, she beat about in an effort to escape. Her prowess was amazing. The dress ripped and the hat came off. The beautiful red hair which had at one time so dazzled the detective came loose upon

the forehead, disclosing the short dark hair of a man beneath. The eyes were like a panther's in a fury of hate. The
teeth were dangerous, the feet flying to take the place of
subjugated hands. The four threshed about in a panting
struggle: it was a full minute before the prisoner was so
closely held as to be helpless.

With a sweep, Rankin totally removed the wig, revealing in full the man beneath the disguise. It was the boy
of the picture at Marcus's, with seven years' development
added to the features. The woman's dress, the painted lips,
and jewelry were incongruous with Girard's appearance.
The landlady gave a scream of surprise.

"Well, you've got me, Rankin," said the prisoner, bitterly. "I didn't give you credit for being able to do it."

For a moment a smile crossed Girard's face, making
them the same attractive features that he had possessed as
Miss Ruth Graham.

"But I led you a merry chase while it lasted—you must
admit that."

"I do," Rankin returned, "but now that's over, you and
I are going to keep that date of ours at last. And it is going
to be a very long date for you, I'm afraid."

29
CONFESSION

"I may as well confess to the killing of my cousin. Rankin seems to have been too much for me. I underestimated his ability, and I believe that is what caused my final downfall. But I had an amusing time of it while it lasted, watching him follow false trails I set in his path, and traveling in circles at my suggestions, ever in greater confusion. As a ladies' man, I must say, he had nothing to be proud of, though I admit he has a way about him. Certainly I almost had him at the end of my string, even though he did his best to resist me."

Lieutenant Thomas looked up from the document he was reading, across his desk, at Rankin, who watched him in silence. There was a light of amusement in his eyes, but his words did not express his thought.

"So you finally got him to write this, Tommy," he said. "Well, that makes things much easier for you, when it comes to conviction."

"Girard had no choice," the detective replied, "and he knew it. He was caught red-handed. That's why I had to get him when I did. You see, when I remembered that remark of Mr. Darrow's, of how clever Girard was, especially in dramatics, I knew exactly who he was. The principal was telling me at the time, though I barely listened, that Girard's impersonation of female parts was something to be wondered at. He fitted into girl's roles perfectly; he could so modulate his voice that, though it was husky, it sounded feminine."

"Well, I wouldn't have believed it possible if it hadn't happened, as it were, so close to home."

"Why not?" Rankin returned. "There are some very famous female impersonators. It's simple enough to cultivate a type of walk peculiar to a soubrette. Then put on woman's clothes, a wig, paint yourself a bit, and manicure your nails. And there you are."

"But to keep it up for several weeks," Thomas objected. "It's not so easy."

"He didn't have to do it steadily, remember that. During the time when he was presumably working he was wandering about the city in men's clothes so he had to keep up the deception only at Mrs. Schmidt's—no one knew him elsewhere. And he certainly had practice. Mr. Darrow went on to mention that when he went to Columbia for two years he continued his activities and was the leading lady for the shows that the Asbestos Club gave twice a year.

"Then knowing who he was—although at first I rather think it remarkable that I saw any resemblance at all in the pictured face, because of the disguise—I knew he'd escape me unless I got to Mrs. Schmidt's in time. Driscoll had let me know that Girard was coming West from Philadelphia and would arrive Tuesday afternoon. Once he got on that train at six-thirty I knew my task of proving him guilty would be doubly hard, if not altogether impossible. On the way he would change into men's clothing, and then where would I be? I had to catch him red-handed, and I could not afford to take the chance of missing him at the station."

Thomas nodded gravely and returned his attention to the written confession.

"My motive for the crime is so obvious that there is no use going into details. I was greatly in debt and the prospective heir to four million dollars or more, as well as the prospective husband of a girl who controlled equally as much. Mildred cheated me out of both. Revenge would have been a sufficient excuse for my act, but there was also my hopes for the fortune, should she die before my uncle. From Dr. Sanford, who attended the old man, I learned that he had no more than three months to live. Death within that time was almost certain; and that meant that I had just a little less time to find my cousin and save my fortune.

"I will not relate how I located her; it was as much good luck as any special ability on my part. It took more than a month to find her at Mrs. Schmidt's boarding-house. Then, in some manner, I had to get the 'lay of the land,' so that I might accomplish the deed without giving myself away. My entire concern was to make myself safe, so that, if any investigation started, there would be no discovery that a man had ever been seen about, preparing the setting for the crime.

"At school and at college I had always been famous for my female impersonations. My voice possessed a certain pitch, susceptible to soft modulations, which I always affected in my feminine parts. It was not my natural tone, but I could control and modify it to sound natural. My manners and affectations as a woman were perfect in their femininity, so that I have often deceived people into believing that I was of the opposite sex. I played the leading roles in all the plays of the Asbestos Club, including that of Lady Windermere, in the Oscar Wilde play that we gave.

"Accordingly, I adopted a disguise to gain admission to Mrs. Schmidt's sanctum. Fortune favored me in that I got the room neighboring that of my intended victim. Thus I gained her acquaintance undiscovered, though it was indeed doubtful whether she would have known me even without disguise. Remember, she had not seen me since she was but eleven years old, and I was thirteen. Ten years at that period make the greatest changes of all. How she hated me when we were youngsters!

"Mildred Yaeger made the crime easy for me. In her attempt to escape that hated marriage with me she had changed her name and completely destroyed her identity. While she was out to work I often examined her room and I discovered how thoroughly she had carried this out. Ostensibly, meanwhile, I worked in Wanamaker's; in reality, I put in my days either planning the crime or in trips to New York. Though if you go to Wanamaker's you will find an actual Ruth Graham working there. I merely borrowed the name.

"Daily I took a Gary paper from the Germantown post office, taking good care never to bring it to the house with me. So, daily I was informed of Lawrence Yeager's condition. And when the reports said that he was fast sinking, they told me that the time to act was growing short. Soon it would be too late and useless.

"Then came the day of the crime. As I have said, my main concern was to make myself safe. But when, in the afternoon, my cousin came into my room with her tale of how she quarreled with her lover, I changed my plans entirely. I could place the blame upon James Norris and be doubly safe. Furthermore, I had plenty of cause to dislike him, because he took my place with her, however unconscious this act of stealing was. Call it a peculiar jealousy on my part if you will. But I think the added safeguard it would supply caused me to act as I did more so than the other.

"I told Rankin the truth as to the events of that afternoon but not the entire truth—only in so far as it suited my purpose and would throw suspicion on Norris. Mildred Yaeger did come into my room to confide her troubles, and

I did my best to comfort her. But she told me more than I admitted. She informed me of the cause of the quarrel; she narrated how her lover was bootlegging and that, furthermore, he proposed, that very night to carry off his final coup. Accordingly, he had to go to the shore. She also mentioned that, during the quarrel in the taxi the preceding night, he had dropped his cigarette lighter, unknowingly, and that she had picked it up and held it in her room. And finally, that she was going to seek him at his apartment to prevent him from going on with his dangerous errand.

"I saw at once how I could turn this all to my advantage. But if I desired to throw suspicion upon Norris, it must appear that a man had killed her. Certainly I wanted no suspicion to rest on a woman, living, as I was then, next door. This, as is apparent, was quite different from my original scheme. Nevertheless, I carried it out.

"At 7:30 Mildred came in, unsuccessful in her quest for her lover. I told Rankin that I did not see her again—that she merely spoke to me through the door. But as a matter of fact she came in and told me of her failure. She was so downcast and troubled that I proposed something to cheer her, and, though she was in no mood for cheerfulness, I persuaded her to regard as a lark and welcome a little trip to Woodlawn, just to forget her troubles.

"Ordinarily that would have been impossible; she was hardly the kind to enjoy a vulgar excursion. But again there were the circumstances. She felt she could never be happy again; nevertheless, in her sorrow she experienced a grim defiance, as though to show the world that she could smile even though her heart was breaking. It was as though she were laughing at the power of any one to take from her the joy that was already gone. Coaxing and cajoling caused her to succumb, and when I promised her obliteration of her sorrows—how true that was!—she finally surrendered. She welcomed the other extreme then, and entered into the fun at the park with abandon. I knew it was a desperate abandon.

"How did I come into men's clothes? By the simplest of all excuses. It was another part of the deviltry in which we two girls were to indulge. I told Mildred that we could hardly go to a park like Woodlawn without being annoyed. Two girls alone were sure to be pestered by the 'sheiks' and riffraff of men that hang out there, seeking to make up to those of the opposite sex. I therefore proposed that one of us, I, in fact, should dress as a man, and thus we would both escape annoyance and trifling. The idea appealed to her mood. So I dressed myself normally, leaving a few feminine touches remaining so that the change would not be too startling. As I expected, she failed to recognize me.

"Not wishing Mrs. Schmidt or Mrs. Edgecomb to see us together, especially in my masquerade, I proposed a meeting outside, at the corner of Reed and Morton streets. That is less than a block away from the boarding-house. Once I saw Mildred leave, I entered her room and purloined the silver lighter. We met at the corner at precisely nine o'clock and proceeded to the park.

"'Thrills in the Dark' was the very place to commit so baffling a crime. For days previous the papers had been full of its opening at the park, the latest and most daring of the amusements. I knew it would be crowded. There was the pitch darkness, the screaming, and the general panic about us both. So, while we clung close to each other in the passageway, after making the first descent, I took the weapon I prepared—

"It was all over in a second. Before the car had come to the end of the ride I pocketed the knife and propped up the body firmly. When I got out it was with perfect nonchalance; I paid my cousin's second fare and casually strolled off. The crowd swallowed me and I watched the proceedings afterward for a short time. In one thing I was fortunate—no one had attempted to get in beside the dead girl on the next ride, else the crime might have been discovered before the cars started off again.

"At ten-thirty I called up New York, and provided myself with an alibi. Curse the old woman for betraying me! If she had kept her mouth shut I believe I would have gotten away with it altogether. Once in men's clothing, Rankin could never have proven anything. As Robert Girard I could not even be connected with the events; only because I was still Ruth Graham did my position become hopeless. If I had only left five minutes earlier!

"To the Enderley Apartments I proceeded at eleven o'clock. As I expected, Norris was out and it was the work of a few minutes to get into his rooms and deposit the knife there, wrapped in one of his towels. Of course I was careful to destroy all fingerprints. What with the weapon, the lighter left in the car, and the quarrel, I felt I had built up an excellent case against him.

"After returning to Morton Street, I could hardly leave at once. That would inevitably attract attention. Furthermore, I had to remain and guide the gullible young man who was investigating the murder, and witness its course, even while I directed it. When it became necessary, I dropped hints about Charles Bond, of whom Mildred had told me, and thus set him worrying on another track. The Rogers incident was an unforeseen windfall and assisted me a good deal.

"Giving Rankin leads was, I believe, the only humorous phase of the entire affair. Perhaps I carried it too far. During the following week Mrs. Schmidt learned I was leaving for a new position, so that when I finally did go, the following Monday, the change did not appear too abrupt. Meanwhile, there came the news of the death of

my uncle and I thought it high time to appear on the
scene. On Monday I communicated with my family lawyers that I would arrive the following day. How Rankin
discovered that is more than I can conceive.”

The confession ended there, its detailed panorama giving
a sufficient picture of the entire crime. Thomas calmly
folded the paper.

“Damnably diabolical and clever,” he commented, “and
absolutely heartless. Of course I’m used to it, but there
doesn’t seem to be the slightest remorse or concern about
the deed.”

“You can’t tell whether he’s altogether to blame for
that,” said Rankin, seeking to find an excuse for the man.
“You don’t know what sort of life he led. Certainly his
heritage wasn’t of the best. Even Mrs. Murchison couldn’t
take from him the qualities his parents left him, though
I’m sure she did her best. Girard’s mother was a wild one
to run away; and the father who deserted them both must
have been a bad egg. So you see it may not be so much his
fault as his people’s.”

“Uh! . . . Perhaps you’re right. At any rate, you certainly
did yourself proud, in the end.”

“In what way? Certainly not in discovering the solution. As a matter of fact, I was quite stupid all the way
through. Twice I had Girard in my hand and didn’t know
it.”

“When?”

“The first time was when Miss Minsey, the school-
teacher, told me of the man she saw coming from Mary
Young’s chambers at ten minutes to nine, or so, Sunday
evening. That was Girard when he went in for the silver
lighter. The second time I paid no attention to it, for it
was when Miss Victhers, the operator, mentioned a friend
who called on Norris on Sunday night, at eleven o’clock.

That was when Girard finished the dirty work. I didn't see anything to it, so I merely passed it over."

"But you can hardly blame yourself for that," said Thomas consolingly. "They were just chance remarks, and you couldn't possibly attach any importance to them."

"Well, perhaps not. But I should have followed them up. Unknown men who appear on the scene are always worth a suspicion or two. What puzzled me the most in the entire case were the two problems of the weapon and that meeting at the street intersection at nine o'clock. After Mr. Bond, who I rather think has learned a lesson in caution, explained away the note, I still had to worry about that rendezvous. From the policeman's testimony, you know, Mary Young did wait on that corner on Sunday night to meet some one. The confession, of course, explains that. And it also explains how the weapon got into Norris's apartment. I always believed it had been planted, but I thought Rogers had done it. Then when he was out of it, I was up in the air."

"Why worry about the details, Rankin? It's the final result that counts, and you came across with the goods in a corking manner. The Superintendent is very pleased. I'll wager you're slated for promotion."

MURDER
THROUGH THE WINDOW

FRANCIS EVERTON

THE
DESERT LAKE
MYSTERY

KAY CLEAVER STRAHAN
Author of THE DESERT MOON MYSTERY

The Ticker Tape Murder
by MILTON M. PROPPER

HENRY JAMES FORMAN
THE REMBRANDT
MURDER

COACHWHIP PUBLICATIONS

COACHWHIPBOOKS.COM

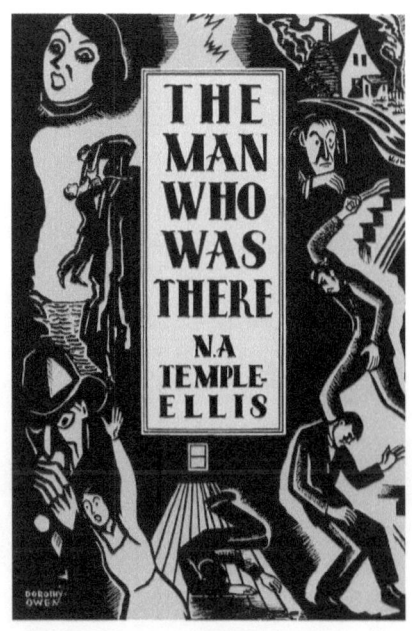

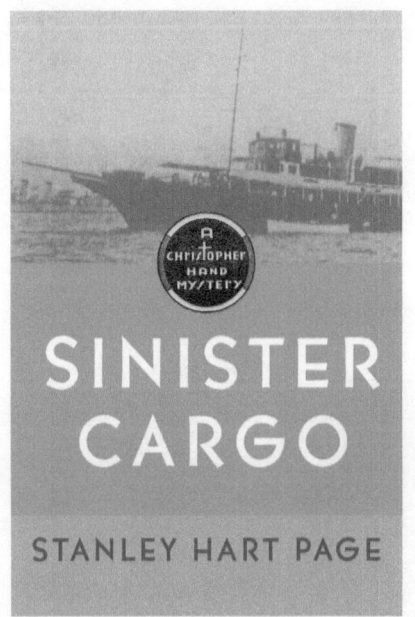

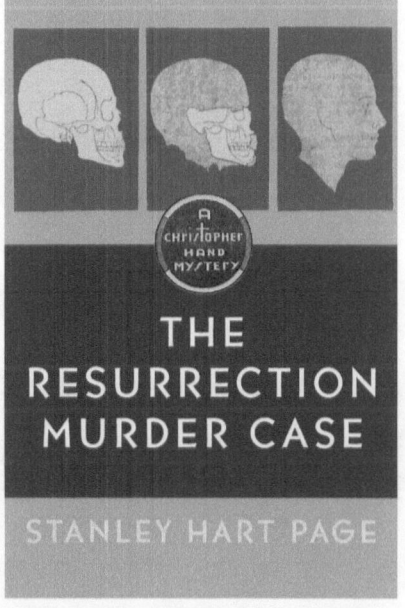

COACHWHIP PUBLICATIONS

COACHWHIPBOOKS.COM

CLUES OF THE CARIBBEES
being certain revival investigations
of Henry Poggioli, Ph.D.

T. S. Stribling

MURDER
IN A WALLED TOWN

KATHERINE WOODS

THE CASE OF THE
UNCONQUERED
SISTERS

TODD DOWNING

LOUIS F. BOOTH

THE BANK VAULT MYSTERY
BROKERS' END

COACHWHIP PUBLICATIONS

COACHWHIPBOOKS.COM

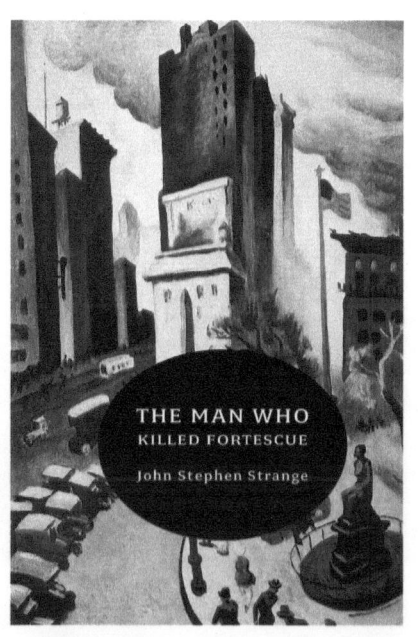

THE MAN WHO
KILLED FORTESCUE

John Stephen Strange

POISON CASE
NUMBER 10

MURDER CASE
NUMBER 33

*FROM THE FILES OF
THE MICHAEL JOYCE AGENCY*

LOUIS CORNELL

3 DETECTIVES
FEMMES AUDACIEUSES
MERWIN • SOMERVILLE • FOOTNER

MEDORA
FIELD

WHO KILLED
AUNT MAGGIE?

COACHWHIP PUBLICATIONS

COACHWHIPBOOKS.COM

BLAIR'S ATTIC

Joseph C. Lincoln
Freeman Lincoln

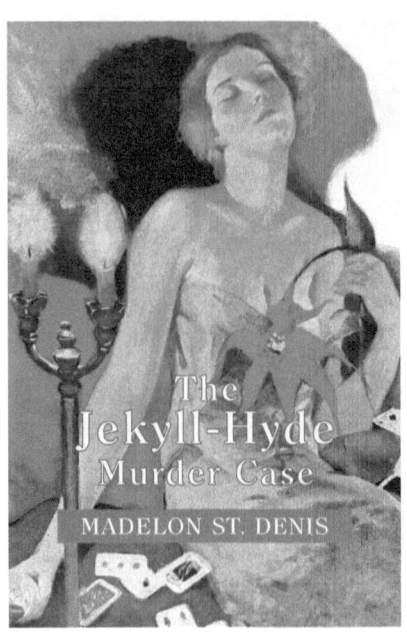

The Jekyll-Hyde Murder Case

MADELON ST. DENIS

VIRGINIA RATH

DEATH AT DAYTON'S FOLLY

THE 5.18 MYSTERY

J. Jefferson Farjeon

COACHWHIP PUBLICATIONS

COACHWHIPBOOKS.COM

COACHWHIP PUBLICATIONS
COACHWHIPBOOKS.COM

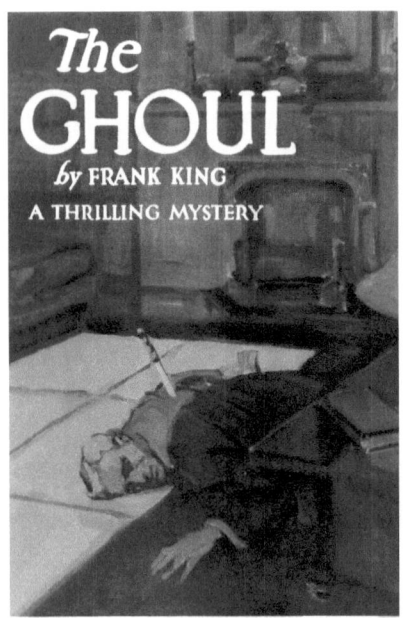

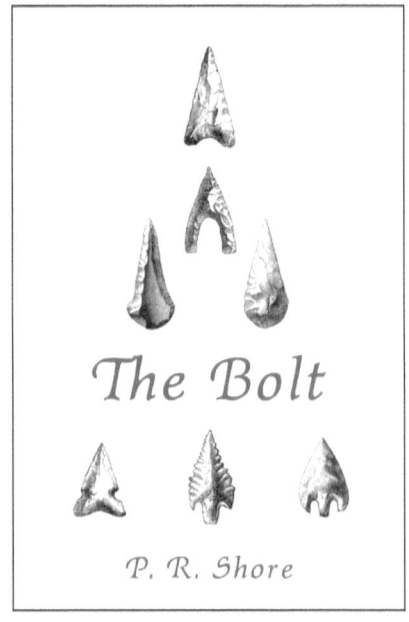

COACHWHIP PUBLICATIONS

COACHWHIPBOOKS.COM

THOMAS KINDON

MURDER
IN THE
MOOR

A JUDGE MASSIE MYSTERY

THE CORPSE IS INDIGNANT

DOUGLAS STAPLETON
and HELEN A. CAREY

hot tip JACK DOLPH

THE MAY DAY MYSTERY

OCTAVUS ROY COHEN

COACHWHIP PUBLICATIONS

COACHWHIPBOOKS.COM